ONE SUMMER BETWEEN FRIENDS

TRISH MOREY

First published Australia and New Zealand 2020

This edition Copyright © 2020 by Trish Morey

ebook ISBN 978-6488359-6-7

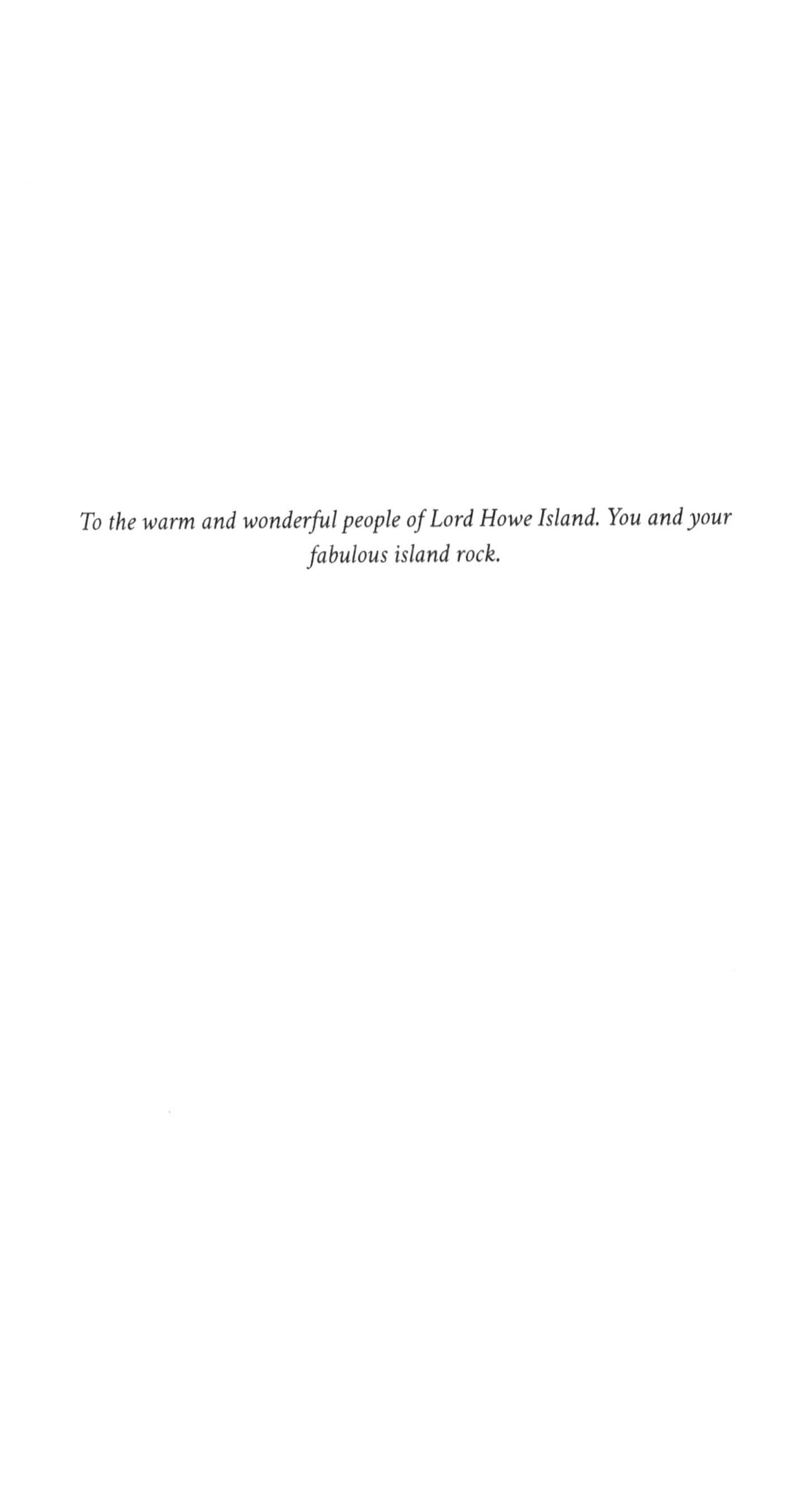

To the warm and wonderful people of Lord Howe Island. You and your fabulous island rock.

PREFACE

Looking back, you never quite knew when or where or how it began, whether with a hairline fracture that grew like a crack in an ice shelf until something snapped and broke free, or with a sudden seismic jolt that shifted the plates of friendship so hard and thrust them so far apart that there was no going back.

Did it begin with the betrayal? Or was that merely the final act, and the seeds had been planted much earlier? Waiting through the decades. Biding their time. Invisible.

Trying to pinpoint the root cause was the sort of thing that a person could beat themselves up about, replaying every conversation they'd ever had, trawling through memory after memory, searching for a clue. A sign that your world and all you'd ever held dear would be blown apart by those you'd trusted the most.

But when it all came down to it, there was no point knowing. Because however and whenever it had begun, whatever you'd missed or not missed, the outcome was the same: loss. Devastation. Hurt that cut so raw and so deep that the wound would never heal and the pain would never go away.

Life went on, of course. Even if you had to read every self-help book you could get your hands on. You pored over pages about death and betrayal and forgiveness. You worked your way through all five stages of grief that the dying and bereaved were said to endure, because you knew grief and this was a kind of dying too. You worked your way through denial and anger, bargaining and depression, until you came to a wretched, uncomfortable acceptance.

This was your lot and there was no changing it.

And so you dragged yourself up, put one foot in front of the other, until one day you could even manage a smile again. To everyone else, you looked normal. But you were forever changed inside. You were harder. Stronger. And determined that nobody was ever going to mess with you again.

But forgiveness?

There was no room in this hard-won existence for something as generous as forgiveness.

No room at all.

1

North Sydney

You just knew some days were going to be special. Days when you knew that all the hard work you'd put in was going to pay off, that you'd turned a corner and your life was finally about to change for the better. Days when anticipation fizzed in your blood like the bubbles in champagne, and the air around you shimmered with expectation.

Like the day Richard had proposed to her in the most magical place on earth. And like the day she'd confirmed what she'd felt deep in her bones and her belly—she was pregnant.

Precious days. All too rare days. But today, Sarah Thorpe knew, was one of those days.

A partnership at Fortescue, Robbins and Lancaster, Chartered Accountants.

After more than a decade and a half of slog, and in spite of being told it would never happen, she'd made it.

At least, that's what Gerard Fortescue had hinted ten minutes ago when she'd bumped into him coming out of the lift. 'Ah, Sarah!' he'd said, seeming delighted to see her as he'd shaken off his wet umbrella, his eyes darting from side to side before he'd smiled and tapped the road map–veined end of his nose. 'Red-letter day for the firm,' he'd whispered conspiratorially. 'There will be celebratory drinks in the boardroom after the meeting, of that you can be sure.' And then he'd smiled again and winked at her.

He'd actually winked at her.

What else could that mean?

Sarah shuffled papers on her desk and rechecked her appointment schedule, not that she registered any details. Just for once she cursed her lack of social media skills. If she'd been the type to Facebook or Twitter, she might have seized her phone and posted something short and sweet that reflected her heady mood and the anticipation that was bubbling in her veins:

Just desserts, here I come! Or *#TakeThatGlassCeiling! #Smashed!*

But Sarah didn't Facebook. She didn't tweet or Snapchat. She did nothing on social media that might reflect badly on the firm or attract the adverse attention of the partners. She did nothing on social media period. She was squeaky clean and above reproach and that—and the fact she'd worked her butt off for years—was finally about to pay off. Big time.

A partnership!

There'd been talk of Gerard stepping back to concentrate on his directorships for the last three years. It's what she'd focused on to keep her sane. It was what she wanted, more than anything. The first woman to make partner in a firm filled with dinosaurs would be a red-letter day indeed. She was about to drag the company into the twenty-first century, even if it had taken the best part of two decades to do it.

God, how could she wait until this afternoon's partners' meeting to find out?

Sarah checked her calendar again and this time her first appointment registered. She headed for the kitchen. There was just enough time for a cup of tea before her client arrived.

She dangled a chamomile and honey teabag in a mug, thinking it might work some serenity and calm into her over-excited brain before she had to turn it back to the intricacies of the recent changes in legislation governing self-managed superannuation funds.

Which meant ten delicious minutes to indulge herself with thoughts of what it might mean if she was right.

Like an office with a door and a view over Sydney Harbour instead of a partitioned-off dog box in the middle of the building. A serious company car—maybe she could finally get that little Audi TT she'd been lusting after?

She looked down at the teabag she was jiggling and snorted. Who she was kidding? All the chamomile in the world wasn't going to calm her, not now when her every career dream was about to come true.

Her only regret was that her ex wasn't around to see this.

'*No ambition,*' Richard had told her when she'd refused to follow up the job leads he'd sprinkled in front of her like fairy dust. '*That mob will never make you partner. It's a boys' club. All they care about is the status quo and golf.*' And maybe he'd been right about the boys' club and the golf, but the firm had been good to her when she'd needed it and surely they would reward her loyalty eventually? Besides, why should she have thrown away a job that was a thirteen-minute commute from their home in Turramurra? This was Sydney —a thirteen-minute commute was like working from home. If Richard didn't like working in the same office as his wife, he could move on.

Which was exactly what he'd done.

Still, it would have been nice to be able to tell him he was wrong.

'Deep in thought?' asked a resonant voice behind her.

Tea sloshed over the rim of the cup and splashed on her hand. 'Oh, Dillon, hi,' she said, switching hands and shaking her fingers.

'Sorry,' he said with a grin, as he fossicked in a cupboard for his mug. 'I didn't mean to startle you.'

She smiled back despite the sting in her fingers. Impossible not to return a grin like Dillon's really, not when it came gift wrapped in a tall, dark and square-jawed twenty-something footballer package. No wonder all the pretty young things had sat up and taken notice when he'd joined the firm a few months back.

'You caught me lost in the hidden delights of self-managed super-annuation funds.' Which was only a tiny white lie.

He cocked an eyebrow as he reached for a coffee capsule. 'There are hidden delights in self-managed super funds?'

'No,' she said. 'Sorry, I just made that up.'

'Damn. And there was me about to ask for a transfer from insolvency to come play in your superannuation sand pit.'

She laughed. This day was getting better and better. She knew better than to think Dillon was flirting with her—she had something like a decade on him and he was clearly just a natural-born charmer. But right now she felt like being charmed. It had been too long since she'd felt so light-hearted. She sipped her tea. 'So, how are you settling in to FRL then?'

He took a moment to answer, a slight frown pulling his brows together as the coffee machine hummed into life. 'Not bad. But then, I've been here more than twelve months. I'm all settled in.'

'Twelve months already? Wow. Time flies.' She felt the phone in her pocket vibrate and glanced at the clock over the fridge. It was probably Frankie on reception advising that her client was here.

'I've got to run,' she said, emptying her mug into the sink as she pulled out her phone. 'Catch you later.'

Except when she looked at her phone on the way back to her office, it wasn't Frankie. It was her mother. Great. Sarah sighed and ran her hand over her hair to give her bun a reassuring squeeze. She really didn't have time for whatever or whoever her mother wanted to snipe about right now.

'Hi, Mum,' she said, 'listen, can I call you back? I've got a client due any minute.'

'It's your dad here, love,' said a voice heavy with gravel and an innate sense of when to pause for effect. 'Your mum's had a fall. Broken her hip.'

Sarah stopped walking. 'What?'

'And so the doc ordered the air ambulance and of course I forgot my bloody phone in all the panic or I would have called up earlier. Dot said not to bother you last night, but I thought you might want to know that your mother went under the knife.'

She put her hand to her head. Good grief. At least one of her parents had the sense to let her know. 'Thanks, Dad. Where are you?'

'Royal Sydney. They did an MRI, or whatever it's called, the minute we got here, and whisked her straight into surgery.'

'I better come in.'

'Didn't you just say you were expecting a client?'

'Yes, but—'

Frankie appeared from behind a partition, saw Sarah standing, phone in hand, and pointed towards reception. *Your client*, she mouthed.

Sarah nodded and held up two fingers and Frankie disappeared again.

'Look, lovey, there's no need to rush,' her father said. 'You get what you need to get done there. Dot will be here when you're ready.' He gave a low chuckle. 'It's not like she's going anywhere.'

Sarah bit her lip. Part of her was relieved she didn't have to make an emergency dash. Another part of her was asking why this had to happen today. Trust her mother to shove an oar into what should be the best day of Sarah's life. But it was still early and her appointment shouldn't take any longer than an hour. There was plenty of time to get out to the hospital and back before this afternoon's meeting. She was definitely not going to miss that.

'Okay, I should be able to get there around lunch time. How's she coping?'

'Bloody unimpressed with it all, I can tell you. You know your mum doesn't like to be slowed down.' Sam Rooney gave a long sigh. 'Gonna be interesting to live with for a while, she is.'

Interesting to live with. That was her father, always master of the understatement.

'Does Danny know?'

'No, your mother doesn't want me to bother him either.'

Sarah rolled her eyes. How where they expected to find out their mother was in hospital? Osmosis? 'Want me to let him know? It won't be for another hour or so, though.'

'Oh, love, I've got to get back to your mother. I'd be ever so grateful if you would.'

~

It was late morning by the time Sarah and the arrangement of pink, purple and white lisianthus she'd picked up from the florist made it across town to Royal Sydney Hospital and into her mother's room.

Dot Rooney grumbled what could have been a welcome. 'And after I specifically told your father not to bother you.' She sighed and shook her head. 'But I suppose it's just as well you're here now.'

Sarah put the vase containing the flowers on a shelf and leaned over the bed to kiss her mother, careful not to put any pressure on her or interfere with any of the tubes going in and out of her.

'It's good to see you too, Mum,' she said, thinking that whoever said, 'The more things change, the more they stay the same', was bang on the money. Sam rose from the visitor's chair in the corner to give his daughter a kiss and a hearty hug, and as she breathed in his familiar dad scent and felt his big arms squeeze her, she knew at least one of her parents was genuinely pleased to see her. She suspected in her heart that Dot was too, Sarah just wished that she was able to come out and say it. 'And don't blame Dad. Of course I needed to know so I could come visit you both. I haven't seen you since you came over for Easter.'

Dot sniffed. 'Well, whose fault is that? My own daughter always too busy to visit us so that I have to break my hip to get to see her.'

Sarah let the barb slide by. She had used the 'too busy' excuse a lot, especially when it involved spending extended time back on Lord Howe Island. But not without good reason.

'So,' she said, perching herself gingerly on the side of the bed nearest her mother's good leg, 'how are you feeling?'

Her mother assumed a pained expression. 'Like I've been run over by a truck. The surgeon had to bolt me together with plates and pins.'

'Ouch. How did you do it?'

'I didn't do it. It was that wretched rail in the shop that did it. I was coming down the stairs with a box of tomatoes and when I reached for the rail, it wasn't there and I missed the step. And the next thing I know, I'm lying on the floor in agony and there's tomatoes rolling every which way, and not a hope in hell that I could get myself up off the ground to pick them up.'

'You missed the handrail?' Sarah inserted what she knew of her mother and of the sturdy timber handrail her father had built into the story. 'Were you in a hurry?'

Sam chuckled. 'Have you ever known your mother to operate at anything less than warp speed?'

Dot bristled. 'I don't like wasting time, if that's what you mean. But that handrail definitely needs to be fixed. It's dangerous the way it is, Samuel Rooney.'

Sam patted his wife on the arm. 'Don't worry, love, I'll have a look at the handrail. Make sure it's a bit easier to get hold of. We can't have people tripping down the stairs.'

Her mother looked suitably mollified.'Least of all me.' Dot nodded, looking suitably mollified.

'Least of all, you,' Sam agreed.

'Oh,' Sarah said, remembering, 'Danny sends his love and best wishes for a speedy recovery.'

'Oh, he does?' At the mention of her son, Dot's eyes lit up. 'Isn't he a lovely boy, to think of his mother like that? Wasn't that lovely, Sam?'

'Yes, that's nice.'

'Just such a shame he has to live all the way down in Melbourne,' she continued. 'I do wish he could have got a job on the island.'

'Not enough work for all the young 'uns, unfortunately,' Sam said, turning his head at the sound of a trolley clattering its way down the corridor.

'But he didn't have to go all the way to Melbourne. If he had to work at Myer, he could have got a job right here in Sydney. At least he'd be closer then.'

'What do the doctors say?' Sarah asked, knowing there was nothing to be gained by pursuing that particular topic. 'How long before you can go home?'

'The surgeon's been this morning, hasn't he, Sam? Such a nice man too. He had a holiday once on Lord Howe with his family. Stayed just next door at Sullivan's. Thinks he even popped into the shop once or twice. Imagine that! Although he didn't remember me. I think Deirdre must have been on duty that day, don't you, Sam?'

Sam looked at Sarah. 'He thinks five to seven days in hospital.'

'I was just getting to that,' Dot said, sounding put out. 'Who's story is this anyway?'

'Yours,' he said, leaning back in his chair, arms crossed over his chest.

The trolley rattled closer, vague wafts of roast chicken crossed with tuna casserole drifting down the hallway. 'I do hope that's the lunch trolley,' said Dot. 'Soggy toast for breakfast and nothing but a biscuit for morning tea after having to fast for hours—it's appalling service here. I could eat the leg off a chair.'

'I don't think our insurance covers us for that.'

'For heaven's sake,' snapped Dot, 'I wasn't serious!'

Sarah caught her father wink at her. Her second wink of the day. She felt the bubbles rise in her blood again. Her mum was going to be okay and there was so much to look forward to. It was still a great day, despite this minor hiccup.

A few moments later a catering woman bearing a tray stopped at the door, checking the number before addressing the patient. 'Mrs Rooney?'

'You've found her,' said Dot, lighting up like a Christmas tree. 'How lovely of you to bring my lunch.'

'All part of the service,' said the woman, putting the tray on the table and carefully manoeuvring it closer.

'I was just telling my family I could eat the leg off a chair, I'm so hungry.'

'Well, now you won't need to. Will you be all right from here?'

'Yes, thank you. But please leave your name and number, because I'd love to take you home with me.'

'Enjoy,' the woman said with a laugh, turning to Sarah on her way out. 'Your mother?' Sarah nodded. 'She's lovely, isn't she? I wish all the patients were so delightful.'

Sarah gave her a thin smile. 'She has her moments.' Unfortunately, mostly with strangers who didn't know her.

Sam was busy uncovering plates as the trolley lady disappeared. 'Do you want me to stay and feed you, Dorothy?'

'Good heavens, I'm not an invalid,' Dot said, batting her husband's hands away. 'No, you and Sarah go and find something for lunch. And don't worry, I won't run off with the surgeon while you're gone.'

'She actually made a joke,' Sarah said to her father as they walked the tortuous route towards the cafeteria.

'She still cracks the odd one,' her father replied. 'Mostly to her customers rather than to me.'

'Or me.'

Sam sighed, pushing open the cafeteria door for her. The hum of conversation over the scrape of chairs and the clatter of hospital crockery and cutlery greeted them. 'I know she can be difficult, love.'

'I know. It would just be nice one day to have a conversation with my mother that didn't involve her sticking a fork in my eye.' But she managed to smile as she said it, and her dad gave a rueful smile in reply as they joined the queue. He passed her a tray.

'So,' Sarah said when they were seated at a table, 'Five to seven days doesn't sound that long for a broken hip.'

'That's what I thought too, but that's just until she's released. That bit's not the problem,' Sam said. 'It's what happens when we get your mum home.'

'What do you mean?'

He unwrapped his ham and salad roll, muttering while he pulled off the top and fished out a couple of rogue kale leaves. 'The occupational therapist called in shortly before you arrived. Your mum won't be able to do half of what she normally does for a while, so she's going to need someone to help her in the shop. Could be six months before she's back to rights.'

'That long? What about Deirdre? Can she do a few more hours?'

'Well, she could, except she's no spring chicken herself and she's been making noises lately about winding back her hours. We can't ask her to do more.'

'Tricky.' Sarah agreed, peeling back the top of her yoghurt, scooping it over her fruit salad and stabbing a piece of rockmelon.

'But I guess there must be plenty of people on the island looking for work.'

'Sarah—'

'It could be an opportunity for someone,' she said. 'Someone young who doesn't want to be forced to head to the mainland for work. It's such a drag when you have to leave.'

'Look, Sarah, the thing is ...'

She looked up from scoping out the next piece of fruit. 'What?'

'Would it be at all possible?' he said. 'I mean, I know your job is important to you, but ...'

And Sarah felt a cluster of spiders crawl down her spine as she realised where this was heading. She put her fork down. 'But what?'

'Your mother thought that you might be able to do it. That you might have some leave saved up and you can come home a while.'

Her breath hissed in through her teeth. Her mother knew all the reasons why that would never happen. 'Why would she possibly think that?'

'Well, because you're family.'

Family? This was supposed to be her day. Her day! When every career dream and aspiration she had finally came true. Instead, a lifetime of injustice boiled over inside her. She'd always been the one who was called upon when someone responsible was needed, whether to help out in the shop or to sit with Gramma or Gramps for the night, because she was more sensible and her brother was too young.

'No,' Sarah said, knowing she had to shut the lid on this hard and fast. 'Sorry, Dad, but it's not possible.'

'You won't at least think about it?'

'There's nothing to think about. I can't do it.' *I won't do it.* 'I can't just walk away from my job, especially not now. You'll have to ask Danny.'

Her father looked at the table and shook his head like a man searching for an answer. 'That won't work.'

'Why not? You are going to ask him, aren't you? Because he happens to be family too. And he already works as a shop assistant—

he's got the personality for it. He'd be perfect in the shop. The customers would love him.'

Her dad sighed and rubbed the back of his neck. 'I know he's your mum's favourite, love, but even your mum thinks he's about as useful as tits on a bull when it comes to anything practical.'

'Then she should have got him to work in the shop like I had to. He could have learnt. He still could learn given he works in retail now. But instead, she expects me to do her bidding the minute she clicks her fingers.'

'Well, you are the oldest.'

Sarah sat back in her chair. 'For heaven's sake, Danny's thirty-five years old. That argument might have cut it twenty years ago when he was just a brat, but not anymore.'

'I know,' Sam said, nodding, looking exhausted. 'I know.'

'Look, Dad,' she said, because she knew her dad was the pacifier in the family, and being stuck in the middle was not always a comfortable place to be, 'maybe someone should actually ask Danny. He's been living away from home more than for ten years. He's bound to have grown up a bit.'

'One would expect so, but it's not just serving customers, is it? It's the stock control and accounts as well. And you're the one with accounting qualifications—you could do it in your sleep. And, well, Dot thinks you're the answer.'

'You should ask him. I'm sure he could handle stock control, it's not that big a deal. And who knows, he might actually like a six-month break on the island.'

Her father heaved another sigh as he rested his elbows on the table and held his hands out. 'Okay, you're right, you're right. But don't you see? If Danny did come, he'd expect to bring Silvio with him, and you know it would kill your mother knowing they were sharing a room.'

'So that's what it really came down to?' Sarah shook her head. 'Don't tell me she still hasn't given up on her dream for him to find a nice girl and get married and give her the grandchildren she's so desperate for?'

'Something like that.'

'She's in denial, that's what she is.'

He nodded. 'It hit her hard, when he brought Silvio home that Christmas, remember?'

Sarah remembered all right. They hadn't had to wait for New Year's Eve to watch the fireworks. 'He might have warned you that he was planning on bringing Silvio.' But that was Danny, always looking for maximum shock value. She just wished he'd stopped at fart jokes. 'And she wonders why he chooses to live so far away.'

Sam put his salad roll, barely touched, on his tray. 'Look, Sarah, I know it's asking a lot, but could you at least give it some thought? You don't have to make a decision right away. Think it over.'

She took a deep breath, wondering why they were still having this conversation. 'It is asking a lot, now that you mention it. You're expecting me to drop everything for six months to look after her.'

He held his hands up. 'You wouldn't have to look after her. You'd mostly be in the shop while she recuperates. She'll have a lot of physio to do too, and I know that if you were there in the shop, you'd stop her from taking on too much.'

Sarah let her head drop back, noticing the chequerboard of ceiling tiles above her head, some stained brown in places from who knows what, others askew in their brackets, dirty smudges left by the hands of some tradesman who couldn't be bothered to put them to rights or care how they looked after he was gone. It struck her that her life was a bit like those ceiling tiles: stained in places and with other bits all askew. Over the years, she'd done her best to disguise the blemishes. To appear normal. In Sydney, she could get away with it.

But if she went back to the island, she'd be exposed to everything and everyone she'd ever tried to forget. All her smudges and stains in plain sight.

Today's meeting was the chance to finally make something of herself—by herself. Could she say no to that? She stabbed at a piece of apple with her fork, trying to find some enthusiasm for it, before giving up and pushing the bowl away.

'I'm sorry, Dad. But no.'

'I'm so sorry, Sarah. I know you've got a very important job.'

'I have.' She licked her lips. She didn't want to tell him about the offer she was expecting. She didn't want to jinx herself. But she had to make her father understand that she wasn't just being selfish and that what he was asking was impossible. 'Dad, there's a partnership meeting later this afternoon—and I have it on pretty good authority that I'm going to be offered a partnership in the firm. There's no way I can simply walk away from that. It's what I've been working towards for too long.'

Her father's eyes misted over, although whether from pride or disappointment, Sarah couldn't tell. She settled on thinking it must be a mix of both.

'A partnership. I can see how that would change things. Congratulations, love, you've worked so hard for this.'

'I have.' No pretence. No false modesty. She'd worked her arse off for Fortescue, Robbins and Lancaster, and it was time that she was rewarded for it. 'But you know more than anyone that it's more than just this promotion.'

'I know she's not easy, so help me I do. But she's still your mother.'

Her reluctance to go back to the Island wasn't only down to her mother, but that part was the easiest for her father to understand, and with good reason. 'The mother who's never forgiven me for being unable to bear her a grandchild.'

Her father reached his hands across the table to take hers, his brow furrowed, and for the first time Sarah realised there was more than tiredness infusing her father's features. He looked older than she remembered, more crumpled.

'I'm sorry, Sarah. She'll get over it one day.'

'She hasn't shown any sign of getting over it so far.' And while she could understand why her mother might find it hard to come to terms with something that she'd found so difficult to deal with herself, it was the implication that Sarah must have done something to have caused her infertility that stung the most. That she was somehow to blame. Always, Dot had to find someone or something to blame.

'Ah, well,' Sam said, clearing his throat, 'I s'pose we'll come up with something.'

Sarah didn't say anything; there was nothing left to say. She looked at her watch, and then at her father's lunch. 'Don't you want to finish that?'

He shook his head and glanced at her abandoned fruit salad. 'We both seem to have lost our appetites. Come on, we better be getting back to your mum.'

~

'What took you so long?,' Dot said, when Sarah and Sam returned to the room. 'My tray got taken away ages ago.'

'The cafeteria was busy,' Sam said, settling back into the visitor's chair and picking up the paper where it was folded to the crossword, fishing a pen from his top pocket. 'It took a while to get served.'

'Did you have something nice?'

'Not really. A soggy roll.'

'So what did you talk about?'

He wasn't so quick to answer this one.

'Oh, this and that,' said Sarah noncommittally. 'We had a nice catch up, didn't we, Dad?'

'We did. It was very pleasant.'

'How lovely,' Dot said, and it was clear that she thought it was anything but. It took another ten minutes of discussion about her mother's lunch, how disappointing it had been, and how the only highlight had been the return of the lovely lunch lady and how much she'd love to visit Lord Howe Island herself, before Dot turned, exasperated, to her husband.

'So, did you ask her?'

'Ask me what?' Sarah said, as she watched her father shrink further into his seat.

'If you'll come home and look after the shop. The therapist said it could take six months for me to be back to full mobility.'

'Why don't you just ask me yourself?'

'Because if I ask you, you'll say you're too busy.'

'Well, yes, you know I'm busy. Have you asked Danny if he can do it?'

'Why would I ask Danny?'

'Because he's your son, and if you're going to ask your daughter to put her life and career on hold for six months, don't you think it's reasonable that you should ask your son too?'

'Here I am, lying in hospital with a broken hip, and you're telling me what I should or should not do?'

'Calm down, Dot. She's not telling you what to do.'

'You keep out of this, Samuel Rooney. If it wasn't for that handrail, none of this would have happened.' Dot turned to her daughter. 'Just think, six months on the island—you can catch up with your old friends again. It'll be lovely.'

Lovely? Sarah blinked. There were no words.

A nurse arrived to check the wound and take the patient's vitals, and Dot Rooney found her world's best patient smile again.

Sarah figured it was as good a time as any to escape. 'I probably should leave you to it, I'll see you later, Mum.'

'I'll see you out,' said Sam.

He walked her down the corridor towards the exit.

'I don't know how you can stand it sometimes, Dad. How do you put up with her?'

He shrugged. 'I signed up for the long haul, for better, for worse. Sometimes things are better. But to be fair, she's in pain and she's on drugs and she's worried about the shop. Cut her some slack. She's not like this all the time.'

Sarah took a deep breath as the exit doors slid open, delivering them into the afternoon. It had rained earlier and now a watery sun was ramping up the humidity. She stepped to one side, out of the way of a couple with a pram heading in, and turned to her father. 'Yeah, you're right. Sorry, Dad.' She reached up to kiss him on the cheek. 'I'll bring you both some of my famous lasagne tomorrow, save you from hospital food. How does that sound?'

Sam's eyes lit up. 'I'd be mad to say no to that.' He was about to head back inside when he said, 'Oh, and congratulations. I can't wait to hear all about your promotion.'

2

Lord Howe Island

The Lord Howe Island Visitor Centre-cum-museum-cum-café-and-gift shop was quiet today, but that was hardly surprising. June was one of the island's quietest months and today's gusty rain squalls had kept all but the hardiest tourists off their hire bikes and the roads and hunkered down in their accommodation. Jules Callahan didn't mind. She loved the quiet months, when tourists preferred Bali or Thailand for their winter escape, and residents outnumbered holiday makers for once. It gave everyone on the island a breather, and a chance to go on holidays themselves, or to renew or rejig accommodation and machinery.

At the museum, it gave the volunteer staff a chance to spring clean the displays and the gift shop bookshelves (even though it wasn't yet spring), review what had and hadn't sold last season, and think about changing things up on the café menu.

It also gave Jules a chance to think, because there was nothing like having a four-year-old with boundless energy and endless demands to make you appreciate having time to think. Counting and restacking island cookbooks (always a solid seller, since who could resist a book that contained a recipe for the banana cream pie they'd eaten at last night's buffet?) presented the perfect opportunity.

And there was plenty enough for Jules to think about. Della was growing up fast. She'd be at school next year and Jules would be able to increase her hours without having to rely on her mum for childcare so much. Maybe she could even look for a better-paying job—but she'd need to get herself some qualifications for that. There weren't a whole lot of administration jobs on the island, so competition was fierce. Maybe she should look into doing some kind of diploma?

Funny—she'd never been ambitious. She'd grown up on the island and thought it the most perfect place in the world to spend her life. Why would you need to strive for more when you had all you wanted?

But then, she'd never wanted kids, either. Never planned on having them, and never understood how some women rushed headlong into motherhood without a second thought, like it was an inevitable part of life or like they didn't have a choice. Jules had never felt the urge to breed. Weren't there enough people already on this planet, let alone this island? And with all that was wrong in the world, all the predictions of doom and gloom, why would you bring children into it?

But then she'd had Della, and somewhere along the line her daughter had done what Jules had thought unimaginable. Della had turned her into a mother.

Now it was no longer enough to drift through life, satisfied with scraping though Year 12 because it was all she'd thought she'd ever need here on the island with only herself to take care of. Her daughter deserved more. Better.

Especially given she was growing up without a father.

Maybe it was time she stopped thinking about it and did something about it. She'd look into administration diplomas by correspondence, after Della had gone to bed. There had to be something she could find that would earn her some extra money.

A car pulled up outside, doors slamming over the sound of the wind. Voices, and the sound of a child running. If she didn't know better, she'd almost think—

The museum door flung open.

'Mummy!'

'Della,' Jules said, opening her arms for her daughter, her favourite bear wedged under her arm, to hurtle into them. 'Hello, this is a surprise.'

Her mother appeared behind Della, pushing the door closed against the weather as she stamped her feet on the mat. Pru Callahan huffed out a breath. 'Well, it's certainly wild and woolly out there.'

Jules stood, her daughter's hand in hers. 'What brings you both here? It's only fifteen minutes until I finish. Is something wrong?'

'No, no, nothing's wrong,' said Pru, waving her concerns away. 'It's just that I had to go out for something. I thought that I might as well drop off Della on my way, in case you turned up and I wasn't there.'

Jules eyes narrowed, her senses prickling. 'What did you suddenly have to go out for in this weather?'

'Onions,' her mother said. 'I was short on onions.' Her lips pursed tight.

'And you couldn't have just called me to pick some up on the way?'

Pru smiled too brightly. 'I didn't want to bother you, dear. And I didn't think you'd mind me dropping Della off here.'

'Yeah,' said Jules, 'it's so inconvenient and all, living—what? Seven hundred metres apart?'

'Exactly. So now you don't have to bother. I knew you wouldn't mind.' Pru leant down to give her granddaughter a kiss. 'I'll see you tomorrow, Della. Be good for your mummy.'

'I will, Nana,' Della said, winding her thin arms around her grandmother's neck for a squeeze. Then she asked if she could go and see Horny, and darted off once she had her mother's approval to see her favourite exhibit. The dramatic bones of the long extinct armoured turtle, with its horny skull and spiked tail, were captured as if in mid growl.

'You shouldn't let her call it that,' said Pru once Della was out of earshot.

'Why not? It's got horns. Besides, Della gave it that name.'

Her mother's lips tightened into a thin line. 'Well, I'll be off then.'

'To fetch your onions.'

Pru gave a weak smile and turned. Jules watched her go. *Onions, my arse*, she thought. She didn't believe it for a second.

3

It was 3.45 when Frankie called to say the partners were ready for her. Sarah's breath caught, the summons to the boardroom like a shot of adrenaline to the heart. The waiting was over. It was happening.

'Good luck,' said Frankie, giving Sarah a thumbs up as she headed to the rarefied air of the partnership floor.

The boardroom had been fitted out sometime in the eighties, with black leather and chrome directors' chairs, a smoked glass table and beige vertical blinds to screen the glass walls. A dusty artificial plant languished in the corner. Sarah had no doubt that the current fashion for retro was going to give this particular look a wide berth. If she was promoted today, she'd put a boardroom makeover at the top of her to-do list.

'I suppose you're wondering why we asked you here,' old Gerard Fortescue said as he welcomed her to the table where the three principals of the chartered accounting firm to which she'd devoted her entire working life sat.

Philip Robbins and Simon Lancaster smiled at her encouragingly, nodding like reporters during a television interview.

Sarah took her cue from them, and smiled back—if they were smiling and nodding, that had to be a good sign, didn't it?—before giving the obligatory response: 'Yes, I did wonder.' No point telling the others that Gerard had all but given the game away hours ago.

Philip cleared his throat, twirling a fountain pen in his hands. Twenty years younger than the seventy-something Gerard, but rapidly assuming the self-assured mantle of elder dinosaur, he leaned back in his chair and said, 'Tell us, Sarah, how long have you been with us at Fortescue, Robbins and Lancaster?'

Sarah tried not to let her impatience show. Clearly they were intent on making her work for this. And even though they were all still smiling at her, she tried hard not to get ahead of herself. Crushed hopes were a fact of life in the dinosaurs' club that was this accounting firm, a world where diversity and equality hadn't yet squeezed in through the seals in the glass walls.

Until today?

Please let today be the day things changed. She deserved it. She knew she did.

'Seventeen years,' she answered, before adding, 'Eighteen next January.' Might as well pile it on thick and make them see how much she deserved this promotion. 'I joined as a graduate accountant, earned my chartered accounting qualification, and I've worked here ever since.'

'And you seem to have a good rapport with the clients—and the staff too, for that matter.'

'I'd certainly like to think so.'

More nodding. More fountain pen twirling. Vague murmurings and eye glances.

Simon said, 'We knew you were the right person to ask.'

Sarah held her breath, fruitlessly willing her heart to slow the cartwheels it was turning in her chest. Surely this time …

'As you're probably aware,' Philip said, removing his glasses, 'Gerard is thinking of pulling back from the coal face. That's going to create quite a vacuum at the top.'

'I see,' she said, licking lips suddenly, impossibly dry.

'And so, the three of us got together and decided that perhaps this was time for a little cultural change at FRL.' He smiled benignly. 'I don't think any one of us would argue that it's not before time.'

Gerard guffawed, the white shirt covering his pot belly shuddering under his clasped hands.

'Which is where you come in,' said Simon, leaning towards her, forearms on the table, hands clenched, making her every last nerve quiver in anticipation. 'We respect the relationship you have with the staff and clients, Sarah, and we trust your opinion. So with that in mind, we want to get your thoughts on Dillon Crombie.'

Sarah blinked, her quivering nerves scrambling into a sudden U-turn and colliding into each other in confusion. 'Dillon?' she managed in what sounded like a squeak. 'What?'

'You see,' Philip said, 'a partner under the age of thirty—nobody could accuse us of being stuck in the Stone Age then.'

'A partner? Dillon?' But Sarah suspected nobody heard her over the chortles and the chorus of 'Hear, hear.'

'And he's on top of all the social media,' Simon said. 'He did an excellent job on—what was it? Twitter?—during the last inter-firm golf day.'

Philip nodded sagely. 'Not to mention golfing off a nine handicap. Most competitive we've been since Richard left.'

Sarah blinked, not just at the firm's sudden embracing of social media, but because mention of her bastard ex put him right back in her head, telling her she'd been stupid to ever think she'd get promoted by this lot. And maybe you shouldn't think ill of the dead, but sometimes it was impossible to think nice thoughts of them, especially when it looked like they'd been right all along.

She shifted in her chair, keeping her features neutral, rather than displaying the increasingly gutted feeling gnawing at her insides. But that was the trouble with experiencing such a jubilant high: the low following it was so much deeper. And the stupid thing was that she knew that the magic never lasted. That it could turn to despair. Look at Richard's proposal. Look at learning she was pregnant. Why had she imagined today would be any different, when neither of those had ended well either.

'So,' she said, needing to put a lid on the tidal wave of the past before it overwhelmed her, 'why do you need me?'

'Because you've been on the office floor so long,' said Gerard, without a hint of irony. 'You've got your finger on the pulse. This is a big change to how we usually do things. How do you think promoting Dillon to partner will go down with the staff?'

They had to be kidding. Surely they were kidding? But no, nobody was laughing. Instead they were watching her intently. Waiting for her to tell them what a stroke of genius this was. She crossed her legs, clasped her hands over her knees and sniffed. 'Well, perhaps it's not such a big cultural change, is it? It's not like you're promoting, say, a woman.'

The three men blinked at each other, until the light dawned and, almost as one, they looked suddenly aghast.

'No, no, Sarah,' said Philip, with a pathetic little laugh. 'You don't think—surely you don't think we're overlooking you?'

'Oh dear, it's not like that at all,' Simon added, appearing decidedly earnest. And shifty, as he glanced at the men seated either side.

'That never even entered our heads,' said Gerard, and for the first time, Sarah actually believed one of them. He frowned. 'Is there a problem, Sarah? We thought you were content, beavering away running the superannuation section.'

What he meant was she'd been here so long they considered her part of the furniture.

'Oh, no problem,' she lied, crossing her legs and parking her clenched hands over her knees. 'No problem at all. In fact, I'm sure that someone who can tweet like a champion and tee off like a pro has exactly the qualities this firm needs in its the next partner. Nobody could possibly accuse Fortescue, Robbins and Lancaster of being a bunch of dinosaurs then, could they?'

Much shaking of heads and grunting ensued, until Simon twigged, and his head suddenly angled towards her, his eyes narrowing in question.

But Sarah was already up and out of her chair.

'If that's all then, I really should get back to work.'

She left with a bad smell clinging to her clothes: the rank smell of crushed hopes and shattered dreams. But there was no shedding the scent just yet, because when she stepped out of the boardroom, there he was. Dillon, waiting to go in. Dillon, the wunderkind with the social media skills and the enviable golf handicap.

Not to mention the requisite pair of Y fronts.

'Sarah,' he said with that bloody bleached-tooth smile and easy charm, 'we have to stop meeting like this.'

Sarah didn't make a habit of snarling, but it took everything she had to turn her lips into something approaching a smile. 'Dino, I suspect you might be right.'

His smile slipped. 'Dino?'

'Oh, sorry, Dillon,' she said. 'I was a few million'—*years*—'miles away.'

Sarah dropped her mobile phone onto her desk and flopped into her office chair. So that was it. No just desserts. No smashing the glass ceiling. No promotion to partnership. Nothing but 'we thought you were content'. And was she content? Hell no.

There was a brief knock and Frankie stuck her head into the room. 'How'd it go?' she said, and in the next breath, when she'd had time to take in Sarah's expression: 'Shit,' she said, leaning back against the door to close it. 'What happened?'

'Gerard is leaving, like everyone's been expecting.'

'And?'

'And they're offering Dillon Crombie a partnership.'

'What?' Frankie pushed herself away from the door. 'And not you? Dillon's barely out of short pants.'

'Closer to thirty, by all accounts.'

'Still, he's only been at the firm about ten minutes.'

Sarah shrugged. 'More than a year.'

'And that makes him more qualified than you?'

'He also tweets a mean inter-firm golf day. How does one compete with that, exactly? I don't even like golf.'

'They're idiots.'

'Yeah, well, they're partner idiots, so they get to call the shots. Thing is, Frankie, I've been hanging out for this promotion for the last three years. I really thought this was it. I just don't know where to go from here.'

'Well, I hate to say this because I'd hate to see you go, but you need to find somewhere else, somewhere they might actually appreciate you and your expertise. Let this lot try to figure their way around the minefield of the superannuation provisions without you.'

'I should,' she said, gnawing on her bottom lip, wishing she felt more confident about the idea of applying for jobs, but she'd scored this one after an information session she'd attended at uni. Looking back, it had been a kind of speed dating event between an auditorium full of accounting firm representatives and a queue of hopeful soon-to-be graduates. She'd earned herself three offers from which she'd selected FRL. She'd never had a real job interview before. She'd never even had to knock up a CV.

God, maybe she was the dinosaur ...

But she could hardly stay at Fortescue, Robbins and Lancaster. Not now. She had to do something.

Her father's request from yesterday drifted into her mind like a seaweed-choked net drifted down from the surface of the sea.

Your mother thought you might be able to do it ... come home a while ...

She swallowed. Just because she'd missed out on this promotion didn't mean anything had changed. She could hardly swan off now when she still had a mortgage to pay.

'Are you going?' Frankie said.

'No.' Because it was more than being in close proximity with her mother for six months. It was about lies and hurt and betrayal and the evidence of all three, and she wasn't sure she was strong enough to face up to it all. 'I can't.'

Frankie angled her head. 'But they'll be wanting to make the announcement shortly and if you're not there ...'

'Oh, that.' Because she knew the moment Dillon's promotion was announced, every female employee would turn to Sarah for her reaction. She was supposed to be a role model to them, encouraging them to do their best. And she'd tried to be. But what kind of role model got rolled by a guy a decade her junior? If she didn't go, people would think she was hunkered down with a box of tissues, mopping up her tears and licking her wounds.

'Let me know,' said Frankie. 'I better get back to reception. Will you be okay?'

'Thanks, Frankie, but I'm pissed off, not suicidal.'

'Good thing too.'

'Besides,' Sarah said with a weary smile, 'I wouldn't give the bastards the satisfaction.'

Frankie punched the air. 'Atta girl!'

Frankie wasn't gone ten seconds before Sarah was on her feet, too restless to sit, wandering the confines of her office. It didn't take long, there wasn't a lot of space between the desk and bookshelf and filing cabinet. God, she'd been a fool to believe it might actually happen today, but then, she'd been a fool to think it would ever happen. Richard had tried to tell her, but she'd believed that if she kept her head down and did her work, sooner or later the cream would rise to the surface and she'd be rewarded.

Idiot.

Therapy, Sarah told herself as she stirred the pasta sauce for the lasagne late that evening, the kitchen smelling of garlic, herbs and tomatoes. After what had happened today, after the crashing disappointment of a decision that had gone the wrong way, after the humiliation of fronting up to the promotion announcement, she badly needed some therapy. The afternoon's meeting had been every bit as excruciating as she'd known it would be, especially when she'd gone to fill her glass and found Dillon standing next to her at the bar and she'd had to find a smile and congratulate him.

Not that she hadn't had plenty of practice hiding what she really felt over the years. Putting on a brave face. Smiling when the inner fabric of your world was being torn apart and all your hopes and dreams shattered along with it. She'd become a master at putting on a mask and hiding what was going on inside.

She just hadn't been expecting to employ those skills today. She'd been so damned sure.

And so damned stupid to tell her father that she was being made a partner. How the hell was she going to tell him the truth without him thinking that meant she'd be going home after all?

The sauce simmered on the stove. Her mother's words simmered in her head.

You can catch up with your old friends again. It'll be lovely.

Lovely.

As if all Sarah had been waiting for these last five years was an opportunity to reconnect with Floss and Jules.

Okay, so the three of them had been inseparable as kids. They'd ridden their bikes to a tiny school where shoes were optional and friends were just as likely to be your cousins, whether once, twice or three times removed. After school they'd search for fragments of coral in the nearby lagoon overlooked by the slumbering giants of Mount Lidgbird and Mount Gower, or they'd ride their bikes to Ned's Beach and feed the trevally and silver mullet and bright blue parrot fish swirling around their legs, their meaty, slick bodies surprisingly warm.

They'd been inseparable in spirit, even when Sarah had taken off to Sydney and boarding school to complete her higher school certificate while Jules and Floss had finished their schooling by correspondence, preferring to stay on the island. But Sarah had still come home and they'd spent every holiday together, the long summer breaks filled with the promise of tomorrow.

Then the boyfriends appeared, and a threesome had become three couples.

It had been wonderful for a while.

But that was back then.

There was nothing lovely about being forced to confront a past that was so badly broken there was no way to fix it.

And her mother thought it would be lovely to catch up with her old friends? Not likely.

No. Better to stay as far away from the fallout as you could get, raise the drawbridge, and protect yourself.

The chirp of her phone interrupted her thoughts. Sarah checked the caller ID and gave a wry smile. So it wasn't just the sauce she was stirring?

She turned down the gas and answered her phone.

'What the hell are you playing at?'

'Hi Danny, I'm well, as it happens, thank you. Is there a problem?'

'Did you tell Mum you expected me to move home to look after her?'

Sarah rolled her eyes. 'No, though I have no doubt that's the line she spun you.'

'She said you suggested it. Why the hell would you do that?'

'Hang on, little brother. I simply told her that if she was going to ask me to put my life on hold, then she better make sure to ask you too.'

'Why?'

'Because it's only fair she'd ask us both, don't you think? And who knows? Maybe you've had enough of the big smoke and would like six months downtime? The fact is she needs help in the shop. Deirdre's looking to cut her hours, and besides, they need someone younger and fitter.'

'You didn't have to drop me into it. You know she hates Silvio.'

'For a start, I didn't "drop you into it". She's your mother too, so this is something that concerns us both. And for the record, she doesn't hate Silvio. She likes him. She just hates that you're gay.'

'And that's going to change any time soon?' He snorted. 'Fat chance.'

'Maybe it will. Give Mum time to get used to the idea, rather than drop in and blow her world apart. Let her see you together and realise that you love each other.'

'You actually believe that bullshit you're spinning?'

'Okay, so it's a long shot, but seriously, why shouldn't you step up when your parents need you?'

'It's easier for you. You're the one who hasn't got a partner to worry about.'

'Thanks, bro, for pointing that out, and you're right, I don't have a partner, just the noose of a massive mortgage around my neck keeping me cosy at night.'

'Whatever,' Danny said dismissively. 'I'm not going. I told her it was impossible. I've got my career to think about.'

She didn't mean to snort. She really didn't. But if her brother was going to be so unhelpful, she couldn't find a good reason not to. Mind you, she really hadn't meant him to hear.

'What the hell did you mean by that?'

'Nothing.'

'Like hell.'

Sarah sighed. 'Okay, Danny. I don't mean to be rude, but seriously, you sell men's underwear in Myer.'

'That is such a cheap shot. We can't all be hotshot accountants in Sydney, can we?'

'Give me a break. Our mother is demanding someone go home to look after the shop—'

'Well too bad, sis, because it won't be me.' And the connection was cut.

Marvellous, she thought, as she put her phone down, braced her hands against the benchtop and looked out onto the dark of the back-yard and the sleeping bush of the steep valley beyond. Was there any relationship in her life that wasn't fucked up?

4

Lord Howe Island

'It's chilly tonight,' said Floss, listening to the sound of rain on the tin roof and the wet slap of palms in the wind. It was chilly and it had been a long day and she could really do with a bit of comfort.

Andy grunted as he climbed into bed alongside her.

She reached out a hand to touch him under the covers. 'Are you going to turn off the light?'

'In a minute. I'm going to read a bit,' her husband said, smelling minty fresh as he picked up his book from the bedside table.

She ran her fingers up and down his side, as much to let him know the direction of her thoughts as for her own pleasure. Because even through the cotton of his pyjamas she could feel the rippling skin-scape of his ribs and abs. Andy might be on the cusp of forty, but he still had the body of an athlete, and just touching him up made her thighs clench in anticipation. 'Are you sure? Because you have to leave early in the morning on the supply ship and I won't see you for two weeks and …'

'And what?'

'And I'm wearing this …' She flipped down the covers, exposing her red silk negligee. Andy's favourite, he'd once told her, because it had shoestring straps instead of sleeves and he'd reckoned he could peel it off quicker than he could a banana skin. It was way too cold this time of year to go without flannelette pyjamas but the night air sure worked a treat on her nipples. She looked over at him. 'And don't you want to make love to your gorgeous wife before you go? In case she forgets you when you're gone.'

He didn't spare Floss a glance. He just sighed as he fished out the bookmark and placed it flat on the quilt lying over his chest. 'I'll be back Wednesday.'

'Hey, you haven't even looked.' And maybe she had stretchmarks where Andy had muscle tone, but she had a couple of things she knew he liked. She waggled her chest, the bullet points of her nipples jiggling under the silk. 'Are you sure you don't want to come and play?'

'Not now,' he said, still not looking as he turned the page.

It was the turning the page that did it. That and the fact he couldn't even spare her a glance. Couldn't bother to say sorry or that he'd like to make love but he was too tired. Because no way was she giving up yet. He just needed some encouragement.

'There's always two ways to do things …' Floss said, as much to herself as to the inanimate object that was her husband beside her. She sat up. 'The easy way, and—' She yanked the book out of his hands before rolling over, shoving the book under her nightie and curling into a ball. 'The hard way!'

He roared, rearing up in the bed, plunging his hand beneath her, and she squealed with delight at finally having his hands on her and his heat around her. Any second now he'd be sure to see it was much more fun playing bedroom games with his wife than reading some dreary book.

He wrestled with her, his hands busy trying to snatch the book back. He was strong, but she was no slouch, and she wriggled some more and shoved the book inside the band of her knickers. 'Come and get it!'

He didn't bother. He flopped back against his pillow, abandoning the chase. 'Bloody hell, Floss,' he said. 'I get all of ten minutes a night to read.'

'And how much time do I get? How much time do you allocate to me every night?'

'We had sex.'

'Three weeks ago!'

'There you go. So give me my book back.'

She wrangled it out of her knickers and hurled it at him, whacking him hard in the chest. 'There's your sodding book,' she said, as she clambered out of the bed and pulled on her fleecy dressing gown, lashing the tie tight. 'Enjoy your uninterrupted nights with your boring novel. I hope you're both very happy together.'

'Where are you going?'

She pulled on her slippers. 'Anywhere you're not.'

'Fine. So maybe we'll both get a good night's sleep for once.'

'You really are an arsehole, sometimes.'

'Yeah,' he said, 'an arsehole who just wants ten minutes' peace and a good night's sleep.' He put down his book and punched his pillow. 'Deal with it.'

A sound came from down the hall, a jerking staccato cry that quickly escalated into a wail.

Floss groaned. 'Now look what you've gone and done. It took me half an hour to get Mikey settled.'

'You're blaming me? All I was trying to do was read. You're the one who had to turn bed time into World War Three.'

'So I guess I'll take care of our child's needs. As usual.'

He switched off the light. 'Makes sense to me, seeing you're the one—'

'I'm the one what? The one who wanted him? Don't you ever let him hear you say that!'

'Relax. I was going to say, seeing you're the one who's already up.'

'Bullshit,' she whispered as she padded down the hallway towards their youngest's room before his cries woke the rest of the family.

But she was too late, because Annie was there before her, her three-year-old baby brother in her arms, singing the boy a soft lullaby to calm him in the glow of the nightlight.

'Oh, Annie, I'm sorry,' Floss whispered, transferring her baby from her eldest child's chest to hers. He grabbed her and clung like a monkey, like he never wanted to let her go, and she kissed his head, rocking him from side to side to calm him and wondering, because he felt hot. She hoped there was nothing more seriously wrong with him than a temperature. She turned to her daughter, who was watching, her lip caught between her teeth. 'You should go back to bed, lovey.'

'I was already awake. I was doing homework.'

'So late?' But now she looked harder, she could see Annie's jeans poking out the bottom of her dressing gown before disappearing into her ugg boots, and she gathered she was still dressed under her gown. 'Well, you better get off now. It's too cold for us both to be up and you've got school tomorrow.'

But the girl didn't move. 'What were you and Dad arguing about before?'

Annie had heard that? Floss put a hand to Mikey's brow. Definitely warm. 'Do you think Mikey's running a temperature? Maybe I should take him to see the doctor.'

'Mu-um.'

'Oh, don't worry. That was nothing.'

'It didn't sound like nothing.'

'Okay, then, it was nothing you need to worry yourself about. Grown-up stuff.'

'Don't fob me off with that crap,' Annie snapped and even in the low light her blue eyes were as sharp as Ball's Pyramid, the blade of rock that speared from the sea some twenty kilometres away. 'I'm sixteen, Mum, I'm not a kid anymore.'

Sixteen. When had that happened? The child in her arms hiccupped, his sobs gradually subsiding, though Floss knew it would take some time before this little one properly settled again. She'd have to find him some children's paracetemol, if he could keep it down.

She put a hand to her daughter's cheek and sighed. Her skin was so smooth, so perfect. Suddenly Floss felt old, more like fifty than the thirty-seven she was turning next week. Everyone said Annie looked like her, and sure, she could see vague similarities, but was she ever as pretty as Annie? She couldn't remember ever being that young, let alone that pretty. Then again, she couldn't remember anything much. It suddenly felt like she'd been sleepwalking her way through the last twenty years. 'No, you're not a kid.'

'Are you and Dad going to get a divorce?'

'What?' She laughed. Or tried to as she sat in the rocking chair where she'd nursed all five of her children. A good thing she and the rocking chair were well acquainted—it was likely going to be her bed for the night. She tucked a crocheted throw around the child at her chest. It was too early to put him back to bed, he'd whimper at the first hint of separation. 'No. Of course not. Why would you even ask that?'

'Because you're always arguing. I hear you at night when you think we're all asleep.'

'Every old married couple argues,' Floss said, because it must be true. 'Besides, we don't argue that often.'

'You do lately.' Annie took a step closer and her eyes softened. 'You'd tell me if something was wrong, wouldn't you?'

'Oh, Annie, nothing's wrong. It's just—married stuff. We're busy with our jobs and sometimes it all gets a bit hard and we get a bit snippy. That's all.' She shrugged. 'It's normal.'

Her daughter shuffled a bit, her expression uncertain, as if unsure whether to believe her or not.

'Hey,' Floss said, 'give me your hand.' And when Annie hesitated: 'Do you want me to try to get up with Mikey plastered to my chest?' That earned her a half-smile.

Annie came closer, slipping her hand into her mother's.

Floss sighed and let her eyelids close as she squeezed her daughter's hand. 'I love you, sweetie. I loved you from the moment I knew you were coming. I loved you the day you were born and first wrapped a hand around my finger, and yourself around my heart. And I've loved you more and more every day since. And I love your dad, because he gave me you and your brothers, and I wouldn't be without any of you for all the world.'

'So—everything's okay then. Between you and Dad, I mean.'

Floss pressed her lips together in what she hoped passed as a smile and nodded. 'Of course it is, silly billy. Come here and give your mum and Mikey a kiss goodnight and then get off to bed. You've got school tomorrow.'

Annie smiled softly and leaned down. 'Night, Mum,' she said, holding back her hair as she planted a soft kiss to Floss's cheek and then her brother's hair. 'Night, Mikey-boy,' she whispered.

Floss heard her footsteps recede down the hallway and then the snick of her bedroom door, and then there was nothing but the spatter of rain on the roof and the wind swirling through the trees, rattling the palm fronds. Sixteen already. No, definitely not a baby any more, and yet, so different from how Floss had been back then. She'd had her life pretty much mapped out at Annie's age. Marriage to Andy and a houseful of kids—so she'd made a slight miscalculation with the actual number and the four kids had become five—but what was one more when you already had a mob to chase after?

She'd got what she wanted and more.

But was this it?

Was this all there was?

Because she really didn't think she could stand another forty-plus years of sleeping with a man who didn't want to make love to her.

Then again—divorce? The thought had never once crossed her mind. She loved Andy. She always had. She always would.

She just didn't know if he still loved her.

Another heavy shower of rain pounded the roof. Mikey snuffled against her chest. The air around them seemed to quiver, heavy with questions to which there were no answers. A shame she was wearing her nightie instead of her repel-all-boarders flannelette pyjamas, because they also managed to repel all cold, but it was impossible to go and change into them now.

But the cold tendrils worming their way under her dressing gown and around her legs were good. The cold was pain. And right now a little discomfort was the perfect accompaniment to wondering how it was that things had gone so wrong.

She hugged the bundle clinging to her chest tighter as the cold needled into her bare legs and salt water squeezed from her eyes.

How the hell had they come to this?

5

Saturday morning sleep-in. Were there any more beautiful words in the English language? Jules stretched under the doona and blinked an eye open, wondering what had woken her. Outside was still the dark of a winter morning, the wind already up, rattling the shutters and slapping palm leaves together so it almost sounded like the crick of cicadas, but inside her bed was blissfully warm, aided, no doubt, by the little bundle that had wormed its way alongside her sometime during the night and now lay pressed hard against her back, a wayward elbow wedged painfully into one shoulder.

Cheeky girl.

Jules smiled as she shifted the offending joint and settled back down for another doze. There was no rush to get up, her shift at the museum didn't start until twelve. It was so nice to sleep in for once. So nice to be able to drift back off …

The water in the lagoon was warm. Weird, seeing it was the depths of winter, weirder still to be swimming, but the water was blissfully warm and luxurious until she moved and something stuck to her skin. Seaweed. No, she realised in horror, suddenly wide awake. Her pyjamas.

'Oh, Della!' she said, throwing the covers back, the smell of freshly unleashed urine hitting her nostrils, banishing any thoughts of dozing any longer.

The girl rubbed her eyes into wakefulness, her face crumpling when she realised what she'd done. 'I'm sorry, Mummy,' she wailed.

'I know,' Jules said, scooping her daughter's sodden form out of the bed, kissing her cheek and cursing Pru for boasting that her children had been out of day nappies at eighteen months and night nappies at two and insisting that Della should be dry by four. Why had she listened? It wasn't a bloody competition.

But she was madder with herself. She should have taken her daughter to the bathroom when she'd first realised she was there. Della hadn't been sleeping dry through the night for that long.

'It's okay, sweetie. How about we go have a shower together?'

They passed the hall table on the way to the bathroom. 'I hope you're satisfied,' Jules growled half-heartedly to the photo there. 'Wherever you are now.'

'Who's satisfied?'

'Your father, my sweet,' Jules said as she put her daughter down and turned on the shower to let it warm up before peeling off Della's sodden pyjamas, one leg at a time. 'Yuck,' she said, as the urine-soaked pyjama bottoms hit the tiles with a wet slap.

'Yucky,' her daughter mimicked, holding her nose. Which made it all the harder to tug off her pyjama top, but Jules managed, checking the water temperature in the shower before she lifted Della into the stall and under the spray.

Her own pyjama bottoms met the same fate. A good thing she had a twelve o'clock start, because she'd sure be giving the washing machine a work out this morning. It was when she was cross-armed and reefing off her top that she brushed something odd with the back of a fingernail. Something that didn't belong there at the side of her breast. A pimple.

She backed up to the mirror, arm raised, examining it with her eyes, feeling it with her fingertips.

No, not a pimple.

A lump. Only about the size of a baby pea, but very definitely a lump.

What the hell?

'Are you coming, Mummy?'

Jules turned to look at her daughter, holding her arms over her chest as the water rained down over her, flattening her strawberry blonde curls against her head. Her four-year-old daughter who'd lost her father and who had a mother with a lump on her breast, and a thousand horrific scenarios lit with neon lights flashed their way through her mind. Could life be that cruel?

She smiled at the child she thought she'd never have. The child she'd had more for other people rather than for herself. And yet, this was the child who had wormed her way into Jules's life and enriched it in ways she'd never imagined possible.

Damn it, no.

Life wouldn't be that cruel.

She wouldn't let it.

'Coming,' she said, assuming a villainous crouch the way she did when they were playing hide and seek. 'Ready or not.'

Della shuddered in faux terror as her mother sprang into the shower and grabbed her under the arms to lift her high under the spray, where she squealed with delight until they were both laughing. And when the girl was done with laughing, she wrapped her arms around her mother's neck, pulled her face close, and kissed her on the nose.

'I wuv you, Mummy.'

Jules was glad she was in the shower so Della couldn't see the moisture that had sprung unbidden to her eyes. She squeezed her girl tight. 'I love you too, Della Bella.'

It was just a lump. That was all it was at this stage.

It didn't have to mean anything.

6

Sydney

'How soon does your mother get out of hospital?' asked Frankie during Monday's lunch at the busy sushi restaurant around the corner from the office.

'How soon does she escape from Alcatraz, you mean.' Sarah gave a wry smile as her eyes followed the parade of little covered dishes on the conveyor, pouncing on a dish of steaming prawn dumplings to add to their small collection. 'At least that's what Mum calls it. It would have been later this week, but they're keeping her in longer.'

'Oh. That must be frustrating for her.'

Sarah nodded. 'Oh, yes.' The novelty of smiling at every doctor, nurse and dinner lady was rapidly losing its gloss, and Dot was reverting to type. Sarah had taken her father home to her place for a night over the weekend, ostensibly to let him sleep in a real bed and give him a break from the fold out chair, but they both knew it was to let him have a mental health break from Dot. And meanwhile she had fed him the lie that the partner's meeting had been postponed because someone was ill. It was only a tiny white lie, really, but she didn't feel good about it because she'd been feeling sick ever since. 'But the

40

physio's not happy to send her home to the island until he's satisfied she's on top of her exercises.'

Frankie nodded, aiming her chopsticks at a dumpling. 'That would do it.'

'It did. So she demanded a second opinion.'

The dumpling hovered just short of Frankie's mouth. 'She did? Wow, she's ballsy. How did that go?'

'She got one, all right, but the second said the same as the first, so now she doesn't like either of them.'

Frankie chuckled, reaching for a plate of chicken karaage, and for a while they concentrated on the assortment of dishes between them. 'So I guess that means you've got a bit more time to work out what you're going to do, huh?'

Sarah sighed. 'Yeah.' What was she going to do? The question had been plaguing her all weekend. It was the last thing swirling around in her brain when she went to sleep at night. It was there the moment she woke up—which she did several times a night. Her visits to see her mother in hospital were painful because Dot already considered the matter settled. There was no escaping the decision she'd have to make, and soon.

But right now she was feeling pleasantly full, and that didn't make it any easier. 'I don't know, Frankie, how could I possibly leave Sydney? I seriously don't think I could survive without our weekly sushi fix.'

Frankie nodded sagely. 'Well, there is that,' she said, topping up their tea. 'Although …' She put the pot down. 'If you don't mind me saying so, would it be so bad, going back? I know you don't get on with your mother, but after what's happened, surely it would be better than staying at FRL?'

Sarah screwed up her nose.

'I'm not staying at FRL,' she said. 'I can't, after being shafted like that.'

'There you go, then,' Frankie said, her tea cup cradled in her hands, expression thoughtful. 'So that much is settled. But I don't know, six months on Lord Howe Island—it sounds like paradise to me. It could be like a mini sea change.'

Huh, Sarah thought, skewering a piece of chicken fair in the middle with one pointed chopstick, an act that felt strangely therapeutic. She was under no doubt that her colleague was imagining sandy beaches and palm trees and fancy cocktails complete with little umbrellas. Whereas for Sarah, it would be less of a sea change and more like an up-shit-creek change, where she'd be at the mercy of the ghosts of her not-so-distant past with not a single swizzle stick let alone a paddle to fend them off.

She chewed on the tender chicken like she'd been chewing on her problem, grateful to have a few moments to think before answering. But when all was said and done, there was no point trying to explain.

Nobody, it seemed, could understand what going home to Lord Howe Island actually meant to Sarah. Not her mother, not her brother —though maybe he just didn't care—not even her father, who she was probably closer to than anyone else in the world, seemed to grasp what was holding her back from committing.

It wasn't a sea change.

It was a sentence.

And Sarah wasn't even the guilty party.

And then she thought about Floss and added an addendum.

She wasn't the guilty party—*mostly*.

But even as she swallowed the chicken, even as the little sushi train kept moving, a little place at the back of her mind kept chewing away at her resistance, exposing the weaknesses and vulnerabilities.

Because no. She didn't want to go. But she'd been kidding herself even thinking she had a choice. That was what was keeping her awake at night. It wasn't having to make a decision, it was knowing she'd never had a choice at all.

Her entire life she'd been the one called upon to step up, to help out when someone needed help. Her whole life, she'd been the one to do it. And now, when she wanted more than anything to challenge the status quo, to pass the baton and let somebody else do their bit, she had no excuse.

All this time, she'd been fighting the inevitable—and for what?

She tossed back her tea, trying hard to swallow the last shreds of chicken that suddenly felt like they were stuck in her throat. There was nothing to keep her in Sydney now. Nothing to prevent her from leaving, no matter how much she tried to pretend there was. No brother to suddenly—magically—pull up his big boy boxer shorts and come to her rescue.

'Oh,' she said, slamming down her chopsticks on the bench. 'Fuck it!'

Heads swivelled all around them. Frankie's eyes opened wide. 'I have never once heard you swear.'

Sarah looked around unapologetically, directing death stares at the glaring patrons until they turned back to their sushi. She picked up her chopsticks and ordered another plate of prawn dumplings, determined that if this was her last Japanese meal for six months, she was going to enjoy it. 'I guess I never had good enough reason.'

'Listen, Dad,' Sarah said that night when she visited the hospital and took him off in search of coffee. 'I told a bit of a white lie the other day when I said the partners' meeting had been deferred.' She licked her lips. 'It wasn't.'

Sam said nothing. He'd raised an eyebrow and made all the right noises when she'd told him, but she'd always been a crap liar and her dad knew it, but unlike Dot, he also knew better than to dig.

'You see, the thing is, I didn't get the promotion.'

The skin on Sam's face settled deeper into its creases. He patted the back of her hand. 'Oh, lovey, I'm sorry. Maybe next month.'

She shook her head. 'No. They promoted someone else—a guy about ten years my junior. Someone who's only been with the firm for a year. And I'm sorry I couldn't tell you before, but it hurt, Dad. It made me feel like a failure, like a has-been. A bit like I'm on the scrap heap at thirty-seven.'

This time he took her hand and squeezed it. 'No,' he said. 'Don't think like that.'

Sarah sucked in a deep breath, fighting back the cursed sting of tears. 'Anyway, it got me to thinking. I can't stay in that job. I have to find another one. But that might take a while. And so meanwhile …'

Hope infused Sam's eyes, a hope that Sarah knew he was too reticent to put into words. She smiled encouragingly. 'I spoke to the senior partner this afternoon,' she said, 'about taking some leave—I've got heaps due, as it happens.'

'You'll come home, then?' Her father took her hands between his. 'You'll really do it?'

She nodded. 'It might take me a few days to get myself organised—I'll need to find a tenant or a house sitter. I can't just lock the door and walk away. But, yeah, I'll come.'

Sam looked like he'd just won Lotto. 'Thank you. From a purely selfish point of view, I'll be happy to be seeing more of you.'

Sarah was ashamed to see the glint of tears at the corners of his eyes. 'It'll be good to spend more time with you too.'

'And I'll do whatever it takes to make sure your mum doesn't give you too much grief.'

'Thanks, Dad,' Sarah said, knowing she that at least she had one relationship that wasn't messed up. The knowledge lent her strength. 'I'll hold you to it.'

Although she knew that when it came to the reasons why she'd prefer not to have to spend the next six months on Lord Howe Island, her mother was only the tip of the iceberg.

7

Dr Bennett had finished his phone call and was busy with the paper-work by the time Jules had put her clothes to rights and was sitting opposite him at his desk again. It was strange to be here without Della on her lap getting antibiotics for an ear infection or a bad cough checked out. It was strange to be here for herself.

The doctor's fountain pen scratched on a radiology request pad, the appointment already made.

'So you think it could be ...'

He stopped writing and looked up, forty years of patients' stories etched deep on his face, a lifetime of understanding in his eyes. 'I think it's something you want to have checked out. I'm sending you to see a radiologist to have a scan and I'm giving you a referral to a surgeon in case they decide you need a biopsy.'

She swallowed. 'And then?'

'And then we get the results and we take it from there. One step at a time. But whatever happens, Jules, you've done the right thing. You've come in early, and that's the best thing you could do.'

She nodded, her addled brain trying to absorb his words, trying to take comfort from his calm and measured delivery, when all she could hear in her head were the what ifs he wasn't addressing. What if the scan showed something disturbing? What if the biopsy came back positive? What if the worst happened and—

'Try not to get ahead of yourself,' Dr Bennett said, as if he could read her mind. But of course he probably could. He'd done this before, said the very same thing any number of times when he sent someone for tests. He knew his patients must feel like an animal caught in the headlights, unable to move for indecision.

'Have you got someone who can take care of Della while you're in Sydney?'

'Yeah. Mum.'

Dr Bennett didn't say anything, just looked down again, signing the forms with a flourish.

'She'll be fine, doctor.'

He looked up. 'I'm sure she will be,' he said and Jules felt herself relax. God, she was jumpy. Even the harmless stack of papers he passed her felt like an unexploded bomb in her hands.

'Any other questions?'

She forced a smile. 'All good,' she said, as if he'd told her it was nothing that a salt-water gargle wo uldn't fix.

She knew he wouldn't be convinced. He would have heard that a thousand times before too, and besides, the quake in her voice didn't lend her any credibility.

'You'll be well taken care of, don't worry,' he said as he stood up to open the door.

'I know. Thanks, doctor.'

Her head was spinning so hard she didn't register who was waiting outside until the nurse said, 'Floss, you and Mikey are next.'

Jules blinked, her vision clearing to see her former friend clutching the whimpering boy to her chest. And then she knew she was really off her game. In an island the size of a postage stamp, the art of avoiding someone you didn't want to run into gave you skills akin to those of a chess master, and yet here they both were.

Checkmate.

'Floss,' Jules said awkwardly, because this time there was no chance of turning away unseen. But she couldn't meet Floss's eyes, so she looked at the child instead. 'Mikey's sick?'

'Yeah.'

'Poor kid.'

'Yeah. You?'

Jules shrugged. 'Can't complain. Good luck then.' She nodded towards the child.

She didn't hear a thank you or goodbye as she left, but then, she really didn't expect one.

Outside the wind was rising, dark clouds building on the horizon, but the beauty of living on a subtropical island was that it never got too cold. Even in the depths of winter, the temperature barely dropped below fifteen degrees Celsius. But she neither saw nor felt the beauty today. Today she was compelled to zip her jacket all the way up, chilled from the inside out by words that swirled in her mind.

Cancer.

It couldn't be cancer. She wasn't old enough to have cancer. She had too much to do and Della was too young.

God, why did she have to notice that bloody lump in the first place? If she hadn't, she wouldn't have been at the surgery, and she certainly wouldn't have run into Floss.

She wished she hadn't. Because seeing her made her realise how much she missed her old friend.

She missed having someone who knew everything about her, going back to school days. She missed having a confidante, someone she could visit and have a coffee with and talk about anything and everything.

She ached for the easy friendship they'd once shared. She missed the way Floss would stay so calm and measured and see the positive in everything and the good in anyone.

Until the day she'd stopped seeing the good in Jules and had cut her off as cleanly as a surgeon amputates a gangrenous limb, leaving Jules to feel the loss every day since.

~

Pru was busy making pastry when Jules let herself in to collect Della. 'How's the head?' she asked, surprised to see her mum dressed in a navy blue tracksuit and looking so active; Pru Callahan had been shuffling around in her pyjamas and looking sorry for herself when Jules had dropped Della off.

'Oh, no time for that,' Pru said with a wave of her floured hand as she reached for her rolling pin. 'I've got a half-dozen banana cream pies on order for Sullivan's Buffet Night tonight.'

'Yummy,' said Della, playing with Duplo at the same kiddie table where Jules had played all those years ago.

'Nice,' said Jules. 'Do we get one?'

'Not this time. Not unless you want to pay me what they do.' Pru looked up. 'So how did you get on with the doctor? Everything all right?'

Jules took a moment to answer. She hadn't told her mother why she'd needed the appointment, because there hadn't seemed any point in worrying her unnecessarily, but there was no way she could avoid telling her now.

She looked at Della, back to playing happily in the corner, singing to the Duplo animals for which she'd constructed a zoo. 'He's sending me to Sydney for tests,' she whispered, too softly for her daughter to hear.

'What tests?'

Jules glared at her mother, who immediately put her fingers over her mouth. Della was still singing, a giraffe in one hand, a polar bear in the other.

'Sorry,' she whispered.

'I have to get something checked out. A lump.'

Her mother's eyes opened wide. She put one hand to her daughter's wrist, and used the other to cover her own breast, the question plain in her eyes.

Jules nodded. 'Can you look after Della a couple of days later this week?'

Pru looked at the girl, her eyes misting over. 'Oh, Jules.'

'Mum, it'll be fine,' she said with a certainty she didn't feel, but she had to say it, if only because she knew her mother was running through the same scenarios that had flooded her own mind. And Jules really didn't need her mother imagining the worst—she had enough imagination for the pair of them. 'Really. It'll be fine.'

'What are you talking about?' Della demanded, suddenly sitting to attention, animals paused mid-action.

'Nothing,' said Pru, and Jules rolled her eyes, knowing that saying the 'nothing' word only made a kid more suspicious.

'It's a surprise,' Jules said, crouching next to her daughter. She pushed a wayward curl behind Della's ear. 'You're going to have a little holiday with Nana this week. Is that okay?'

'Why?' Della's blue eyes darted suspiciously from her mother to her nana and back again. 'Where are you going?'

'Only off to Sydney for a couple of days.'

'In the pwane?'

'Yes, in the plane.'

Della frowned, her bottom lip sticking out as her unfairness radar kicked in. Going on the plane was a special treat that didn't happen anywhere near enough in her books. 'Why can't I come?'

'Because I'm going to be very busy and I need you to look after Nana for me while I'm gone to stop her from getting too lonely. Do you think you can do that?'

'Will Nana make banana cream pie for me?'

'Of course Nana will,' said Pru.

Della looked from her mother to her nana and burst into a fit of giggles. She pointed at Pru. 'Nana looks silly!'

'What?' said Jules and Pru together.

'There's a hand on her booby.'

Jules saw there was: a flour print of Pru's hand neatly cupping one breast. She joined in the laughter.

'I'm such a silly billy!' Pru said. 'I forgot to put my apron on.'

'Put one of those on the other side,' Jules said, 'and you could almost be the Little Mermaid.'

'Ariel!' said Della gleefully, clapping her hands, because she'd watched Jules's old videos a thousand times.

Pru patted the flour from her top. 'I always thought I was more of an Ursula.'

8

Floss blinked into the grey light of early morning. Thirty-seven years old. In three years, she'd be forty. In thirteen, she'd be fifty. In another thirty-seven she'd be seventy-four. Would she make it that far, or had she already used up more than half her life?

Whoa! She had to get herself out of this funk.

She knew what would help. She looked hopefully over at Andy, but he was still sleeping, a dark shadow in the gloom, his breathing slow and even. She'd been on tenterhooks all yesterday, wondering what kind of mood he'd be in when he got home after his days away on the supply ship run, but he'd breezed in, pecking her on the cheek before being buried alive under the deluge of their children's welcome-home hugs. And if he gave a toss for the acrimony that had accompanied his departure, it hadn't shown—he'd acted like their argument had never happened, like he'd dispensed with it as easily as flicking a bug from his arm. Half his luck. She'd spent the last three days replaying every sentence, trying to work out what she should have said to turn their problem around.

After dinner Andy had read a couple of chapters of Harry Potter to the kids and gone to bed at nine o'clock. He'd been asleep and snoring by the time she'd finished her chores and slipped in beside him.

But today was her birthday, and he had no excuse. If he didn't display some kind of affection towards her beyond a peck on the cheek, she'd burst.

Exactly the way her bladder would if she didn't get out of bed this minute.

She snapped on the kettle in the kitchen on her way back from the bathroom and stood at the sink, her arms crossed, gazing unseeingly at the wall of greenery swaying outside the window. It would be nice to linger in bed on her birthday, but there were kids to get ready for school, and three rooms to clean and change over before today's plane came in.

She squeezed her arms and looked around her simple country-style kitchen with the big table in the centre, every horizontal surface cluttered with lunch boxes and water bottles and whatever the kids had last got out the fridge or pantry and left there and that she hadn't had the energy to put away, and felt a wave of despair wash over her.

Because this was half the problem. It wasn't just the sex, or lack of it.

It was this. *The same thing.* The same cycle of wake up, get the kids up, breakfast, school, cleaning rooms, washing, making dinner, home-work, bed. The same view of swaying palms outside her kitchen window. And the next morning she got out of bed early to face it all over again.

And if she couldn't even look forward to having sex with her husband to relieve the monotony?

She spooned coffee into two battered mugs as if on autopilot, one heaped spoon for him and one rounded for her, and two sugars for him, and there was no preventing the words of an old Marianne Faithfull ballad worming its way into her mind, a ballad written before she was born that she'd found in her mother's music collection when she was young.

A song she wished she'd never been curious enough to listen to, because the older she'd got, the song had become harder to forget. 'The Ballad of Lucy Jordan'.

Today Floss was the same age as Lucy in the song. Thirty-seven years old, and with a husband who disappeared to work and whose kids went to school and who'd never get beyond the prison-like walls of her tiny island home.

The way her life was going, she'd never get to Paris, never ride in a sports car, never feel the warm wind in her hair either.

Floss had seen pictures of Paris, of course. She'd talked to guests from all over who'd told her it was the most romantic city in the world. But what was it really like to experience it for yourself? Or, for that matter, what about London and New York? Rome and Istanbul? All of these places that were just names on a map to her. Foreign. Exotic.

She looked down at the mugs, surprised to see she'd already put milk into them. Autopilot again. Her life in a word. Not having to think, just to do: the dishes, the cooking, the change overs. The sheer bloody drudgery of her existence. Day after day after bloody day.

She sniffed as she picked up the coffees, and headed back to her bedroom.

There was a birthday card–sized envelope on her pillow. There wasn't a present to go with it. They hadn't done presents for each other in forever. Why buy something just for the sake of it? Andy had said they had everything they ever needed already.

Back then, she'd agreed with him. But now?

She put down their coffees and sat on the bed, picking up the envelope and flicking it over. Andy was still lying under the covers, watching warily.

'I thought you were asleep,' she said.

'I was.' One corner of his mouth kicked up, a concession to a smile as he raised himself to kiss her. It was a little stab to her heart that he missed her mouth. 'Happy birthday, Floss.'

She smiled anyway and pulled out the card. It had a bouquet of flowers on the front and 'To my wife' in fancy gold lettering. On the inside were more sprays of flowers scattered around the kind of sugary-sweet verse that made your teeth ache, but that was okay, because Andy had never been great at expressing his emotions. He'd written 'To Floss' above the verse, and 'Love from Andy' below it.

She raised her eyebrows. Okay, so once upon a time he might have addressed it to his 'favourite wife' and added a kiss or two under his name, but at least hadn't signed it simply 'from Andy'. That had to be worth something, surely?

'Okay?' he asked, looking at her with such sad eyes, almost like he was afraid of her, like he was afraid she was going to start another argument.

'Thank you,' she said, adding a smile, because she meant it, but also because she mustn't appear disappointed. He'd remembered it was her birthday, after all. And she didn't really care that Andy hadn't chosen to break their rule about not buying each other presents. She just wouldn't have minded if he had.

She stood the card on her bedside table and picked up her coffee.

'Got a surprise for you tonight,' Andy said, reaching for his coffee, his bare chest on full, glorious display. He was such a fine-looking specimen for his age, fit from his physical work, was it any wonder that the neglected place between her thighs went all tingly as her mind turned to sex?

'Ooh,' she said, leaning closer, propping herself on one arm. 'Tell me more?'

He looked supremely smug. 'I'm not saying anything, other than to say that tonight, you don't need to worry about making tea. It's all taken care of, all right?' And then he patted the back of her hand where it rested on the doona. Like she was the family pet.

What about after tea? she wanted to ask. But she mustn't start a row. She mustn't look ungrateful or needy. Dinner out was good. It just wasn't what she really wanted. It wasn't enough.

They piled out of the van and into the Halfway Café at six pm for her birthday tea. Eating at a café that mostly catered to the visiting tourist trade was a rare treat, not least because it was expensive. Andy set down the guidelines for choosing a meal: they weren't about to pay for the local kingfish or steak at restaurant prices so their choices were limited to pizza or burgers, and the nut sundae selection of the dessert menu. All apart from Floss, because it was her birthday, and she could choose another dessert if she wanted.

Annie immediately took umbrage. 'I'm too old for a frickin' nut sundae,' she said, tossing the menu on the table and crossing her arms. Floss looked at their sixteen-year-old daughter and was sympathetic. Tonight she looked more like twenty-one, although that probably owed more to the skilful cat's eye curl at the ends of her eyeliner and the impressive bust under her peasant blouse. A bust ably assisted, Floss knew, by the push-up bra that Annie had requested for her own birthday.

Floss's DNA didn't run to a steady hand with eyeliner and she didn't own a push-up bra, but she had made an effort tonight, taking more time with her hair so her messy up-do looked more designer chic than struggle bun. She'd chosen her favourite blue and pink paisley peasant blouse and even broken out the mascara and lippy, feeling pretty good about herself until she'd made the mistake of asking Andy how she'd looked. 'Yeah, all right,' he'd said, barely sparing her a glance, before yelling at the kids to hurry up and get in the van.

'You can share my cake,' said Floss to Annie.

'What about me?' grumbled Brodie, gangly arms angled on the table like grasshopper limbs. 'I'm not a kid any more.'

'Do we have to have nut sundae?' piped up eleven-year-old Cameron, who was making noises to younger brother Ben about the chocolate brownie listed on the menu.

'You'll have what I say you can have,' said Andy, laying down the law. 'There's nothing wrong with nut sundae.'

'I *hate* nut sundae,' said Mikey, buying into the mood and looking thoroughly dissatisfied at an upside-down menu he had no hope of reading even the right way up.

'No, you don't,' snapped Annie. 'You love it when we have it at home.'

'Have I had it before?'

Annie rolled her eyes.

'Of course, you have, you drongo,' said Brodie. 'Mum makes it all the time in summer.'

'Brodie called me names!' cried Mikey.

'Maybe we could just sort the pizzas out first,' Floss suggested, 'and worry about dessert afterwards if anyone's still hungry.'

'I'll still be hungry,' said Brodie.

'And me!' said Cameron.

'I don't want nut sundae!' yelled Mikey.

'Shh,' said Floss, feeling a vague drumbeat behind her eyes. Dinner out with the kids. What a brilliant present.

'All right?' said Andy.

She looked at him. He'd dressed up tonight too, as much as Andy did—a rare open-neck shirt under his crew jumper—and with his six weeks' overdue hair flicking over his ears and an unshaven jaw, he was definitely the best thing on the menu tonight. That is, if he was on the menu.

'How about we order dinner and get this lot home,' she said. Because the sooner they got home, the sooner they could get the kids to bed and think about going to bed themselves. Surely tonight, for her birthday, he might forget about his book for once?

Andy's eyes did a sweep at the already bored bunch of kids around the table. 'Yeah, let's do it. Okay, kids, how many for ham and pineapple?'

An hour later, full up on pizza and ice cream, the family dived through a rain shower and climbed back into the van. Annie buckled Mikey into his booster seat while Floss and Andy jumped into the front, brushing off the rain.

'Not such a great idea, then,' Andy said under his breath. He took her hand and squeezed it. The acknowledgement and the feel of his hand around hers were so unexpected that Floss couldn't help but smile.

'It was okay.'

He snorted. 'It was a disaster. I'll make it up to you somehow.' And before she could respond, he looked over his shoulder, and said, 'Everybody in?'

'Mikey says he doesn't feel well,' Annie said, sliding the van door closed and clicking her seat belt.

'Hang on, Mikey,' said Andy, 'we'll be home before you know it.'

They were halfway home, Floss busy working out ways to tell Andy exactly how he could make up for tonight's disaster, when she heard the sudden gush, felt the splatter, and heard Annie's scream followed closely by, 'Oh, Mikey, gross! Stop the car!'

To Andy's credit, he hosed out the van (it wasn't like it was new, but they'd been so right to get rubber mats rather than carpet) while Floss bathed Mikey and collected up the vomit-splashed clothes, now reeking of regurgitated ham and pineapple pizza and chocolate sauce. It wasn't half as appetising second time around.

She was still settling Mikey when she heard Andy come inside and hit the shower, no doubt needing it after sorting out the van. He was just getting in bed by the time she got to the bedroom to grab her dressing gown and head for the shower herself.

'Quite the night,' she said, feeling battered by the events of the evening. Though if Andy was still determined to make up for the disaster of the evening, she wasn't going to be unwilling. She'd already waited too long.

He sighed and picked up his book from his bedside table. 'That's one way of putting it.'

She clutched her dressing gown against her belly. 'It's still my birthday—at least for another hour—if you still want to work out a way of making up for it.'

For a moment he looked like he wanted to argue, and then he seemed to relent, and said, 'Sure. I'm sorry your birthday got fucked up. Go have a shower. I'll be waiting.'

It was the fastest shower she'd ever had, her clothes kicked into a corner of the bathroom rather than being rinsed out.

Except when she got back to the bedroom, Andy was already snoring.

'Oh, give me a break,' she said, as she slipped in beside him, punching her pillow because it would have been bad form to punch her husband while he was asleep, no matter how much she felt like doing it.

Andy snorted, oblivious, and rolled over, putting his back to her.

Floss squeezed her eyes shut and rolled over likewise, 'The Ballad of Lucy Jordan' playing on an endless loop in her mind, words she'd like to erase from her memory, because—god knows—that story hadn't ended well.

She hugged her pillow tight. 'Happy birthday, Floss,' she muttered as she waited fruitlessly for sleep to claim her. 'Happy freaking birthday.'

9

Jules hated turbulence. Stupid really, when the only practical way off the island was by plane, but she would never get used to the way the small plane was tossed around on the wind currents, dropping into holes in the air and landing with a thump before juddering along towards the next invisible booby trap.

She sat with her seat belt firmly fastened, willing herself to relax, telling herself that staring at the propeller outside her window wouldn't be enough to prevent an engine falling off, all the while trying to believe that a plane in turbulence was no different to a car on a bumpy road. But how could that be anywhere close to the same when there was no shoulder to pull off onto if you broke down, just thirty-thousand feet of empty, unhelpful air under your wings instead?

No, she hated turbulence.

She hated the turbulence in her head even more.

Don't get ahead of yourself, the doctor had told her, but how did one do that exactly? How did you maintain a zen-like calm and think, *Well, if it happens—and the tests come back positive—then it happens and I'll just have to deal with it then?* How did you restrain yourself from using what little internet allowance you had to consult Doctor Google and search for terms like 'needle biopsy'? 'Lumpectomy'? 'Mastectomy'? 'Radiotherapy'? 'Chemotherapy'?

Cancer.

How did you stop the bubble of panic that was wedged right at the back of your throat from rising further until it damn near choked you with panic?

How could you not be more aware of your own mortality?

And even though the sites were full of happy-clappy stories of smiling people wearing scarves over bald heads who had won the battle against breast cancer—even though there was article after article saying the odds of overcoming this thing if discovered early enough were tipped massively in your favour, there were other stories too, of women who weren't so lucky—or who had considered themselves lucky and counted themselves among the survivors, until they'd discovered secondaries a year or two on and it had all turned to custard. It was those other stories that nibbled and gnawed at Jules's threadbare confidence, like the rats that until recently had chewed off every green shoot from the island's forest floor.

Jules leaned her head back against the rest and closed her eyes.

If she'd never got pregnant and had Della, then the fishing trip would never have happened. She would never have lost her father, and her mother wouldn't have lost her husband. Her father was always the stronger of her two parents. He would have supported Pru, whatever happened to Jules.

Bottom line, they would have coped.

But Pru alone with Della?

Jules swallowed. God—and the doctor had told her not to get ahead of herself? How could she *not* get ahead of herself? How could she not join the dots? All she had at the moment were dots. Possibilities. And if those dots joined up and ended up somewhere she didn't want to go…

She pinched her nose and took a deep breath as the plane lurched and bounced. The intercom crackled into life and the pilot apologised again for the conditions and said they were trying to find smooth air but meanwhile, to stay seated with seat belts fastened.

Smooth air. Jules could do with some of that. Already she knew more about breast cancer than she ever wanted to. And the crazy thing was, if she got lucky, she might be able to forget it all in a week. It might be nothing. A cyst. Benign. Because she'd searched those words as well, joined those dots and followed them until they took her home in a couple of days, to hug her daughter and kiss her mum and say with a smile of relief, 'False alarm.'

Which dots should she believe? The ones she dearly wanted to, or the ones that scared the shit out of her?

The plane pitched and bounced and a woman the other side of the aisle gasped. 'Oh, god,' she whimpered, more a cry of resignation than prayer for help. 'When will it stop?' Her partner at the window seat said nothing, clearly trying to put on a not entirely convincing brave face given his complexion was a pasty grey.

Jules found a smile for the drama queen across the aisle, the woman who might once have been her, before she sat back in her seat and closed her eyes again.

There was more than one kind of rough ride in this world, and right now a little air turbulence was the least of her worries.

Sydney's atmosphere felt heavy and scented with petrol fumes and industry, so different to the fresh island air she'd left behind on Lord Howe. Jules found herself sniffing unappreciatively as she left the lodge the next morning on her way to the nearby clinic, a fresh wave of nerves welling up from the pit of her stomach and tingling its way along her limbs.

This was it. The lump on her breast was still there. She'd checked this morning of course. How could she not? But no matter how hard she'd wished it away, no matter how many times she'd wished it would shrink to nothing in the night so she could say to the doctor, *Nothing to see here!* it was still there. There was no getting out of this.

She snorted, her hand poised on the clinic's door. As if wishing it away was ever going to work. She'd wished her pregnancy away, hadn't she? Wished it would disappear in the night? That hadn't got her far either.

A stab of guilt pierced her heart. What kind of mother was she that she could ever have wished her daughter away?

But things were different now. Having Della had been a game changer. When Jules looked back, she'd been drifting through life until she'd had Della. No cares, no responsibilities, nothing but herself to worry about. But when Della was born, Jules had realised in a thunderclap just how empty and purposeless her life had been. More than that, how selfish her life had been.

Maybe this—whatever *this* turned out to be—might end up being a game changer too?

She took a deep breath before she pushed open the door.

Hold that thought.

Jules had never had a mammogram. She'd had ultrasound scans when she was pregnant with Della, so she was familiar with the feel of the gel and the slide of the probe over her skin, and while she was more than thankful she didn't need to be holding a litre of water while the breast ultrasound happened, she'd never experienced the womanly delight of having her breasts squeezed by a machine until they were spread between the plates like hot cakes. Both breasts, one after the other.

'I thought I was just going to have a needle biopsy on the lump,' she said, feeling overwhelmed that it wasn't just the breast with the lump that was getting attention.

The technician smiled. Jules had come to expect it, because everyone smiled here, from the people managing the accommodation to the receptionists at the desks. 'No doubt the specialists want a good look at what's going on in both your breasts.'

'Fabulous,' Jules said, feeling like she'd unwittingly fallen into a rabbit hole in which she could travel only one direction—deeper.

Her lips pulled into a grimace as the two plates clamped tight on her breast and then kept right on pressing.

'Okay?' asked the operator.

'Never felt better,' Jules lied through teeth gritted almost as tightly as the plates, her body tilted unnaturally, armpit rammed into a corner of the machine as her arm bent over it at an awkward angle. 'You are going to pump this baby up again afterwards, aren't you?'

The technician gave a lilting laugh. 'It won't be for long, I promise.'

Why did everyone have to be so nice? Why did everyone have to be so positive and empathetic?

Everything she'd read in the brochures, all the stories and testimonials she'd read online, were true. Everybody she met was so friendly, compassionate and caring that, frankly, it was disarming. So okay, she was a cynic from way back, but why would they be so nice unless they were trying to distract you from thinking the worst?

'Back in a moment,' the technician said, before she disappeared behind a screen to press a button and capture the image.

'It's okay,' Jules called after her, more than a little frustrated that finding out if her lump was cancerous or not wasn't going to be as straight forward as she'd expected—as she'd damn well wanted. 'I'm not going anywhere.' Certainly not with her breast—and by extension, the rest of her—held hostage by this modern-day instrument of torture.

'We're done,' the operator said with a smile on her return. Another smile. And sure, it was nice, but it was unnerving too.

'Can you tell anything from the shots? Could you see anything?' Jules asked hopefully as the machine released her and she tenderly peeled her flattened breast away from the plate. Because surely if something looked bad it would show up?

This time the technician's smile was soft and sad. 'I'm sorry, I just take the pictures. Don't worry, it won't take too long.'

After that, the needle biopsy was almost a formality. Jules went willingly, thinking, *Finally we're getting somewhere.* 'This was the reason I came,' she said, as the doctor guided the needle into the numbed skin of her breast. 'And so far I've had everything else but.'

'It can seem a bit of a conveyor belt,' the doctor said unapologetically, focusing on her work. But then she pulled the syringe back and the requisite smile followed. 'Once we get hold of you, we don't like to let you go.'

Jules sighed. 'I was kind of getting that impression.' She looked at the needle in the doctor's hand. 'I don't suppose you can tell anything from that already? I don't know if I can wait two days to get my results.'

The doctor shook her head. 'The hardest part is the waiting for test results to come back, I know.'

'But if it does show—' Jules wasn't able to finish the sentence.

The nurse by Jules's side stroked her shoulder while the doctor said, 'The biopsy is just a test. It's a tool, nothing to be afraid of in itself. But what you need to know, and to focus on, is that at least seventy per cent of breast biopsies came back negative for cancer.'

Seventy per cent!

Jules had never been crash-hot at maths in school. Percentages, decimals, fractions—such baffling concepts had been Sarah's domain. Jules had preferred playing sport to playing with numbers, but clearly she'd missed something, because numbers could be truly beautiful. She'd been freaking out about a thirty per cent chance of getting a positive result. She could handle that kind of math, because on the flipside, it meant she had a seven in ten chance of getting back on that plane in two days and putting this all behind her.

After the test, Jules dressed quickly, feeling more hopeful than she had all day. She didn't want to start counting chickens, but seven out of ten was far more positive than three out of ten. All her imaginary dots seemed ridiculous and overblown now, and when the results came in, there was a good chance she'd have confirmation of that.

Back at the lodge, she was in the kitchen making herself a cup of tea when a woman trailing a piece of blue wool from a tapestry bag tucked under her arm joined her at the bench, found herself a mug and helped herself to coffee. Jules recognised her. She'd seen her a couple of times in waiting rooms, or passed her in the clinic's corridors. More noticeably, she was also the first person Jules had seen today who wasn't smiling.

'Hi,' she said, squeezing her teabag before putting it into the bin. 'Are you another inmate then?'

The woman looked up at her, her startled eyes circled with shadows.

'Sorry, bad joke,' Jules said. 'I saw you on that conveyor belt they call a clinic today, so I figured you're stuck here having tests too, although you were busy knitting so you probably didn't notice me. I'm Jules, from Lord Howe Island, hoping to get the all clear in a couple of days and go home.'

'Oh,' the woman said, nodding, sandy-coloured tendrils of hair moving listlessly around her face. 'Yeah, I'm Molly. From out past Narrabri. And snap. Waiting on results too.'

'It's the pits, isn't it,' said Jules, sitting down at the table and picking up a Scotch Finger biscuit. 'I hate waiting. And meanwhile everyone keeps on smiling and saying, "Don't worry."'

Molly smiled thinly and put her bag on the table as she sat down next to Jules. 'I noticed that—the smiling thing.'

'I mean,' said Jules, 'it's nice and all …'

'Yeah,' agreed Molly, nodding. 'It's nice.'

'Just—weird.'

This time Molly laughed. She dropped her head into one hand and sighed, and when she looked up, Jules could see tears in her eyes. 'Thank you. That's the first time I've laughed all day. I needed it.'

Jules looked around. Most of the other patients seemed to have someone with them, a partner or friend to keep them company. But this woman didn't look like she was waiting for anyone.

'Are you here by yourself?'

'Yeah. Mum's looking after the kids while Wayne's managing the farm.' The woman rested one hand on her knitting bag. 'I think knitting is the only thing keeping me sane at the moment. I figure if I concentrate on a pattern, I can't think too much. How about you?'

Jules nodded. 'My mum's looking after my daughter. There's no-one else.' She took a sip of her tea. 'How many kids do you have?'

'Four under seven.' Molly looked numbly into the coffee she hadn't touched. 'Stuey's only eighteen months old. I hate being away from home. I hate—' She looked around. 'Look, don't get me wrong, it's fantastic what they do here, and everyone's wonderful. But it's not home, is it?' She turned to Jules, and in the cold light of the downlit kitchen, Jules could see how stress was pulling the skin over Molly's cheekbones taut. 'And everyone is so nice and saying don't worry, only how can you not worry when you get sent to a place like this and you could have cancer and you've been here since yesterday and you still don't know?' She looked beseechingly at Jules like she was waiting for an answer, or at the very least reassurance, and then she seemed to cave in on herself as her shoulders sagged. She shook her head. 'Oh, I'm sorry. You've obviously got your own shit to worry about. You don't need anyone else's.'

'It's okay, I get it,' Jules said, feeling the pull of her own daughter, knowing Della was at home with her grandmother when Jules should be the one looking after her. And she only had one child to worry about, not four. 'I feel like I'm stuck in no man's land. There's this lump on my breast and nobody knows exactly what it is yet, but until they work it out, my life has been consumed by it. It's like being stuck on a roundabout and not knowing when or where you'll get off. I kind of wish I'd never found it.'

'Huh,' Molly said. 'Wayne found mine. I wish he'd kept his mouth shut too.'

'But then, it could be a good thing that he did find it,' said Jules. 'If it is something, I mean.'

'I know. I still don't have to like it, do I? You're right, it's a bloody roundabout and I'm stuck on it, and I don't care how many people tell me not to worry, bottom line is, worry or not, I don't want to die, Jules. Jeez, I haven't got time to die. Too many people are depending on me.'

Jules looked at the woman on the verge of tears beside her, the woman from western New South Wales whose suntanned face and sun-bleached hair spoke of the outback, a world of which Jules knew little, but a woman with whom she had more than a little in common, and she knew that spending a night fretting over what tomorrow would bring would do neither of them any good. 'Bugger it, Molly, you know what we need?'

'What?'

'We need to go and get royally pissed.'

Two proseccos and two margaritas down and one thing was clear: Molly was even worse at karaoke than Jules, but they didn't let that stop them. Together they'd murdered 'Dancing Queen', made a screeching abomination of Whitney Houston's 'I Will Always Love You', and rounded out their set with a heartfelt rendition of Queen's 'We are the Champions' before collapsing onto their seats in fits of laughter.

'Can you believe it?' Molly said, gasping for air. 'A couple of people in the audience even cheered.'

Jules snorted. 'Only because we sat down.' She picked up margarita number three that Molly had insisted they order before they got up to sing, clinked Molly's glass and raised her own in a toast. 'Here's to you and me, Molly. Fuck cancer.'

Molly looked conflicted. 'We don't even know we've got it yet.'

'What's it matter? Fuck it anyway.'

Molly lifted her glass, shoulders back, chin up. 'Yeah, fuck cancer,' she said, and downed the lot.

Jules woke the next morning with the pressing need to pee, a list as long as her arm that she really needed to get stuck into and a hangover that felt like a jackhammer had been let loose in her skull. She groaned as she eased herself upright. Way to fuck cancer all right—she was going to die of this hangover before she even knew if she even had cancer. She groaned as she eased herself upright. She hadn't felt this bad since Sarah's twenty-first party. She'd danced and sang and got seriously pissed that night too. God, you'd think a woman would learn. She was getting too old for hangovers.

All she needed was to find some painkillers, because her list wouldn't wait. It was the shopping that made this whole unexpected trip kind of worthwhile. And if she managed to visit a couple of TAFEs she'd found on-line that offered an administration course and speak to someone who could give her more details, that would be a bonus.

Once her headache was less jackhammer and more thick dullness, she tackled the shops. She dragged herself around the children's wear department at Myer, buying new summer clothes for Della, not even batting an eyelid that she was paying full price, when usually she'd scour the online catalogues for bargains, because she figured she was already saving on delivery.

She hit the kitchen shops next, feeling a bit brighter as she drooled over a glossy red KitchenAid mixer that would have cost an arm and a leg in freight, even if she'd had the dollars to buy it, before she bought her mother some new non-stick flan tins for her pies, and then she left kitchenware and hunted down some fancy undies (she wasn't getting ahead of herself or jinxing herself by buying bras just yet) and a new pair of jeans.

With her hands full of shopping bags, Jules found a café over-looking the mall and nursed a latte. She gave up on achieving anything else for the day, she didn't have the heart or the energy to go chasing up course counsellors. That could wait. Instead, she popped another painkiller to take the niggling edge off her headache, and wondered how Molly was coping at Taronga Zoo, where she'd gone to take videos to send to her kids. Jules wasn't sure she envied Molly. Now that her shopping was done, she was content to sit and drink her coffee and watch the city spin by. So different from home. So many people. All so busy. All so fast, dashing to and fro. And high above the mall loomed the towers like giant anthills, where all the worker ants spent their days.

Her gaze shifted to some buildings behind which she figured the coat hanger of Sydney Harbour Bridge must be. Somewhere beyond that, on the other side of the harbour, stood another tower, the office tower where Sarah worked. Guilt squeezed Jules's gut so tight that the pain of it drowned out her headache. Guilt that would never leave her, guilt that only ever eased because Sarah lived two hours and an entire world away, where Jules didn't have to see her. On a good day she didn't even have to think about her.

But here in Sydney, it was impossible not to think about Sarah. This was her city. Her home.

And Jules knew that Sarah hated her. Still she couldn't help but wonder: what was life like for Sarah now? How was she coping? *Was* she coping?

Jules stared at the mug of half-drunk coffee, a feeling in her throat like the milk had curdled in her gut.

Sarah hadn't looked like she was coping the last time Jules had seen her. God, was it really three and a half years ago? But it had to be. Richard's memorial service. Sarah had looked like a ghost of herself, her face gaunt, her eyes hollow and haunted. But when Sarah's eyes had fallen on her, Jules had been able to look right in, and had seen that they weren't hollow or empty, but filled with a world of pain. And Jules had known then that Richard's death was only part of the reason for the pain, and that she herself was to blame for the lion's share.

She'd ached for her old friend then. She still ached for mistakes she wished she could erase. Mistakes that had set off a chain reaction like dominoes falling, heading to a place nobody had wanted to go. A place impossible to avoid.

There was no way that she could fix all that. There was no way to undo what had been done. There were no words that could explain. But she'd wanted to reach out that day—*needed to*—if only to give Sarah the letters. One she'd found when she was going through Richard's papers, one she'd written herself. But by the time Jules had parked Della with Richard's mother and plucked up the courage to approach her, she'd discovered Sarah had already gone.

Jules pushed the dregs of her coffee away, wishing she could push the memories away as easily. Wishing she could find an end to the ever-present guilt. There was no way past the guilt. Around her conversation hummed, a baby cried, plates and cutlery clattered and an uncomfortable thought wormed its way into her brain.

She could always go and see how Sarah was coping herself. After all, she was in Sydney, her shopping was done and she didn't have anywhere to be until tomorrow morning.

Besides, it wasn't like she'd have to go to Sarah's house and invade her privacy and risk having the door slammed in her face. She could turn up at her office, somewhere less personal. Less confrontational. And without Della by her side to complicate matters ...

Although Sarah still might refuse to see her.

Jules sighed, looked at the mound of shredded paper that her anxious fingers had created from the empty sugar sachet without realising, and swept it into the centre of the table. Fair call too. If she were Sarah, would she want to see the woman who'd blown her marriage apart? Not likely.

And of course Sarah would be coping. She was strong. Turning up at the memorial service proved it, even though it must have been the last place on earth she'd wanted to be. No, Sarah would be fine. Coping and coping well. And no doubt coping all the better for not seeing Jules.

Shaking her head, Jules collected her bags to return to the lodge. Being in Sydney for this bloody breast thing must be messing with her head for her to be considering such foolish notions. There was no point going to see Sarah. Far better to go home to Lord Howe Island and leave the past behind her where it belonged. There was nothing to be gained by stirring it up.

10

It didn't matter how many times Sarah flew into Lord Howe Island, the sight of that tiny jewel appearing as the plane slipped through a hole in the clouds never got old.

Even today, when she couldn't help but think about what might be waiting for her when she got there, the sight of the island's cloud-topped mountains and ridges curling almost possessively around its turquoise lagoon, all fringed with the white lace of crashing waves, inspired a kind of pride. She'd been born here, right there in the tiny hospital on that speck of an island, in the days before pregnant women were dispatched early to the mainland to deliver their babies.

Maybe it wasn't her choice to be going home today, but there was no stopping the tug on her heartstrings, nor the message it carried, which mocked her as if to say, *And you thought you could stay away?*

All around her, heads craned for a better glimpse of their island-paradise destination as the plane descended.

Sarah sat back in her seat and supposed it was a kind of paradise—if you weren't descending into the tangled remnants of your past.

She thought about the last time she'd felt this nervous approaching the island. She'd been at university and was bringing Richard home for Easter. She'd already told everyone all about Richard and how amazing he was and how much she knew they would love him as much as she did. And while Floss and Andy had immediately absorbed Richard into their little group as though he'd always been part of it, Jules had surprised her. From the start, she'd been cool and standoffish, like she was weighing Richard up and constantly finding fault. Challenging his opinions. Snidely putting him down every chance she got.

Not that Richard had done himself any favours. He'd never been a shrinking violet and he was always up for a challenge. If anything, he delighted in baiting Jules. They'd rubbed each other up the wrong way from the beginning.

And yet Sarah had persisted, because both of them were special to her and sooner or later Jules would see, just like Floss and Andy had, that Richard was okay, and once she relented, Sarah was sure he would too.

She pulled the strap of her seat belt tighter, her lip curling.

They'd relented all right.

Six months, she told herself. Maybe even less if her mother behaved herself and did her exercises religiously. Meanwhile she'd scour the online job agencies and put out some feelers and find herself a new job to go to when she was done.

Six months. She could do that. It wasn't as if it was a life sentence.

Sam was waiting for her at the airport, and he wrapped her in a bear hug as soon as she passed the gate into the arrivals area. 'You, girl,' he said, 'are a sight for sore eyes.'

'How's Mum?' she asked, giving him a squeeze back.

'Cranky as all get out.' His weathered face broke into a grin. 'Situation normal.'

She laughed and planted a kiss on his cheek. 'Oh, Dad. Come on, let's go grab my bag.'

He filled her in on how Dot was getting on with her exercises ('You'll notice she's cursing a lot more than usual') and her walker

('She calls it Frankenstein—but don't ask me who's the real monster') while chatting to a couple of locals as they waited: the bus driver who'd come to pick up guests for Sullivan's and a member of the island board who'd been to Sydney for a meeting. Sarah knew them, if only vaguely, and was happy for her dad to do all the talking. She was too busy scanning faces for others she recognised.

It was a tiny island, she knew, but the airport was public. Anyone could be here. Her palms were sweaty and she all but pounced on her bag when the luggage trolley finally arrived.

It was only when they got out to the car park that she started to relax. The air was cool and crisp here, the smell of avgas left behind, and Sarah sucked the air into her lungs. Wow. She'd forgotten how fresh this air was, so different from Sydney's leaden humidity, the air flavoured with sea spray and lush vegetation grown in rich volcanic soils. Then she got a whiff of something else, and smiled as her eyes found the cows grazing across the road. That was something else that made this place unique.

'You right to go?' Sam Rooney asked, tossing her bag into the tray of his battered ute.

'Ready when you are.'

'Only I got the impression you were looking for someone.'

She pulled at the door handle. Had she been that obvious? 'Making sure the coast is clear, more like.'

He climbed into the driver's seat, put his hands over the wheel and sighed. 'Jeepers, Sarah, is it that much of a problem being back?'

She smiled tightly and pushed her hair behind her ears. 'There are some people I'm in no hurry to catch up with, yeah. One in particular. You can probably guess who that is.'

Her father blew out a long breath, the air whistling tunelessly through his teeth, before he scratched his head and turned to her. 'I'm sorry, love, if coming home is causing you grief. In a way, I guess I was kind of hoping …'

'Hoping what?'

'That things might sort themselves out, given a bit of time back on the island.'

She suspected what was coming, but still she had to ask, 'What "things"?'

He shrugged. 'With Jules and Floss.'

Sarah snorted.

'Only … you were all such good friends once. And I don't know all the ins and outs of everything that happened, but seeing you're back on the island, it'd be a good chance to maybe mend a few bridges.'

'I thought the ins and outs were pretty obvious, given the little bundle that Jules popped out.' Sarah made no attempt to disguise the bitterness infusing her voice.

Sam gave a gruff cough. 'Right. Well, there is that. Even so, Richard's no longer in the picture, is he?'

Her breath caught in her throat, and she wondered if there would ever come a time when she didn't feel that sudden stop-start hitch in her chest. She knew Richard was dead. She knew she'd lost him even before the game fishing boat had gone down and taken him and Jules's father to their watery grave. And yet every time someone mentioned it, it was like hearing the news all over again, when she'd forgotten for one instant everything that had happened, other than that he was her husband and that he was gone. A time capsule that vomited out its pain and disbelief and incomprehensibility every time the lid was cracked open.

'It still doesn't change what happened.'

'No, nothing can change that. But maybe, instead of hiding away—'

'I'm not hiding. I'm here, aren't I?'

'Okay, so now you're here, instead of trying to avoid Jules, maybe try talking to her?'

She crossed her arms. 'Dad, I just got off the plane. Don't make me climb out of this car and get right back on.'

He held up a hand in surrender and turned the key in the ignition with the other, as if he feared she might do just that. 'All right. All right. It was just an idea. A daft idea, maybe. But I care about you, love, and I hate that being back home causes you heartache.'

'Which is why I'm not keen on piling on more.'

'All I know is that there's wrongs been done, and if nobody talks to each other, nothing's ever going to change, and nothing's ever going to be resolved.'

'Enough, Dad,' she warned. 'You've said your piece. Enough.'

He reached over and patted her leg. 'You're right, lovey.' He put the ute in gear and pulled out of the carpark.

Sarah exhaled, letting go of at least a little of her tension. It was weird being back. The same but different. Colours seemed brighter, more intense. It could have just been that she'd been in the city too long and grown used to the concrete and glass jungle of the city. Then again, it could be the knot pulling tight in her belly that was working to heighten her senses.

What was going on behind the palm-lined roads? Had the news of her homecoming spread? Lord Howe Island was like a country town, with all the benefits and foibles that came with that. Word got around pretty fast. Did Floss and Jules know she was coming? Were they sensing the foundations of their world starting to shudder a little?

They wouldn't be delighted by the news, she knew that much.

A police ute topped with red and blue lights passed them going the other way. Her dad gave the driver a two-finger salute and the officer acknowledged him with a nod of his head and a wave.

'New copper?' Sarah asked, not recognising the dark-skinned man at the wheel.

Sam gave a quick shake of his head as he changed down gears and turned the car away from the lagoon and up a steepish hill. Tourists on rented bikes passed them going the other way, free-wheeling down. 'Not for long. Barry's on three months long-service leave so we've got ourselves a locum. Noah something's his name. Been here a couple of weeks now. Seems to be fitting in all right.'

'He looks nice,' she said.

Sam looked her way. 'I hear on the grapevine he's not married.'

'Geez, Dad,' she said, rolling her eyes. 'I didn't mean it like that. I didn't come here to find a man. I think I'm over men.'

'I hope that doesn't apply to your old man.'

She smiled and said, 'Of course not.'

It was Sam's turn to smile as he steered the ute into the store's car park. The shop was exactly as Sarah remembered it, the squat timber building with the adjoining house behind hunkered down against a background of graceful kentia palms.

'So, how's business?'

'Reasonably quiet,' he said. 'But then, it's winter. Should pick up come September.'

She nodded. Winter was the off-season, when tourists were thinner on the ground. It never got really cold, but the weather was less reliable, more prone to storms and winds, and less appealing for beachgoers and tourists wanting to climb the island's many walking tracks. That's if the changeable weather let them get to the island at all —tourists waiting on the mainland had been known to miss their entire holidays due to the wacky weather, the lucky ones being those stuck on the island and forced to ring their bosses to say they couldn't get back to work. Nobody ever seemed to mind when it worked out that way.

'Given that's the case,' her dad said, 'I'm thinking that running the shop should be a doddle for a bright girl like you. You should even manage a bit of a holiday while you're here. Reckon you're probably owed one.'

Wasn't that the truth? Not that she couldn't think of a dozen other places in the world she'd choose to visit first. But Sarah threw him a smile and spared a thought for her useless brother. Danny could have handled a doddle if he ever bothered to get off his behind to do something for someone else. Even their mother would have known that.

She climbed out of the car, noticing the signs in the windows advertising fresh fish and vegetables—the same signs that had been there since she was a child. 'Not much has changed lately, then?'

'You know what your mother thinks about change,' Sam said, fishing in the tray for her bag.

'If it ain't broke, don't fix it.'

Sarah recited the mantra along with her father and they both laughed, until her dad clapped a hand on her shoulder and said, 'Oh, Sarah love, it is good having you home. I'm sorry if it's going to cause you any grief.'

'It's okay, Dad,' she said, injecting her voice with as much confidence as she could muster. 'I'm a big girl now. I can't run away from my past forever.' *Much as I'd like to.*

'That's the spirit.' He gestured towards the building. 'Come on in and reacquaint yourself with the shop, and then we'll go out back and see how your mum's getting on. She was having a nap when I left.'

Stepping into the store was like stepping into the past. Nothing had changed inside either. Not the tinkle above the door, not the all-pervasive scent, a mix of washing powder and candle wax, spices and a sugar hit, courtesy of the bags of mixed lollies that graced the counter. Wooden shelves still lined the walls, wooden shelves she'd grown up with that still bore packets of dried fruit or flour or tins of tomatoes or spaghetti sauce.

It was like being transported back in time.

'It hasn't changed inside either,' she said, more delighted than surprised, spinning around, taking it all in.

'I guess it all seems a bit old fashioned to you,' said Sam, 'with all the fancy supermarkets you're used to in the big smoke.'

'Coming!' they heard from the store room out the back, and then Deirdre's head poked out. 'Oh, you're here!' She bounded down the stairs in a way that probably wasn't wise for an ample sixty-something woman if they were the same stairs that had brought Dot undone. But there was no time to utter a caution before Sarah felt herself enveloped in a squishy hug that felt like being wrapped in a feather doona.

'It's so good you could come,' Deirdre said, 'You're a life saver. You have no idea how much we all appreciate it.'

'Thank you,' Sarah said, not sure how to disentangle herself.

It was Deidre who relented and let go, her chubby-fingered hands immediately going to Sarah's shoulders to look at her. 'But it's not just that,' she said, her fingers squeezing. 'It's so good to have you home.'

Sarah returned the smile, unexpectedly touched and just as unexpectedly feeling crappy that she'd had to be dragged all but kicking and screaming back to the island. 'It's good to be home,' she said, and strangely, it wasn't all a lie. She had enough happy memories of her years on the island that part of her would always belong here. It was just a shame that other memories had come along to get in the way.

'Deirdre's just about to become a grandmother again,' Sam said, watching from where he leant one hip against the counter. 'That'll make three now, hey, Dee?'

Sarah blinked. 'Tammy's third?'

The older woman smiled an apologetic smile. She knew Sarah's history. She understood the despair and desperation that came with being unable to bear a child. Her Tammy had miscarried twice before she'd managed to have her first baby—Sarah had chatted with Tammy about it on one of her visits when their families had got together for a fish fry. And Tammy had understood better than anyone the depth of the hurt you felt every time you saw a pregnant woman or a baby or received yet another invitation for a baby shower.

There weren't many people who understood that level of loss, that level of grief. Even your best friend, who'd chosen to remain childless, could listen and lend a shoulder, but still had no concept.

Then Tammy had succeeded where Sarah hadn't and they hadn't spoken since. And now she was just about to have her third …

So bloody unfair!

Dee squeezed her shoulders. 'All right, love?'

Sarah forced a smile and nodded That was the way it was. It wasn't as if her dad had said or done anything wrong, it was just that one innocent remark, one tiny reminder could make a bone-deep hurt well up. A hurt she was doing her best to come to terms with, but one she knew would never let her go.

'That's wonderful news, Dee,' she said, willing her voice not to crack, because it *was* wonderful news and she was truly happy for the girl. 'Please pass on my congratulations.'

The other woman's face creased as she pulled Sarah into another hug.

Don't cry, Sarah told herself, clamping down on her throat and forcing back the tears. *Don't cry!*

Still, a couple of tears squeezed out. Sarah brushed them away as inconsequentially as she could, listening to Deirdre filling her in on where the shop was with regard to stock and showing her the exact same order book system that Sarah remembered using when she worked in the store as a high school student.

And as Sarah listened, she thought that maybe her time here wouldn't be wasted, that maybe things weren't completely 'broke', but that she could streamline operations, or at least bring them into the twenty-first century.

She might as well spend her six months here constructively.

After Sarah was brought up to date, Deirdre shooed them off with a final hug to check on Dot. 'You don't know how happy your mother is to have you home.'

'She is?' asked Sarah.

Deirdre smiled benevolently, her hands clasped before her, and Sarah thought Deirdre would have made the perfect nun in another life. 'She doesn't like to be too effusive, of course,' Deirdre said, 'but I can tell how delighted she is.'

A perfect nun, complete with the art of understatement. Sarah smiled and promised to report at eight am the next day, ready to begin work.

Halfway through the door that connected to the house, Sam hesitated. 'I'm sorry for what I said back there, about Tammy and the baby,' he said. 'It just came out. It was clumsy. I didn't think.'

Sarah smiled, even though it was yet another tiny needle to her heart. 'It's okay, Dad. I really don't want people to be walking on eggshells around me for the rest of my life. It's just something I have to learn to deal with.'

He nodded as if he understood before he turned and kept walking. But he didn't understand, she knew. Nobody could understand unless they'd been there.

Dot Rooney was sitting up in bed doing a crossword when Sarah and Sam found her. Sam kissed his wife's head. 'Look who I found,' he said.

'Hello, Mum.'

'Ah, here she is.' Dot allowed Sarah to kiss her cheek before she said, 'Deirdre's been frantic about when you were going to arrive.'

'She didn't seem too worried just now.'

'What? You've talked to her?'

Sam looked apologetic. 'We called by the shop on the way.'

'Well, take it from me, Deirdre's been worried sick.' Dot smiled at her daughter. Not the full-blown smile she'd thrown a doctor or physio or even the tea lady on their first visit, but it was a smile nonetheless. 'She wouldn't want to show it, of course, not in person. But you're here now, and that's the main thing.'

'How's the hip going?' Sarah asked, already exhausted. 'Is it getting easier walking around?'

'Well, it might be,' Dot said, 'if I didn't have to deal with that thing.' She threw a snarky glance at the walking frame standing near the bed.

'Isn't it helping?'

'I don't want a walking frame. I just want to be able to walk. Why is that so hard for the doctors to understand?'

Sam squeezed his wife's shoulder. 'I'll be right back to help you with your exercises, Dot, I'll just help Sarah to the studio with her luggage. Okay?'

'See you soon,' Sarah said, and waved.

They'd barely gone five steps through the kitchen before her father said, 'And no, you are not getting on the next plane.'

'Ha. How did you know?'

'I live with her, don't I? There's not a day goes by at the moment I don't think about getting on that plane myself.'

'Oh, Dad, I'm so sorry.'

'It'll get better. She'll get better. And then I'll only be thinking about getting on that plane every other day.'

He smiled as he said it, before they both laughed.

'You deserve a medal.'

'That I do,' he said, leading her into the studio where she'd be spending the next six months. He snapped on the lights. 'Now, your mum wanted to give you your old room, but since it's right next to ours, I figured you might want a degree of separation. This room is a bit chillier than the main house, but it's got its own loo and external access. Might be handy.'

'In case I have a secret love tryst?'

Her father's face didn't even twitch. 'In case you're trying to avoid your mother. Trust me, you'll thank me for this.'

She kissed him on the cheek. 'Thanks, Dad, I think I already do.'

Sam showed her the old bike he'd cleaned up for her to use and left propped up outside, and then returned to go look after his wife's needs.

Sarah wandered around the room, added for shop workers when the house was full of her and Danny. A simple add-on with plain walls and louvred windows but with the bonus of a bathroom and easy access. What more could she ask? Her dad was indeed a gem.

Sarah sat on the double bed, the mattress a little smaller and less grand than what she was used to, and gave a long sigh of relief. She'd survived the airport and the drive here without any disasters. She could survive whatever else was coming. She had to.

11

If there was one thing Floss had learnt it was that, whatever happened, life went on. Just … sometimes not in the way you wanted.

Feeling a sense of gloom about the unfairness of the world, Floss steered the van out of her parents' driveway, watching her dad in the rear-vision mirror as he gave one final wave from the top step before heading back inside their cottage.

Life went on.

Even when it wasn't easy.

It hadn't been easy when she'd discovered she was pregnant with Mikey. Four kids, they'd agreed on, albeit reluctantly on Andy's part—more of a going along with Floss to keep the peace, rather than an enthusiastic endorsement, she knew. When they'd got married, neither of them really had any concept of what a large family meant, but four kids later, they sure as hell did. So when Mikey happened along, things between Floss and Andy got tense for a while. But what was one more, Floss reasoned, when you already had four? And how could you not have this child, when your other children had magically expanded your heart so you could fit them all in? So they'd made it work, even when she knew it could have been easier.

Life went on.

Even when you couldn't change things, no matter how much you wished you could.

How much did she wish she could change things for her folks? Her dad hadn't complained when he'd called to say he couldn't get to Beached today because her mum's MS had flared up overnight and she was in too much pain for him to leave her. He'd actually apologised that he couldn't come in, and apologised again when Floss had dropped by with a corned beef dinner for them both, because he didn't have time to cook.

Life went on.

And even if her mother's illness didn't make her feel any better about her own problems, it sure put them into perspective.

Floss had been operating on autopilot since the birthday-night fiasco, doing what she had to do, looking after Beached, her guests, her kids, and even Andy when he was home to be fed and watered (because he certainly didn't ask for anything more). But she was numb inside, and her relationship with her husband had to change or she'd go on being numb forever. Or worse, the numbness would thaw to a bitterness that would taint their marriage irreparably.

If it hadn't already.

For better, for worse. For richer, for poorer. In sickness and in health ...

The words of the wedding vows—the words her father was living by yet had apologised for—weighed heavily on Floss as she drove slowly down the road, watching out for cyclists and pedestrians in the half-light. A new, even gloomier thought wormed its way into her mind: maybe that was the difference between her parents' situation and her own; her mother and father still loved each other, while her union with Andy seemed like it was teetering on the edge of something cataclysmic. Something terminal.

She rounded a bend, or tried to, but the van didn't want to go with her. It was suddenly unresponsive. Floss pulled over as best she could.

One look at the tyre had her cursing Andy and his insistence that the tyres still had a good couple of thousand kilometres in them and didn't need replacing just yet. Of course he was out on the supply vessel right now. And she could hardly ask her dad for help.

'Shit,' she said, and kicked the tyre for good measure.

Her toe connected with the rim and pain shot up her leg. 'Ow!' She hopped to the back of the van.

She was a dab hand at looking after most things mechanical—when she had to be. She had this. But when a car pulled up as she was lifting out the jack and someone offered to help, she wasn't about to say no.

It was the new copper she realised when she looked up, the teeth in his wide smile all the whiter against his dark skin. 'I take it you're a local?' he said as he climbed out of the cab. 'I've been looking forward to meeting everyone. I'm Senior Sergeant Noah Lomu.'

'Floss Miller,' she said, taking his hand. 'I run Beached.' She pointed over her shoulder. 'Just up the road, with my dad.'

The policeman nodded as he crouched and ran his hand over the flattened tyre. 'Well, this is well and truly flat.' He stood and wiped his hands. 'Come to think of it, I reckon I might have met your daughter the other day. Angela, or maybe Annie? Met her with a friend.'

'Annie's our eldest,' Floss said, pulling out the rest of the tool kit. 'And if she was with anyone, she was probably with Trent. They're a bit of an item.'

'That's the name,' Noah agreed, as he unhitched the spare and got to work. 'They seem like nice kids.'

'They are.' Floss looked at him suspiciously. 'You're not going to tell me you caught them doing something they shouldn't have been doing?'

He laughed. 'You would have heard from me before now if that were the case.'

Floss liked the man instantly. 'That's a relief. With kids you never know what's coming next.'

'I'll take your word on that,' he said. 'I haven't got any.'

'I can't imagine what that's like. We've—that's Andy and me—got five.'

'Five kids?' He blew out through pursed lips. 'I'm not sure I *want* to imagine that.'

Floss laughed, and together they changed the tyre, or more

correctly, Noah changed it while Floss watched. It was no hardship: the man was all muscle under that uniform.

She turned away, suddenly uncomfortable with the direction of her thoughts. What the hell was she thinking, ogling another man?

As Floss got back behind the wheel, and she waved the policeman goodbye, she found herself wondering what it said about her precarious marriage that she was.

'I hate you, you bitch,' said Molly, grinning as she sat down next to Jules in the waiting room, her knitting bag tucked under her arm. 'I haven't had bed spins since my first B&S ball.'

'Hey,' Jules said, happy to see her new friend. They'd arranged to be at the clinic to support each other, but after the amount of alcohol they'd consumed, she wasn't sure Molly would remember. 'You were the one who insisted on that third round of margaritas.'

'I was drunk, you fool. Why would you take any notice of me?' Molly leaned her head against the wall, eyes closed. 'I made it to Taronga Zoo, for your information, but only after I'd thrown up over the side of the ferry. Not my proudest moment. Then I was in bed by four.'

Jules chuckled. No wonder she hadn't seen Molly around the lodge last night.

'But at least it took my mind off all this crap. I haven't had so much fun in forever.' Molly looked sideways at Jules as she reached into her bag to retrieve her knitting. She pulled a ball of wool off the end of her knitting needles and started knitting, her needles click clacking. 'How are you feeling today? Nervous?'

'A bit, yeah.' She'd turned up twenty-five minutes early for her appointment. just wanting it to be over. She was done with Sydney. She was done with shopping and thinking about old friends. She wanted out and she wanted out fast. Already she couldn't wait to hug Della and her mum, and show them all the surprises she'd bought. Today, this afternoon, if all went well.

There was one seat left on today's flight to Lord Howe and she wanted so much to be on it. She had her suitcase already packed and waiting at reception. Timewise it would be tight to make it to the airport, but all she needed was the green light. 'How about you?'

'Same. I wish they could just text us when they get them. They're our results aren't they? It's not like we're kids.'

'Probably worried we might not take it well. Jump off a bridge or something. You know, while there's one close handy and all.'

Molly's needles stopped clicking. She turned to Jules, aghast. 'You're kidding! They think we might be capable of that?'

She shrugged. 'Makes sense they'd want to reassure us, you know, in case—'

Jules's name was called and apprehension scorched a trail along her nerves. 'Oh god, that's me.'

'All the best,' said Molly, putting her knitting onto the seat next to her. 'I'll wait for you.'

'Thanks,' she said. 'Me too.'

'Only if it doesn't hold you up getting to the airport if you get the all clear. *When* you get the all clear, I mean.'

Jules smiled. 'I knew what you meant. But in that case, if I don't see you, all the best.'

The two new friends hugged, bonded over the same nagging uncertainties, if not their similarly appalling inability to hold a tune, and then Jules went to get her results. She had her suitcase already packed at reception. All she needed was the all-clear.

She didn't get it.

'But you said the lump is benign?' Jules said, winding back the words, trying to make sense of why that good news wasn't the end of it. The lump was what she was here for.

'Yes,' said the doctor, a slim, kindly faced woman in her sixties. 'That's the good news. But the tests also showed an area of concern ...' She turned her computer screen towards Jules. 'It's actually in the other breast. Can you see those white dots? They're tiny calcifications in the milk ducts, and they could be nothing. We'd like you to stay for a biopsy, so we can take a closer look. Like I said, it could be nothing, but until we can take a look inside ...'

'Stay? But I'm going home today. There's one seat left on today's flight ...'

'We appreciate you want to get home, but we'd prefer that you didn't leave just yet. The procedure won't take long and we'll have your results back as quickly as we can.'

Jules shook her head. She'd thought she'd considered everything. She'd joined dots and thought about percentages, but this had never figured as an option. What was the point of joining dots – what was the point of figuring percentages when you were on the right side of them and things still went wrong? 'I didn't sign up for this,' she said. 'I didn't ask you to look at the other breast. I just wanted you to look at this lump and this lump is fine. All good. So why should I stay?'

'Jules, I understand this is a disappointment. Try to see it also as an opportunity. There is no lump to feel with calcifications like these, so you're way ahead of the game. If there's nothing suspicious happening within the calcifications, you'll be on the next plane home.'

'And if there is?'

'And if there is, then you'll have the satisfaction of knowing you caught whatever it is early.' The doctor smiled sympathetically. 'We can't make you stay, but you've come this far. Do you really want to go home without knowing?'

'No, but ...' As much as she needed to be at home, the doctor was right, because there was no way she'd be able to relax knowing they'd found something else lurking in her breast. When it all came down to it, she just didn't want this to be happening, period.

The doctor patted the back of Jules's hand. 'Do you want me to call your family and talk to them about it?'

Jules took a deep breath, the leaden press of disappointment in her gut no match for the cold hard knowledge that she didn't have a choice at all.

'No,' she said, already resigned to the fact that today's plane would be taking off without her. 'I'll do it.'

Jules wished Molly better luck as she was called in for her consultation. 'I'll be here when you come out,' she assured the other woman. And why wouldn't she? Her biopsy—a core biopsy this time, just for something completely different—wasn't scheduled until later this morning and the only other thing she had to do was unpack her bag again.

She went outside, sat on a garden wall, and waited while the phone rang on an island two hours off the coast. 'It's me, Mum,' Jules said, dropping her head into her free hand when Pru picked up and talking over her before she could ask. 'Look, it turns out I'm not coming home today.'

She heard her mother's intake of air, could all but see her hand fluttering to her chest. 'The lump?'

'Is benign. But they've found something else they want to check out.'

'Like what?'

'They called them calcifications. They could be nothing, they say, or they could be something. They're doing another biopsy today.'

'Oh, Jules. And you there all by yourself.'

'I'm okay,' she lied, swallowing hard as she turned her head towards the sky. 'How's it going? How's Della?'

'She's good. But she was so looking forward to you coming home today.'

Jules bit her lip to stop herself from shedding the tears that were right there, pricking at her eyes. 'Can you put her on?'

'Is that wise?' her mother asked. 'She'll be upset.'

Jules rapidly blinked. Della wouldn't be the only one. 'Look, Mum, she's going to find out sooner or later that I'm not coming home. I'd like to be the one to tell her.'

Pru huffed agreement down the line, and a few seconds later Jules heard her daughter's voice.

'Mummy! Nana and me are going to meet you at the pwane!'

Jules heart squeezed tight as she tried to find words her daughter would understand to explain that she wasn't coming home today but she'd have lots of presents for her when she did. Of course, no amount of future presents was going to make up for immediate disappointment, so the conversation ended in tears, on both sides of the ocean. Somehow her mother managed to prise the phone away from her wailing granddaughter to say goodbye.

Jules could tell Pru was annoyed with her. 'Are you okay, Mum?'

'Nothing a stiff drink wouldn't fix,' Pru snapped.

'Mum!' Jules growled.

'Forget it, I was kidding. Now you go and get yourself fixed up and be home as soon as you can. We're fine here.'

Jules dredged up a smile of relief from the bottom of a tank that was running on empty. 'Thanks. I will.'

She'd been back in the waiting room ten minutes when Molly emerged with red-rimmed eyes. 'It's a cyst,' Molly said, when Jules had found them both a settee to share away from other ears. 'But it's a complex one and there's a chance it could turn cancerous, so they recommended surgery.'

Jules squeezed her new friend's hand. 'God, I never knew such things existed.'

'Same here. We're all getting an education this week, whether we want it or not.' Molly dragged in a breath and swiped a hand at the tracks of her tears. Tears of relief, Jules now knew. 'But that should be the end of it hopefully, so I said yes. They've put me on a surgical list for Tuesday and I should be okay to go home the day after.'

Jules nodded as her phone buzzed. The summons to her second biopsy. They sure weren't wasting any time. Her stomach flipped. 'Here I go again.'

'Back on that bloody roundabout,' said Molly as the pair quickly hugged. 'Here's hoping it flings you off somewhere you want to be this time.'

How many different ways could you stick a needle in a breast to pull something out? Jules pondered this question as she lay perfectly still on her side with one breast stuck between the plates of the mammogram machine while a needle pumped up and down through the hole the doctor's scalpel had made in her (thankfully numbed) breast. It was like being stitched up by her grandmother's old treadle sewing machine.

'Just a little while longer,' the nurse sitting at her head and holding Jules's shoulder said when the needle stopped thrusting. 'We're almost done, but we just have to make sure we've got enough of the calcifications for pathology.'

'We're good,' someone else said beyond the range of Jules's vision.

'You can release the prisoner?' Jules asked hopefully.

'As soon as we place a tiny marker at the spot. Just in case anyone needs to find it again. Once that goes in, you'll be free to go.'

'A marker?'

'Made of titanium. This one's in the shape of a top hat.'

'Isn't that a metal? My boob won't go off when I go through airport security? Because that might be hard to explain. Not to mention prove.'

The nurse laughed. 'No. No sirens. No alarms.' The needle moved again. 'That's the marker going in now.'

And then she was slowly unhitched and had dressings applied to her wound.

And when, finally, she managed to get vertical after being so long lying still, they showed her the slide of the calcifications they'd retrieved—tiny white egg-shaped dots they'd plucked from her breast. So tiny and yet the cause of so much trouble.

She was definitely getting an education, Jules thought, remembering Molly's words. A pity it was an education she'd never wanted.

~

Jules and Molly went to dinner together that night, to a tiny Thai restaurant that thankfully didn't serve margaritas or offer karaoke, where they compared family reactions to the news. Molly's kids were just as upset as Della had been, and Jules couldn't imagine having to cope with the tears of Della times four.

But when she went to bed that night, Jules wasn't thinking about home. Instead, her thoughts returned to Sarah, wondering what her former friend would think if she knew what Jules was going through, with her life suddenly full of questions with no easy or quick answers.

Sarah wouldn't be too cut up about it, that was for certain. She'd probably be feeling a little smug.

Jules rolled over, trying to get comfortable. Maybe it was good she hadn't been tempted to look Sarah up. Because whatever happened and wherever this whole breast thing ended, while Sarah had lost everything, Jules still had Della. When it all came down to it, what right to sympathy did she have?

And then, somewhere along her train of thought, Sarah morphed into Floss and the atmosphere closed in, and it was suddenly raining. Or maybe it was just that everything looked misty through Jules's eyes. Misty, dull and hopeless. Exactly how she'd felt when she'd found out she was pregnant.

Jules had desperately needed to tell someone and there was no way she could reach out to Sarah. Goal-oriented Sarah. Confident city-slicker Sarah. Horrifically betrayed Sarah.

So she'd turned to Floss, hoping that she might understand. Level-headed Floss, mother of four, would know what to do. Wasn't that what level-headed friends were for? So she'd told Floss that she was pregnant and her friend's shoulder had been everything Jules had needed and more. Sympathetic. Understanding. Full of good advice and support and the balm to her soul that she'd needed. Until she'd asked who the father was, and Jules, in a fit of honesty, had tearfully confessed, and Floss had turned from supportive confidante to appalled and horrified antagonist.

She woke up in a sweaty tangle of sheets with an ache from the wound in her breast and a horrible sense of why this was happening to her.

This was payback. Justice. The gods were exacting their revenge for what she'd done, and they were exacting it right under Sarah's nose, in her town.

And maybe, Jules thought, as she unravelled her tangled sheets and flipped her pillow over to find a cooler side, it was exactly what she deserved.

1 3

It felt strange being back on Lord Howe. It was the same as it had always been, and that made sense, because strict development controls meant the island never changed dramatically, but it felt different too. It was as if nothing had changed, yet everything had. Everything had shifted.

Or maybe it was just Sarah herself who'd changed.

No surprise there, she thought, as she closed the store. You couldn't expect to drop a brick on a concrete floor without a few corners chipping off. Maybe even breaking in two. And she'd been dropped from a great height, after all.

She switched off the lights, mentally patting herself on the back for getting this far. She was here, she'd survived her first few days, and she was coping. Her brand of coping might come with counting down the days until she could leave again, but she was coping. She'd imagined a roll call of ghosts calling by the shop, a bit like in Dickens' *A Christmas Carol*, but nobody had. By accident or design, her ghosts all seemed to be keeping their distance. Exactly the way she preferred it.

Back in the house, the kitchen was filled with the scent of a casserole she had softly bubbling away in the slow cooker and the sound of Dot complaining to Sam as he helped her with her physio, punctuated by Sam's gentle words of encouragement. Sarah smiled. Her father had the patience of a saint. She gave the casserole a stir—not too long now—and added green beans.

Through the kitchen window she could see the sky was painted with streaks of red, the trees swaying into shadow, and the simple beauty called to her. Dinner was at least half an hour away and she wasn't needed here.

'I'm going out for a walk,' she called, as she shrugged on her jacket and pocketed a torch. 'Back in a little while.'

She closed the door on her mother's protest that it was getting dark and her dad's 'Cheerio!', and set off up the road. She was on her feet all day in the shop, but it was good to really stride out now. She was puffing by the time she got to the top of the hill, grateful when the road flattened as it curved around to follow the ridge along the top of the island.

The air was fresh against her heated face, the bitumen a dark ribbon beneath her feet. Amid the stir and rustle of palms and the call of a settling bird, she could hear small waves breaking nearby and turned right when the road divided, heading towards the beach. The whoosh of waves was louder here, the smell of salt and sea on the air. She walked across the park to where the grass met the sand and stood in the gloom, looking out over the darkening sea and the slumbering bulges of the Admiralty Islands before turning her eyes to the inky sky above, lighting up now with the Milky Way, the sky like velvet dusted with diamantes. She couldn't remember seeing stars in Sydney. Star soup, she used to call it, like the fish soup Ned's Beach became when tourists turned up to feed the fish from bags of pellets they'd bought.

Ned's Beach. She hadn't been down here for years, not since her twenty-first. They'd all staggered to the sand the day after the party, her and Richard, Floss and Andy, and Jules, who seemed to be nursing the biggest hangover of the lot and so grumpy with it she was almost toxic, but not just with Richard for once. Richard reckoned it was because the Swedish chef from Halfway Jules had been seeing had flown off the island the day before the party without telling her.

Sarah wasn't so sure; Jules hadn't seemed too cut up about it at the party. But like a dog with a bone, Richard hadn't let go.

'Maybe if you weren't such a grumpy bitch,' Richard had said to Jules, 'you might manage to hold onto a boyfriend for a change.'

'Stop it,' Sarah had told him.

But Jules had delivered the final word when she'd given him the finger and told him to fuck off, before storming away.

'Good riddance,' Richard had called after her.

And Sarah, whose head had been pounding after too much cheap wine and too much drunken dancing, was so relieved the sniping might stop now that Jules was gone, had been glad to see the back of her too.

Sarah raised her head to the stars and sighed uneasily. Should she have gone after Jules that night to find out what was wrong instead of just letting her go? Would it have changed anything if she had? Would things be different now?

She turned her back on the beach. There was no peace for her here.

When she got to the main road she wasn't ready to head home. Her thoughts were still unsettled, memories rattling loose. Her feet took her down the road towards the lagoon, past Halfway, which was already bustling with the dinner crowd. Past the little store where she and Jules and Floss had hung out eating ice-creams or hot chips after school and gossiping about boys, safely away from the eyes and the ears of her mother. Floss full of talk of Andy and how they were going to marry and have four kids. Jules stating, with a certainty that was unnerving, that there were enough people in the world and on the island and that she was never having kids. Unlike Sarah, who'd assumed it was an inevitable part of life, like growing up and getting married, and that one day she was bound to end up with a couple of kids of her own.

Funny how life turned out.

Sarah blinked, swallowing a surge of grief, and kept walking, accompanied by the surf booming over the coral reef that fringed the lagoon. She switched on her torch, pointing it at the road, more to let drivers know she was there than to light the way ahead.

She stopped at the T-junction that would take her back up the hill to home. Stopped and looked out at the sea and the thin line of beach that glowed under the risen moon and stars. She recognised the dark shadow on the water as the pontoon the three of them had raced around before flopping onto the grass that flanked the sandy beach the day before she'd left to do her HSC in Sydney. That perfect summer day when she'd sworn to her friends that she'd be back.

The three of them linking their index fingers together the way they'd done since year one.

Best friends in the world.

Best friends in the universe.

Best friends forever.

Sarah shook her head. So close they'd been back then. The three of them together, standing tall and solid, a foundation upon which their young lives had been built.

The three of them linking their index fingers together the way they'd done since year one.

The breeze set the palm fronds rattling above her, almost like voices chattering in the treetops. Sarah looked up and listened. These palms had watched her grow up. These palms and their tangled vines had seen her leave the island, and then return. And she realised it didn't matter how far she walked on this island, the past was all around her here.

She shivered.

And so too were her ghosts.

14

Time dragged. By the time Jules's appointment to get her biopsy results had come, she was over waiting. She'd given up thinking in percentages and was prepared to think the worst. And why shouldn't she? Didn't she deserve it after what she'd done?

So when the oncologist told her they'd found cancerous cells within the walls of the calcifications, earning her a diagnosis of ductal carcinoma in situ, it came as no surprise that she wasn't getting off this roundabout any time soon.

A nurse sitting in the corner smiled sympathetically and Jules felt ill. She watched as the oncologist pulled a sheet from a pad that had a diagram of a woman's breasts and started scribbling over it, showing her where her dots had been found, pointing to the cross sections of ducts with their various stages, circling the one that equated with her condition.

'DCIS can be a precursor to more invasive breast cancer. The trouble is, we can't predict which cases turn invasive.' There was a lot more information, then the doctor asked, 'Do you understand?'

Jules nodded. 'So what happens now?' she asked, almost numb to the disappointment and shock.

'We remove it surgically,' said the oncologist. 'It's only a small focus, and from what we can tell, your lymph nodes aren't compromised. We remove it in what's called a wide local incision, which means we only take as much surrounding tissue as we need to ensure we've got it all. At this stage I'm ruling out chemotherapy, and whether we need to think about a course of radiotherapy will depend on the histopathology report. Of course, that wouldn't happen until your wound is healed, so you can go home for a few weeks.'

'A lumpectomy.'

'Exactly.' The oncologist nodded, then looked down at her notes, a slight frown marring her perfect brows. 'Do you have anyone staying with you? Or any family you can call on to be with you? It's not major surgery, but it's still surgery, with all that entails, and it always helps to have family on hand, especially after a diagnosis like this. It can be upsetting, and that's normal.'

'No,' Jules said, her throat tight and dry. 'They're all at home on Lord Howe.'

'No friends a bit more local you could call upon to keep you company while you have surgery?'

And again Jules thought of Sarah. Sarah was local. Jules gave a half-smile, imagining how Sarah would feel getting a call from Jules to ask her to hold her hand while she was getting part of her boob cut out. Sarah would probably say yes, but only on the condition she could wield the scalpel.

Maybe not a good idea.

Then there were Richard's parents in Goulburn, but she'd only met them a couple of times, and one of those was at Richard's memorial service. When it all came down to it, she barely knew them. They were lovely, and no doubt they'd come if she asked them for help, but they'd expect to see their grandchild, and then they'd be disappointed and uncomfortable and Jules would only end up feeling guilty that Della wasn't here.

'I'll be fine,' she said, forcing a smile. 'Let's do it. I want to go home. I want it to be over.'

'I understand, but as I said, you might have to come back for a course of radiotherapy.'

'But no chemo.'

The oncologist shook her head. 'Recent research is showing that in cases like yours, chemotherapy doesn't provide any further protection from recurrence of the disease. And we don't believe there's any point making your recovery any harder than it has to be.'

No chemo? No hair loss or mouth ulcers or all those other horrid side effects she'd read about while she'd been doing her research? Jules found a weak smile in the midst of her disappointment. 'So that's actually a win, isn't it?'

The oncologist left her with the nurse to answer any further questions and give her advice about support services.

Jules found Molly waiting for her when she got out.

'How did you go?' Molly asked.

'Crap,' Jules said. 'They've found cancer in those dots. So—snap—they're going to cut it out. Only bright side I can see is that I'm on tomorrow's list with you.' Jules held up the pink brick that the nurse had given her. 'Meanwhile I have this to refer to if I have any more questions.'

The other woman's eyes narrowed. 'What's that?'

'A "My Journey" kit. Apparently it comes with the diagnosis, kind of like a show bag without the junk food. It's got all kinds of information, apparently, and there's a diary in case I want to write down my feelings.'

Molly pulled a face. 'Not my idea of a journey. Think I'd rather go on a cruise.'

'I know,' Jules said. 'Right now I'd settle for going home. A journey I actually want to take.'

'Come on,' Molly said. 'I figure we're both fasting from midnight. So how about we journey to that pub over the road and I'll buy you a beer.'

Jules found a grin. 'They're the happiest words I've heard all day. Let's do it.'

The pub was filled with workmen still wearing their hi-vis vests after knock-off time, so the bar was noisy and smelt of stale beer, forlorn hopes and despair. To Sarah, it was perfect. She and Molly laid claim to the booth of a vacating group, high-fiving as they sat down. They weren't leaving Sydney without learning something about city life.

Jules went to the bar for their first round. By the time she came back, Molly had her knitting out, needles furiously clacking. She put it aside as she took her glass, clinking it with Jules's. 'Cheers,' she said, before they both downed a decent gulp.

'Are you nervous? I mean about tomorrow and all.' Molly put her glass down and resumed her knitting.

Jules nodded, more interested right now in Molly's needles moving rhythmically as a memory of her nan—Pru's mum, long lost—floated to the surface. She remembered the jumpers and cardigans her mother had pulled out when Della had been born, items that had been knitted for Jules by her grandmother. Something about the click-clack of Molly's needles was calming. Pru had never been a knitter, but Molly made it look so easy.

And if there was a way to make all this hanging around waiting for things to happen a bit more productive, Jules was all for it.

'Do you think you could teach me to do that?' she asked.

'Do what?'

'Knit.'

Molly laughed as she took a sip of her beer. 'Anyone can knit. There's no secret.'

'So you could teach me then?'

'Of course, I could,' Molly said, pulling a spare pair of needles and ball of wool from her bag, 'It's not like it's rocket science.'

Which is how two women got to spend the night before they both underwent surgery in a Sydney bar, one teaching the other the rudiments of casting on. Of knit and purl and stocking stitch. Casting off.

'I'm going to make Della a jumper,' Jules declared a while later, putting the idea out into the universe as she proudly held up her wonky square, even though it had more holes than stitches. Even if she didn't have a handle on this knitting thing quite yet, she wasn't going to waste her time just sitting around.

15

There was a stiff wind giving the airport wind sock hell when Floss drove by, heading for the car park. She'd seen the plane land on even windier days so she wasn't worried, although she knew the wind might give the passengers a few anxious moments as the plane bucked and bounced on its way down. She had five guests arriving for Beached today, one couple coming to celebrate their twenty-fifth wedding anniversary, along with a party of three sixty-something women who were almost regulars—this was their third visit.

She parked the car with a few minutes to spare, and found Bill from Sullivan's already waiting inside the terminal. They talked a while about the weather and the rain they were looking for to fill up their water tanks, and before long the grunty sound of an approaching engine could be heard through the gusty wind.

They ventured out to the fenced lawn that served as both departure and arrivals gate to watch the plane come in. It was descending crablike, sideways to the wind, like a shopping trolley with a broken wheel that refused to roll in a straight line.

'Reckon there might be a couple of passengers in need of a change of pants when they get down,' muttered Bill.

Floss couldn't help but smile. The sight of that rock wall at the end of the short runway could be daunting on a calm day; on a day like today, it was easy to wonder how the plane could actually clear it. Especially side on.

But the pilots who operated flights here were the best in the business. They had to be. At the last possible moment, the plane straightened, touching down with only a couple of bumps, before taxiing to the small terminal.

'All righty,' said Bill. 'Prepare yourself for incoming.'

The stairs were wheeled into place, and in no time the doors were opened and people were disembarking front and rear, and luggage being removed from the hold. Floss held her BEACHED sign in front of her as the first passengers climbed down. She recognised two of her group of three—one waved to her—and then the third emerged from the plane. Great. Now she just needed to find her couple. She was scanning the twenty or so passengers when her gaze passed over a woman walking alone. Her eyes flicked back, because she looked like

...

Jules.

Wow, their second inadvertent encounter in as many weeks. Imagine that.

The first of Floss's booked group of three reached her, all smiles, almost old friends the way she hugged her, and then they were all there, Alison, Rosslyn and Barb, talking nineteen to the dozen about the landing, about how happy they were to be back.

Jules passed by and for just a moment their eyes met. Floss heard a 'Mummy! Mummy!' and turned her head to see Pru with a tight grip on the hand of a young girl.

'Be careful, Mummy's a bit sore,' Floss thought she heard, before she noticed a couple looking around uncertainly as they entered though the arrivals gate and there was no time to wonder about Jules any more.

'Beached?' Floss offered, holding out the sign that had been obscured during the mini reunion. The man smiled with relief and Floss knew she'd found David and Jill Jones.

'Come on, honey,' he said to the grey-faced woman beside him.

'Here's our shuttle. You'll be fine now.

My wife isn't feeling too well,' said the man to Floss and she swung into action.

'Let's get you inside,' she said, 'and we'll get you a drink of water while we wait for the luggage.'

'I'm so sorry to be a problem,' said the woman weakly.

'You're not a problem. You had a bit of a rough approach. You'll soon be feeling a whole lot better, I promise.'

By the time the luggage was loaded into the van, Jill was starting to look human again: there was colour in her cheeks and she was starting to appreciate her surroundings. 'It's quite beautiful here, isn't it?' she said, staring up at the looming heights of Mounts Lidgbird and Gower, and Floss knew she'd be fine.

Floss barely had to say boo on the way back to Beached as the three walkers started offering advice to the first timers about all the sights they simply had to see and all the places they had to eat, pointing out the landmarks along the way. It was fun listening to people doing her job and doing it well, and she only had to insert a footnote every now and then, mostly details about opening hours. And then David and Jill started talking about why it had taken them so long to discover Lord Howe—they'd been busy tripping to other places all around the world, and they got into a discussion comparing their favourite travel destinations: San Francisco, Istanbul and Venice, even the lost temples of Angkor Wat buried deep in the jungles of Cambodia. These people had been everywhere, it seemed, and as Floss listened to them recount their adventures, a part of her envied their freedom to explore any part of the world they chose.

Floss knew this island like the back of her hand, but there was an entire world out there she'd only every heard about. It didn't help that their discussion was punctuated by comments about how beautiful this or that was on the way.

She shoved her discontent aside as she pulled off the road. Beached was tucked down a hibiscus-lined driveway in the sub-tropical forest behind Ned's Beach. The three walkers were telling the newbies that for an unmissable experience, they had to go and stand in the low waves and feed the fish as they swam all around them.

Floss smiled. The walking group had just about mapped out the Jones's itinerary by the time she pulled up. Beached's dozen cabins were sprinkled between rolling lawns and stands of swaying kentia palms. The units were simple but comfortable, their timber steps leading to small verandas furnished with outdoor chairs and tables. To Floss's eyes they looked fresh and inviting after their recent lick of paint.

She sorted the luggage and showed them all to their rooms, reminding them to come to the office if they wanted to book a restaurant for dinner (the three walkers were full of recommendations for the first timers here too) then left them all to settle in. It was her dad's day with her mum and she had whatever booking requests that had come in to deal with, and then she had a bolognaise sauce to get simmering for dinner.

Dinner time at the Miller residence was loosely referred to as feeding time at the zoo. It was a noisy affair, with kids talking over, reaching past and annoying each other and generally trying to eat the most in the least possible time before clearing out, using the excuse of homework, before it was time to do the dishes.

Floss didn't mind that she was left with the cleaning up. She'd tried once upon a time to establish a roster system that shared the washing and drying up around, but over the years she'd grown sick of waking up to a dirty sink because someone had been too busy the night before to do their bit, so it was just easier to do it herself and be satisfied it would get done. The kitchen sink. The one bit of mess in the kitchen she figured she could control.

It gave her ten minutes of quiet because no child was silly enough to interrupt her or they'd be press-ganged into drying, and was often her favourite part of the day. Especially if Andy was home to help out, which he was tonight.

'I saw Jules again today,' she said. Annie had gone off to do homework with Trent and, as expected, the boys had all cleared the decks so they could pretend to do homework.

'Yeah?'

'She was getting off the plane. She must have been to Sydney.'

'Maybe she took Della to see her grandparents. Don't they live in Canberra or something?'

'Goulburn. But no, Pru and Della met her at the airport.'

He shrugged. 'So maybe she had something to do in the city.'

'That's what I was thinking. The last time I saw her was at the surgery.'

'So?'

Floss put one hand on her hip and pondered the fog the steam was leaving on the window. 'She didn't have Della with her then, either.'

Andy brought over the plates. 'And you think these things are somehow connected?'

Floss rinsed them in the second sink before sliding them into the sudsy water. 'They could be. I mean, Jules goes to see the doctor alone and then the next thing, she's coming off the plane from Sydney, also alone. You don't think something's wrong, do you?'

'So, Detective Floss,' Andy said, scooping up a fingertip of suds and depositing them on her nose, 'why don't you just ring her up and ask her what's going on?'

She laughed at his unexpected silliness, and swiped the froth from her nose. 'You know I can't do that.'

'So stop worrying about it.'

'But I can't do that either.'

'Why not?'

She shrugged. 'Because we used to be friends and if something is wrong ...'

'Hey,' he said, taking hold of her shoulders and wheeling her around to face him in a way that made her heart race. 'You just said it. You *used* to be friends. If you were still friends, wouldn't you both have stopped and said something when you met at the surgery or when she came in on the plane?

Floss could barely think. His eyes might be laughing at her, but the hands on her shoulders were big and warm and it had been so long since he'd touched her that she almost forgot what she was talking about. She blinked, trying to find her place in the conversation. 'But still…'

He dropped his hands and moved away, collected more plates and brought them over.

She smiled as she watched him work, his movements smooth, his reach long as he bent across the big table. No wonder this was often her favourite part of the day. She turned back to the sink and washed a couple of glasses while the water was clean. The mornings were crazy getting the kids organised and off to school, while after dinner offered a precious few minutes to catch up with her husband.

And lately, it had become their most intimate part of the day.

How sad was that? But tonight Andy seemed to be in a playful mood.

She turned back to the sink and washed a couple of glasses while the water was still clean.

She licked her lips. 'Andy, do you think we could go on a holiday one day?'

'Where to?'

'Somewhere we haven't been. Maybe overseas. Really overseas, not just to Sydney or Port Macquarie.'

'What? With this lot? How could we afford that?'

'No. Just you and me. Somewhere romantic maybe. The couple who came in today were talking about Istanbul and saying how wonderful it was. But there's always Paris, or even Hawaii.'

He grunted. 'Still going to cost a fortune.'

'Maybe, but if we saved up a bit every week, maybe we could afford something for our twentieth anniversary. It's only a couple of years away.'

He picked up tea towel and started drying the dishes in the rack. 'I don't get it. Why do you suddenly want to travel? You've never mentioned it before. I didn't think you were interested in travelling.'

'Maybe I wasn't. Does that mean I can't be interested now? Is it so unusual to want to visit somewhere else for a change?'

'But why? People come here from all over the world because this place is so special. We're the lucky ones, that's what everyone tells us. We get to live our lives here.'

'Yes, our entire life. I'm thirty-seven years old, Andy, and I've never been out of the state. I'd really like to see something else of the world before I die.'

He snorted. 'Now you're just being melodramatic.'

'No, I'm not. Will you think about it? There must be somewhere you'd like to see.'

'I don't know,' he said. 'I reckon everywhere is kind of the same when you get there.'

'That makes no sense,' she said, shaking her head.

'Why?'

'Because if everywhere was the same, nobody would ever want to come here, let alone keep coming back.'

'But they do, because this place is special.'

'Good grief, Andy, you're not listening.'

'Yes, I am, I just don't get what your problem is.'

She slammed the balled-up washcloth down on the sink and crossed her arms. 'You want to know my problem is? I feel trapped, Andy. I feel trapped and bored and taken for granted—and yes, that includes by you. And I feel like if I don't have a chance to go somewhere else and see something else, I might just go mad.'

There was a commotion in the bathroom, rapidly escalating to physical blows. Cameron and Brodie arguing over who should have first shower.

'That's bullshit,' Andy said, his eyes cold as flint, before the tea towel in his hands hit the table and he strode off to sort them out.

Annie appeared at door to the laundry, her eyes haunted, almost like she'd been crying. Floss wondered how long she'd been there. And how much she'd heard.

'You're home earlier than expected,' she said, trying to inject normality into her voice while Andy was barking orders as he sorted out World War Three in the bathroom.

Annie didn't say anything, just headed to her bedroom and slammed the door.

It suddenly hit Floss that Annie might have been right, and that she and Andy could be sliding towards divorce without her even realising.

1 6

What was it about a brush with your own mortality that made you spend the wee hours of the night tossing and turning instead of sleeping? By the end of her second night home, Jules was over it, unsettled and cranky. Sure, it didn't help that her stitches were pulling, and that she knew, once healed, she'd probably be heading back to Sydney for radiotherapy, but in reality, she had nothing to be cranky about. Life was good. She'd had a close call. Less than that really—a mere brush with something that could have been a whole lot uglier, and she'd got off lightly. She was one of the lucky ones.

You're so lucky.

The tourist she'd been sitting next to on the plane home to Lord Howe Island had said as much when she'd learned Jules lived on the island. She and her two friends had been to Lord Howe twice before, and all of them said that if they lived there, they'd never leave.

But they were right. She was lucky.

Funny how your perspective could change almost overnight. Jules had never considered herself a lucky person. She hadn't felt lucky when she'd found herself pregnant, and likewise she'd felt anything but lucky when Richard and her father had been lost at sea. She certainly hadn't thought herself lucky when the doctor had packed

111

her off to Sydney because of the lump she'd found, a lump that, while benign, had led to the discovery of something sinister going on in her other breast.

But maybe that's what facing your own mortality was supposed to do—stop you from dwelling on what was wrong with your life and what you were missing, and got you concentrating on what was right with it.

For starters, she did live on the most gorgeous island in the world, a fact most people seemed to envy.

She had a beautiful daughter in Della, and a supportive mother in Pru. And to top it off, her cancer had been nipped in the bud.

Clear margins. Her new favourite words.

Because they meant the surgeon had got everything. Along with a sizeable chunk of her breast that might see her nipple pointing in a slightly different direction than her other one, but hey, Jules still had a breast and a nipple, even if the wound would be tender for a while. All in all, it was a small price to pay.

And so what if she hadn't got off as scot-free as she'd been hoping? It could have been worse.

So okay, her cancer journey may still have a way to run, but right now she was back on Lord Howe Island with Della and Pru, why shouldn't she just count her blessings and concentrate on the good in her life?

She flipped her pillow over, searching for a cool spot to lay her overheated face.

Damn it, but she knew what was bugging her. Because there was a flip side to appreciating what was good in your life. There was also an appreciation of what you had left undone, of things that refused to stay buried in the past--things had to be put to rights while you still had time, however hard it was or impossible it seemed.

Because if there was one uncomfortable fact this brush with cancer had rammed home, it was that nobody knew how much time they had on this earth.

So - lucky?

Maybe, but it was another kind of luck—dumb luck—that had

seen her run into Floss, first at the surgery and then at the airport, after managing to avoid her for years. And now Jules kept seeing her face—kept remembering the questions and the concern in her eyes when they'd met at the airport. Only for a moment, before Jules had had to turn her head away, because it had looked like Floss had almost cared, and once again, Jules had been reminded of all the words that had been said and all that she had lost. But it was the words that played over and over in her head, like they were stuck in a loop.

'You slept with Richard?' Floss's shrill words still stuck her with pain. 'How could you do that?'

'I didn't mean to, it just happened,' Jules had told her. Because it had. 'He was devastated about Sarah losing the baby. About everything really. He was a mess, Floss, and he needed comforting, and one minute I was consoling him and the next—'

'The next you were bonking each other's brains out. Yeah, it's obvious how devastated he must have been feeling. It's obvious how you thought you'd console him.'

'It wasn't like that! You make it sound dirty.'

'How do you expect it sounds? We grew up on this island together, we went to school and Sunday school together, we played together. What part of that upbringing told you it's all right to sleep with your best friend's husband? That it's not wrong? That it's not sordid?'

'Don't you think we know it was wrong? But it was a mistake. It shouldn't have happened, I know that, but it did. Only now it's suddenly more complicated.'

'Yeah,' Floss had said, chewing on her lip, 'babies can do that.' Jules had got a sense then that maybe things weren't all right in Floss's world, but there was no time to think about why, not when she was being hit with a barrage of questions she'd already been angsting over.

'So what happens now? What are you going to do?'

'I honestly don't know. I thought about having an abortion. I was so tempted. But Richard wants to keep it.'

'Is that so hard to understand? He's desperate for a child. Except Sarah—remember Sarah, his wife? *Your friend?*—is the one who was supposed to give it to him.'

Jules had dropped her head, clasping her hands behind her neck with the weight of it all. 'I know! I know. But I can't change that now!'

When she looked up, it was to find Floss watching her thoughtfully, condemnation in her eyes. 'This is going to kill Sarah. You know that.'

Jules had known that, had lost sleep knowing it, had wished her baby away a million pointless times so that Sarah never had to find out. And while she'd also known that her confession would be met with shock and dismay, still she didn't understand why Floss couldn't be just the tiniest bit sympathetic, when Jules knew the grief Sarah had dished out to her over the years.

So Jules had lashed out. 'Why are you so worried about Sarah? What's she ever done for you but made you hide your children away and pretend you don't have them? Every time she looks at you, envy all but drips from her eyes. You can't tell me you're still friends after the way she's treated you.'

'Are you serious? Whatever happened between Sarah and me, she's still human. She's still got feelings and deserves respect. And I thought you were best friends. But you go and do this heinous thing—' She shook her head. 'I don't know. I thought I knew you, Jules. But it turns out I don't know you at all.'

'Floss—'

'No. I don't want to hear it. Nothing you can say is going to make me change my mind. I hate that you've done this. I hate what you've done to us. I'm sorry, Jules, but I don't think I can be friends with someone who could do something so low to someone who's supposed to be their best friend.'

Jules wrestled with her quilt some more before giving up on sleep.

It was still dark outside as gingerly she pulled her dressing gown up her arm and over her shoulder and headed to the kitchen to make herbal tea. She stopped at Della's door on the way, saw her daughter sprawled face down on the bed, and stood there, watching her breathe a while, feeling swamped by a sudden sadness. If the stars had lined up and all had gone right in the world, Della would be Sarah's child. But the world had tilted like a chess board, mixing up all the pieces, and it was Jules who'd ended up with a child, along with a stifling burden of guilt for the hurt she'd caused and the friendships she'd destroyed.

With a sigh, she pushed herself from the door frame. Curse these sleepless nights and this endless soul searching. What point was there in rehashing the past – of remembering what had gone wrong in your world - when you couldn't see a way to fix it? How could you ever make things right, when there were simply some things you couldn't undo?

'You look tired,' Pru said when she dropped in with a basket of clean washing at eleven the following morning and found Jules huddled over a coffee pot at the kitchen table, her knitting pushed to one side. Della was sitting at her table, playing with her Duplo, an empty cereal bowl and spoon at her elbow. Both were still in their pyjamas.

'I can't sleep,' Jules said, pushing the coffee pot her mother's way. 'Help yourself. I'm all caffeinated out.'

'Thanks, I could do with a coffee.' Pru found herself a mug and poured. She pulled a pack of Panadol from her purse and popped a couple of blisters, tossing them back with a swig of coffee.

Jules watched, bleary eyed. 'You okay?'

'Oh, I'm fine. It's you we need to worry about. Is your wound hurting?'

'No, it's tender and the stitches are pulling, but it's okay. It's my brain that won't switch off.' She sighed, her gaze falling on the basket. 'Thanks for the washing, by the way.'

Her mother waved her gratitude away. 'Least I could do.' Her hands cradled her mug. 'How's the knitting going? Lost interest already?' Jules had shown her the pattern Molly had helped her find on the knitting website Ravelry, a simple striped scarf on which to practice her stitches before launching into anything more adventurous.

Jules gave her mug a swirl, before thinking better of it. 'Can't concentrate.'

Pru nodded. Neither said anything for a while, until Pru put her mug down with a decisive rap, and said, 'Did you hear about Dot?'

'What about Dot?'

Pru gave her a quick run-down of Dot's broken hip and her arrival home a few days ago.

'Really?' Jules said, 'Why didn't you tell me? I could have visited.'

'You were busy with your own issues,' her mother said. 'Besides, I wasn't sure it was wise. The last thing you needed when you were already emotionally vulnerable was to run into Sarah while you were going through all that.'

Not for the first time, Jules thanked whatever gods or powers that be that had given her Pru for a mother. Sure, no mother was perfect, but a girl could do a lot worse. Because Pru was right, Jules would have worried about Dot. She would have tried to visit if she could fit it in. There was something about knowing another islander was in trouble, that country town thing that tied them all together—until those ties were irrevocably broken, of course.

Dot had never broken ties. They'd never exactly been close—Dot had always been a bit overpowering for Jules—but Dot hadn't frozen her out like some.

'I'll have to take her some flowers.'

Her mother shifted in her seat. 'Jules,' she said, 'before you do, there's something else you should know.'

'What?'

Pru hesitated a moment. Just enough for Jules to feel like she really didn't want to know. But still she had to ask. 'Tell me.'

Her mother's expression turned bleak. 'I hear Sarah's back.'

The seismic jolt that zapped down her spine and left her quaking deserved more of a response than Jules was capable of delivering. 'Oh.'

'She's come home for six months to look after the shop.'

Jules reached for the plunger, poured what liquid was left from the dark depths of the pot into her mug, took a swig of the bitter dregs, and sat back.

'Right.'

'I thought you should know. Save you from getting a shock if you bumped into her somewhere around the traps.'

'Yeah. Thanks.' First Floss, now Sarah. What were the chances? She looked at her mother. 'Does Dot know I was in Sydney? Would Sarah know?'

Pru shook her head. 'I didn't tell anyone.'

Jules sighed. 'Floss was at the airport when I came in.'

'Was she? I didn't see her.'

'She was surrounded by a group that had just come in and you were busy with Della. But she saw me, all right.'

'Well,' Pru said, getting to her feet. 'I really should be going. You'll let me know if there's anything else I can do for you, won't you?'

'I will,' Jules said.

It was only after Pru had gone, with the caffeine was buzzing in her blood, that Jules realised it wasn't just dumb luck that was seeing her toss and turn at night – and it wasn't just dumb luck that had chosen this particular point in time for her present and her past to collide.

It was a sign.

17

The tops of Mounts Lidgbird and Gower were hidden under a big donut cloud when Floss went to pick up the solo guest checking into Beached, some journalist doing a piece on the island. While it was part of every islander's DNA to make guests feel welcome, Floss had mixed feelings about journos. This one had been treated to free flights and four nights' accommodation and he'd no doubt sample the best the island had to offer.

Lord Howe had a constant stream of return visitors but you couldn't afford to stand still in the world of hospitality so the island needed to keep the positive articles and good reviews coming. She knew Lord Howe would provide a jewel of a holiday on any day, rain or shine, but you never knew when somebody had a chip on their shoulder or would blow some tiny mishap out of proportion and into a major blight on their stay.

They'd had one such reviewer who'd called Beached's accommodation 'rustic at best, outdated in a world expecting five-star', said that the fresh hibiscus left in the room to welcome the guests were 'twee' and that high-speed internet would be more useful.

Reviewers like that completely missed the point of Lord Howe and what it offered. There was five-star accommodation on the island for those who craved it, and Floss had got the impression that he was just sour he hadn't been offered it.

They didn't need bad reviews though. There was already so much competition out there, so many much cheaper holidays to the likes of Bali or Fiji, and people didn't need another reason to look elsewhere.

All of which was in the back of her mind when she picked out the only single man disembarking the plane among the couples and family groups, and saw that he was heading towards her BEACHED sign. With long legs clad in red skinny jeans and lace-up shoes, a check shirt under a brown leather bomber jacket and a carry-on bag slung over his shoulder, he looked more like some hipster film star than any journalist she'd ever met. The ponytail that captured the long hair from the top of his head and curved over short back and sides and a short, squared-off beard just sealed the deal. She'd bet there was a tattoo or three emblazoned on a well-honed shoulder.

Red jeans. Floss sniffed as she waited inside the arrivals area, feeling drabber than usual in her khaki work pants and stone-coloured top embroidered with the Beached logo, her blonde hair that hadn't seen a hairdresser in forever tied back in a real ponytail.

Annie would no doubt think their visitor looked hot, but Floss wasn't a fan of hipsters, even if half the itinerant workers who worked in the restaurant kitchens or behind the espresso machines seemed to be held hostage by the same lumbersexual fashion. Give her a man decked out in denim jeans and work boots with windblown, collar-length hair any day. Someone like Andy.

Even if he hadn't been much good in the bedroom department lately.

She sighed. Ah well, better not to go there when she had work to do.

'Floss Miller?' the visitor said as he approached, treating Floss to a broad smile under piercing blue eyes. Eyes older by a decade than she'd thought at first glance. Intelligent eyes. And Floss thought that maybe he wasn't all bad. At least he looked genuine.

'You must be Matt Caruso. Welcome to Lord Howe Island,' she said, holding out her hand. 'Do you have luggage to collect?'

'Nope,' he said, shaking her hand warmly as he swung his bag off his shoulder. 'Got everything I need right here.'

'Great. Let's get going.' She waved to a couple of locals as she led him through the tiny airport to the mini-van. 'Your first time on Lord Howe?'

'Yeah,' he said. 'But I can already tell it won't be my last. What a view coming in. Just spectacular.'

She felt a zing of pride then. She never got sick of hearing visitors' first impressions, and for a moment she forgave him for being a journalist. 'It is pretty special.'

'Although are the mountains always hidden by clouds? I'd like to see what they look like underneath.'

She changed gears as she pulled out onto the main road that curved in a loop around the runway. 'It's a bit tricky this time of year, but I'll see what we can arrange. No promises, mind.'

He turned to her, gave her one of his smiles again and said, 'Don't worry, I won't hold you to it.'

Floss felt a disarming burst of warmth. She turned her attention back to the road. Okay, so maybe she could give her paranoia about unfavourable articles a miss this time. He didn't look like the cynical type who might be carrying a chip on his shoulder.

She drove slowly along the lagoon road, sticking to the maximum of twenty-five kilometres an hour, so there was plenty of time to point out the local landmarks, the bowling club that put on a good feed (just make sure you book well in advance), the local school, the hospital where the GP ran a surgery until two in the afternoon if needed, and the museum that boasted a café and internet access as well.

She showed him where to pick up the hire bike that had been arranged for his stay, and the shops and store that formed the centre of the tiny town, and Halfway Café, which did a great line in burgers and pizza if you wanted something quick.

He looked at her. 'Halfway Café?'

She smiled. 'Because that's what Lord Howe Island is: halfway to heaven.'

'I like it.'

Floss turned inland from the lagoon towards Ned's Beach. 'Unmissable,' she told him. 'Feed the fish, snorkel over coral or go for a paddle on a board. You'll love it.'

He nodded. 'Thanks. It's on the list.'

Minutes later they arrived at Beached. She led him to unit eight and stopped at the foot of the steps. 'Here we are. I'll leave you to settle in, Mr Caruso, and I'll see you at six to take you to your restaurant.'

'Thanks, but, um.' He put his hand out. 'The key?'

'I'm sorry,' she said with a smile. 'There are no keys. We don't lock anything here on the island.'

He looked a bit taken aback. 'For real? I'd read that, but I wasn't sure whether to believe it.'

'Believe it. We don't have a theft problem, mostly because there's nowhere for a thief to run to,' she said with a laugh. 'Don't worry, you won't need to lock anything up here.'

'But my laptop?'

'I've never lost one yet and I certainly don't plan to start with yours.'

He gave her such a wide and genuine smile with his thank you that she was doubly determined not to start with his, and left him to settle in.

Her father was in the office when she got there. 'Six queries about summer bookings already today, Flossie,' he said in his gruff voice. 'It's looking good.'

'Excellent,' she said, heading to the small kitchenette to fill up the kettle. 'Coffee?'

Neill Beckinsale's eyebrows shot up appreciatively. 'Is the Pope a Catholic?'

Floss smiled at her father's chronic inability to say, 'Yes, please.' He'd retired and handed over the running of Beached to his daughter four years ago on his sixty-fifth birthday, but that didn't stop him turning up to work every other day. Floss wasn't about to object because it had always been a family business and it meant there was always another person to share the load. But most of all she knew her dad needed a break from being with her mum. It was three years since Sue had been diagnosed with multiple sclerosis, and she had good days, and then not-so-good periods. One day there'd come a time when her dad would be needed to care for his wife twenty-four-seven, but until that day, Floss wasn't going to deny him something productive to balance the load he was increasingly having to take on.

'So how's our guest?' he asked. 'Any first impressions?'

'Okay, I think. He seems happy enough to be here. I think he's going to be positive.'

'Excellent. We need to keep the punters coming.'

The kettle boiled and Floss filled their cups, fishing the milk from the fridge.

'Did Andy get off okay?' Neill asked when she put his coffee down beside him.

'He did,' she said, sitting at the desk alongside his and blowing on her coffee. Andy and two of his colleagues had had left that morning on a flight to Norfolk Island to help out a cargo company that was short staffed after a flu outbreak. He'd actually volunteered to go and it had almost seemed to Floss like he'd welcomed the chance to get away.

When it all came down to it, Floss couldn't say she was sorry to see him go. Already she felt the tension in her shoulders dissipating, the tightness in her chest loosening. A couple days of clear air would do them both good. A couple of days when she could stop trying to put some spark back into their marriage, only to see her attempts end in tears.

'Lovey?'

She looked around to see her dad standing behind her, holding the tin of chocolate chip biscuits. 'I asked if you wanted a biscuit.'

'Oh, sorry, Dad,' she said, reaching for one, 'I was lost in thought.'

～

It was around midday the next day when Floss came upon their journalist guest sitting on his veranda, tapping busily into his laptop, his ponytail jiggling with every keystroke. He looked up before she'd drawn even, tossing her a smile that landed in the pit of her belly and warmed her from the inside out.

'Hello,' he said with a wave.

'Hi, yourself,' she said, slowing her steps. 'How are you enjoying your stay? I thought you'd be out and about.'

'It's amazing,' he said. 'I've already been up to Kim's Lookout this morning—just writing it all up now. Hey, do you fancy a coffee? I just made a pot. I figure I owe you something after the one-on-one tour you gave me when I arrived.'

'It was no trouble,' she said. 'Besides, you look pretty busy. I don't want to interrupt you.'

'I promise, you won't. To be honest, it'd just be nice to talk to another human for five minutes or so. I mean, it's nice going to cafés and stuff, but when you're in a place like this, it's a bit weird having no-one to share it with and say, hey, check that out. I'm so full of stuff I've seen if I don't download to someone, I'll burst.'

She smiled, feeling tempted. She'd sat with guests before, shared a coffee or tea or even a glass of wine on their veranda while they talked about their day and all the discoveries they'd made. So why was she hesitating now?

Maybe because it wasn't a couple or even a group asking her. It was a single man who smiled at her like she wasn't invisible and whose eyes twinkled when he laughed. And whose lumbersexual get-up, complete with ponytail, was becoming more appealing by the minute.

But most of all because she was so wanted to say yes.

She smiled. 'Thanks, but I've got to make up a couple of rooms before the next flight comes in. Maybe next time?'

'Sure.'

Was that a flicker of disappointment skating over his eyes or just resignation that once again he would be stuck with his own company?

She'd lied about the rooms needing to be made over, she'd finished early today.

And she wasn't entirely sure why she'd lied except she'd remembered the way she'd surprised herself the other day by ogling the new policeman. She'd never looked twice at another man, but now it seemed she was not only noticing other men but wondering what they made of her.

Call it a hunch, Floss told herself as the screen door swung shut behind her, or maybe a sneaking suspicion, but she really shouldn't want to be alone with a man who seemed to have an uncanny knack of being able to generate such warmth in her with just one smile.

Given the attention deficit she was experiencing, she wasn't sure that she was up to dealing with that kind of superpower.

Shame, because he seemed like a nice guy.

The office was empty when she entered, Neill home with Sue today. Floss headed through the office to the bathroom where there was a mirror above the sink. She flicked on the light and stood there looking at her reflection, appraising it. From the time she was a toddler she'd recognised the word cute and had figured out early that was the way people described her. Not pretty—her nose hovered too long at the end and she liked photos where the photographer captured her from the front rather than in profile, when she looked how she wanted people to see her. Andy had almost divorced her when she'd nixed three-quarters of their wedding photos because she'd been caught in profile.

So pretty? No. Never pretty.

And that was when she'd been skinny. Having babies had put an end to that. She'd been hovering five to ten kilos over her recommended weight ever since. She really should say no to those chocolate chip biscuits in the office.

But cute? Was there still a shred of that going on under the lack of sleep? She angled her face this way and that and pulled free the blonde shoulder-length hair from its scrunchie, fluffing it around her face, batting her eyes and pouting like she'd witnessed guests and even Annie do for a selfie.

What did Matt Caruso see when he looked at her? A weary, heading-for-middle-aged manager of a guesthouse who was running a few kilos overweight that he just wanted to shoot the breeze with? Or could he see some remnant of cute?

She turned away from the mirror, tying her hair back in its ponytail again. It was all kinds of pathetic, but she kind of hoped he did.

18

Sarah shut up shop, feeling a sense of optimism. She was getting an idea of what was needed in the store and had begun making plans. She'd ordered orange oil to treat the timber shelves after they'd all been emptied and wiped down, and was drawing up plans to turn the little veranda into a proper outside eating area, with café-style tables and chairs rather than just long benches against the wall. She'd order in some gelati rather than the bog-standard ice-creams the shop had always stocked and have a look at installing a decent coffee machine for real espresso coffee—although she knew that expense was going to meet with some resistance.

But overall, small changes, small improvements, and all without affecting either the core integrity or the retro charm of what was essentially a general store supplying the basics to those in self-catering accommodation, plus a few treats for cyclists passing by. The visitors who came to Lord Howe weren't short of a dollar and were used to the best of everything, especially their coffee, and in peak tourist season there were more than enough tourists to go around. It could work, she knew it could.

Feeling more optimistic than she had for weeks, Sarah was heading into the kitchen to check the slow cooker she'd put on this morning when she heard her father's voice. 'Jesus. That's rough. All right, then, I'll have a word.'

'What's rough?' Sarah asked, looking from Sam to Dot as she lifted the pinny from the hook on the back of the door and slipped it over her head. It couldn't be the curry that was causing ructions, that was smelling amazing.

Her father shuffled his feet, looking like he'd been caught in the act, but she could make no sense of her mother's expression. Dot looked like she was almost in pain, her lips tight, her eyes almost accusatory.

'Your mother had a call just now,' Sam said, 'from Pru.'

'Oh?' Sarah turned and picked up the wooden spoon from the rest where she'd left it. 'I didn't realise you were still friends with Pru.'

'Pru and I grew up together,' Dot snapped. 'Why wouldn't I still be friends with her just because you had a falling out with her daughter?'

'Oh, give me a break!' Sarah said, spinning around. 'It was hardly a "falling out"!'

'Sarah,' Sam interrupted. 'It is actually about Jules. She's got breast cancer.'

'Oh.' Sarah blinked, myriad thoughts flashing through her brain, not all of them entirely sympathetic, at least one of them featuring karma in a starring role.

'Is that all you've got to say?' Dot said.

Sarah turned back to the slow cooker, lifted the lid and sniffed appreciatively as she gave the rogan josh a stir. Just about there. The lamb was falling apart, and a swirl of yoghurt and a sprinkle of parsley and it would be ready to serve once she'd steamed some rice. She replaced the lid and set the wooden spoon down on its rest.

'Well?' prompted her mother.

Sarah had been brought up with the principle that if you couldn't say anything nice, then you shouldn't say anything at all. But this was probably not the time to remind her mother of her own (do as I say, not as I do) teachings. 'Yeah, Dad's right. That's rough.'

'That's it? When she's got a four-year-old child to think about!'

'Don't you think I know that?'

'Then you could try to be a little more sympathetic.' Dot sniffed. 'It's a very trying time for Jules and Pru. First losing Greg and Richard in that terrible boating accident, and now this—it's just one thing after another.'

Sarah sucked in a deep breath—still better to say nothing—and went to the pantry to find the rice.

'Anyone hungry?' she said, putting it on the bench and digging out the steamer. 'Dinner won't be long. Nothing better than a warming curry on a winter's day.'

'Oh, I give up,' said her mother, struggling to her feet and shuffling towards the bathroom on her walker. 'You talk to her, Samuel.'

'What?' Sarah said, catching sight of the look of resignation on her dad's face before she bent down to search for the yoghurt in the fridge. 'What does Mum expect me to do? Bake Jules a cake or something?'

Her father curled his hands around the back of a chair, and shook his head. 'Nobody expects that. But it's Jules - she's asked to see you.'

An electric snake slithered its way down Sarah's spine before suddenly snapping tight. 'But you said that was Pru.'

'Jules asked, via Pru, via Dot. She thought it might be better coming that way.'

Sarah made another attempt at finding the yoghurt, succeeding this time. She snatched the tub out from the depths. 'I've got nothing to say to Jules.'

'That may be true enough, but from what I gather, she's got something she wants to say to you.'

'Tough.'

'Would it be so hard to hear what she has to say?'

She found a spoon and put both it and the yoghurt down on the table, and set about straightening the knives and forks on the place-mats. 'Actually, yeah, it would be.'

'Sarah—'

Her head jerked around. 'She's made no attempt to reach out to me before now, not once. But suddenly, because I'm back on the island, she feels a desperate urge to talk? What's so different that she has to seek me out now? And why would I want to listen to anything she has to say? There's nothing she could say that would undo what she did to me and to my marriage.'

Sam shook his head, straightening from the chair where he was leaning to go to the window and pull down the blinds. 'I can't answer that, or talk for her, but I can imagine that, given her diagnosis, she's had a bit of wake-up call. Health scares, and thinking about your own mortality, can do that to a person. After all, grievances and resentments are of no use when you're dead.'

Maybe not, Sarah thought, *but they were pretty damn inescapable when you were alive.*

She raised her chin. 'She's got no reason to have any grievances or resentment against me. I'm the injured party here, remember?'

'I remember. So maybe it's something else she's looking for.'

'Like what?'

He shrugged. 'Who knows? A chance to clear the air? Maybe she wants to explain her side of the story?'

'Her side is hardly defensible.'

'Then maybe she's looking for forgiveness.'

'Forgiveness? How could I ever forgive her after what she did, not just to my marriage, but to *me*?'

'You keep asking me questions I don't know the answer to. But for what it's worth, I reckon it'd be tough. But they say there's five stages of grief, so it makes sense there'd be a similar few stages to forgiveness. I mean, it doesn't just happen, does it? You don't say to an arsonist, oy, you bastard, you've burnt down my house, but whacko, I forgive you. It can't be that easy.'

Normally her father's homespun ways of explaining things would leave Sarah smiling. Normally. But this time his wisdom had one huge flaw.

'The trouble is, Dad, I don't want to forgive her. And even if I wanted to, I'm not sure I could.'

'Well, love, you won't know if she's even looking for that unless you talk to her. Would it be such a stretch to at least meet up and listen to what she has to say? It's not a sign of weakness to talk to her. It's not like you'd be letting her off the hook.'

~

Sarah tossed and turned in bed that night, and it had nothing to do with either the curry or a mattress that was more a Volkswagen than the Porsche she slept on at home. But she'd promised her dad she'd think about Jules's request, and now she could think of nothing but. It was three and half years since she'd seen Jules. A good three and a half years of shoving her past into an iron box she'd welded shut with white hot tears and hidden away, never to be opened. Forgetting had been getting easier this last year.

But now the iron box refused to stay shut, and the life she'd thought she was finally getting back to rights had started unravelling all over again.

Sarah rolled over and wrestled with her pillow. Outside a gusty shower of rain sent palm fronds slapping into each other, much like the thoughts slapping inside her head. The last time she'd seen Jules had been at Richard's memorial service in Goulburn.

A memorial service.

There was no coffin. No interment and no cremation. There was no body.

Sarah hadn't wanted to go—Richard had left her more than a year before—but her mother had said she should, and reluctantly, Sarah agreed.

Because whatever Richard had done, he'd been her husband—and a good husband at that—for ten years.

Besides, it was only a couple of hours' drive down the highway from Sydney and Richard's parents would be there, and they'd been good to her. They'd lent her their support when she and Richard were undergoing IVF. They'd been there with words of sympathy when it had failed time and again to produce the grandchild they were hoping for. They'd told her that it didn't matter, that she shouldn't keep trying for their sakes, although she'd seen the same yearning she'd felt reflected in their eyes. She knew that it did matter, and that they wished things could be different.

So Sarah had gone, only to feel that she didn't quite deserve to be there, because Jules had turned up. Jules, with the dark circles around her eyes because she hadn't just lost the father of her child, she'd lost her own father too. Jules, with a six-month-old baby in her arms.

And when the eyes of the two women had met, nobody looking on could have said which woman was the sadder.

How was the wife of a dead man supposed to react to the presence of his lover and his child at his memorial service? What was the protocol? Where were the guidelines for that? This was a time to respect the dead. A time for serenity and peaceful reflection. But how did you show respect? How did you remain serene when you wanted to scratch out the eyes of the woman who wasn't his widow but his lover? The woman who made it look so easy to bear someone else's husband's baby?

And even though Richard's parents had told Sarah time and again that they didn't care if she could never have a child, that it didn't matter, clearly it did. Because there they were, clustered around Jules and her baby—their grandchild—cooing and clucking. How could they not be, when Jules's baby was like a gift from the gods? When she'd delivered them a miracle, and given them something of their lost son, something they'd all but given up on. The child her once-best friend carried like a trophy.

It had been impossible to watch.

Each and every gesture had been another a slice off Sarah's bruised and battered heart, another brick in the wall separating her from her former in-laws, while her empty womb ached for the child she would never have. So

The child her once-best friend carried like a trophy.

she'd fled, leaving the service early, slipping away without saying goodbye to anyone. It wasn't like she was needed, and she'd paid her respects, hadn't she?

So what did Jules want now?

Forgiveness?

Absolution?

Fat chance.

She sniffed. Her father had likened forgiveness to grief. Wrong again, because grief was something Sarah knew all about. She'd lived every one of grief's five stages during every failed IVF cycle and through the months that followed. The threads of denial, anger, bargaining and depression were woven through the fabric of her life. There was even acceptance there too, but that was the flimsiest thread of all, the thread that threatened to snap and unravel at the slightest hiccup, the thread she had to fight with all her might to keep together, lest she fell apart with it.

And as if that hadn't been enough for one person to bear, then had come betrayal of the worst possible kind, and the frayed and fractured fabric of her life had been indelibly stained.

She'd had so much stolen from her. The thought of giving something away now was anathema to her. She had nothing left to steal. Nothing left to give.

Least of all forgiveness.

19

Life seemed so much easier when Andy was working on the supply ship. So much less stressful. The mornings ran more smoothly, the kids fed and off to school before she did the housework and checked out guests and cleaned rooms in preparation for incoming guests. It was so much better than spending her days angsting about what Andy had or hadn't said or done the night before. Besides, cleaning rooms and changing sheets gave her time and space to put the various pieces of her life together and work out the bigger picture.

So she was married to a man who couldn't see the point of travelling and wouldn't even consider going somewhere new with her, not even to celebrate an occasion as special as their twentieth anniversary. A man who preferred to read a book in bed than make love to his wife. A book about the history of the internal combustion engine— Floss had checked in case he was getting his thrills there. A man who didn't seem very interested in being married and who was becoming more distant and short tempered by the day.

She'd tried to be a good wife and, for the most part, she thought she had been. Okay, so they'd had that one big slip-up when she'd found herself pregnant with Mikey when they'd settled on having four children, but what was one more when you already had four? For the most part, she'd been a pretty decent wife. She'd cooked and cleaned and managed the guesthouse, and if she had to give herself a ranking out of ten, she'd probably be around a seven-point-five to eight. But only because nobody was perfect and you had to take marks off for something. Even if just for her few extra kilos or a less than perfect nose.

But what would Andy say if she asked him if he still wanted to be married? Would he admit the very same question had been playing on his mind, and maybe they should talk about where things were going wrong so they could fix them? Or would he be relieved and simply say, no—he didn't want to be married any more, but he simply hadn't known how to tell her?

After the past few weeks and months, she didn't put much hope in the first option. When Annie had asked her if she and Andy were going to get divorced, Floss had been blindsided, the idea too ridiculous to contemplate. But the more she examined their relationship, the more she could understand why Annie would have thought that.

But the really scary thing? The prospect of him saying that he didn't want to be married to her any more didn't frighten her half as much as she thought it should.

On the contrary, it would kind of be a relief. Like getting a diagnosis on a tricky medical issue and finally knowing what you were dealing with. Because it was never the disease itself that was the problem, it was the not knowing.

She finished the room she was working on, gave the bed cover one last tweak, and arranged a welcoming assortment of fresh hibiscus on the dining table. She looked at them, their bright colours mocking her mood.

She turned away.

The flowers wouldn't last of course.

They never did.

～

Floss never went for a walk after dinner, she was always too busy doing the dishes, but tonight she surprised her children by saying she was going out. Someone else could worry about the dishes for a change—if they did.

'Mum?' said Annie.

'Where are you going?' Mikey demanded.

'Just out,' she said, wrapping a scarf around her neck before pulling on her jacket. 'If I'm not back, Annie will put you to bed.'

Annie pulled a face but Floss ignored her and headed out the door. She turned into the wind, pulled her jacket hood closer around her face and walked down the driveway.

Today's revelation had rocked her, then haunted her. It had played on her thoughts and tugged on her heartstrings all afternoon long. Was she really ready to be done with Andy? High school sweethearts. Marriage. Five kids. And then, *bam*! The world blows apart. Even just thinking about it seemed like sacrilege.

But was that the problem, being together since high school? Never being with anyone else? Tying yourself to just one other person and expecting it would last the distance? Floss marched down the road feeling lost and out of her depth, while the wintry wind flipped back her hood, icy fingers snatching at her hair.

Because there was definitely a problem. And if she didn't out what it was, and find a solution, she might just go mad in the process.

20

It was quiet in the shop, so Sarah had let Deirdre go home early to help out her daughter with the witching hour. Sarah wasn't entirely sympathetic. More than anything, she was baffled that anyone who had been through the disappointment of miscarriages would be complaining about a little disruption and inconvenience in your day when you finally had the children you wanted. Sarah had sworn black and blue that she'd never complain about a little upheaval in her day, if and when she finally had a baby. She'd promised the IVF gods that she'd never whinge or make a fuss, she'd be the perfect mother, a picture of serenity. Not that any of her promises had made a shred of difference, but still …

Tammy, though, didn't seem to mind calling on her mother for help. But maybe when you were onto your third baby, you could forget how much you wanted even just one.

God, how amazing would that be?

After Deirdre had gone, it was quiet in the store, the perfect time to think about what Sarah was going to do about Jules's unexpected request, and get something productive done at the same time. That's why she was bum up, head down wiping out the bottom of the big fridge while she mulled over whether she even wanted to see Jules, let along talk to her, when the bell over the door tinkled. Sarah sighed. That'd be right.

'Be with you in a minute,' she called over her shoulder. 'Yell out if you're in a rush.'

'No rush,' said a deep voice. 'Take your time.'

And if she wasn't wrong, whoever was talking wasn't wandering around looking for something, but standing at the counter with a perfect view of her arse. Marvellous.

She tried to get up too fast and hit her head on a shelf.

'Bloody hell,' she said, rubbing her head as she stood and found herself face to face with a policeman, the same one she'd seen the day she'd arrived. He was smiling widely and she had a pretty good idea why.

'Sorry about that,' she said, peeling off her gloves and wiping her hands on a towel.

'Are you okay?' he asked, still flashing that amazing smile.

'Let's just say my ego's been in better shape. Now, what can I help you with?'

'I heard Dot had got someone in the shop to help out,' he said. 'I just wanted to come by and introduce myself. Senior Sergeant Noah Lomu.'

'Wow,' she said. 'I recognise that name. Any relation to Jonah Lomu?'

He laughed, a rich sound that curled warmly in the air. 'I wish. My football skills are rock bottom and he would have no doubt disowned me if we were related. It's why I had to find a real job.' He paused. 'And you are?'

'Oh god, sorry. Sarah Thorpe. I'm Dot and Sam's daughter.' She held out her hand and when he took it in his, she realised the warmth didn't end at his laughter.

Almost reluctantly she let go, and he put his hand on the counter. A big hand. Big arm for that matter.

'So you're a rugby tragic then?'

'Not me. My husband—well, he's gone now. He was a big fan.' God, she was babbling. She took a deep breath. 'Anyway, that's neither here nor there. Dad said you're only here temporarily.'

Noah's tilted head and raised eyebrow asked the question.

'Oh, Dad was filling me in. We passed you coming from the airport.'

'I remember,' he said. 'I saw you too.'

'You did?'

'I try not to miss too much.' He gave a wry grin. 'Kind of goes with the territory.'

She smiled, wishing she looked more respectable and not like she'd just been dragged out of the bottom of the fridge. 'Fair enough.'

'How's Dot getting along then?'

'It's fair to say she's a bit impatient with it all. She's not a fan of the physio.'

'Well, who is, when you're forced to do it?' He pushed himself back from the counter and rubbed his hands together before he gave her that dynamite smile again. 'You'll pass on my regards to your parents?'

'I certainly will. Thanks for dropping by, Senior Sergeant—'

'Nope.' He shook his head. 'Noah, please. I'll see you round, Sarah.'

Sarah bade him goodbye and went back to her cleaning, grateful for the interruption but still no closer to working out what to do about Jules's request. She got down on her hands and knees and cleaned and scrubbed and removed sticky bits that had been stuck to the shelves for who knew how long while her mind wrestled with the problem.

She knew what her father thought: that accepting Jules's invitation to talk wasn't a sign of weakness. That it wasn't letting her off the hook.

But why should she listen to anything the woman said? What difference could it make? None. None at all.

In the almost five years since her world had been turned upside down, Sarah had done her best to raise the drawbridge and protect what was left of her shattered emotions. That had been possible— manageable—while she'd lived in Sydney, throwing herself into her work and striving to pretend that the soul-destroying events of the past had happened on a distant galaxy, rather than an island a mere two hours off the coast.

But now she was back on Lord Howe, it was impossible to keep that drawbridge up, impossible to keep the pain at bay. The memories were too raw here. They merged to crash over her like the ocean waves against the coral reef that fringed the lagoon. They boomed inside her skull.

And all she knew was that things could have been so very different.

She sniffed at the truth in that, remembering the exhilaration of discovering she was pregnant. She'd known from the minute she and Richard had signed up for IVF that it was going to work. She'd always succeeded at anything she'd tried, she always won everything she'd ever put her hand to, so why should this be any different? She and Richard would be one of the success stories whose photos lined the clinic walls, who inspired other infertile couples to try. People would read their story and know that it would work for them too.

After the first failed attempt, Sarah had tried to be practical. It didn't always work the first time. She understood that. She was good with numbers and IVF was a percentage game. She knew thirty-two per cent of women in their thirties succeeded through IVF, as opposed to thirteen per cent of women in their forties—so she was on the right side of the percentages. She was sure she'd be one of those thirty-two per cent.

She also knew it took an average of three treatment cycles to get a baby. Which meant some people would undergo only one, others more than three. She understood that too. It was an average after all, though she'd been better than average all her life. It wouldn't take long.

She also knew she wasn't the type of person to be crushed by one setback. So it hadn't happened this time—but it would happen.

After five failed attempts, on the wrong side of average, Sarah was a mess, her weight had ballooned from endless injections and hormones and her skin and hair looked like shit, but she knew that their story would be all the more inspiring for having to go the extra distance. Persistence. Never giving up. Never losing sight of your goals. And everyone would be all the more thrilled for her and Richard, because they knew the rough road they'd travelled.

And then, on their sixth attempt, the stars lined up, and the magic happened.

She remembered the words so clearly, she remembered the joy of the doctor, who'd called to give her the happy news herself, because she knew what it meant. She remembered the joy, the excitement, the sheer exhilaration of the high, that after a string of keenly anticipated but ultimately fruitless attempts, after all the heartache and despair, finally success.

She was pregnant.

With child.

In a few months she'd meet their baby and hold it in her arms.

And for a blissful few days, a few precious weeks, things were perfect. Her body had done all the right things. Her sense of smell rebelled at the aromas of freshly ground coffee and meat cooking, and she'd delighted at its rebellion. Her breasts had grown more tender, as had the relationship between her and Richard. It had shifted, a load taken off. Richard took her out for dinner and to the Opera House for a Vivaldi concert. He treated her like she was the most precious thing in the world, and then, just to top it off, he'd wanted to make love to her. Not because it was the right time of the month or the right temperature or the right damned moon, but because he'd wanted to.

Even morning sickness hadn't prevented it from being the most wondrous few weeks of her life, made all the more special because it had taken them so long to get to this place, and finally—finally—their long held dreams were about to come true.

Ten weeks came and went, one-quarter the way through, and Sarah was feeling on top of the world.

Until she'd woken in agony to find her sheets wet, stained with the lifeblood of her pregnancy, together with her hopes and dreams for this child.

In hospital, while Richard had held her hands as she'd cried her heart out, she'd blubbered, 'We can try again. We were so close this time, so close. We can try again.'

'Shh,' he'd said. 'You need to rest and get well. Let's talk about that later.' And he'd squeezed her hand, even as he hadn't quite met her eyes.

They'd been booked to fly to Lord Howe Island four days later, ostensibly to perform the audit of the Island Trust, but the timing had been perfect: they'd wanted to share the news of their pregnancy. To celebrate success, rather than to receive commiserations for a change.

But Sarah pulled out of the trip. She wasn't well enough or strong enough to face her mother and her well-meaning and not-so-well-meaning homilies. Not face to face. She'd had enough of them over the phone.

'Never mind, dear, you never really seemed the motherly kind.'

'Best to forget all about it. After all, a baby would just get in the way of your career.'

'These things only ever happen for a reason.'

'There, there, it's all for the best.'

And then the kicker: 'But I don't know what's wrong with you. Nobody else in the family has had any trouble having children. I never did ...'

No. Sarah had known she couldn't handle it. She was too emotionally fragile to withstand her mother's half-baked wisdoms, well-meaning or otherwise. And she was too emotionally raw to see Floss and her brood, and see how easy it was for some. How unfair it was.

So she'd cancelled her flights. And when Richard had asked if it was still okay that he went, she'd told him she would be fine, that it would give him a much needed break, although she was worried about his accommodation plans.

'Are you okay staying at Jules's, though? I know you two don't get on.'

'Hey, I'm a big boy,' he'd assured her. 'I can handle a cantankerous woman as easily as the next guy.'

'In that case, you might as well stay with Dot.'

He'd pulled a face and said, 'I said I was a big boy. I didn't say I had super powers.'

And she'd laughed, for the first time in what had seemed ages. 'Seriously,' she'd told him, 'you could always stay somewhere else. Floss might be able to put you up.'

'I'm not afraid of Jules,' he'd said.

And she'd kissed him goodbye, and said, 'That's the spirit.' And sent him straight into the arms of another woman.

The woman who was asking to meet up with her now.

And why?

Nothing could change what had happened and no words could make up for it. Whatever motivated Jules to reach out now was hardly Sarah's problem. So why should she do Jules any favours? What was the point?

It wasn't like they could ever be friends again.

Sarah pulled her head out of the fridge and rocked back on her knees, puffing a little. She nodded as she surveyed the results of her efforts. Stainless steel gleamed, glass sparkled. Tomorrow she'd rearrange the shelves. But for now, as she put away her cleaning gear and washed her hands, she wished it was as easy to remove the stains and blemishes from her own life.

21

Floss put the phone down. Matt Caruso had asked her to make a booking for dinner that night but the restaurant had a generator problem and had to cancel, so they'd recommended a couple of places where they were directing their guests.

Floss followed the palm-lined path towards Matt's unit to ask what he'd prefer. It was after four, and she had no idea if he'd even be around. But there he was, sitting on his veranda, tapping away on his keyboard.

'Hey,' he said, raising his hand as she approached.

'Hi yourself,' she said, feeling ridiculously pleased at his welcoming smile. 'I'm afraid I've got some bad news on the dinner front. Echoes has generator problems and has had to cancel tonight, so we'll have to find you another place to eat.'

His hands abandoned his keyboard as he sat back, his forearms resting on the chair's armrests. He blew out through his teeth. 'That's too bad. I'd heard good things about Echoes, too.'

'All is not lost. They gave me a couple of suggestions.'

He picked up his bottle of wine. 'In that case, can I offer you a glass of white while you run through the options?'

Floss hesitated. There was no reason why she shouldn't say yes. It was Tracey's turn to run the guests to their dinner bookings tonight and Floss wasn't planning on going out. In any case, a glass of wine was neither here nor there.

He cocked an eyebrow. 'I hear it's not good to drink alone, and you did say maybe next time.'

Yes, she had. She also remembered the reason why. Because this man looked at her in a way that made her feel like she actually mattered.

'Seriously,' he said, 'it would help flesh out my article a bit. To have the human touch. A local's touch. I mean, not just about what it's like to be a visitor, but what it's like to actually call Lord Howe Island home.'

'An interview, then,' she said.

'That's it,' he said. 'I'd love to interview you. If you've time, that is.'

There was nobody around to ask her questions, directions or advice, and nobody who needed her attention. Annie would be home by now to see to Mikey—god, what would she do without that girl to help with her brothers and Mikey in particular—so she didn't have to be anywhere in particular ... and it was kind of nice to have a man interested in her for a change, even if it was only for an article he was writing.

'Sure,' she said, climbing the steps. 'Why not?'

And he smiled again and asked her to sit down while he went to fetch her a glass.

She sat on the veranda and enjoyed the view of the palms and flowering hibiscus trees as her guests were used to seeing them, noticing the rustle of the leaves in the breeze. The promise of rain hung in the air. There would be showers later in the afternoon, but for now it was mild and pleasant and it was nice to sit down.

In a flash Matt was back and pouring her a wine, then he lifted his to clink glasses. 'Cheers.'

'Cheers.' She took a sip. Very nice wine, not too sweet, not too dry, and not too chilled for a mild winter's day. 'Wow,' she said, 'that's like the Goldilocks version of wine. The just-right version.'

'It's good, isn't it?' he said, raising his glass to examine it in the light. 'I found it at the store.'

'Which one?' Floss didn't drink a lot, but she wouldn't mind getting hold of a couple of bottles to put away for special occasions.

'Oh, the one just up from the museum.' He frowned. 'Short name—'

'Dot's?'

'That's the one.'

He put his glass down and turned his gaze on her, holding it for a beat too long, and Floss got the impression that, like the wine a moment before, he was examining her. She crossed her legs and tucked her hair behind her ears, wondering again just what he saw.

'It's good to catch up with you for five minutes,' he said. 'I see you darting around everywhere, so it's nice to pin you down for once.'

She shrugged, trying not to read too much into his comment. 'When you're in the hospitality business, there's always something that needs doing.'

'And you're the chief cook and bottle washer.'

She smiled at the ancient expression, something she'd expect her father's generation to come out with. Maybe his father's too? 'Something like that,' she said, and took another sip of her drink. The wine was warming her from the inside, coiling into her senses, and she could feel herself relaxing. So nice.

'We'd better get started on that interview before this wine goes to my head,' she said, only half joking.

He nodded. 'So tell me, how long have you lived here, Floss?'

'My whole life,' she told him. 'I was born here, same as my mum, and her mum before her.'

'Wow,' he said, 'you're so lucky to live in such a special place.'

'Yeah,' she said, unable to prevent a sigh, 'that's what people tell us all the time.'

He angled his head. 'You sound like you don't believe it.'

'No, it's not that. It's just—limited, I guess. You can't go too far in any direction without falling off the edge. And it's beautiful and special and visiting Lord Howe is on just about everyone's bucket list,

I get that, but sometimes it would be nice to be somewhere else for a change.'

He chuckled, the deep notes of the sound combining with the wine to send ripples of warmth through her veins. 'The grass is always greener, eh?'

'Yeah, maybe that's it,' she said. Though it was much more than the grass being greener elsewhere. Because the ocean that separated this island from the world and made it so special to visitors, was the same ocean that held her captive and prevented her from just getting in a car and driving somewhere different. Anywhere different. 'What's it like where you come from?'

'I live in Melbourne now, but I grew up on a dairy farm outside Tatura, cow country not far from Shepparton. I don't think you'd want to change places with either of those, at least, not permanently.'

'Why not?'

'Because the city is crowded and busy and smells like there's a bazillion people shoved into a shoebox.'

She smiled. She'd been to Melbourne for a school trip once and it had been crowded and the city air full of fumes, but it had also been exciting to kids that came from an island with less than four hundred permanent residents. 'And Tatura?'

'Is flat and dry and smells like there's a bazillion cows shoved under your doormat. Although in all fairness, that's probably because Dad was always wiping his muddy boots on it.'

She laughed. 'Okay, so maybe I'll cross Tatura off the bucket list.'

'Hey, don't get me wrong,' he said, refilling her glass before she could say yea or nay. 'There's a lot going for the place too.'

Floss smiled. She wouldn't have said no to a second glass, but it was such a rare treat to be sitting and chatting over a glass of wine that she wasn't about to argue. Especially with a good-looking man who knew how to hold a conversation. She was enjoying herself for the first time in what seemed forever and she felt ten years younger in the process. Better still, she'd stopped wondering what he thought of her. He made her feel good about herself, and that was enough.

'There's a lot going for the place too.'

'So tell me what Tatura has going for it.'

'For a start, it hosts the second biggest international dairy festival in the southern hemisphere every January.' He paused to let the import of that sink in. 'And if that isn't grand enough to impress you, I'll have you know the local bakery won a prize in the Great Australian Vanilla Slice contest two years running.'

'Wow, I am impressed! But who gets to host the biggest international dairy festival?'

He screwed up his nose. 'We don't like to talk about it back in Tat,' he said. His eyes were brown, she noticed. A much darker brown than she'd first thought, almost mocha, and crinkled at the edges when he smiled. It took her a couple of beats and the final sip of her wine to remember where she was in the conversation.

'You didn't want to be a dairy farmer, like your dad?'

He shook his head. 'No, I was always better with words than with animals. I was the only kid in the family who didn't have a pet, let alone who wanted to get up close and personal with the cows, a big disappointment for my father, let me tell you. It was just lucky my younger brother made up for my failings. Travis is a natural. We called him the cow whisperer from the time he was a little kid, and it was kind of a joke then. But not anymore.' He held up his hand, curling his pinky. 'He's got those girls wrapped around his little finger. He gets the best yields in the district. Nobody knows how he does it.'

She had precious little knowledge of cows, beyond the existence of the small herds that grazed the fields by the airport and down near Old Settlement Beach, and whose sloppy cow pats you had to dodge on your way up the hill to get to the remains of the Catalina flying boat that had crashed in 1948. He might as well have been talking about a different planet, but he was easy to listen to and he made it all sound fascinating. He stood and disappeared inside and she was just thinking how wrong she'd been about him when he'd stepped off the plane, and that he was far nicer than she'd assumed, when a moment later he was back with a second bottle and topping up her glass.

Another one? She glanced at her watch. How long had she been here?

'I've got it,' he said as he filled up his own glass.

'Got what?'

'Who you remind me of.'

She blinked and sat up straighter. Is that why he'd been staring at her? 'Who?'

'Nicole Ritchie.'

'Oh.' She grimaced, not entirely sure whether to be flattered or not. 'Is that a good thing?'

He smiled, almost apologetically. 'I think she's kinda cute. I thought you looked familiar when I met you, but it's the way you've got your hair up today with all the ends coming loose around your face that made me realise.'

Was he flirting with her? Was he saying she looked cute? Floss had two ways of doing her hair: scraped back in a ponytail when Annie hadn't stolen all her hair ties, or pinned in a messy bun when she had, like she'd had to do this morning. She put her hands to the loose ends now, trying to poke them away.

'Don't,' he said, putting his hand on hers, not holding it, just resting it there, warm and real. 'It looks good like that,' he said, his fingers now at her hair, undoing her repair work while his eyes returned to hers. 'You look good.'

The world seemed to stop. All she knew was the tingle of her scalp where his fingers had brushed and the thudding of her heart, and dark eyes so compelling she could fall into them. Eyes that seemed to be coming closer, so there was every chance she would.

A sudden squall riffed violently through the trees as the heavens unleashed a burst of rain. Big fat drops hurling onto the veranda at a forty-five-degree angle and splatting hard against anything in their way. Against them.

'Quick,' he said, grabbing the wine and bolting for the door, 'let's get inside.'

They were half drenched by the time they made it under cover, the rain coming in sheets now, tearing through the vegetation and thundering on the roof. They stood there dripping wet and looking at each other in disbelief, then started laughing.

And somehow, suddenly, she was in Matt's arms and he was kissing her. Only she was kissing back. He tasted of the wine they'd shared, he tasted of man, he tasted of heat, and it was intoxicating. It felt so good—so bloody good—to have his hands on her back and skimming over her breasts because it had been so bloody long.

She had no idea how long they stood like that, how long they kissed, but when finally he pulled away, his breathing ragged and hard like he'd run a marathon, she didn't want to let his mouth go, even if it was to nuzzle at her ear and send his warm breath down her collar.

'It's my last night on the island,' he whispered, his hands roaming low down her back, his fingers squeezing, 'and I was wondering …'

22

It was one of *those* days—the days Jules dreaded because of what it could do to bend her mother emotionally out of shape. Birthdays, Father's Day, Christmas. But she was getting in early and hopefully heading off any trouble. She fashioned a bouquet of bright hibiscus flowers and fern fronds from the garden to give Pru. She knew exactly where it would end up, but she didn't mind. Whatever made her mum feel better on a day like today was all right with Jules.

She called Della, who came running to pick up the box of cookies they'd made together. Two batches. Della had chosen chocolate chip, because they were her favourites, while Jules had chosen raisin and oatmeal, because she'd figured they were packed with goodness and half a meal in themselves and if her mother only ate those ...

'Okay,' she said, 'let's go see Nana and Papa.'

They drove past Dot's Store on the way and Jules felt weird thinking Sarah was probably somewhere inside. She thought about her unanswered invitation and felt her irritation spike. Sure, Sarah could ignore her and not answer if that's what she wanted to do, but how hard was it to give a simple yes or no? The non-answer pissed Jules off. She had a week before she had to be back in Sydney to start her radiotherapy and she wanted to deal with this before then.

And really, what could Sarah do if Jules just turned up at the store out of the blue? She would have to deal with Jules's request then.

Besides, it wasn't as if she'd never shopped at Dot's before now. Why shouldn't she simply turn up?

Just not today. Today she had more important things to do.

Finally, they were past the store, and she flexed her tight fingers on the steering wheel and exhaled a long breath. That was the trouble with a twenty-five kilometre an hour speed limit, it took too long to drive past anywhere you didn't want to be.

A minute later, she pulled up in Pru's driveway and unclicked Della from her child seat. Immediately her daughter ran inside, calling for her nana, while Jules collected her bag and the biscuits and flowers. She was just shutting her door when Della came running out again, her little face stricken.

'Mummy, Mummy. Nana won't wake up.'

Dear god, no. Enough already!

Jules wasn't overly religious, she'd attended Sunday school and services at the local Anglican church for years growing up, before she'd turned into a rebellious teenager and tossed religion aside. But it was an appeal to any higher being that ran through her mind as she rushed inside behind her daughter, an appeal that her worst fears weren't about to be realised.

'See, Mummy?' Della said, as she stopped in the living room.

There was Pru, lying on her face on the sofa, one arm dangling. Motionless. Until all of a sudden she snorted loudly and then kept on snoring.

Jules's stalled heart found a reassuring beat. So not dead. *Thank you, God, because even if you're not there, someone answered my prayers.*

And then she got down on her knees next to her mother. There was a wine cask on the coffee table. Empty. An empty glass fallen beside it. No prizes for working out how or why her mother had passed out.

Oh, Mum.

'What's wrong with Nana?' said Della, looking serious now, pulling out the two fingers she'd had wedged in her mouth just long enough to ask.

'She's not feeling well,' said Jules, patting her mother's face. 'Come on, mum, wake up.'

It took a few more attempts before Pru snorted and stirred. 'Wha?' she said, blinking into the midmorning light.

'It's Jules and Della. We were going to visit Papa's memorial. Remember?'

Her mother blinked again, before her face creased and she made a keening sound. 'I was trying to forget,' she said, when at last she could talk, beating one hand against the sofa. 'I was trying to forget.'

'I know,' Jules said, reaching down to hug her mother and draw her up. 'I know. Come on, sit up. You'll be much more comfortable then.'

With a mighty effort, Jules got her mother upright—but only because Pru was such a lightweight now.

'I'm so thirsty,' Pru said, eyeing the empty glass. 'Is there something to drink?'

'I'll get it,' Jules said, whipping the glass and carton out of the way, returning with a glass of water.

Her mother drank it down quickly. 'Oh, you don't have a painkiller to go with another one of those, do you?'

'Are you all right, Nana?' Della asked as Jules refilled her glass and searched through her bag for painkillers.

'Just a bit muddle-headed today,' her mum said. 'I'll be fine.'

'Here,' Jules said, handing Pru a couple of capsules and another glass of water.

Her mother took them. 'There,' she said, with too bright a smile to be real. Especially when her hair and the rest of her looked completely shell-shocked. 'I'm sure I'll feel better in no time.'

'You were asweep,' said Della, with the gravity of a four-year-old who knew this wasn't quite right.

'I know,' Pru said with a wobbly smile. 'I got very tired and suddenly it was way too far to get to bed, and I decided to curl up on the sofa instead.'

Jules sighed, relief dragging through her veins. Her mum was okay. She picked up the flowers and handed the cookies to Della to deliver.

'I'm sorry, Mum, because it's so not right, and it's so not happy, but happy anniversary anyway.'

'It would have been our fortieth anniversary today,' said Pru to nobody in particular as she knelt in the damp sandy earth by the memorial, the empty grave, that bore her husband's name. Palms bordered the small cemetery that was so close to the beach that the sound of the waves hitting the sand melded with the sound of the breeze rattling through the palms and her mother's lost and lonely voice.

'Forty years, Greg. Who would have believed you could put up with me for that long?' Her mother sucked in air, 'Except you didn't, of course. I'm not blaming either of us for that, but I do miss you, Greg. And I wake up every day, wishing you were here.'

Jules waited a distance away, resting her hand on Della's head while the girl clung to her leg, fingers in her mouth while her nana spoke to a papa Della would never remember meeting.

For Pru and Jules, the day Greg had been lost was impossible to forget. It had been blowy, but nothing out of the ordinary, nothing Jules's sea-faring father couldn't handle with both his hands tied behind his back. So when the boat didn't come back at the appointed time, everyone assumed they'd hit the mother of all fishing grounds and were making the most of it while the light lasted.

But as the hours stretched out and there was no sight of the returning vessel and no contact, concerns grew. As dark fell, Jules went over to her mum's place so she wouldn't be alone as they waited for news.

But, as the long night hours eked out, there was none.

The search crews were out early, a police rescue helicopter from Sydney, planes from Port Macquarie, along with the police cruiser from Lord Howe. For hours Jules waited with her mother, hanging out for the phone to ring, dreading it at the same time. As friends dropped by in the following days to lend support, Jules had clung to Della. 'We'll find your daddy and your papa,' she'd told the tiny infant, who was too young to know what was going on, but sensitive enough to the vibes to know that something must be happening.

When the call finally came, it was the local policeman.

'Jules,' he said. 'They've found wreckage from a boat. A bucket and some fishing gear. A life buoy. It's from *Snapper*.'

A thump of her heart before she could ask, 'And the crew?'

'I'm sorry.' He paused and again her heart thumped before it seemed to stick in her chest. 'There's no sign.'

Nobody gave up hope of finding survivors—at least, not at first. But eventually the search wound down, and their hopes died with it. No boat. No bodies. Nothing but a few random items and some shattered pieces of hull.

But Pru hadn't given up. She struggled up to the Intermediate Hill lookout every day for a week to search the horizon herself, because she couldn't believe that Greg was gone and wasn't coming back, and she couldn't just stay at home and do nothing but wait.

They'd been married for the best part of forty years, after all. You didn't just accept that your life partner was gone and get on with it.

When the inquiry finally came, it pointed to a catastrophic failure of the engine, leading to an explosion, so sudden that there would have been no warning, no time to get out a Mayday message.

No hope, which meant no answers.

And that was half the problem, Jules figured. The not knowing.

Her mother had never been averse to a glass of wine before. A moscato or a bit of sweet fizz. But after Greg had gone, she'd really settled into drinking. For escape. For relief. For company at night until she collapsed into bed, and for sleep that came with no dreams. Filling the void that came with not knowing.

For a while, Jules had understood. She could see how it had happened. She'd felt the same kind of shell shock, but she'd had Della to take care of to keep her grounded, to hold her together when otherwise she could have fallen apart. She missed her father so very badly. She missed him every day. But she'd never loved Richard. Not like Pru had loved Greg.

Her mother laid the flowers Jules had brought at the foot of the headstone.

But right now, unlike her mother, Jules wasn't concerned with the dead. She was increasingly worried about the living. Not just for herself and her own ongoing treatment. And not just because she knew Sarah was back on the island and, sooner or later, Jules was somehow going to have to face her and the past. But also—mostly—for the way her mother was trying to drown her grief within the cardboard walls of a wine cask.

Because she had no idea how to fix that.

23

Sarah was up a ladder in the store, hard at work applying orange oil to the stripped and cleaned shelves when she heard a car pull up outside, followed by the slide of van doors opening then slamming shut. She heard voices, young ones, and the clumping of feet up the short flight of steps to the veranda, before the door flew open, the bell rendered redundant as a clutch of kids burst in, talking potato chips and Twisties as they scattered through the shop.

Not tourists then, Sarah thought, as she backed down the ladder and pulled off her gloves. Unless they were the kind of tourists who could afford to bring the whole family on holidays with them.

'What can I do for you?' she said to two teenagers who were standing at the counter with a collection of snacks.

They peered at her strangely, a blonde girl about sixteen who looked almost familiar and a boy just as tall but who looked younger, and who Sarah assumed was the girl's brother, while from the back of the store came the tinkle of bottles and a firm, 'No. Put that back,' from a voice she'd grown up with. A voice she hadn't heard for something like five years. 'You can't have that. Here, take this, will you?'

A sizzle went down Sarah's spine. She looked at the girl again and realised why she looked familiar. She was looking at an almost Floss;

from back in their high school years and with the addition of a stud in her nose, but yes, Floss, with her clear blue eyes and wayward hair.

And suddenly the real Floss was there too, her mouth half open, flanked by two more boys. She held a basket weighed down by wine bottles in one hand while the other braced a child on her hip.

Floss blinked, looking like a mutton bird recently crash landed and wanting to run away and hide but confused about which hole to run into. 'Sarah,' she said. 'I didn't—'

Sarah attempted a smile that was almost crushed under the weight of their history. 'Hi Floss. I'm just helping out a while Mum recovers from her hip operation.'

'Oh. I'd heard, but I didn't realise …'

That she was back? The island telegraph definitely wasn't what it used to be. Or maybe people had figured Floss wouldn't want to know, because of what Sarah had done to her.

The poisoned cloud hung in the air between them, fat with the memory of the day the hairline crack in their friendship had turned into a chasm. The day Floss had disclosed to her and Jules that she was twelve weeks pregnant with her fourth baby. The day Sarah's jealousy—the jealousy that had been brimming under the surface and that she'd battled so long to contain—had turned toxic and spilled over.

Sarah momentarily closed her eyes, wishing she could blot out what had come next, but there was no forgetting her ugly words. She'd ended up screaming at Floss that it wasn't fair that she could get pregnant so easily when she already had three babies, and when every period was another slap in Sarah's face, especially when she'd tried so hard—so damned hard. That she was sick of trying to be happy for everyone else when happiness was so unequally shared. And why did Floss have to be such a fucking fertility goddess when Sarah had to miss out? She'd completely lost it that day, her anguish and rage and jealousy gushing out. A flood of envy and heartbreak. Unrelenting. Unforgiveable.

Especially when Sarah had told Floss that they were done, and that they couldn't be friends any more.

Across the counter, Floss seemed to rally herself, her eyes wary.

'Kids,' she said. 'Get in the car. Annie, look after Mikey for me. I'll be there in a minute, okay?' She passed the child on her hip to her daughter.

'Lollies!' protested the child she'd called Mikey, who'd spotted the packets in the jar and didn't want to go anywhere.

Floss snatched up two packets and handed them to Annie. 'Go, get in the car, all of you.' To Sarah, Floss said, 'Add those to the total, okay?'

'Please,' Sarah said, 'don't make them go. It's fine, I swear.' She took a deep breath. She was older now. Hopefully wiser. Stronger than the emotional wreck she'd been then, just two weeks after yet another failed IVF attempt.

She tried her hardest to find a smile.

'So, these are all your kids?'

Floss looked at her wide-eyed, almost guilty, and worried. Definitely worried. 'Yeah,' she said tentatively, her mouth twisting as if the admission was as uncomfortable to make as it must be for Sarah to receive it.

'I've met the eldest two, I think,' Sarah said, doing her best to keep her voice even. 'Although ages ago now.' She'd met number three too, although he'd been little more than a toddler. She vaguely remembered now her mother announcing some time ago that there'd been a fifth, but she'd repressed that unwelcome information, kept it buried until now.

'I remember,' said the girl, stony faced.

Sarah winced. Of course she'd remember, because she'd been there that day. She'd heard every bitter and twisted word that had spewed out of Sarah's ugly mouth.

'Me too,' said the boy, although his eyes were nowhere near as hostile. More like wary.

'Anne, was it?' said Sarah, looking at the mini-Floss, trawling through memory after painful memory. That was the worst of trying to forget the fact everyone else in the world was happily popping out babies—you blanked their children's names too.

'Annie.'

Sarah nodded. 'Annie. Of course. Great to see you again.' She turned to the girl's brother. 'And, Brad?'

'Brodie,' he said.

'Sorry,' she said, 'it's been a while. Nice to see you again, Brodie.'

Floss finished the introductions. 'And these two are Cameron and Ben,' she said, 'and this little monkey's called Mikey.'

'Wow.' Sarah was being too cheerful, she knew, too false. But she couldn't help herself, couldn't stop making out like everything was perfect and that nothing was wrong. 'And now, I suppose, I should ring up your groceries.' She was being too cheerful, she knew, as she added up their purchases on the till. Too false. But she couldn't help herself, couldn't stop herself from making out like everything was perfect and that nothing was wrong.

While Sarah totted up the purchases, Floss just as hurriedly packed them into a string bag. 'So … how long are you back?'

'Only six months. I'll be gone before you know it.'

Floss nodded.

'How's Andy?'

Floss looked away and reached for her wallet. 'He's, um, good.'

'Good.'

Sarah told Floss the total and watched as she pulled out some notes.

'Oh,' Floss said, 'you forgot to add the lollies.'

Sarah shook her head. 'They're on the house.'

Floss pressed her lips together and nodded before she turned and started herding her family towards the door. She held it open while they trooped through, the younger ones bolting down the stairs to get to the van first.

Floss turned at the door.

'I'm sorry, Sarah.'

Sarah bit her lip but couldn't stop the moisture from leaking from her eyes. 'No, I'm the one who should apologise. I'm sorry. For everything. It's nice to see you again, Floss.'

'Yeah. You too.' And if Sarah wasn't wrong, Floss almost managed a smile.

Sarah listened as the van's engine kicked into life then let herself slump onto the stool behind the counter. God, she'd been such a bitch. So jealous and bitter and making out like it was Floss's fault that Sarah couldn't conceive.

But Floss was at the other end of the fertility spectrum. The one for whom getting pregnant was as easy as breathing.

And it had hurt so very bad for such a long time.

But now it hurt to face up to what she had done. Sarah walked to the window and looked out at the cloud-scudded sky and the ever-shifting palms that screened the guest house across the road, and felt … alone.

She'd been alone forever it seemed. She stood at the window, her mind a jumble of thoughts. She'd wronged Floss, and it had helped ease the pain to see her again. Jules had wronged her. She squeezed her eyes shut. The situations weren't the same. They weren't equivalent. What Jules had done to her was a thousand times worse.

But would it help to see her?

To talk?

Floss hadn't wanted to be confronted by Sarah, she'd wanted to flee, Sarah had seen it in her eyes and sensed it in her body language. And yet she hadn't run. She'd held her ground and they'd talked. Briefly.

Maybe she should do the same, just go and listen to what Jules had to say. Walk away again, head held high. Nothing given away. Nothing lost. After all, in Jules's case, Sarah wasn't the one in the wrong.

The scent of orange on the air reminded Sarah of what she'd been doing before Floss's unexpected visit, and she turned away from the window, her heart thumping loud at an unlikely decision made, already dreading their meeting, half suspecting she was going to regret it.

'This can't go on, Mum.' Jules said, putting a cup of tea in front of Pru. 'It has to stop.'

It was eleven in the morning, two days after her parents' wedding anniversary, and she'd walked in and found Pru snoring on the sofa again.

'I know, dear,' Pru said, wafting one hand in the air. 'It will. As soon as you stop shouting at me.'

'I'm serious, Mum. You have to do something about your drinking.'

One eye blinked open and her mother ran a hand through her hair. 'Please don't make it sound like I've got some kind of problem.'

'You do have a problem! Which means I have a problem, because I have to go to Sydney next week for radiotherapy, and I have to leave Della in your care for four entire weeks. I can't have you passing out on her. I won't expose my child to that kind of abuse.'

'I'm hardly abusing her.'

'But you are, if she's seeing you attached to a wine cask from morning till night. What do you think you're teaching her?'

'That's enough,' Pru said, sitting up, her tone firming. 'I dragged *you* up all right, didn't I, in spite of all my obvious failings?'

'You didn't have a drinking problem then.'

'Della's my granddaughter. I'm not going to do anything to harm her, am I?'

Jules wanted to shake her. 'How am I supposed to be sure she'll be okay if you keep this up? You can't go on like this.'

Her mother dropped her head into her hands. 'If I hadn't lost Greg,' she wailed. 'If things had been different ...'

'But we did lose Greg,' Jules said, thinking that it was time for some tough love and for her mother to face up to the truth that he wasn't coming back, and that she had to live in a world without him. 'We lost Greg. We lost Richard. They're gone, Mum, no matter how much we wish it had never happened, no matter what either of us wish we could change.'

'I know,' said Pru, looking like a puddle of herself on the sofa as she descended into sobs. 'I know.'

Jules sat down beside her and wrapped her in her arms, because she hated being this hard on her mum. Even if Pru needed it, it hurt Jules too. 'It's okay, Mum. It's going to be okay.'

It was only when she'd tucked her mother up in bed to sleep it off that she saw the answering machine blinking with a message. She picked it up, thinking it might be something important. She was not prepared to find that it was Dot. She was even less prepared to find that it was Dot calling to ask Pru to let Jules know that Sarah had agreed to talk to her, the sooner the better—anything to get it over with. ('But don't tell Jules Sarah said that.')

Jules sucked in air as she put the phone down.

Help!

25

After Andy being away so long this time, his homecoming was like a celebration for the kids, so Floss didn't have to work at avoiding him. But when she was doing the dishes he picked up a tea towel and then a plate from the drainer.

'Everything all right?'

She stiffened at his closeness. 'Sure. Why wouldn't it be?'

'Only you seem a bit—' he shrugged, '—I don't know. Quiet?'

'It's impossible to get a word in edgeways with this lot, you know that.'

'That's true.' He picked up another plate and started wiping. 'So there's nothing wrong?'

'I've got a lot on my mind, that's all,' she said, hands deep in the soapy water, 'Tomorrow's going to be busy with six change overs and there's Mikey's party to think about.' *As well as all the stuff on my mind I'm not going to tell you about.*

'Mikey's birthday's not for ages.'

'It's in a three weeks, and the fundraiser the weekend before that. I've been asked to help out with the raffle. It's not like I'm standing still here.'

'All right, all right, I was just asking.'

She closed her eyes and rocked a little over the sink. God, it was impossible standing next to him. How could he not smell her fear? 'Sorry,' she said. 'There's just a lot on my mind.'

'Okay,' he said, and continued drying dishes in silence for a while, until: 'I know what I was going to tell you. I saw Sam Rooney at the airport picking up some produce for the store. Did you know Sarah was back?'

'I know. I turned up at the shop and got the shock of my life.'

'Yeah? What happened?'

'Nothing. She was nice. Trying too hard, especially seeing all the kids were there, but she was all right.'

'Jules must be shitting herself.'

She wasn't the only one. If Andy had any idea what Floss had done … But the mention of Jules reminded her of something she'd heard today. 'One of the mums at school who works part time at the museum said she heard that Jules had to go to Sydney for some tests.'

'Oh? What for?'

'She didn't know. Jules didn't say. But apparently she's back already.'

'Can't be too serious in that case,' he said, moving a stack of plates into the cupboard. 'Mind you, you fuck around with someone you shouldn't be fucking around with, you probably deserve a bit of grief.'

Floss's stomach churned. She swayed a little on her feet before she picked up the abandoned tea towel. 'Tell you what, how about you go read Mikey a story, and I'll finish these.'

'You serious?' She knew he was sizing up the rest of the dishes in the rack and thinking she was mad.

'Yep,' she said, 'Mikey's missed you. Go read to him and ask what he wants for his birthday, because he hasn't told me.'

He went, and Floss slumped against the bench, her head in her hands. What the hell was she going to do?

'What's wrong with you?' she heard Annie say a few seconds later.

She straightened slowly and turned. 'Just thinking.' She took in the damp coat her daughter was peeling off. 'Where've you been?'

'I had to take a book over to Trent's. He needed it for homework.'

'You see a lot of Trent lately.'

She shrugged, thrusting her hands deep in her jeans pockets. 'He's cool.'

'Well, just make sure you concentrate on school. There'll be plenty of time for boys later on.'

'Says my mum, who got married at twelve.'

'Excuse me, I was nineteen.'

'But you knew Dad way before that, didn't you? You went to school together.'

'We grew up together.'

'There you go.'

'There you go, what?'

'I dunno.'

Floss balled up the tea towel and lobbed it at her daughter. 'Come on, now you're here, you can give me a hand with the drying up.'

That night in bed, Andy threw an arm over her. And in spite of craving physical attention for as long as she could remember, Floss froze.

'Are you angry with me?' he asked, lying behind her.

'Why would I be angry with you?'

'I don't know. You just don't seem very happy to see me.'

'Are you planning on making love to me?'

He said nothing for a while. 'What's that got to do with anything?'

'Self-defence, really. I'd just like to know before I get all worked up and hopeful and then it turns to nothing like it usually does.'

His thumb made small circles on her arm. 'Well, maybe I am.'

She squeezed her eyes shut. 'In that case, too bad. It's that time of month.'

'Lucky,' he said, rolling over and turning his back to her, 'that saves us both a heap of disappointment.'

And Floss wondered, in the long, lonely hours afterwards, what would become of them.

26

It was one thing to invite Sarah to talk. It was another thing entirely for her to agree. Now Jules couldn't claim the high moral ground (however shaky that might be), couldn't claim that she'd tried to reach out to her old friend, only to have her efforts rebuffed.

Jules sat in a chair on the veranda, waiting, knitting needles click-clacking, trying to look more relaxed than she felt. Pru had taken Della for the morning. Jules had wanted her nowhere near here when Sarah turned up.

Della, the proof of her betrayal.

Della, the child who should never have been.

Della, who she loved more than she'd ever thought possible of something or someone you'd never before realised you'd wanted.

She'd been shattered when she'd discovered she was pregnant. Devastated. But at that stage the fact it was a child hadn't registered. At that stage her pregnancy had been a problem she hadn't wanted, because she'd known what it would cost.

Oh Della, she thought, rubbing her forehead with her hand. If she'd had her way, Della wouldn't even be here. It was Richard who'd begged her not to go down that route.

God, if she hadn't told Richard. If he'd never known and she'd gone ahead, she'd never have become a mother and her parents would never have discovered the wonder and joys of being grandparents.

So it was Richard she had to thank for Della. She hadn't felt like thanking him then or most times since. He'd turned her life upside down and broken irreplaceable bonds. But he'd been Della's father and she'd mourned his loss because of what Della had lost. What Jules had lost was already long gone.

But now she couldn't imagine her life without Della.

Instead of a curse, her daughter had turned out to be a gift. A gift that had destroyed friendships, true, but a gift without equal.

She looked down at her knitting to find her needles still. When had she stopped? She checked where she was up to on the pattern and resumed.

She'd finished the scarf and moved onto Della's jumper and was working on the sleeves, and what seemed a continuing saga of casting on and then casting off. Whoever had invented raglan sleeves, she'd decided, was some kind of masochist. She forced herself to concentrate.

Knit. Purl. Knit. Purl. Knit two together ...

And meanwhile clouds rolled and roiled overhead, and palm fronds slapped wetly as the wind pushed its way through the rain splattered treetops. Jules's gut churned.

She looked up, her eyes searching the approach to the house. Where was Sarah? Had she changed her mind? Part of her wondered why Sarah had even agreed. Jules had been prepared for Sarah to go on ignoring her. If the circumstances were reversed, Jules wasn't confident she would have agreed to a meeting. But Sarah had. Because of the cancer? Because Sarah felt sorry for her? Or because she wanted to witness the evidence of Jules's illness for herself?

Her knitting needle stabbed at a loop, picked it up and promptly dropped it, threatening to cause a run.

Damn!

Jules took a deep breath. She was determined to finish this jumper for Della before she had to return to Sydney, but she was so tense. She used a crochet hook to snag the lost stitch and thread it back on to the needle like Molly had taught her. Tried the stitch again.

She had to talk with Sarah.

Explain. Apologise.

Because if Jules didn't try now—if they couldn't try to make some kind of peace while Sarah was right here on the island—then it would never happen.

27

It was a decent walk to Jules's house, although nothing was too far on the island, but Sarah was in no mood to rush. Still, she arrived at Jules' driveway far sooner than she was ready. She took a deep breath as a pair of tourists cycled by, wobbling precariously and laughing as they waved a greeting to Sarah. But while she waved back, she couldn't find an answering smile. Not while voices banged around in her head, asking questions that had no answer, and singing sweet Siren songs suggesting that there was still time to change her mind.

God, she was tempted.

Yet still she forced her feet up the driveway, the pavement damp from earlier rain, the clouds still hovering low like dark sentinels. The cottage was all but hidden from the road, only coming into view as Sarah rounded the curve between the kentia palms. And when it did, it was as cute as she remembered, white timbered with a green tin roof and cedar-framed windows, and wrapped with a veranda edged with green railings and posts and cream-coloured slats that matched the house.

This was where Richard had come that time, to stay with Jules. This was where Sarah had sent him, practically with her blessings.

And this was where her husband and her one-time best friend had betrayed her.

It looked far too charming a cottage to be the venue for such a crime.

Bile rose hot and sour in Sarah's throat. She swallowed hard against its bitterness, shaking her head. 'What the hell am I even doing here?' she whispered, and turned to leave.

'Sarah?'

She stiffened at the plaintive sound of her name being called, and turned back, searching in the shadows of the veranda until she saw her—Jules—seated in a rocking chair.

'I wasn't sure you'd come.'

'I almost didn't.'

'I know.' Jules rose from the chair then, slowly, deliberately, as if not to disturb the tension that pulled the air taut between them or, if she felt anything like Sarah, as if held hostage by it. She put something down on the table beside her. 'Thank you for not changing your mind.'

I still could, Sarah thought, her jaw achingly tight. She still could turn around again and walk away and leave Jules standing there.

Except she didn't. Her feet remained glued to the driveway, her eyes taking in the changes in the pixie-like features of her one-time friend's face: the shadows under her eyes, the flesh of her cheeks drawn tight over her bones.

'It's been a long time,' said Jules. 'You look good.'

Sarah knew her professional persona had been unravelling ever since she'd been on the island, her grooming routine relaxing, but she still looked a damn sight better—healthier—than the woman on the veranda. That knowledge didn't prevent the lie from slipping out. 'So do you.'

'I look like crap,' Jules said with a laugh, and the palm fronds around them rustled and swayed, as though it were her unlikely laughter that sent a breeze through the trees to dance with the loose tendrils of Sarah's hair and tug on her heartstrings. Because for just a moment, the spell was broken and the woman standing on the veranda was Jules again, instead of that other woman.

Sarah pressed hard against that thought. Jules was gone, along with Sarah's husband. Along with friendship and trust and all that was good in the world.

Jules took a deep breath. 'Do you want to come inside, where it's a bit warmer?'

Sarah had been inside Jules's cottage plenty of times before. "Before" being the operative word. She looked around, testing the air. 'It's not cold outside.'

The other woman nodded and Sarah was a bit miffed that she seemed so readily to understand—as if she didn't want her inside either. 'Come on up, then, and I'll get us something to drink. Tea?'

Something stronger would have far more appeal, but Sarah just nodded. Her mouth was so dry, she would have said yes to a poisoned chalice.

Her feet came unstuck as Jules retreated inside, like the women were performing a dance, mirroring each other's movements, three steps forward, three steps back, maintaining the distance between them. Tentatively she made her way up the steps to the veranda, leaning her hands on the railing and taking a moment in which all she could hear was the thudding of her heart. Should it be racing after such a short flight of steps, or was there something else happening? Stupid question really. How had she let herself be guilted into this? She owed Jules nothing.

The clatter of cups signalled Jules's return. Sarah breathed deeply, steeling herself. Jules put a tray down next to a bag on a low table. A knitting bag, Sarah realised. That was new. But then, what did she know about Jules anymore?

'I heard you're back for six months,' Jules said, sitting down again.

'That's the plan.'

'How's your mum coping?'

'She's not the best patient. She doesn't like doing her exercises and she's frustrated because she's not progressing like she thinks she should be.'

Jules nodded and picked up the teapot. 'Sounds like Dot.'

Sarah was inclined to agree, but that would be to offer too much, too soon. She didn't like that this woman knew her mother almost as well as she did.

'She's incapacitated and she's worried about the shop.'

'I get that.'

Sarah sighed and looked out over the driveway, wondering if there was any point to this, or if their every future contact was going to be edged like a sharply honed blade.

'Look,' she said, not even bothering to pick up her cup. 'Let's cut to the chase. What is the point of this meeting? I don't want to be here, just as much as you, no doubt, don't want me here.'

'I got diagnosed with breast cancer, Sarah.'

'I heard.'

The woman opposite blinked slowly, then said, 'They cut it out and they think they got it all, but I still have to go back to Sydney for a course of radiotherapy.'

Sarah wasn't entirely sure what she was expected to say. 'Congratulations' hardly seemed the appropriate response under the circumstances, but if Jules was looking for sympathy, she was looking in the wrong place. So she said nothing.

Jules waved at the air like it was in her way. 'Anyway, it got me to thinking. About life, and stuff.'

And karma, Sarah thought, nodding. *Don't forget karma.*

'And that's why I wanted to see you.' She paused, her blue eyes searching out Sarah's brown ones, holding them, not letting them get away. 'I wanted to say sorry. In person.'

The air around them seemed to shimmer into stillness, as if holding its breath. Waiting.

'What?'

The muscles bracketing Jules's mouth pulled tight. 'I said I'm sorry, for everything that happened.'

'*Sorry?* Are you kidding me? You slept with my husband. You got pregnant to him. You had his baby and you took him from me—' her voice was rising, becoming more shrill, '—and you have the nerve to tell me you're *sorry*? Like that makes it all *okay*? Well, I've got news for you—it doesn't!'

Jules reeled back in her chair as though she'd received a body blow.

'I didn't mean to get pregnant. If it's any consolation. It was an accident.'

Sarah's cry came unheralded, a keening wail of devastation that lifted the lid on the pain of five failed IVF attempts and one even more soul-wrenching miscarriage.

Jules ventured a hand across the space between them. 'Sarah—'

'No!' she yelled, pulling away. 'Don't you dare touch me! Do you know how hard I tried to get pregnant? How many injections I had to endure? How many invasive procedures? And every time, to hold onto the tiniest thread of hope that this time it might work—that this time would be the one.

'And you—*you* have the gall to tell me that you didn't *mean* to get pregnant? That it was an accident? You think that might be some kind of comfort? That it might somehow help? *Nothing* can make up for the hurt you caused.' Sarah put her hands over her mouth and shook her head, tears stinging at her eyes. She turned away, looking out over the balcony into the gardens, looking anywhere to get that woman out of her line of sight. If she didn't get out of here now, it was going to get ugly. 'I have to go.'

Sarah made a move towards the steps, but Jules was already there barring the way, her features confused.

'But you knew this. I told you.'

'What? When?'

'I wrote to you. I wanted to talk to you at Richard's memorial service but you left early.'

Oh, Sarah thought, *that* letter. 'I—burned it.'

Jules looked stricken. 'Look, Sarah, I've handled this badly, I know—'

'I really have to go.'

Rain was starting to fall. Fat drops that splattered on the palms and ricocheted in a dozen different directions, slowly first and then faster, but any concerns about getting wet were no match for her need to get away.

'You think you're so perfect!' she heard through the din of rain hitting the metal roof. 'You think you're the only one hurting here? The only one who matters?'

Sarah didn't turn around, just kept walking, uncaring of the rain pelting down on her.

'I didn't seduce him, you know,' Jules said. 'If that's what you're thinking.'

Sarah closed her eyes, her steps faltering, and this time she did spin around. 'Do you really think it matters who seduced who? What matters is that I trusted Richard. I trusted you. You were the one I turned to when I felt heartsick. When I'd just had a failed IVF attempt and Floss declared she was having another baby. You were the only one I could tell. You were the one I cried my heart out to.' Her voice cracked and she had to drag in air to recharge her lungs.

'You *knew* what having a baby meant to me. You, more than anyone! And yet you not only slept with my husband, you *gave him a child*—the child I couldn't, no matter how hard I tried. So do you really think it matters how it happened?' Her head flopped sideways, rain soaking into her collar, trickling down her neck in slithering snakes of cold, but she couldn't care less. 'My god, Jules. No. Because it did happen. You slept with my husband. How could you do that to me?'

'I didn't want a baby,' Jules cried through the rain. 'I never wanted a baby and I would have done anything not to have had it so you would never know. But Richard said no. Richard wanted it.'

Richard wanted it. Finally, something that made sense. Something she could believe. *Richard wanted it.* Of course he would. He'd wanted a child from the outset—but his child, it had to be *his* child. Adoption would be to admit failure. So he'd been her biggest cheer squad and said when it came to the cost of treatments that money was no object. But it didn't change the fact that it was one of *her* best friends who'd given him what he'd craved.

It didn't change the fact that he'd wanted to go ahead with a pregnancy that he knew would be her undoing, and that Jules had gone along with him.

It was all too much. 'You know what I don't understand? What bothers me more than anything? You didn't even *like* Richard,' she said. 'He didn't like you.'

The other woman shook her head. 'Do you think he liked you, at the end? Do you think he liked the person you'd become? He felt trapped, Sarah. Helpless.'

The words lashed at her, more stinging than the rain, piercing her skin, digging their way into her soul. 'You're lying! You're just trying to make yourself feel better, to justify what you did to me!'

'Am I? I'm sorry I asked you here today. It was a mistake.'

'Yeah. It was.'

She spun on her heel, marching blindly down the driveway. The squall disappeared as suddenly as it had hit, but it didn't matter, she was already drenched.

She rounded the bend in the driveway to see a woman carrying an umbrella coming the other way, a child skipping alongside her.

The woman stopped dead, her hand tightly clasped around the little girl's.

The little girl had two fingers in her mouth, a teddy wedged under her arm—and Richard's eyes.

Air punched from Sarah's lungs.

'Hello, Sarah,' said Pru Callahan, sounding hesitant, her eyes anxious. 'Are you all right?'

'Pru,' she managed, without taking her eyes from the child. The child had curly hair and her mother's heart-shaped face but Sarah kept coming back to Richard's damned eyes. She hadn't got close enough to either Jules or the baby at the memorial service to notice details, but there they were now, looking up at her in total innocence. But if she'd ever had a glimmer of a hope that Richard hadn't been the father, simply a convenient place for Jules to hang paternity from, that hope died a rapid death.

'Hello,' she said, suspecting she must look half demented, yet somehow managing to dredge up a smile. 'My name's Sarah. What's yours?'

The fingers came out of the girl's mouth, but moved no further than her chin. 'Della.' The fingers went right back in.

'That's a pretty name.'

The girl regarded her seriously before pulling her fingers out again. 'You're all wet.'

'I know. I got rained on.'

'You need a 'bwella.'

Cute. So damned cute that the loss of what she'd never have surged over Sarah in a tidal wave of pain. But Sarah wouldn't give in to it. She simply nodded, raised her eyes to Pru's concerned face, and said goodbye.

The rain had stirred the forest floor, infusing the air with the rich scent of nature, and Sarah breathed it in, willing it to calm her as she walked the narrow road. No other place on earth had air like this, she knew, that seductive blend of sea and salt and lush vegetation. Life giving air. Fertile air.

For some.

She sniffed, swiping her nose with the back of her hand, and thought of the day Richard had come home in a weird mood. But Sarah had considered it understandable; she herself was still battling to come to terms with their loss. They were like orbiting planets, avoiding each other's gravitational pull. But she needed him if they were going to get back on the IVF treadmill and try again. Yet when she'd tried to reach out, he pulled away. Nothing was wrong, he told her every time, but there were moments when she saw him watching her, an unfathomable expression on his face, looking like he was about to say something. 'What?' she'd said, more than once, but he'd closed his mouth and shaken his head, as if he'd thought better of it.

And then, four weeks later, like someone or something had flicked a switch, everything had changed.

He'd come home from the gym, his movements feverish, an excitement she hadn't seen for a long time lighting his eyes. He'd pulled open the fridge door, seized the milk and guzzled it straight from the bottle. And she'd laughed, because it was such an unusual sight, but more so because it was good to see him happy. He'd suggested dinner out that night, their favourite restaurant, champagne, and she'd thought that things had turned a corner and would be better from now on. He'd drunk too much red and she'd driven home and he'd made love to her—or tried to—and then he'd cried in her arms and told her he was sorry. She'd thought he was apologising for being a lousy lay, but their night together had been enough to convince her it was time to try again.

So the very next day she'd called the clinic and made an appointment to come in. Having been so close last time, they'd be crazy to give up.

And when she'd told him the exciting news, he'd looked at her aghast. 'I can't go through this any more,' he'd said. 'I want a divorce.'

She'd thought then that things couldn't get any worse. She'd pleaded with him. He was tired of the effort, emotionally exhausted, just like she was—it was understandable. But it would get better—it would change—a baby would fix everything.

And when she'd refused to believe that he'd meant what he'd said, Richard had dropped the bombshell that had blown her world apart. He hadn't just stayed at Jules's place on his trip to Lord Howe—he'd slept with her best friend.

Now Jules was pregnant with his child. And he was leaving Sarah to be with her.

In that moment, and all the moments that followed, Sarah's future had stretched out in front of her, a long and bleak ribbon of emptiness.

'Who was that lady, Mummy?' asked Della.

'An old friend of your mother's,' said Pru, looking concerned as she undid the snaps on Della's raincoat.

'That's right,' said Jules, because that was less confusing than telling her daughter that it had been Della's dead father's wife. There are some things a child her age didn't need to know.

'Are you all right?' Pru asked, when Della had run off into the kitchen for a biscuit.

Jules pushed herself away from the veranda railing. 'I guess I had that coming.'

'She wasn't very receptive?'

'Oh, she listened. And then I suppose you could say she had a few things to get off her own chest.'

'Oh, Jules. But at least you did the right thing. You reached out.'

'Yeah, but I didn't do the right thing, did I? That's what the problem is.'

'For heaven's sake,' Pru said, 'what's done is done. You can't change it. So what can she possibly expect from you now? Blood?'

Jules nodded. 'I think that's exactly what she'd like.'

'You did the right thing, and I know it can't have been easy. Now you have to forget about Sarah and concentrate on you, and on making a full recovery.'

Jules turned away. She'd tried. What more could she do?

29

Sarah changed out of her wet clothes and dried her hair before she went back into the store. Deirdre was happy to see her and soon bustled off to help Tammy with her kids while Sarah returned to oiling the shelves. She tried hard to imagine Dot being so keen to help Sarah out if she'd ever managed to have kids, but drew a blank.

Her mother might like to imagine herself as a martyr, but she wasn't the type to actually muck in. Dot was more the type who liked to stand back, organise and criticise, and she would have found plenty to criticise in Sarah's mothering skills.

Maybe it was just as well she'd never had kids. Her arm stopped. Her breath hitched. Had she really just thought that?

Bloody hell, that was a turn up. The run-in with Jules must really have affected her. Unless it was the island. Or maybe it was just being with her mother that made her glad she didn't have yet another reason for Dot to find fault with her.

Yeah, that was probably it.

~

'Did you have a nice visit with Jules?' Dot asked when Sarah had shut up shop and let herself into the house. She finished off the gravy beef she'd prepared that morning, mashed some potatoes and served it all with green veg.

'Not really.'

'That's a shame.'

Not in Sarah's book. The shame was that she'd wasted her time. When had saying sorry ever really changed anything? It wasn't like you could rip out the pages from the book of the past. And when Sarah had refused to give her the absolution she was so clearly seeking, Jules had struck back in a way she'd known would hurt. Talk about picking the scab off a wound. Sarah had been stinging ever since.

'Because I know Richard was hoping you two could be friends.'

Some connection in Sarah's brain shorted. Her right eye twitched. 'What?'

'It's not nice to say what,' said Dot. 'Richard hoped one day you two could be friends again. Well, all of you, really—Floss as well. You all used to be such good friends.'

'How would you know what Richard hoped?'

'Because he told us,' said her mother, sounding exasperated that Sarah had to ask. 'Right here at this dinner table. Didn't he, Samuel? He said that he was sorry for what happened, but what else could he do?'

'Are you kidding me?'

She looked from her mother to her father. 'Dad, please tell me this isn't true. Richard was never here saying any such thing?'

'Of course he was,' said Dot. 'He brought Jules and baby Della for tea one night. Cute as a button she was too then, just a couple of months old and full of smiles. He sat right where you're sitting and all but gobbled down my fish pie. Richard always had a weakness for my fish pie, didn't he? Even you couldn't argue with that, Sarah.'

Sarah's gut churned. She couldn't look down at her plate because the thought of food would make her throw up before she'd even eaten it, so she stared at a flower embroidered on the tablecloth. A tiny violet, the colour deeper at the outer edges, a flicker of yellow at the centre. She licked her lips, focusing on the flower, trying to ignore the fact that her gravy beef smelled a lot like fish pie right now. She looked up at her mother. 'Let me get this straight—you had Richard over for dinner, together with the woman he had an affair with, along with their infant child? While he was still married to your daughter?'

Dot sniffed as if Sarah was making Mount Gower out of Intermediate Hill. 'Don't you think we had a right to meet Della? She was the closest thing to a grandchild we were likely to get. And after all, he was still our son-in-law.'

'Dad,' Sarah appealed.

Sam's chin rested on locked hands, and the sad eyes that looked at her were brimming with guilt. 'I'm sorry, love. It's a small island.' He gave a resigned shrug. 'It wasn't like they were over every other day. It seemed churlish to ignore them completely.'

'After what they did to me?'

'Well, I daresay if you'd been able to bear children yourself,' Dot said, shaking her head sadly, 'he wouldn't have had reason to stray.'

The garbled sound Sarah heard came from her own throat. She cut it off and stood, her appetite gone. 'I should have said this a long time ago, because god knows, every one of us thinks it. But sometimes, Mum, you can be a real bitch.'

Dot Rooney's mouth fell open. Even Sam looked dumbstruck. 'Well, I never,' Dot spluttered. 'If I'd known you were going to be like this, I would never have agreed to letting you come home.'

'You *begged* me to come home.'

'If it hadn't been for that handrail—'

Sarah didn't hang around to hear the rest. The door slammed behind her and she was gone, out into the windy night, the darkness punctuated only by the occasional light of a residence.

She powered her way down the hill, seething and spilling tears. She'd been rubbed raw by her meeting with Jules and her charge that Richard had felt trapped and helpless in their marriage. Putting the blame on her, like Sarah was the one at fault. What kind of pathetic person did that?

Richard had been happy when she'd discovered she was pregnant.

Blissfully happy. They both had been. They could have tried again. They'd been so close.

And yet now she'd discovered she'd been betrayed by all those who should matter most to her. Richard. Jules. Even her mother. *If you'd been able to bear children yourself, he wouldn't have had reason to stray.* Her mother's inevitable blame game dressed up as wisdom. What kind of mother said that to her own daughter? What kind of mother painted the husband who'd slept with another woman as the victim?

But then, what kind of mother invited her daughter's ex over for dinner, along with his lover and the product of their union?

She reached the bottom of the hill and struck left along Lagoon Road, towards the airport. The palms were thick along the sides of the road here, the sky above her head brooding, the road a battleship-grey strip between the gloom. The boom of the waves at the outer edge of the lagoon sounded like thunder.

Perfect.

She held the edges of her cardigan together over her chest, regretting that she hadn't stopped to grab a jacket. But she hadn't needed it then, her blood had been boiling. And soon it wouldn't matter anyway, she'd warm up.

The night was quiet apart from the occasional vehicle, the surf and the wind. Perfect for reflection. Perfect for wishing she'd never come home.

Home.

That was a joke.

She'd feel more at home—more welcome—on Mars.

A car slowed behind her and she sniffed as she moved closer to the side of the road, grateful that at least she seemed to be running out of tears.

'Sarah,' a deep voice called. 'We meet again.'

The car drew level as she swiped at her cheeks.

'Sarah?'

The car pulled up and the driver was out of the car and at her side. For a big guy, Noah sure could move fast. But he didn't make a move to touch her. He gave her space. 'What's wrong?'

She shook her head, keeping her eyes down, wondering why every time she met this guy, she had to look like a total wreck. 'It's nothing. Family stuff.'

'Is it Dot? Is she okay?'

'Oh, she's fine.'

Maybe it was the growl in her voice. Maybe it was the way she shivered in the cool night air, but: 'Hop in,' he said.

'I am not going home.'

'I'm not taking you home. Come on. You're coming to my place to warm up. Unless you don't trust me, of course.'

She looked up at him. He was so tall, so broad across the shoulders, his features so bloody compassionate that it was impossible not to find a grateful smile. 'Why is it that my knight in shining armour is wearing a blue police uniform and riding in a tray-top ute?'

His smile grew wider, his teeth flashing in the moonlight. 'You got lucky, I guess.'

She had got lucky. Noah took her to his house attached to the police station and showed her around. It was simple but homely. He made coffee, and poured a slug of Baileys into hers but she noticed he abstained.

'On shift?'

He shook his head. 'Knocked off for today, but just in case.'

She nodded. When you were the only copper within cooee, that made sense. She sipped her coffee, the heat and the rich liqueur warming her stomach, seeping into her veins, and rested her head against the chair. So good.

'So,' Noah said, sitting down opposite her, elbows resting on knees, coffee nursed in hands, 'I don't want to pry, but something's wrong, and if you want a shoulder ...?'

She laughed a little. Oh god, where to start? She put a hand to her head. 'It's a long and not very happy story. How much time do you have?'

'I'm a good listener.'

She blinked and looked at him. She'd only been half joking. She barely knew this guy but it would be so good to talk to someone. And maybe it was better that it was a stranger.

'Then you first. Tell me about you. Where are you from? Why are you a cop and why are you here? Do you have a wife stashed somewhere? A family? And what are you most afraid of?'

His eyebrows shot up. 'Wow. Okay.' He took a sip of his coffee. 'Let's go right back to the beginning. My mum's from Coffs Harbour and she met my dad while backpacking around New Zealand. My dad was a surfer dude from Tonga. At least, that's what he told my mum. Long after she'd moved on, she found out she had a souvenir. She went back and looked for him, but he'd moved on too, so she went home to her family and had me by herself.'

'But—your surname?'

He smiled. 'Mum picked that. She wanted something that sounded cool.' He grinned. 'She did good.'

Sarah smiled. 'That she did. And now?'

'She manages a supermarket in Port Macquarie where she started out on the registers. She's done okay.'

'And the police thing?'

He shrugged. 'I wanted to help people out.'

'As simple as that?'

'As simple as that. I like helping people out when they get in a fix.'

'And catching crims?'

'Yeah, because that helps people out too, but I much prefer it when I can help prevent a crime in the first place.' He put his empty cup aside. 'And now, Sarah, are you going to tell me about you, and what makes you tick, and what makes you go roaming the streets on a dark and windy night?'

Mellowed by his deep voice as he'd talked about his past—and by the Baileys in her coffee—Sarah spoke. Of the three school friends who'd grown up together, of her infertility and failed IVF attempts, and of the jealousy and betrayal that had blown both a marriage and her friendships apart. She told him about the mother whose speciality was finding fault and who was tone deaf to the hurt she regularly dispensed.

She opened up and told him more than she'd ever told anyone, and she'd been right, it helped that he was virtually a stranger and that, in a couple of months, he'd be gone and then she would too, and they'd never see each other again.

And when finally she stopped, she blinked and looked at the clock on the wall behind him and was mortified to find she'd been talking for more than half an hour. She turned to him, still sitting silently, watching her. 'You were right.'

'About what?'

'You're a good listener, Noah Lomu.' He'd let her talk with barely a word uttered himself, inserting only an acknowledgment every now and then that he was still paying attention.

'You've got a powerful story to tell.'

'I'm sorry.' She felt flustered now, like she'd exposed too much of herself. 'You must think me a complete sad sack.'

'No. I think you're a woman who's had to deal with more than her fair share of the crap life can throw at you. Stuff nobody should have to deal with.'

Okay, so not a complete sad sack then. 'Thanks.' She smiled, because she did feel better than she had when he'd found her striding so purposefully but ultimately pointlessly along the road. Where eventually she would have had to turn around and walk back to the place where she really should be going now. She stood up. 'I've taken enough of your time. I better get going. Thanks for coffee.'

'You're not thinking of walking?'

'It's not that far.'

'It is on a cold, dark night. I'll run you home.'

'You've already done so much.'

'I want to,' he said, with a look that stilled her arguments and sent a little flutter low in her belly. 'And that's the end of it.'

It was a two-minute ride, even at twenty-five kilometres an hour. Two minutes of being intensely aware of the man sitting alongside her, his capable hands on the steering wheel. Two minutes of telling herself she was being ridiculous and she'd read too much into his interest to be feeling this heady and alert. He was being polite, that was all, helping her out because she'd been in a fix. That's what he did.

So when he pulled up outside the shop, she had one hand on the door handle, ready to jump out with a breezy thank you and goodbye. Except she felt his big hand slide around hers where it rested on her leg.

She looked at him, her heart suddenly thudding up a storm.

'Sarah,' he said, squeezing her fingers in his. 'I'll see you at the fundraiser this weekend, right?'

'I—I'll be there.'

'Good,' he said. 'I'll be there to maintain the peace, but afterwards, I'd like to buy you a drink.'

Wow. This time her heart failed to thud when she expected, so the next one was a real boomer.

'I'd like that.'

'Even better,' he said. He gave her hand one last squeeze and glanced over at the house. 'Will you have to see your mother tonight?'

'No. Dad was clever enough to give me a room with a separate entry.'

He smiled. 'Wise man. Good night, Sarah.'

As Sarah let herself into her room and readied herself for bed, she realised that Noah had been right again.

It had turned out to be a very good night.

30

'No, Mummy!' Della screamed, squirming as Jules tried to hand her daughter over to her mother. 'I want to go on the pwane too!'

Jules's heart was breaking and there were tears in her eyes. She was the last to board and the plane was waiting for her to take off.

'No!' the girl squealed, reaching desperately for her mother, as the transfer was successfully, if not altogether smoothly, made.

'Go,' said Pru, 'she'll be fine once you're out of sight.'

Jules knew she was right. Besides, it wasn't like she was going to be locked away in a cave for four weeks. They'd been supplied with buddy laptops enabled for Skype sessions and she'd be chatting to Della and Pru every night, but that wasn't her only concern. She looked at her mother, struggling against the tangle and energy of four-year-old limbs. 'Will you be fine, Mum? Can you promise me you'll be fine?'

'Of course, I'll be fine!' her mother said, a little too stridently perhaps, but then, they'd had this conversation several times already. 'Just go, already.'

Jules nodded, her lips tight.

'Mummy!'

She didn't dare give Della another kiss or she'd never get free of her monkey grip. So she said a final, 'I love you, Della,' and exited the gate.

'Mummmyyyyy!'

The screams of her daughter rang out across the tarmac, pulling hard on Jules's heartstrings. Four weeks. She'd never been away from her baby for more than a few days, and now she wouldn't feel her hugs for an entire month.

She struggled up the steps and into the plane through a veil of tears, not bothering to hide them, not caring how she looked as she was steered to a seat at the back, which she flopped into. Caring only about the child she'd left behind.

The door was closed and the propellers started whining, and before long they were up at cruising altitude, the island far behind them. Then, and only then did it seem to Jules that she couldn't hear Della's cries any more.

She took a deep breath.

Four weeks wasn't forever. It wasn't a life sentence. It was just a few weeks of treatment and then she could go home again.

Four weeks and this brush with breast cancer would be over. Finished. Done. Meanwhile all she had to worry about was that Pru could do it too, that her mother could hold it together like she'd promised. Jules had to believe she could. What other choice did she have?

3 1

It seemed to Floss that the entire island population plus visitors had turned out to support the fundraiser for a flash new X-ray machine for the hospital. The golf club dining room was chockers, with table seating at a premium, and still people were piling in. Her kids had managed to snaffle stools and sat to one side of her, stuffing their faces, as she stood just inside the door, selling raffle tickets to unsuspecting newcomers. Other people perched wherever they could or stood in groups nursing a drink or holding a plate. The volume of conversation in the room almost drowned out the music, but nobody was complaining. The food was fabulous, the buffet groaning under fish pies and mornays, fried fish and chips and a colourful display of salads, with more supplies arriving by the minute.

Sam Rooney entered, slowly leading Dot, who was taking tentative steps behind her walker.

'How are you, Dot? Sam?' Floss asked. 'How's the hip going?'

'It's a long road,' offered Sam, 'but Dot's doing well, aren't you, love?'

Dot sniffed. 'I'll be glad when I can ditch this contraption, that's for sure.'

Sarah followed them in, bearing a large aluminium foil–covered tray. Floss was surprised to see her, given the high probability of her bumping into people she might want to avoid. People like Jules. 'Hi Sarah,' Floss said.

Sarah gave her a smile, even though the look in her eyes said she was still edgy, like she'd been when they'd run into each other in the shop. 'Where do I take the fish pie?'

Floss pointed. 'Kitchen's through that door. They'll put it out when there's a space.'

Sarah looked over her shoulder, uttered her thanks and disappeared with her tray.

'Can I interest you in a raffle ticket?' Floss asked the Rooneys.

'What's the prize?'

'First prize is a return flight to Sydney, second prize is three nights at Beached, third is a dinner voucher for Halfway.'

'How much are they?' asked Dot.

'Two dollars each.'

The woman gave a saintly smile. 'Well, it's such a good cause, isn't it? We'll take one each, won't we, Sam.'

Sam duly fished in his pockets and handed over a couple of coins, and then Sarah was back. She read the flyer for the raffle and said, 'I'll take twenty-five.'

'They're two dollars each!' said her mother, shocked.

'It's for a good cause,' said Sarah, handing Floss a fifty dollar note before starting to fill in the ticket stubs.

Dot sniffed and Floss suspected it was because she'd just been trumped by her own daughter.

'Is this all your brood then?'

Floss looked up to see Dot watching her four boys where they sat in a row against the wall.

'All except Annie,' Floss said.

'Oh,' Dot said. 'Isn't that nice? So lovely to have a big family. Some women are just meant to be mothers, aren't they?'

Floss heard Sarah's rapid intake of air and saw her expression become stony. She ripped her tickets out with a little more force than necessary, and Floss couldn't blame her.

'I guess so,' Floss said, 'it's just so unfair when some women have to miss out.'

Sarah's eyes suddenly met hers. There was an understanding of what Floss had just done in them and, if she wasn't mistaken, a thank you.

Floss smiled back. 'I'll fill the rest of these stubs in. Enjoy your evening.'

The people kept coming. At one stage, Floss looked over and saw that someone had made way for Dot to sit down at a table, and she was now holding court with a group of the island's elders.

She noticed Sarah drifting around the room, looking like she didn't quite belong. It had to be hard on her, being back after so long away, especially with a mother who could be so difficult. She couldn't really blame Sarah for choosing to live in Sydney. It wasn't like her mother made living on the island easy for her.

And then she was distracted by her boys, who were getting bored. She sent them outside to run around, because at least that released some much needed seating, and then turned to see Pru at the door, carrying a box. Della was holding her hand, a fluffy toy jammed under her arm, two fingers deep in her mouth.

'Hi,' she said. It had always been a bit awkward with Pru since she'd fallen out with Jules, but it was a small community and she had nothing against the older woman, and certainly nothing against the child. 'Can I interest you in some raffle tickets?' She went through her spiel, and Pru promised she come back after she'd delivered her pies. The woman made a move towards the kitchen, then seemed to halt, her gaze lingering at the crowded bar.

'It's crazy busy tonight,' Floss said. 'They could probably do with another couple of people behind the bar.'

'Doesn't matter to me,' Pru said, her back suddenly straighter, 'I'm not staying.'

She returned a minute later and began putting her name on some raffle tickets.

'Is Jules coming tonight?' Floss asked. 'It's just that Sarah's here, and …'

'Oh?' Pru looked up and around, found Sarah among the crowd and gave a nod, her lips tight.

'It's all right, Jules is in Sydney.'

'She went on the pwane,' said Della.

'Oh?'

Pru leaned closer. 'She's gone back for four weeks while she has radiotherapy. She had a lump—or something—they had to remove first.'

'Oh.' Floss's hand flew to her mouth. 'I'm sorry. I didn't know.'

'That's understandable. She didn't want everyone to know, not until she was sure what was happening.' She looked around at the crowd, and added, 'Though I expect it'll be all over the island by morning.'

'I won't tell anyone.'

'Oh,' Pru said, 'I didn't mean you. It's just word has a way of getting around.' She pulled the tickets from the stubs and she and Della drifted off, leaving Floss to think about Jules. It made sense of the news that she'd had to go to Sydney for tests. But breast cancer? God, what a nightmare she must be going through.

For the first time in a long time, Floss felt bad for her former friend. Then she remembered Andy wiping the dishes and saying that if you fuck around with somebody you shouldn't, then you deserve a bit of grief.

And suddenly she felt bad for herself.

It wasn't the same thing. Matt Caruso wasn't her best friend's husband, he'd been a visitor to the island. It wasn't in the same league. It was different.

But she doubted that Andy would see it that way.

The evening was going well. Everyone had eaten their fill and the clean-up had begun. Floss circulated through the crowd and mopped up any loose change anyone cared to fling her way before she counted her takings and found a silver bowl in the kitchen that would do for the prize draw.

That's when she saw Sarah sitting by herself on a stool on the edge of the room. Floss wandered over.

'Had a good night?'

'Food was great,' Sarah said. 'I haven't had banana cream pie since forever.'

Floss grinned. 'Classic Lord Howe.'

There was a silence, then Sarah said, 'Thank you for what you said back there with Dot. That was nice of you.'

Floss brushed it aside. What Dot had said was plain cruel, and she'd had enough experience over the years to suspect it wasn't unintentional. 'It was nothing. Dot doesn't seem overly appreciative that you're here.'

Sarah skated her glass to and fro on the bench. 'She's waiting for an apology that's not going to happen. That's why she's in such a snit with me. She has no concept that she's the one who in the wrong.'

'What did she do?'

'Made a comment about Richard not needing to stray if I'd been able to give him a child.'

'Oh my god! And what did you do?'

'I called her a bitch.'

Floss's hands flew to her mouth. 'You didn't? You always said you would one day.'

'And I finally did. I'm thirty-seven years old, Floss, and if I can't call out my mother for bad behaviour at my age, when will I ever be able to?'

'Good thinking, and good timing—if you'd waited much longer, you'd get accused of elder abuse.'

Sarah looked at her, an expression of wonder on her face. 'That's so true,' she said. 'Imagine if I'd missed this opportunity? I'd be kicking myself.' And both laughed. It was like a moment from the past, reclaimed. Then they seemed to realise that they shouldn't be enjoying each other's company, and they stopped.

Floss noticed signals coming to her from across the room. She looked at her watch. 'Oh, damn, it's time to draw the raffle. I have to go.' She went to stand up, but then sat again. 'Look, Sarah, this is really left field, but we're having a birthday party for Mikey this Sunday. It would be really nice if you could come.'

Sarah's eyes opened wide and Floss saw panic flash across them.

'Very low key,' Floss said. 'Mostly big kids and party games and party tea. Just a bit of fun, but it would be great if you could make it. I'd so love it if you could come. Can you?'

Sarah remained silent, almost afraid, and Floss continued,

'It starts at two. Party tea at four. It'll be all over by five. You're welcome to come whenever you can make it. No pressure. I'd just love to see you again. Okay?'

Sarah's head got stuck somewhere between a nod and a shake, and then Floss had to go. It was up to Sarah now.

32

Sarah was still marvelling at Floss's unexpected invitation, glad she was sitting by herself. For a while she'd been drawn into a group of her parents' friends and been plied with questions about what it was like being home and if she intended to stay and, when the group was satisfied, they'd moved on. Sarah had been content to let them. Nobody had protested when she'd drifted away when Sam had taken Dot home.

Meanwhile, it was impossible not to notice Noah in the crowd. Impossible not to notice those broad shoulders of his moving around the room, looking strong and sexy, not to follow him with her eyes. She'd never been one to have a thing about men in uniform before, but she was sure starting to develop a king-sized fan-girl crush on them. Or on one of them, at least.

She'd seen him watching her too. And every now and then he'd shoot her a smile or a wink across the room and her cheeks would heat up. God, she was like a school kid all over again.

And yet she barely knew him. Sure, she'd subjected him to her life story in all its gory detail, but he'd been more of a therapist that night, rather than a love interest. At least until he'd covered her hand with his and asked if she was coming tonight. Which was kind of like asking her on a date—wasn't it?

When she realised he was finally making his way across the room towards her, Sarah felt a bloom of heat that started at her cheeks and whooshed down all the way to her toes.

'How's it going?' Noah said, lifting a leg over a stool to sit next to her. His knee brushed hers, and she got the distinct impression it wasn't accidental. She didn't move away.

'Good.' A million times better, now that he was here. 'So how goes the peacekeeping business? They're a pretty rowdy lot tonight. Any arrests so far?'

He smiled, sending a billion watts of warmth zapping straight across the table and up her spine. It had been nice to see Floss and she'd been heartened by her support, but this man was the real reason she'd come tonight. This man, and the way he made her feel.

'Well,' he said, 'there was an altercation at the buffet over the last piece of Pru Callahan's banana cream pie that almost ended in fisticuffs.'

'And they say there's no crime on the island,' she said, with a grin. 'What did you do to keep the peace, cut it in half?'

He shook his head. 'I took justice into my own hands and ate it myself.'

She laughed.

'So,' he said, 'what are your plans for tonight?' On the surface, they were just having a friendly chat. But below, he was stirring all sorts of long forgotten thoughts in Sarah.

'Dad took Mum home. I told them I'd walk.' She smiled. 'My dance card is free.'

His smile widened, the glint in his dark eyes turning from a spark to a flame. 'Well, if that's not a crime against something, I don't what is.'

'Are you going to arrest me?'

One eyebrow raised. 'I might have to take you into custody.'

'I like the way you think.'

He looked closer at her, and she was glad she'd made an extra effort with her make-up and hair. Nowhere near as much effort as she made to look professional for the office, but a bit more resort casual than island workaday. She'd even piled her hair into a messy up-do.

'I like the way you look.'

Her skin tingled. He was flirting and it wasn't just his words, but the way his deep voice seemed to rumble right through to her bones. She wanted to tell him that she liked the way he made her feel, but it was too early for that. They'd held hands, or rather, he'd held hers, and now they were rubbing knees and on the face of it, that was all. Although she was getting the distinct vibe that was all about to change.

'How long before you finish up?'

He looked around at the thinning crowd, tables emptying and spilling into the dozen or so vans performing the shuttle service back to homes and guesthouses. 'My work is done. I could buy you that drink I promised you, or ...'

'Or?'

'We could go back to my place? Shoot the breeze? Check out my etchings?'

'Sounds perfect,' she said. 'I'm a big fan of etchings.' At this time of night on the island, there really weren't a lot of other options anyway. Halfway would still be open for coffee for a while but after she'd spent the evening watching this man work the crowd, she just wanted to be somewhere she could have him all to herself.

'Then let's go.'

With his fingers at the small of her back and her heart in her mouth, Noah led Sarah through what was left of the crowd, waving as people said goodbye. There were a couple of raised eyebrows as they left and she knew word of her leaving with Noah would filter its way back to Dot and, in due course, there would be an interrogation. Sarah kind of looked forward to it.

They stepped outside into the inky night. Behind them loomed the twin mountains, while the sky above was like a velvet blanket encrusted with diamonds. She shivered a little and Noah put his strong arm around her shoulders to nestle her against his body until they got to the car, where he let her go to open her door for her. She missed his body heat, would have been happy to forget about the car and go right on walking. But she climbed into the cab and he snicked the door shut behind her.

'Who said the age of chivalry is dead?' she said as he slid in the driver's seat.

He glanced at her as he turned the key in the ignition. 'I bet you thought my charms began and ended with my etchings.'

'You're funny. Anyone ever tell you that?'

He gave a brief chuckle. 'Yeah, my year six teacher. She told me off for always making light in my writing exercises. Told me I never took anything seriously and couldn't go through life joking about everything.'

'Are you kidding me? That is so wrong.'

'I know. But she made me believe there must be something wrong with me, so I told my mum, and she marched into the principal's office the next day and told her there was enough doom and gloom about and that the world needed more laughter, and to let me write stories the way I wanted to.'

'Wow, what a heroine.'

'Yeah, she sure is.'

Sarah sat back and wondered how it was that other people could have a mother who was so supportive. Who stood up for you instead of constantly sniping away, undercutting you at every opportunity. Floss seemed to have managed okay, and Jules had Pru.

'I seem to have drawn the short straw in the mother stakes.'

'You seem to have done all right in the father stakes.'

'Oh, I'm sorry,' she said. 'I didn't think.'

He smiled. 'That's okay. I guess the upside is that my dad never gets the chance to give me any grief. Besides,' his hand reached over to take hers, 'maybe someone just figured you were tough enough to deal with it.'

'You reckon?'

'What doesn't kill us makes us stronger, isn't that what they say?

You've put up with a lot and you're still standing. That makes you a kind of heroine in my book.'

'You know … I like you,' she said as the car pulled up in front of the police station and he jumped out.

'Well, that's a coincidence,' he said, opening her door, 'because I happen to like you too.'

He took her hand as she climbed down, then he took the other. And then he leaned down and pressed his lips to hers and she felt his smile on her lips as she tasted him, warm and strong and real.

She trembled then, wobbling a little on her feet. Only because she had her eyes closed, she told herself, although she knew she was kidding herself.

'It's funny,' she said as he led her inside, 'I've only met you a few times, but already I feel like I know you much better than that.'

'I know. I feel the same way. It must be the space–time paradox,' he said.

'What's that?'

'I don't know. But I hope it sounded impressive. Were you impressed?'

She smiled. She was impressed all right. Even if it was simply the way that brief kiss had sent sparks shooting all the way to pool low in the pit of her belly. 'You know I'm only here for your etchings.'

'In that case,' he said, opening the door for her, 'you'd better come inside.'

Noah put on a lamp and some music before he left her to go and change out of his uniform. The song was French and sounded like something you'd hear in a dimly lit bar or a cabaret, husky and sexy, warm and evocative. Sarah liked it. She sat down on the sofa and let the music wash over her.

'Do you speak French?' she asked, when he returned wearing jeans and a jumper that skimmed his powerful torso.

'What?' he said, before he realised. 'Oh, the music. I like it because I don't understand the lyrics. It doesn't get in the way of my thinking. Coffee?'

She nodded. 'Please. So what do you think about?'

'You quite sure you're not a detective?'

She grinned and put on an officious tone: 'Just answer the question, please.'

He chortled and went into the kitchen to flick on the kettle, reaching into a cupboard for a couple of mugs. 'I think about the same things most people do,' he said. 'I think about life and death and taxes and the unfairness in all three of those. And I think about people, and what makes them tick.'

She had not expected that. 'For a guy who says he always makes light of things, that's pretty deep stuff.'

'Call me multi-faceted,' he said, bringing sugar and milk to the coffee table while the kettle boiled.

'But I think you're wrong.'

'What? Why?'

'I don't think people think about those things at all. I think they worry about tomorrow, and what somebody else has got that they haven't, and how they can get it too.' At least, looking back, it seemed that's what she'd spent a decent chunk of her life thinking about. Not the big issues at all, but the excruciatingly personal things that ruled your life and that you obsessed about, and suddenly she felt a bit ashamed that she'd had so blinkered a view—that she hadn't been able to see past her own shrunken world. She looked up to see him watching her, a mug in each hand. And then, because this wasn't all about her, she gave a weak smile and added, 'And football scores. People fret an awful lot about football scores too.'

'Quite rightly, too,' he said, putting their coffees down and sitting next to her. If he'd read anything into her confession, he let it pass.

'How was it for you after I dropped you home that night?'

Sarah pulled a face as she thought back, remembering her mother's pinched expression and her refusal to talk to her daughter. 'Tense. She won't forgive me for what I called her, even if I do apologise, which she expects but which I won't do. She'll never admit she was in the wrong.'

Noah shook his head. 'She certainly comes across as much more genial in public.' He looped an arm around her shoulders as he said it, and maybe because she'd been there before, it felt like the most natural thing in the world to let herself nestle into him.

'That she does. And the thing is, in the past, I've always given in to her. It was easier, I figured, to apologise and keep the peace, even when I knew that she was in the wrong. It's my brother who's always been the one to upset her, but then he's her golden child and she makes excuses for him. Mum doesn't like it that I'm not rolling over any more. She's not used to it.' She shrugged and smiled at him. 'Maybe I should have been more rebellious as a teenager. Instead I ran away to Sydney first chance I got. Talk about a coward.'

'I don't think you're a coward. If you were, you wouldn't have come back.'

'I had no choice—there was nobody else.'

'You would have found a reason if you'd wanted to.' He smiled. 'Believe me, you're no coward.'

Wow. Being with Noah was like taking a dose of self-belief pills, only one hundred times better. 'Thank you.'

'How long before Dot's fully fit again?'

'Three, maybe four months. All going well, I'll probably take off after Christmas.'

'You're definitely going back?'

Sarah screwed up her nose as she picked up her coffee. 'I can't stay here. There are bits I like, bits I'd forgotten, but there's too much history. Too many reminders.' She took a sip. 'How about you?'

'I've got seven weeks left, then it's back to the Port.'

'Will you be happy to get back?'

'Yes and no. But I'm glad I came.'

'Why's that?'

'Because I got to meet you.'

Oh boy. His voice had dropped an octave and the music had changed too. Someone was crooning in Italian now, something that sounded half familiar. 'Angels', she realised. Robbie Williams' 'Angels', sung in Italian, the notes making the air in the room shimmer. She felt Noah's fingers under her chin, coaxing her face closer to his, felt the warm puff of his breath and the heat from his skin, and gave herself up to the press of his lips against hers.

The kiss was warm and wonderful, and just as the first touch of their lips outside had promised, only better, because she knew that brief moment was no mistake.

When finally they drew apart, however many minutes later, she found herself flat on her back with her hands under his jumper and both of them breathing hard.

Gasping, he said, 'Sarah, I'm sorry, but this is going to get out of hand pretty quickly. If you want me to stop and take you home, tell me.'

She knew what he was asking, and respected him even more for doing so. She battled her own ragged breath to say, 'I'm not the kind of girl who sleeps with a man on the first date.'

'Oh,' he said, that lonely syllable laden with disappointment. 'Of course. In that case—' He pushed himself up.

She pulled him back. 'Don't you dare take me home until I say I'm ready to go.'

'But you said—'

'I didn't finish. I'm not the kind of girl who sleeps with a man on the first date—but tonight, I'm thinking it's time that changed.'

He growled and the sound rippled under her skin and vibrated into her bones, then his lips descended again, and she was lost, giving herself up to pleasure.

Logically, Sarah knew all men were different—they came in different shapes and sizes and looked different, after all—but she'd never spent much time thinking how different they must feel. She'd never had to, because Richard was the only man she'd ever really held close. After twenty years together, she was so used to the feel of Richard that the memory of him was imprinted on her: a man felt like Richard; a man smelt like Richard. Naïve, perhaps, but that's all she'd ever known.

But Noah was a world apart. The girth of his arms, the width of his shoulders, the scent of whatever cologne he wore, spiced and exotic, which complemented his own masculine scent. Her fingers traversed his skin, exploring the different textures, the dips and bumps and planes, and the nubble of his hard nipples.

'Hey,' he said between kisses. 'Stop thinking about him.'

'What? Who?'

'Your ex-husband.'

She blinked up at him. 'How did—'

'Because you're touching me like I'm some kind of science experiment and you have to catalogue all the differences. I don't know about you, but in my view, three people in a bed is one person too many.'

She groaned. 'Sorry. I'm just not used to—anyone else. It's strange.'

He smiled down at her, kissing the tip of her nose and then her chin, his thumb stroking her brow. 'This isn't about anyone else. This is about you. All you have to do, is feel.'

He pressed his lips to hers, a kiss as gentle and tender as it was beautiful. A kiss that held the promise of so much more.

A kiss that carried Sarah away with it.

33

The radiation oncologist explained the treatment and the possible side effects—the sunburnt skin, the discolouration, the itching and rashes and fatigue. Why did the side effects always sound worse than the treatment? It seemed a lot to endure for something she'd been thinking of as mopping up—insurance. She had a CT scan to take measurements from which the specialist would make the calculations to determine the area to be treated and dosage. Calculations that normally took a week, but were fast tracked so that Jules didn't have to be away from home longer than necessary.

She felt another fluttery rush of apprehension as she met another strange machine. Her naked breasts were turned into some kind of medical craft project, drawn on, wired and taped, before the strange bed Jules was awkwardly perched upon, knees bent, arms above her head, was slowly conveyed beneath the circular scanner. Then came the crowning glory: three tiny blue tattoos inked left, right and centre of her breasts. Markers to ensure she was placed in the exact same position for every one of her sixteen treatments.

Treatments that would start the day after tomorrow.

Jules breathed a sigh of relief when it was done. She couldn't wait to start counting down.

She texted Molly as soon as she was out.

Back in Sydney for radiotherapy.

You go, girl! You've got this!

Wish you were here. No-one to murder songs with.

Lol! How's the jumper going?

I finished it!

Jules flicked through her photos, attaching one of Della wearing her new red jumper, before hitting send.

Wow! Looks fab! What are you doing next?

A shawl for Mum. Then I don't know.

Check out Ravelry again. Loads of great ideas there. Hey, school run beckons. I gotta go. Take care!

Thanks, I will.

And meanwhile, lie back and enjoy the journey. Hahaha!

Jules couldn't help but snort even as her thumbs tapped out a reply.

Cow!:)

The next morning the sun was shining and Jules had no intention of spending it moping around the lodge. There was a yarn shop not far away that she wanted to check out, to look for something special to make Pru's shawl, and then she was going to take a leaf out of Molly's book and head for Taronga Zoo.

The yarn shop was eye-opening. Walls of shelves bulging from floor to ceiling with balls and skeins of wool in all the colours of the rainbow, and in so many varieties, from the softest, finest baby wool to the chunkiest multi-coloured balls that Jules could see knitted into a throw rug. Her fingers itched with the possibilities. But that would be getting ahead of herself, because her mother's shawl came first.

Eventually she found something that would be ideal: a yarn coloured in graduated shades of blue that reminded Jules of the sea and sky that surrounded the island. The yarn was a blend of wool, alpaca and possum, which promised warmth and softness. She couldn't wait to get started.

But first she took the ferry across the harbour to the zoo.

She wandered the winding paths, taking dozens of photos and videos of the animals for Della. The scents and sounds of the park, the sounds of children's laughter, made Jules smile. How long since she'd been to a zoo? How long since Della had been to a zoo?

Guilt twisted her insides. She shouldn't be doing this alone. She remembered Della screaming at the airport, her cries and tears tugging hard on Jules's heartstrings. She promised herself then and there that the next time she came to Sydney, she was bringing Della with her, and they'd be visiting the zoo for sure.

She rode the ferry home in good spirits. Radiotherapy proper might not start until tomorrow, but today had been a kind of therapy too, first the thrill of finding the perfect yarn, and then the kind that made you laugh and feel happy you were alive. Why shouldn't she be happy? She'd dodged a bullet. Early-detected DCIS, meaning no chemotherapy. Radiotherapy for insurance, to zap any wayward cells left in her breast, and improve her chances that it wouldn't happen again.

So by the time the first of sixteen appointments rolled around the next day, Jules was ready to get started. It might feel like a conveyor belt or a magic merry-go-round, this breast cancer sausage machine she had found herself stuck in, but she was on the way to being spat out. All she needed now was to be cooked.

She lay down on the same awkward table, her bum perched on a ledge, her arms above her head, while the radiotherapists got her in position by tugging her this way and that while checking and calling out numbers. The CT screen above her threw a track of green and red numbers down her chest and abdomen, and in a matter of minutes they were gone, and she was left to listen to the piped music, while the bed was raised and the radiotherapy machine rolled into position.

Six bursts of buzzing on the right, one long, five short, the machine zipping into a new position between each burst. And then it circled over her head, trailing something that looked like a long dinosaur spine, to attack from the other side. Four buzzes this time, before the machine fell silent.

A few moments later she heard the doors open and her attendees reappeared to lower the bed and lift the machine clear. 'All done.'

'That's it?'

'That's it. You did well.'

Jules hadn't done anything but lie there, but it was good to know that treatment was as easy as lying down and letting the machine do its thing. She'd felt nothing.

Later that afternoon she skyped home. 'One down,' she told Pru, 'fifteen to go.'

'How do you feel?'

'Fine. I expect I won't feel the worst of the side effects—if they crop up—for a few weeks.' She paused. 'How are things? With you, I mean.'

'Good,' said Pru. 'Fine, no problems here.'

Jules smiled and breathed a sigh of relief. 'That's great to hear, Mum.'

'Well,' her mother said, 'I've got a very important person to look after. Speaking of which, she's watching a video in the next room, I'll go get her.'

Jules felt herself relax. It was early days, sure, but it looked like her mother was taking her responsibilities seriously.

A few moments later, she was back. 'Look, Della, it's Mummy.'

'Mummy!' squealed Della, jumping up and down as she held onto the table under the screen. 'Mummy, I wuv you!'

Jules had tears in her eyes when they finally said goodbye, and not just because Della was still wearing the jumper she'd knitted. Pru had told Jules that she insisted on wearing it every day. She leaned back in her chair, closed her eyes and blinked away the moisture that was gathered there.

Jules knew she could handle this course of treatment, and if Pru could manage while she was away, she knew she'd made the right decision.

34

Sarah heard the party long before she arrived, the music and the laughter and the sound of excited children's voices telling her it was well underway. She paused a while on Floss's driveway and took a breath. It had been a few years since she'd been here, but Beached looked better than she remembered, the units fresh and inviting among gardens filled with colourful frangipani, hibiscus and swaying palms.

A *thwack* punctuated the air, accompanied by screams of anticipation and then groans of disappointment.

Sarah flexed her clammy hands a couple of times. She could do this. She wanted to do this. She wanted to be friends with Floss. God, she could do with a friend.

With one last breath to fortify her, she followed the path around the office to the residence where an army of children were gathered under the covered pergola. Floss was in the centre, covering a child's eyes with a blindfold. Above them hung a colourful, battered, piñata. Everyone stood back as the boy was spun around and handed the broomstick.

Sarah watched from the outer edge of the group with a few hovering parents. She nodded to a couple of people she recognised then saw Tammy on the other side of the group and quickly looked away in time to catch the broomstick smack hard into the piñata. A crack was made in the side, but, while the piñata swayed and wobbled crazily, it refused to release its cargo.

'My turn!' a child squealed, and the blindfold was duly transferred.

Floss looked up when she was finished, caught Sarah's eye and smiled before spinning the girl around and pointing her towards her target. She had a quick word to Andy, who frowned and then scowled when he saw Sarah. She wanted to hide, but Floss was already threading her way through the group.

'I'm so glad you're here,' she said, her face bright, her cheeks red. 'Thank you for coming.'

'Thanks for inviting me. I won't stay long.'

'Stay as long as you like. You're just in time for birthday tea.'

Another *thwack* and the piñata spun and swayed, and the children sighed, growing impatient with the game. Floss's Brodie took the blindfold next.

'This'll be good,' Floss said, leaning closer to Sarah, as everyone stood clear for the teenager to take a mighty swing.

There was a crash, a tearing sound, and suddenly sweets were raining down onto the ground. There were squeals of delight as they were hoovered up by the waiting children.

Floss laughed. 'Told you so,' she said. 'Come inside, I'll get you a punch before this lot descend on the party food.'

The kitchen was much as Sarah remembered it, with bottles and lunch boxes stacked on one bench, paintings the kids had done at school lining the walls and knick-knacks they'd made decorating the window sill. To Sarah, whose home never had a thing out of place, it felt cluttered and horrific, and yet, at the same time, kind of wonderful. Floss's house didn't feel like a show home, it felt warm. It felt like a family lived here.

Floss ladled Sarah a glass of punch and then began removing cling wrap from plates of sandwiches and fairy bread, and pouring potato chips into dishes. Sarah helped out where she could, but Floss was a one-person party organiser and Sarah felt she was in the way, so she stood back.

'You've done this before.'

Floss laughed, snapping a pot on the stove to cook the little frankies she'd retrieved from the fridge. 'Only a couple of dozen times.' The oven beeped. 'Ooh, can you rescue the sausage rolls? There's a plate all ready.'

Sarah was only too happy to do something to help out. 'I didn't see your folks outside. Are they away?'

'They were here earlier,' Floss said. 'Mum got tired and Dad had to take her home. Mum's got MS.'

'I didn't know that. I'm sorry.'

Floss shrugged. 'Yeah, it's a bitch, but what can you do?'

Sarah was sorry to miss Neill and Sue, she'd always got on well with Floss's parents, although that had been before. Then she remembered the look Andy had given her and thought that maybe it was better that there were two less people to glower at her. She found an oven glove and pulled out the tray of piping hot sausage rolls. Her tummy rumbled. 'Oh, these smell so good.'

'Don't they? You better get in quick if you want one. They won't last long when that lot gets inside.'

Sarah wasn't about to say no. She put the plate on the table and squeezed a dab of tomato sauce on top of a sausage roll then blew on it until it was cool enough to bite into without burning her tongue, while Floss bustled around getting the last few items to the table.

The sausage roll was every bit as good as it smelt, the pastry was flaky and light and the filling delicious. God, how long was it since she'd had a homemade sausage roll? 'Mmm,' she said. 'The best.'

Floss grinned. 'A girl's gotta have a talent for something, I reckon. Queen of the sausage rolls, that's me.' Then she stood back and looked at the table with a critical eye. 'I think that's it. I reckon it's time to let in the hordes.'

Sarah hung back while the children swarmed around the table. *It's okay,* she thought, not feeling the least like hyperventilating, *I can do this.*

Tammy smiled at her as she sat down across the room and Sarah found a brief smile in return before she looked away, training her eyes on Floss moving around the room, topping up a plate here, mixing up another batch of punch there, seemingly oblivious to the din.

Sarah couldn't imagine how she would have coped with making homemade sausage rolls and organising games if she'd ever got to the birthday party stage. She probably would have resorted to a caterer and an entertainer, or at least a bouncy castle or a clown—that's apparently what mothers on the North Shore did, according to the conversations she'd overheard at work.

Annie bounced into the room, holding hands with a curly-haired boy about the same age.

'Where've you been?' said Floss.

'We're here now, aren't we?' Annie said, poking her tongue out and handing her friend a plate. 'Hey, who pinched all the sausage rolls?'

Floss simply smiled and winked at Sarah. 'You should have got here earlier.'

Sarah felt strangely humbled to be included in the joke.

Yeah, she could do this. Maybe when it came to her green-eyed envy, she'd finally worked her way through those five stages of grief. Maybe she was getting to acceptance, at least on this score. She would never have children. Why take it out on those who had?

Andy sidled over to her, a full plate in his hands. 'I didn't expect to see you here, Sarah.' His voice was low and his displeasure was clear.

'I'm lucky to be invited, I know.'

'You hurt Floss again like you did before, and you'll know about it.' He turned and walked away.

O-kay. So she probably deserved that. She could feel her cheeks burning, saw the empty cup in her hands and made for the punch bowl, taking a welcome sip of the cool, sweet drink.

When she sat down again, Tammy's baby was fussing. Without hesitation, Tammy lifted her jumper, released the snap on her bra to reveal her breast, and started feeding her baby.

Sarah couldn't tear her eyes away. The baby had latched on to the nipple, her cheeks moving as she suckled, while her tiny hand clutched the breast and her big eyes looked adoringly up at her mother's face, the mother who was smiling down at her. It was beautiful, the iconic image of Madonna and child. The baby suckled, pausing for a moment, a breath, before resuming. So beautiful. So poignant, Sarah could almost feel the baby suckling at her own breast.

Without warning, a wave of grief-laced want rose up and crashed over her. She couldn't breathe, her throat growing achingly tight, her lungs squeezed flat.

She couldn't stay her a moment longer. Somehow she wobbled to her feet, found a horizontal space in which to park her glass before if fell from her hands, and staggered outside.

She stood under the pergola, arms tight around herself, gulping in the fresh air, feeling the breeze cool her skin and her heart rate settle to something closer to normal. Above her head swung what remained of the shattered piñata, broken and bereft. She knew exactly how it felt. So maybe she hadn't quite made it to acceptance yet.

Floss found her there a few moments later. 'Sarah, are you okay?'

'Yeah, sorry.' She took a deep breath as the pop of a balloon and riotous laughter drifted from inside. 'Sometimes something reminds you, and it all—it all just gets a bit overwhelming.'

'I bet it does.'

'I mean, it's crazy, I know it's crazy,' she said. 'How is it that you can miss something you never had? How can you miss something so badly that it twists you out of shape?'

Floss shook her head. 'I don't know.'

'God, Floss,' Sarah said, putting her hands to her hair, 'I don't know how you can be so nice to me. I shouldn't have come. I'm the wrong person completely to have at a kid's birthday party. I can't believe you invited me. I can't believe I said yes.'

Floss put a hand to Sarah's arm and rubbed it. 'But you did, and you've done fine, you really have.'

'Yeah,' she conceded with a deep breath. She had. For the most part.

'You know, for a while there—for years, actually—I couldn't be around kids at all. I said no to every work Christmas picnic. I said no to every baby shower and refused to visit women who'd just had babies. I sent a present or flowers, of course. But I couldn't see them.

Apart from when I was here on the island.' She gave a wan smile. 'Your kids were harder to avoid.'

'I'm sorry,' Floss said. 'It was kind of hard to hide them. I know it must be hard for you, I guess nobody knows how hard, unless they've actually been there.'

'When you can't have a child, it's like life is mocking you,. Around every corner there's a pram or another new baby. You can't avoid it, no matter how much you try. And I know it's mental and I know it's wrong, but I couldn't face seeing that other women had succeeded in something when I was such an abject failure. I'd never failed at anything in my life until I couldn't have kids. Then everything went pear-shaped with it.'

She looked down at her clasped hands and sighed. 'God, Floss, I was so revolting to you. I was so full of jealousy and envy, I was toxic with it. I'm so sorry. When I look back on what I said, I want to shake myself and slap my mouth and kick myself into next year. So it's really good of you—amazing, actually—to invite me anywhere after the way I treated you.'

'Oh, Sarah,' said Floss with a smile. 'I knew you didn't mean it. I just didn't know how to fix anything.' She paused a beat. 'Do you think we might be able to fix it now?'

Sarah pressed her lips together, tears once again threatening, although this time in joy that her once best friend would want to find a way back to friendship, after all she'd done to destroy it.

'I hope so.'

Floss said, 'Come here, you,' and pulled Sarah into her arms, and it was just like old times. Sarah breathed in the familiar smell of Floss's hair, the same verbena scent of the shampoo she'd always used, and warmth seeped into her. A warmth that made her feel good, that had been absent from her life for too long. She hadn't realising she'd been missing it.

Eventually Floss let her go. She screwed up her nose and smiled apologetically. 'It's probably getting close to cake time in there. Can you bear to stay? I'll understand if you don't want to, but I'd love the chance to catch up a bit more after everyone's gone.'

Floss didn't want her to go? Sarah had to take a moment to process that. Floss didn't want her to go? 'Of course I'll stay.'

'Brilliant,' said Floss, and with a laugh, grabbed her hand and pulled her back inside.

The next half-hour was bedlam. Sarah stood against the wall at the back of the room and did her best to stay out of the way while spills were mopped up, faces were wiped and children were herded back into the room so candles could be lit on the cake and lights dimmed for everyone to sing 'Happy Birthday'.

It was kind of fun to be here and be part of it, Sarah conceded, as the last bars of the chorus rang out, even if she couldn't trust herself to look at Tammy holding her new baby again.

Afterwards, as children and parents filtered away, and Floss and Andy went to see them off, it was no hardship for Sarah to stay inside and gather up the remains and the rubbish and stack plastic cups and plates for washing.

By the time Floss came inside the place looked almost normal, although the sink was loaded with dirty dishes and the floor needed a good mop.

'Andy's taken the kids to Ned's Beach to feed the fish,' Floss said. She stopped and looked around. 'You've done all this?'

Sarah shrugged. 'Consider it partial compensation for past transgressions.'

'Lady,' Floss said, 'you can come to all my parties.' She looked at the dishes piled up next to the sink and the cake smooshed on the floor and said, 'God, I need a coffee before I tackle this lot.' She almost immediately changed her mind. 'No, I don't. I need something stronger. Fancy a wine, Sarah?'

'Yeah. That'd be nice. Thanks.'

Floss took a bottle from the fridge, regarded it strangely, almost like she was having second thoughts, before shrugging and finding a couple of glasses. 'Outside, I think.'

They pulled up a couple of chairs on the veranda, where it was cool rather than cold. Misty rain was falling now, nothing you'd run away from, just enough to soften the edges of the garden, muting the colours and turning it into an Impressionist painting. The two women sipped on their wine while they chatted. Sarah told Floss about how her job had suddenly turned sour and made it impossible to be able to say no to her mother's request to come, and Floss told Sarah about her mother's slow descent into chronic illness.

'It's awful,' she said. 'I feel so bad for my dad. And with this place to run, I can't help him anywhere near enough.'

'At least you want to,' Sarah said, enjoying the wine.

'Is your mum still the same? Even after you've come home?'

Sarah blew out a breath. 'You know Dot. You saw what she was like at the fundraiser. But it is nice being closer to my dad. So swings and roundabouts, I guess.' She sipped her wine. And then there was Noah.

Sarah looked up to find Floss staring at her. 'What?' she said.

Floss smiled. 'I don't know. It's just so nice talking to you again, it's like what happened before never did.'

Sarah bit her lip. It did feel good, sitting here with her old friend. It felt like old times. She took hold of Floss's hand and squeezed it. 'You really forgive me, then, for being such a bitch to you?'

'How could I not forgive you? You were one of my best friends, even if you did go a bit off the rails. I'm just so pleased you came back to the island. I've missed you.'

A bit off the rails? Sarah wondered what she'd done to deserve Floss. 'You know I can't stay forever. I've got to go back and find a new job.'

'I know, but if you hadn't come, we might never have got back to being friends.'

They sipped their wine in silent contemplation, before Floss gave a long sigh. 'I feel bad for Jules, though. Alone in Sydney coping with all that by herself. Do you think that it could be like this with her too?'

Sarah took a big swig of her wine. Not likely.

'I mean, I feel bad,' said Floss. 'With her having cancer and all.'

'They cut it out,' said Sarah, studiously examining what was left in her glass.

'But she's having radiotherapy.'

She sniffed. 'As a precaution.'

'But she's still having to go through it. It must have been terrifying, getting a diagnosis like that. Can't be easy, even now.'

Sarah thought a while. 'You cut her off because of what she did, didn't you?'

'I couldn't stay friends with her after that. I felt like I didn't know her any more.'

'Even after what I'd done to you.'

Floss shrugged. 'Doesn't change anything. What she did was wrong. What they both did.'

'But you stuck up for me when you didn't have anything to gain, and a friend to lose. I can't forgive Jules for what she did, but I can't expect you to feel the same way. I can't tell you not to reach out to Jules. It's just—I'm in a different place.'

The breeze stirred through the palms, a gentle sound. Peaceful. Sarah realised in that moment how much she didn't miss the constant noise of the city. To be able to hear the rustle of leaves, even the flap of butterfly wings against the air, it was like a balm for the soul. She could even think about Jules without feeling that familiar tightening of her chest. Though maybe that was the wine talking too.

She watched Floss pick up the bottle, assuming she was going to top up their glasses, but instead she just seemed to be staring at the label.

Sarah recognised it. 'Is that the wine you bought at the shop?'

'Yeah. More?'

'No. But it's good though. Handy to know.'

'Mmm.' Floss put the bottle down and swirled the wine in her glass before suddenly blurting, 'Can I ask you for some advice?'

'Of course.' Sarah wasn't about to say no to anything Floss asked now, unless it was to do with Jules. 'What about?'

'It's about Andy and me.'

Uh oh. 'I don't think so.'

'Please, because I need to talk to someone, and I'm worried that something's wrong. With our marriage, I mean. And who else can I ask? I can't talk to my mum and I'm certainly not going to talk to my dad. And if I tell anyone else on the island, it's sure to get back to Andy …'

'You want to ask *me* for marital advice? I think you've come to the wrong shop.'

'No, it's just—Andy's been really funny and things haven't been good lately. Not for a while, and—'

'You think he's having an affair?' After what he'd said to Sarah today? 'I'll kill him myself if he is. I am so over bloody men.'

'No. No, at least, I don't think so.' Floss was silent for a few seconds. 'I'd know, wouldn't I? If my husband was having an affair?'

'Next question.'

'Oh hell, I'm sorry,' Floss said, shaking her head. 'That was so stupid.'

'All right,' said Sarah. 'So what's going on between you and Andy?'

Floss threw her hands up. 'That's it—I don't know.'

'You must have some idea. Has he said something?' A note of seriousness crept into Sarah's voice. 'Has he done something to you?'

'You mean like hit me?' Floss actually laughed out loud at that. 'No, he hasn't touched me. He hasn't come near me. That's the problem: he's not interested in me. He never says anything nice about how I look. I don't think he even notices how I look. He's not interested in sex. When he's in bed, he'd rather read a book on motor mechanics than make love to me.'

'Could he be tired? Stressed?'

Floss rolled her eyes. 'God, who isn't? But doesn't that make you want to reach for the one thing you know is going to make you feel better? The one thing that makes everything worthwhile? It does me, but it's not happening and I don't know why.'

Sarah shook her head. It felt weird to be sitting here witnessing Floss's distress when, so many times in the past, it had been Sarah doing the crying. But it wasn't the same, she knew, because Floss wasn't crying out of jealousy. It was nothing to do with envy for what Sarah had. It was all to do with what she was missing.

'But surely Andy loves you? Maybe he just doesn't say it.'

'I want to believe that, but how am I supposed to know? If he doesn't say it, and he doesn't want to make love to me, what else am I supposed to think?'

'Oh, Floss.' Sarah leaned over, put her arm around her friend's shoulders and squeezed her tight. 'You know what? I have a pretty good feeling Andy loves you.'

Floss pulled her head away, wiping at her tears. 'How do you know?'

'Because while everyone was eating, he sidled up to me and threatened me, that's how. He told me if I hurt you again, I'd know about it.'

'Andy said that?'

'He did. Scared the crap out of me, if you want to know, because I knew he meant every word. So I figure he must care about you. Why would he bother otherwise?'

'Wow. I mean, I'm sorry he was mean to you, but—wow.'

The sound of Andy and the kids returning floated up the driveway. Sarah stood up, knowing she should be going and that Floss should be with her family. 'I'll see you later.'

'Will I see you again?'

The two women hugged. 'You can count on it.'

35

Floss lay in bed, exhausted. The birthday party had knocked the stuffing out of her, or maybe it was the bottle of wine she'd shared with Sarah afterwards. But she felt good too. It had been nice to see her old friend. It was so easy to talk to Sarah, a reminder of their yesterday world, when she and Floss and Jules had done everything together.

She thought about Jules, stuck in a hostel near a Sydney hospital, and wished she'd known earlier so she'd been able to say something to her before she'd left. Just a small message of support to let her know she was thinking of her. Pru would know how to get a message to her. She'd ask.

Andy lifted the covers and slid into bed alongside her. It was a rare treat to beat him to bed. 'Thank you for your help today,' she said.

'It was a good party,' he said, beating his pillow into submission before putting his head down. 'I'm knackered.'

'Too knackered to—'

'Oh geez, Floss,' he said, rolling over and putting his back to her, 'I said I was knackered, didn't I?'

She kept a lid on the impulse to snap back. 'Too knackered to talk, I was trying to say.'

'What about?'

'I had an interesting conversation with Sarah.'

He turned his head towards her. 'Yeah? Did she behave herself?'

'She did. Was that because you'd threatened her?'

A pause. 'She said that?'

'She told me you said that if she didn't behave herself, she'd have you to answer to.'

He grunted and settled back down. 'Well, fair enough too. I didn't want her to upset you, that's all. I remember how you were last time.'

'You did that for me?'

'Somebody's got to look out for you.'

'I didn't think you cared.'

'What?' He rolled right over this time. 'What are you talking about?'

'Just that we don't seem to be close lately. I got the impression you didn't want to be with me any more.'

'Oh, Floss, that's garbage.'

'Is it? Because we never seem to make love these days.'

He growled, and Floss knew she was on shaky territory, but she pressed on. 'Annie asked me if we were going to get divorced.'

'What?'

'I know. It shocked me too. At first. But then I got to wondering if that's what you really wanted.'

'Jesus, no.' He sat up and raked his hands through his hair, his breath coming hard and heavy. 'Look, Floss, I know I haven't been exactly easy to live with lately, but I wasn't planning on going anywhere. I—I love you.'

'You do?'

'Of course I do, you muppet. Come here,' he said, reaching for her and pulling her into his arms, snuggling down under the covers with her.

She went willingly. Enthusiastically. He kissed her head and she breathed in his warm, masculine scent. There was a momentary pang of guilt that, if Andy had been like this before, then maybe it would never have happened, but she suppressed it. She didn't want to think about that now. She couldn't afford to think about that now. She wanted to enjoy being held in the arms of the man she'd always loved.

Body heat was a beautiful thing. She wouldn't have said no if he'd asked for sex, but right now, it didn't matter. Knowing she was still loved by Andy was enough. Even if it was probably more than she deserved.

As she lay safely entwined in her husband's embrace, she squeezed her eyes shut and tried harder to destroy the memories of an afternoon that should never have happened. She felt Andy's muscles twitch and his breathing become steady as he relaxed into sleep. God, would she ever not feel guilty about that day?

Would she ever be able to relax and enjoy just being held by Andy again, instead of being beset by self-recrimination and feelings of remorse?

Matt was gone now. Nobody should ever know. Nobody would ever find out. And when it all came down to it, was it that bad, what she'd done? It was only once, and she was sorry.

And yet ...

She turned her face into Andy's shoulder and breathed him in, a scent that was almost part of her. A scent she couldn't live without. Why had she been kidding herself? She loved Andy. Had loved him from their school days together. Would love him always.

She just prayed she hadn't blown it.

Dot looked at the dining table set for two. 'Are you going out again?'

Sarah glanced up from the bench where she was preparing a salad to go with the tuna mornay that was browning under the grill. Anyone would think she was never home, although she'd seen Noah a mere two evenings since the fundraiser. 'Yes,' she said, 'but I'll get this on the table before I go, don't worry.'

'Off to see our policeman friend again?' said Sam with a wink, rolling up his shirt sleeves as he joined them.

'Well, I think you're making a prize goose of yourself,' Dot said. 'It's not like it can lead to anything. He's going home in a few weeks.'

'It doesn't have to lead to anything,' said Sarah, who was feeling way too good to be sucked down by her mother's negative vibes. 'That's not the point. It's just nice to—' *enjoy some hot sex* '—enjoy some pleasant male company.'

'Does he know you're barren?'

'Dorothy!' Sam said, so loud that they almost missed the knock, and there was Noah at the open door.

'Am I intruding?'

'Oh, Officer Lomu,' Dot said, putting on her best so-pleased-to-see-you expression. 'We were just talking about you.'

He smiled charmingly and nodded. 'Yes, Mrs Rooney, I heard.' He turned to Sarah. 'You look lovely, Sarah. Are you ready?'

'I was just about to serve—'

'I'll handle it, lovey,' her dad said. 'You deserve some time off for good behaviour.' He winked as he relieved her of the oven mitts. 'You two kids go and enjoy yourselves.'

'Thanks, Dad,' Sarah said, removing her apron and kissing him on the cheek. 'Night, Mum.'

Her mother mumbled something unintelligible as Sarah grabbed her coat and a bag of groceries and left.

'You okay?' Noah said when they were outside, gently burying a hand in her hair as he drew her head in close for a kiss.

She smiled against his warm lips, and thanked god for strong men who knew how to make an entrance. 'I am now.'

'You know,' he said, 'if I'd realised you were already cooking dinner for your folks, I wouldn't have agreed to this plan of yours to cook for me.'

'That's why I never told you,' she said. 'Come on. You're a man with a healthy appetite. You must be starving.'

He chuckled as he led her to the car, holding her door open for her. 'The way to a man's heart,' he said.

Half an hour later, Noah's kitchen was filled with the aroma of chilli, tomatoes and garlic as Sarah poured more hot stock into the pan. She felt his hands at her hips as he leaned over her shoulder to breathe deep.

'That smells amazing.'

'You do,' she said, because he'd obviously showered before he'd picked her up, and smelt clean and spicy.

'Be careful, woman, or I may not be responsible for my actions.'

Sarah knew that if he kept leaning up against her, she wouldn't be responsible for her actions either, but she wielded the wooden spoon and cocked an eyebrow. 'Do you want to be fed?'

'Well, there is that,' he said, as he grinned and left her to go organise the bowls. 'But after we've eaten, watch out.'

Sarah finished the risotto by adding some Kalamata olives and shaved parmesan,

Noah pulled garlic bread from the oven and they sat down at the table.

'This is a bit fancier than what I'm used to,' he said.

She laughed. 'In which case, my advice is don't go getting used to it.'

Noah finished his first bowl of risotto by the time Sarah was halfway through hers. He sat back in his seat.

'Amazing,' he said.

'It's good,' she said, without an iota of false modesty, sprinkling on extra parmesan. 'It's an easy recipe, one of my favourites.'

'No,' he said. 'I wasn't talking about the risotto, although that, too, is good. I meant you're amazing.'

Her fork faltered on the way to her mouth.

'Being here, having to put up with all the crap you have to put up with ... I heard what Dot said to you.'

'It's not so bad,' she said, staring into her bowl, shifting the risotto from side to side. 'It won't be forever. I'll go home, make a new start with a new job.' She lifted her eyes to his, adding a crooked smile. 'But I'll always have you to thank for making my time here a lot more interesting than it could have been.'

'Only "interesting"?'

'Okay, also sexy and wicked and fun.'

His gaze became suddenly intense.

'I'd like to see you, again. After this is over, I mean. When I'm back in Port Macquarie and you're back in Sydney.'

Sarah swallowed. She'd been thinking this was a brief fling to brighten her stay. A holiday romance with an end date. Thinking longer term had never been on her radar. 'That's weeks away.'

Noah shook his head. 'Not so many weeks that I'm not already thinking about what happens afterwards.'

She was lost for words. They'd both been outsiders here—the short-term locum copper and the reluctant returnee. It made sense that they'd gravitated towards each other, finding something in each other that slotted into their current circumstances: a convenient hook-up.

But the thought of this extending past Noah's leaving sent bubbles fizzing in Sarah's blood. Not only bubbles of excitement, but of panic. She was done with men, or so she'd thought; at least done with long-term relationships and commitment. 'I don't know what to say.'

'Say you'll meet up with me when we're both finished here.'

She took a deep breath to replace the air the bubbles had whisked away. She'd never expected to find something valuable when she returned home for six months—something she might want to hang on to. She'd expected to get in and get out again. So Noah was a bonus. But now that he'd made her feel like she was special, now that he was talking longer term, maybe she should think about his offer to meet up afterwards?

She licked her lips, feeling like she was on the edge of a precipice. She barely knew Noah. She could still say no and walk away. Surely that would be the sensible thing to do?

But sensible Sarah was finding it hard to even think about ending this. She hadn't felt so good in the presence of a man—in the presence of anyone—for years. Why would she give that away?

'If you still feel the same way when it comes time to go home ... ' she said cautiously, because, god knows, she'd managed to fuck up every other relationship she'd ever had, 'I think I'd like that.'

When Noah made love to her that night, it was like coming home. He was no longer a stranger, no longer unfamiliar. He was a safe haven, a place she wanted to be.

And afterwards, when she lay with her head in the curve of his shoulder as he slept, her legs woven between his, she felt the tiny stirrings of something she'd thought long lost to her: a fragile flickering in her chest that whispered of possibilities of a future.

She wanted to laugh at that. She'd been there once before, and delicious as it had felt at times, she wasn't fool enough to want to rush into another relationship. Not now. Not knowing how it had ended.

She was over men, she wasn't looking for anyone, especially not after Richard. She wasn't afraid of being alone.

But a holiday fling that made her feel more desirable than she'd felt in years? She wasn't over that. And if it didn't have to end just yet, she'd take it.

37

The pattern of Jules's days was quickly set, twenty-four hours revolving around one fifteen-minute appointment when she would lie back and allow herself to be tugged and shifted and tweaked until her tattooed dots were lined up before the machine was let loose on her breast, six buzzing bursts from the right that sounded like they were coming from a comic ray gun, before the machine rolled slowly to fire another four bursts from the left, the long dinosaur tail snaking over her head in between.

It was weird, but it was nothing like the biopsies she'd had to endure. When she was done she was free to go and smooth calendula cream over her breast and beyond to cover the area she'd been advised by the nurses would or could be affected. She'd been warned about the possible discolouration, maybe even rashes and itching and burns as the treatment progressed, but for now it was early days. She allowed herself a smile as she worked the cream in. Lovely to have something to look forward to—*not*.

After her treatment she was free to do what she liked again. Walk, or catch the ferry across the harbour, or knit. That wasn't the problem, she was loving knitting more than she'd ever imagined, getting better and faster, and her mother's shawl was growing at a rate that meant she'd be looking for a new project soon.

It was just that every day was the same as the one before.

Buzz. Zap. Buzz.

Knit. Purl. Knit.

Lather. Rinse. Repeat.

The only thing that kept Jules going was her regular Skype sessions with her mother and daughter.

The night after her fifth treatment, already sick of the city, she called home, needing the connection to the ones she loved, relishing the background of her kitchen behind her mother's head as she came into view, the ancient sideboard filled with knick-knacks, Della's artworks lining the walls.

'Della's still in the bath,' Pru said, looking flustered, 'I didn't realise the time.'

'We agreed it, Mum.'

'I was baking and lost track,' she said. 'I'll get her.'

So long as baking was all you were doing. The uncharitable thought —*fear*—came from nowhere. 'Before you do …'

Her mother turned back to the computer. 'Yes?'

'How is everything, Mum?' And then, to be certain her mother understood, she said, 'How are you?'

Her mother fluttered one hand in the air. 'Oh, you know.'

Jules wished she didn't. 'One week already. I'll be home before you know it. No time at all.'

Her mother sighed. 'I just wish you didn't have to be away so long.'

'We both do, but with weekends, it's only another three weeks.' Jules took a deep breath. 'You can do this. You promised.'

'I know, but it just seems so long …'

'It's not that bad. Some women have five or six weeks of it. Men who have prostate cancer can have treatment every day for eight weeks.'

'Can they? Oh, heavens.'

'So you see, it could be worse.'

Pru gave a relieved smile. 'Just as well you don't have prostate cancer then,' she said. 'Hang on a sec. I'll go get Della.'

Jules blew out a long breath once her mother had disappeared, feeling simultaneously relieved and stressed. Bugger this disease. She couldn't fault the doctors and the nurses. She couldn't fault the organisers, the ones who arranged the accommodation and made the patients feel welcome. They all made it as easy as they could, and that was great, but when you were stuck in Sydney twenty-four hours a day all by yourself and the people you loved were far, far away …

It was crazy. People imagined you might feel trapped living on an island like Lord Howe. Trapped by the geography, the tiny size of the island and its distance from the mainland.

And yet people never seemed to consider that you could be trapped in the midst of a huge city.

Suddenly she felt overwhelmed by it all. Why the hell had she agreed to radiotherapy anyway? The surgeon had told her there were clear margins, so she must have got it all. Why was she even here putting up with this?

She closed her eyes and when she opened them it was to see Della draped in a towel, running towards the screen.

'Mummy! Mummy!'

Jules smiled, swiping the tears from her eyes. Because there, dripping wet and grinning wildly, was the reason why. This treatment was insurance against it happening again.

'Tell me,' Jules said, injecting lightness into her voice, 'what have you been up to since we last talked?'

'Nana and me made scones and then Nana took me to the 'seum for story time and then I did a drawing.'

'Oh? Do you want to show me?'

The little girl looked around, pouncing on her latest artwork when she spotted it. Clutching her towel in one hand, she ran back to the screen, holding the picture up in the other. 'It's Horny!' she cried.

'I can see!' Jules said clapping her hands, the ancient hollow-eyed, pointy-skulled turtle unmistakeable. 'That's very good. Well done, you!'

Della beamed as Pru appeared behind her, pyjamas and dressing gown in her arms. 'Come on, Della, let's get you dry and into PJs while you talk to your mum.'

Jules felt redundant, watching her mother wrangling her four-year-old, a bundle of skinny arms and legs and incessant chatter, and then it was bedtime and Della kissed the screen to kiss her mummy goodnight.

'I'll be right back,' said Pru, as Della skipped off to the calendar to cross off another day, and then went to bed.

Jules picked up her knitting while she waited. She was loving the mix of blues.

'What's that you're making now?'

'Oh.' Jules hadn't realised Pru was back. She hid her knitting in her lap. 'It's a surprise. You'll have to wait and see.'

Her mother's eyebrows rose and she smiled. 'Sounds intriguing. You're really getting into this knitting thing, aren't you?'

'It's relaxing. It passes the time, and it's productive. You should try it, Mum.'

'Oh, I don't think I'd be any good—'

'Why not? Grandma used to knit. And if I can, anyone can. Hey, can you take a photo of Della's picture and send it to me? I want to brighten up my room.'

Her mother tsked. 'So help me, she's nuts about that creature. You know she stands there and talks to it?'

'I know,' Jules said. 'It makes me laugh.'

'Ah, well,' Pru said, looking over her shoulder towards the dirty dishes piled up on the sink. 'I suppose I should go and clean up a bit around here.'

Jules felt guilty all over again at what her mother was dealing with while she was away. 'Thanks, Mum. I owe you, big time.'

'You just get fixed up, that's all I ask.'

'I will. Eleven to go. Counting down.'

3 8

Coffee with Sarah at the Halfway Café didn't seem nearly as strange a concept to Floss as it once would have. She leaned back against the corner booth's upholstery, sipping what was left of her cappuccino while Sarah visited the bathroom. In front of her sat a plate with two forks and crumbs, the remains of the lemon tart they'd shared, just like old times. They'd talked about how things were going with the store and Dot and how Sue's symptoms had thankfully eased so Neill was getting a bit of a break.

But they'd shared more than that. Sarah had even 'fessed up to Floss about her budding romance with Noah. Not everything, but enough to have Sarah blushing. Girl talk, so unfamiliar from a woman who hadn't shared anything so personal with her for so long. Floss hadn't realised how much she'd missed it.

It felt good to be friends again. It felt right.

Sarah wove her way back through the tables, the smile on her face good to see. She parked herself down at the table and said casually, 'How's things going with Andy? Better?'

Floss looked into her cup, found it empty, and sat back, frowning a little. 'Okay, I think. He's away on the supply ship right now.' And then she deflected the question. 'Actually, I think I need another coffee. You?'

Sarah looked conflicted.

'Oh, I'm sorry, you've probably got to get back to relieve Deirdre. Don't mind me.'

But instead of taking the easy escape, Sarah nodded. 'Sure, same again.'

Floss went to the counter with their order and spent the walk back biting her lip. She knew this subject was going to be a tricky one to broach.

'Sarah,' she said, sitting down carefully. 'I've been thinking. About Jules.'

'Oh.' And the look Sarah gave Floss told her that she was regretting ordering that second cup of coffee.

'I know. I know. But I've been feeling bad about her going through the treatment all alone.'

'She did bring it on herself.'

'What? The cancer?'

'No. The being alone.'

'Yeah, well …'

A waiter delivered their coffees.

'There you go, ladies,' he said, beaming at them. Sarah smiled weakly back. Floss just nodded.

'Okay,' said Sarah, 'maybe you should get whatever it is off your chest. I really should be getting back to relieve Deirdre.' She plucked a sugar stick from the bowl on the table, briskly ripped it open and stirred the contents into her cappuccino.

'You see,' Floss began, 'I was angry with Jules. Because of what she did.'

'We all were. Still are,' Sarah said, spooning froth into her mouth.

'But the thing is, you know I told you about Andy and me having problems and you asked if I thought he was having an affair …'

'Yeah?'

'Well, it wasn't Andy.' Floss looked at her old friend with worried eyes. 'It was me.'

Sarah put her cup down with a clatter. 'What?'

Floss collapsed into her chair. 'You see, there was this man—a guest—'

'Oh, Jesus, Floss,' Sarah said, her hand covering her mouth. 'Don't tell me. You didn't—'

'No, I didn't. I swear, I didn't.' She stared at the table. And then she looked up, her eyes beseeching. 'Though I wanted to. But only because things haven't been good for a while. Months, to be honest. It has been so long since Andy looked at me as anything more than the mother of his children and the woman who makes his morning coffee, and it was so nice to feel attractive for once. And he was a real gentleman and smelt nice and he even had a beard. I've never kissed a man with a beard. It was different from what I would have imagined. Nice.'

'Oh god,' said Sarah, through the fingers pressed over her mouth. 'You actually kissed him?'

'I know! It was just kind of being close and flirting to start with, but then it moved up a gear—well, a few gears—and suddenly we were kissing. And it was so nice to kiss someone—anyone—that I didn't stop him, but then he started mucking around with my clothes and I froze. Do you know what stopped me?'

'The fact you're married? Your wedding vows? Your kids?'

Floss's face screwed up. 'No, it wasn't any of those.'

'But what else could it be?'

Floss looked at her with a kind of apology in her eyes. 'My stretchmarks.'

'What?'

'I know. Can you believe it? My bloody stretchmarks and what he might think of me when he saw them were what stopped me. And that's what's so wrong. That's what's eating away at me. Because I should have been thinking about Andy and the kids and my marriage vows from the start, but instead I was thinking about how nice kissing this man feels and then how horrible I look naked and how I couldn't bear it if he saw them.'

Floss twisted a sugar stick that was never destined to make it into her cup. 'That's mental, isn't it? Worrying about what some stranger thinks when I don't give two shits what I'm risking with my marriage?'

'You did say you were drinking.'

'But that's no kind of defence for wanting to forget all about my marriage vows, surely?'

Sarah shrugged. 'I don't know if I can help. I was so crazy about Richard I was never tempted to stray. And then, once we started IVF, there was no time to think about anything, least of all anyone, else.' She paused, and then reached out a hand to Floss. 'What are you going to do?'

'I don't know. What can I do? But it got me thinking,' Floss said, not waiting for an answer. 'I judged Jules for sleeping with Richard. I cut her out of my life because she could—and he could—trash his wedding vows. But when it all comes down to it, am I any better than she is? Who am I to judge?'

'It's not the same thing,' said Sarah, whipping her hand away and flipping through her wallet, looking for a note to cover her coffees and extracting a ten before stuffing her wallet back in her bag. 'It's not the same thing at all. You were drunk and he took advantage of you. It wasn't like you had sex with your best friend's husband.' Sarah sniffed. 'When it all comes down to it, you didn't have sex at all.'

'But I could have. I could see how it could easily happen.'

'But you *didn't*. I'm sorry, Floss,' she said, standing up. 'I've got to get back to the shop.'

'But—'

'Listen, Floss, I'm forever grateful that you've forgiven me for being such a cow to you. But when it comes to Jules, you have to do what you have to do. I want to be your friend, but don't try to take me with you. I can't go there.'

Floss nodded numbly as Sarah leaned down, kissing her on the cheek. 'It's okay,' she said. 'It didn't happen, so stop torturing yourself. You didn't do it, and who cares whatever the reason why? You didn't do it. That's the important thing.'

That at least raised a weak smile to Floss's lips.

Sarah smiled back. 'Same time next week?'

And with a nod of Floss's head, Sarah was gone.

'How's my favourite girl?' Andy said as he arrived home.

Floss looked up from where she was peeling potatoes.

'You sound bright,' she said. Brighter than he normally did when he got home from work.

'You better believe it,' he said, slipping his arms around her waist and nuzzling her neck.

'What are you up to?' she asked, secretly delighted. It had been an age since Andy had been anywhere near as playful.

'You'll just have to wait to find out,' he said, as one of his hands slid up to cup a breast.

'Oh, gross,' said Annie. 'Get a room, you two.'

Andy turned and grinned at her. 'Nice to see you too, Annie.'

Mikey came running in next.

'Daddy,' he squealed as he charged into his father's legs.

Andy laughed as he picked him up and gave him a hug. 'Come on,' he said, 'let's go find your brothers.'

Annie and Floss stared after him a while. 'What's up with Dad?'

'I have no idea,' said Floss. But whatever it was, she liked it.

He was reading his book when she got to bed that night. Bugger, she thought, that was short-lived.

But he put his book down and turned off his light. 'I thought you were never going to get here.'

'You were waiting for me?'

'Yeah,' he said, pulling her into his arms. 'I've got a surprise for you.'

Floss was surprised, all right. And delighted and breathless and well and truly satisfied. She lay there in the afterglow of the best sex she'd had for months—maybe years, come to think of it.

Andy's chin resting on her head and she pressed her lips to his chest, slick and salty with sweat. Delicious.

'I'm worried,' she said, still panting as her body hummed back to earth.

'About what?'

'I think someone stole my husband.'

He chuckled a little, then he sighed and kissed her head. 'I'm sorry, Floss. I didn't realise things were that bad. Not until you told me Annie thought we might be getting divorced.'

She pushed herself back from his chest so she could see his face. 'I don't understand.'

'I tried to ignore it,' he said. 'I'm thirty-eight. Too young for, well, you know. And I sure wasn't going to go see our doctor here and ask about it. A mate put me onto his doctor in Port Macquarie.'

'What are you talking about? Too young for what?'

'Jeez, Floss, don't make me say it.' He sighed, and pinched the bridge of his nose with his fingers. 'Erectile dysfunction. I couldn't get it up, and if I did, I couldn't keep it up. And the more I worried about it, the worse it got and the grumpier I got.'

'I thought you didn't want to make love to me.'

'I know. I'm sorry, Floss. I couldn't. And I couldn't tell you. I didn't want to admit it.'

She kissed him and nestled against his shoulder, her hand skimming over his chest and abdomen. 'You poor thing. I'm sorry I gave you a hard time.'

'Not your fault. If I'd known how easy it was to do something about it.' He snorted. 'Thirty-eight years old and already needing Viagra. It's all downhill from here, babe.'

Floss's hand encountered her second surprise of the night. She wrapped her fingers around him. 'You don't feel all downhill to me.'

Breath hissed through his teeth. He pulled her closer. 'You don't mind if we do it again?'

And Floss knew there really was a Santa Claus.

39

The days rolled into weeks, and suddenly three weeks were gone and Jules could start counting down on the fingers of one hand. Just liked the nurses had predicted, the skin of her breast had started to tan. A rash appeared one day and disappeared over the weekend only to reappear. Still, she thought she was getting out of it pretty lightly until her nipple started to crack. It was painful, like starting to breastfeed all over again. Barrier cream became her best friend.

Her calls home only made her more impatient to get there. Every time they skyped, Della would solemnly cross off another day on a calendar, drawing ever closer to the day her mother was due to come home. And Jules would search for signs that Pru was still coping. All the hanging around in Sydney, all the waiting for her treatment to finish, dragged heavily on her bones.

If she hadn't discovered knitting, if Molly hadn't blessed her with this gift and taught her the basic stitches, she would have gone stir-crazy by now. When she wasn't undergoing treatment, or visiting her now favourite yarn store, her fingers were forever busy. She'd finished her mother's shawl and another jumper for Della, a special surprise, and she couldn't wait to see their faces when they unwrapped their gifts.

And now she'd embarked on her craziest project of all, one she was determined to finish in time for their Christmas celebration. The figures might be tiny, but they were proving challenging, and she was learning new skills in the process, embroidering faces and stitching the tiny robes together. But she was loving the distraction from the everyday monotony.

And at least she'd have something concrete to show for her time away.

4 0

Dot progressed from her walking frame to a walking stick on the same day Noah's term on the island expired.

Sarah was at the airport to see him off.

'When will I see you?' he asked.

'I'll be back in Sydney in a couple of months.'

He smiled at her and said, 'I don't know if I can wait that long,' then he kissed her, long and hard, right there in the departure area, uncaring that anyone could see, before he exited the gate and headed for the waiting plane. He waved from the top of the stairs and she felt sad that he was leaving, but she felt good too, because she knew it wasn't the end, just the end of the beginning.

That night, her mother's mood was markedly improved. She even complimented Sarah on her lamb casserole and didn't snipe at her once; not one smug comment about Noah leaving, which Sarah had half expected. It made dinner actually quite pleasant for a change, Dot chatting about her successful doctor's visit and Sam looking visibly relaxed with the improved atmosphere.

But of course her mother would be happy, she was getting stronger by the day, the exercises she'd cursed at the beginning finally paying off. And Sarah also suspected Dot was cheered by the fact that she could see the end of her daughter's problematic stay.

It certainly cheered Sarah.

When the phone rang, Sarah said, 'I'll get it.'

'That'll be Deirdre,' said Dot. 'She promised to call back tonight.'

But it wasn't Deirdre. It was Floss, asking Sarah if she could make it to coffee the next day. Sarah hadn't heard from Floss for a few days, but she figured if Andy was back on the island, she'd have enough on her plate. Besides, they hadn't really parted on great terms the last time they'd had coffee together.

'Sure,' Sarah said, 'so long as Deirdre can cover for me. I'll let you know.'

'Why does Deirdre need to cover for you?' Dot asked after Sarah had hung up.

Sarah told her about Floss's invitation.

'Oh, pooh, I can cover you.'

'Are you sure?' asked Sam. 'It's been months.'

'Of course, I'm sure. It'll do me good having a turn around the store. Be just like old times.'

Which is how Sarah found herself sitting next to Floss at Halfway the next morning. Sarah wondered whether Floss was going to have another shot at attempting a reconciliation between her and Jules, but instead Floss said, 'You know I told you about—you know, that bloke?'

Sarah knew.

'The thing is, do I tell Andy about it? Do you think I should?'

'Oh.' Well, there was a hairy one. 'How are things between you and Andy now?'

Floss smiled so hard she blushed. 'So good. The best they've been for years. He's like a horny teenager all over again.'

Sarah smiled. Floss had poked her hair behind her ears as she'd said it, looking every bit the horny teenager herself. 'In which case, do you really want to put that at risk?'

'God, no. I mean, things were really rough between Andy and me, and even though I didn't have sex with this other guy, I was so tempted.'

'And I guess he'd be angry hearing it, right?'

'Why wouldn't he be? I kissed another man—and I thought about doing more—that's all kinds of unfaithful, right there.' She swallowed. 'But worse than that, I know he'd be disappointed in me. I could deal with the anger, I could understand that. It's the disappointment that would kill me. I couldn't bear it now, not when things are finally looking up.

'What do I do? Should I tell him? I want to be honest with him—I know I should be able to be—but I'm scared of what might happen. I'm scared I'll lose him for good.'

Sarah took a deep breath. She was woefully unqualified to give the kind of advice Floss needed. All she could think of was to try to tackle it from a different direction. 'I often wonder what would have happened to us all if Jules hadn't got pregnant. I mean, if she and Richard had slept together, but they'd never said a word about it to anyone, and Richard had come home and they'd both pretended it had never happened.'

'No!' Floss protested.

'Because it was the baby that changed things. It was the baby— Richard's baby—that meant it couldn't stay a secret. Because he insisted on Jules having it. There was no hiding their betrayal then.'

Sarah looked intently at Floss. 'You would never have known, for a start. You would have stayed friends with Jules all these years. And I would never have known. I mean, things might have been a bit strained and awkward between us all for a while, but look at you and me now. And we were all so used to Richard and Jules sniping at each other that we might not have picked it.

'I'm not saying it would have been right, but would that have been better? Two of us in blissful ignorance and we'd all remained friends?'

Floss sat back, wide eyed. 'Are you saying I shouldn't tell Andy?'

Sarah sighed. 'I don't know. Maybe just that … sometimes wounds take a long time to heal, if they ever do. Maybe sometimes it's better not to know.'

⌇

Sarah's words to Floss sat uncomfortably with her as she restocked shelves in the store. She wasn't sure she believed them. She wasn't sure she would want to live with a man who kept a secret like that. She certainly didn't want a friend who could do that to her.

Whatever Floss decided to do, it was better that Sarah knew about Richard and Jules. Neither of them had been able to hide from what they had done, and that was only fair.

When the computer pinged, Sarah assumed it was a confirmation of the order she'd placed earlier, so it wasn't until an hour or so later that she checked her email. She stared at it a few seconds, read it and reread it, and then punched the air. 'Yes!'

Her first tentative foray into the world of CVs and job applications had come up trumps: she was being invited for an interview. The firm was a medium-sized outfit on the North Shore, even closer to home than her former office in North Sydney. So what that it was a managerial position? From what she'd researched, the firm was young and dynamic, and light years away from the prehistoric world of Fortescue, Robbins and Lancaster.

Better still, she wouldn't have to wait an entire two months to see Noah again.

41

Jules climbed happily but wearily down the plane's rear steps. Because she was still in her thirties, she'd assumed she'd take any of the side effects of radiotherapy in her stride. And yet she hadn't counted on the stress of worrying about what was going on at home while she was away. She'd actually wept in the change room after her last treatment. A quiet shedding of tears of relief that it was over. And now she was exhausted, so completely drained of energy that she clung to the handrail for support.

On the flipside, she'd never felt better in her life, because she was home, and there waiting for her in the arrivals area were Pru and Della. Her daughter was wearing the simple red jumper Jules had knitted her. Jules smiled, looking forward to seeing Della's reaction to the latest treat she had made.

'Mummy!' squealed Della, jumping up and down and clapping her hands. 'There's Mummy!'

It was all Jules could do not to break into a run and gather her girl up in her arms and squeeze her tight. Somewhere in the four weeks she'd been gone, winter had turned to spring, the sun felt warmer and the air held the promise of renewal. It had never felt better to be alive.

'Mummy!' Della cried again, as Jules came through the gate. She leaned down, successfully deflecting one of her daughter's arms from going around her chest and looping it around her neck. Her breast was still sore, the skin feeling like it had been sunburned. It would heal though. A few sore spots on and around her breast was nothing compared to the feel of her daughter in her arms.

'How are you feeling?' said Pru, her voice and eyes filled with concern, rubbing Jules's back as she released Della and stood.

'Tired,' Jules said, half wishing Della wasn't here so she could tell her mother she was absolutely buggered. But only half wishing, because she'd wished Della away once before, and there was no way she was ever wishing her away again.

'Let's get you home then,' said her mother, taking her cabin bag.

Pru had soup on the stove with fresh bread and golden butter on the table, and the smell as Jules walked into her cottage was utterly heavenly.

'I'll just get a bowl of that for you,' Pru said. 'You look like you could do with a decent meal.'

Jules could. Cooking had seemed too much of a chore while she'd been in Sydney, and especially in the last week or so, she just couldn't be bothered. But the smell of her mother's ham and vegetable soup had her drooling, even though it was nowhere near dinner time.

But first things first. 'I have something for both of you,' Jules said, opening her luggage and retrieving the two packages.

'What is it?' asked Della, reaching out for hers, her eyes wide.

'A surprise.'

Della was bursting with excitement as she ripped at the paper. But, 'Another one,' she said, and Jules heard the slightest tinge of disappointment in her daughter's voice as she unfurled the blue jumper. A tinge of disappointment that turned into a squeal of delight when she found what Jules had knitted on the front. 'Horny! You made me a Horny!' And promptly ran into her bedroom to put it on.

'Well, I never,' Pru said. 'However did you do that?'

'I made a design from the picture you sent me. Almost went mad in the process, but I think it came up okay.' To be fair, she'd only tackled the skull, with its prominent horns, big empty eye sockets and nose, but she was more than satisfied with the result. So was Della, from the way she came charging back into the room, proud as punch of her new jumper.

'Remarkable,' said Pru.

'Open yours, Nana,' said Della, and Pru obliged, much more carefully than Della had done, but no less delighted when she pulled the multi-shaded blue shawl from its wrapping. 'Oh,' she said, holding the knitted fabric to her face. 'It's exquisite. It's so soft.'

'It's the possum fur,' Jules said, 'soft like angora but without the scratchiness. It's got alpaca in the blend too, so it should be toasty warm.'

'I love it,' said her mother, wrapping the shawl around her shoulders. 'It's the most beautiful thing I've ever owned.'

Jules doubted it, but she accepted her mother's hug of thanks, before Pru announced that Jules must eat.

Della was gorgeously attentive, slathering butter on slices of bread for her, more than she could eat, but Della helped her there too, and polished them off.

'Thank you, Mum,' said Jules, after she'd eaten what she could, feeling her eyelids growing heavy and weariness dragging at her after the long day and the flight and the huge emotional release of coming home.

'Nonsense,' said Pru. 'It was only a bit of soup.'

'No,' Jules said, putting her hand over her mother's. 'I didn't mean the soup.'

Pru slid her hand out and patted her daughter's arm and Jules knew her mother understood.

'All in a good cause,' Pru said. 'Now, are you sure you're going to be all right tonight, just you and Della? You're welcome to come back to my place.'

Jules shook her head. 'No. I want my own bed tonight. We'll be fine. I've got Della to look after me.'

'I'll look after Mummy,' the girl said, a toy tucked tight under one arm, fingers poised to go back in her mouth. 'I can put Mummy to bed.'

'You see?' Jules said, tweaking the peach-skin perfection of her daughter's cheek. 'We'll be fine.'

It was only when she was saying goodbye to her mother that Jules noticed the flowers on the sideboard. A bright arrangement of the best of island colour.

'Oh, Mum, I didn't notice these before. They're beautiful. Thank you.'

Her mother cocked an eyebrow and gave a smile. 'I didn't bring them. Floss did.'

42

Floss had good intentions and a spring in her step. Life had never been better and she wanted to share the joy. Bookings were picking up and the indications were that summer was looking good. The kids were behaving—mostly—and the nights with Andy were a revelation. It was like they were teenagers all over again, and she felt more wanted than ever. The days he spent away on the freight ship only heightened his desire, making departures and reunions something special to look forward to.

So when Andy came into the bedroom like a charging bull, his aggression was as unexpected as it was terrifying.

'You should have been more careful!' he bellowed. 'It's not like we're bloody millionaires.'

'What on earth are you talking—'

But he'd already thrust something under her nose—a stick with two bold pink lines. 'I found this in the bin!'

She looked up from the stick to him, relief swiftly swamped by the shock of realisation. 'It's not mine.'

'Then who the hell's is it?'

As Floss looked at Andy, together they shared a moment of panic. Who else's could it be?

~

Floss found Annie crying on her bed. 'Annie,' she said gently as she eased the door open after knocking.

'Mum,' Annie wailed, sitting up and throwing herself into her mother's arms as she sat down next to her on the bed. 'Mum, I heard Dad shouting.'

'Everyone on the island did.'

'And it's all my fault,' she said.

'Why is it your fault?'

'Because I'm going to have a baby.'

Oh god. Floss closed her eyes, feeling suddenly sick to her stomach, because it was one thing to stumble upon what was going on, another thing to hear the words out loud. She stroked her daughter's hair and swept her hand down her back, looking at the walls adorned with posters of boy bands and Pink, the stuff of a teenage girl littered around the room. There was a picture of Trent in a heart-shaped frame on the side table. Funny how Floss had never thought twice about that before; they'd been a double act for some time, but Floss had assumed that it was no more than a teenage crush. Never thought it could lead to something so life changing. At least, not yet.

'Mum?' Annie asked, when Floss still hadn't spoken.

'You're so young,' she said. 'You have your whole life ahead of you. You know this will change things if you decide to go ahead and have the baby.'

Annie's eyes lit up with equal measures of defiance and horror. 'Of course I'm going to have the baby. Would you have got rid of any of us?'

'No. No, of course not.'

'I thought we were being careful.'

'Things happen.' Floss swallowed. 'I take it Trent's the father.'

Annie nodded, her sobs now turned to hiccups.

'And how does he feel about it?'

The girl sniffed and wiped her cheek with the back of one hand. 'Same as me—we want to get married and keep it.'

'I didn't realise you two were so serious.'

Annie lifted her head from Floss's shoulder. 'I love him, Mum, and he loves me.'

'That's a good start when you're going to bring a baby into the world.' Still Floss ached for her daughter, who thought she knew what she wanted at sixteen. Maybe she did, but what if she was wrong? What if she grew up wondering about other men? What if she was tempted? Floss had been lucky with Andy, and lucky that when things had become strained, they hadn't snapped apart. 'You know, you don't have to decide any of this yet. You're young. There's time to work it out.'

'No, Mum, we have worked it out. Don't make it sound like we don't know what we're doing.'

'But to get married so young—'

Her daughter pulled away. 'You and Dad got married when you were teenagers! I thought you'd understand. Why should it be okay for you but not for us?'

Floss wanted to say she hadn't been pregnant at sixteen with limited options, but it didn't seem like the time. Instead she pulled her daughter closer and they sat there a while, before she asked, 'So you've thought about the practical things, then, like school and what you're going to do after?'

Annie nodded. 'I'm going to finish. The baby won't be born until June sometime. And then, I thought—I wondered if I could work with you here at Beached. Trent's going to work at his dad's bike hire shop.'

'You have got it all worked out. So why were you crying?'

'Because I heard Dad yelling. I didn't think anyone would look in a bathroom bin. Funny thing is, I've known about it for a little while now. I only did the test to make sure I was still pregnant before I told you. But then Dad found it. And he sounded so angry.'

'He wasn't angry with you. He was yelling because he thought it was mine.'

The girl blinked up at her. 'Seriously?'

'Seriously. He thought I was hiding a little secret. I think he figures five is enough.'

Annie laughed briefly before her eyebrows creased into a frown again. 'So he's not angry with me?'

'Well, I guess you could say he's a little shell-shocked. We both are.'

'I was going to tell you, really I was. Trent was going to come over after school today and we were going to talk to you together. I just wanted to make sure I was really pregnant first. That it hadn't been a mistake.'

From outside the room came the sound of cupboard doors and drawers banging in the kitchen, no doubt the boys wondering where the breakfast chef was. 'There you go. I like him better already.'

'He's really nice, Mum.'

'I know.' Floss kissed her daughter's forehead. 'You wash your face and get ready for school. I better go make porridge for the masses.'

Annie hugged her tight. 'Thanks, Mum.'

Floss went back to being mum for the next hour, serving breakfasts and organising lunchboxes, and when it came time to send the kids off to school, Annie looked herself, her hair in pigtails. A kid again, if only for a while.

And Andy, who'd rung work to say he'd be in late, sat down next to Floss on their bed, one arm around her shoulders, the other tucking her head against his chest, cups of tea he'd brought going cold on the side table while they both came to terms with the revelation.

'My baby is pregnant,' Floss sniffed.

'That's just it,' said Andy, 'she's not a baby any more.'

'But she's so young.'

'Is she?' he said. 'It could have been us, way back when. We were having sex at their age.'

'At least we didn't get pregnant then.'

'Yeah, we were lucky. But would it have made any difference anyway? We were always going to get married.'

'But her and Trent?'

'They've got a few things to work out, sure. Meanwhile we have to support Annie the best way we can.'

'I'm going to be a grandmother,' she said, staring blindly at the faded carpet. 'Aren't I too young to be a grandmother?'

'You'll be the sexiest grandmother on the island.'

'Only on the island?'

'On the planet.'

She smiled at that. 'I'm not sure I'm ready to make love to a grandfather.'

'Don't worry, we've got a few months to get you used to the idea.'

'You know some people are still going to say they're too young, and that they're throwing their lives away?'

He paused. 'Yeah, there is that, but have you had a chance to think about how your mother is going to react to this? She's going to be a great-grandmother. And she's not well and she doesn't have a whole lot to look forward to, and she's not going to give two hoots about Annie being sixteen and her and Trent not being married yet, but a baby—she is going to get such a kick out of that. She always loved it when you had a baby. I can't wait to see her face when she holds Annie's.'

Floss looked up at this man she'd thought she'd lost, looked at his too long hair and his craggy features and whiskered jaw he still hadn't had time to shave, and in that moment, Floss had never loved him more.

Jules was snoozing in a recliner chair with a rug over her knees, her knitting put aside for now, when someone knocked on the door.

'I'll get it,' yelled Della, and Jules smiled, grateful that she had such a willing slave, even though it was probably only Pru checking in.

'Mummy,' said Della, running back. 'It's a lady.'

Jules cocked open an eye and pushed herself higher in the chair, cursing the sting from her burnt breast. She'd been told the side effects peaked a week to ten days after concluding her treatment, and the nurses were spot on. She got herself halfway to standing when Floss walked into the room, a casserole dish in her hands.

'Oh, please don't get up,' said Floss. 'I didn't mean to disturb you. I just brought a pasta bake, in case you don't feel like cooking.'

Jules was lost for words. Floss, right here in her living room? 'That's really nice of you.' Then she remembered. 'You brought flowers too. Mum said.'

Floss nodded.

'I haven't had time to thank you for those.'

'It's not necessary. I just hoped it might be a nice surprise when you got home.'

Jules licked her lips. Definitely a nice surprise.

'Shall I put this in the fridge?'

'Oh, yes, of course. Della will show you the way.' Even though the cottage was no different from the last time Floss was here.

Floss disappeared with Della into the kitchen and returned a few moments later.

'I should offer you coffee or tea or something,' Jules said, at a loss as to what to make of this.

'No.' Floss shook her head and gave a small smile. 'I won't stay. I just wanted to let you know people are thinking about you, and to ask if there's anything you need.'

'I'm good,' Jules said. 'Or I will be once the side effects wear off.'

Floss smiled and was almost at the door when Jules asked, 'Why did you come? Is it the cancer? Did you come here because you feel sorry for me? Because it's nice of you to bring a casserole and all, but I don't need people feeling sorry for me.'

The other woman sighed, her eyes raking the ceiling as if searching for the words. 'It's partly the cancer, that's true. But it's not because I feel sorry for you. It's because it turns out that nobody is perfect, least of all me.' She took a deep breath. 'I'm sorry, Jules. It's probably years too late, but I'm sorry for what happened between us.' She pressed her lips together, sniffed, and then said, 'I'll see you later. I hope you feel better soon.'

Della looked bereft. 'Is the lady gone?'

'She had to go.'

'She was nice, Mummy. Is she coming again?'

Who knew?

Then Pru bustled through the door with a basket filled with treats. 'Goodness,' she said, 'was that Floss I just passed coming in?'

'It sure was,' said Jules.

'Well, that's nice,' said Pru. 'First flowers and then a visit.'

'And a casserole.'

'Wow. That is nice. Isn't it?'

And Jules thought about her unexpected guest and her cryptic comments, and said, 'Actually, it is.'

~

Pru put on a load of washing while Jules made a batch of scones with Della and after her mother helped Della with the washing up, they all sat on the verandah eating scones with jam and cream.

'Mmm,' said Jules, 'I could get used to this. Shame I have to go back to work in a couple of days.'

'You sure you'll be ready for it?'

'I'll be fine. It's so nice being home in my own bed, and being spoilt by Della and you. But I have to get back to work. It's only part time.'

'Actually,' Pru said, brushing scone crumbs from her skirt, 'there's something I need to talk to you about then. Something you need to think about for the future.'

'This sounds serious.'

'It is.' Pru looked over her shoulder to where Della was busy riding her pedal car around the veranda, cheerfully engaged in her own fantasy world. 'I need you to think about who you'd want to be guardian for Della if something happened to you.'

Jules wasn't up to moving at warp speed just yet, but she sat to attention in her chair pretty bloody fast. 'What?'

'I said, you have to think about—'

'I heard what you said. I just don't understand why.'

Pru fixed her with a steely-eyed stare. 'You know why.'

'You were fine. I was away the best part of a month and you managed fine. No problem.'

'Not for you, maybe. For me, every night was a struggle, even with those tablets the doctor gave me to help with cravings. Every bloody night, I had to look at Della, and think, *No*.'

'But you made it. Why don't you just keep going?'

Pru shook her head. 'Oh, love. If only it were that easy.'

Jules's throat tightened. 'You don't want Della? I can't believe it.'

'Don't you understand? It's not a matter of not wanting her—it's about not trusting myself. I'm not proud of having to tell you this, but I thought it better to be honest. Because in all seriousness, I don't want to go through life never having another drink. Surely that's my choice? Besides, Jules, I'm sixty years old. She's four. When she's twenty-one, I'll be nearly eighty. What kind of life is that for a child, growing up with an old woman?'

'She's your granddaughter! The only one you've got!'

'Don't you think I know that?' Pru sucked in a breath, and when she spoke again, it was with her regular clipped tones. 'Which is why I'm suggesting you think about it. Look, it's probably all academic anyway. Health-wise, you're fixed now, but if you've got all your ducks in a row, the i's dotted and t's crossed, then you'll probably never need to resort to whatever you decide.'

Jules sat back in her chair, blindsided.

'There must be someone,' Pru said. 'Someone better than me.'

Jules shook her head, still trying to come to terms with her mother's announcement. 'Richard's family are in Goulburn. Too far away and they're a similar age to you, why would they want that? Besides, I want Della brought up on the island.'

'Well, that's one thing we agree on. I'm selfish enough to want to have regular contact, even if I can't be her guardian. But that just means that you'll have to find someone here. Like I said, it's probably academic, but you have to get it sorted out, just in case.'

'More scone, Mummy? I get you one.'

Jules looked over to where Della stood, wearing her new jumper and keenly awaiting her answer. She smiled. 'Yes, please. That would be awesome.'

Her daughter beamed, then pulled a scone apart and slapped jam and cream onto each half, before holding one out to her mother, the other held fast in her hand. 'I look after Mummy really well, don't I, Nana?' she said before scoffing her own half.

'You do, Della,' Pru said, regret running deep in her eyes. 'You look after your mummy really well.'

44

———

Once the interview date and time was locked in, Sarah could make other plans. Given she'd be in Sydney, it seemed as good a time as any to go and tender her formal resignation to Fortescue, Robbins and Lancaster. Then there were just the flights to organise, into Port Macquarie and out of Sydney.

It was all booked when her phone rang again. She picked it up, laughing, thinking there must be something she'd forgotten to give the agent.

'Sarah,' said the caller, and her laughter died in her throat. 'It's Jules.'

'Oh?' Sarah had heard from Floss—and Dot, via Pru—that Jules was back after her treatment. But after their last encounter, Sarah was surprised that Jules would bother to contact her again. 'What do you want?'

She heard a half-laugh. 'At least I can't accuse you of feeling sorry for me.'

'What?'

'Doesn't matter. Look, Sarah, I know the last time we met it didn't go so well.'

'Right.'

'So I thought we could try again.'

'Why?'

'Because it's important.'

'Again, why?'

'For old times' sake?'

'Which old times are you referring to, Jules? The old times when we were friends, or the old times when you decided to sleep with my husband?'

'God, Sarah, can you give it a break? We need to talk.'

'I don't think so. Thanks for calling.' Sarah put the phone down. For all the pleasant moments on the island enjoying the quiet and the sunsets, it was going to be one hell of a relief to get back to Sydney.

Sarah had just delivered two cappuccinos, one long black and a soy latte to the group sitting on the veranda and was wiping down the coffee machine when she heard the door swing open and the tell-tale tinkling of the bell. 'Sugar's right here at the counter,' she called over her shoulder, because someone was always coming in looking for more.

'I'm not here for the sugar.'

Electricity zapped down Sarah's spine. 'Jules,' she said to the woman standing just inside the entrance looking so serious and gaunt. 'What are you doing here?'

'You wouldn't come to me.'

'I have nothing to say to you.'

'That's too bad, because I've got something to say to you. Something to ask you. A favour, if you like. An important favour.'

'You want to ask me for a favour?' Sarah fought the urge to laugh. 'I don't see why I'd want to do anything for you.'

'You haven't heard what it is, yet. At least do me the honour of listening first, before you decide if you can help me out or not.'

The bell tinkled as the door opened behind Jules. Sure enough, a girl from the table outside. She'd barely got the words out before

Sarah waved at the area of counter laid out with serviettes, sugar and spoons. The girl helped herself and left again, apparently totally oblivious to the tension that had Sarah and Jules pinned to the spot.

'We need to talk,' Jules said. She looked out the windows to where the group were laughing. 'Somewhere private.' She wasn't asking this time, Sarah noted.

'Can't you see I'm busy?'

'The shop has to close sometime.'

'And I have to get dinner for my folks.'

'Jesus, Sarah, what are you so afraid of?'

Sarah thought about what Noah had told her, that she wasn't a coward or she wouldn't be back here on the island, and took a deep breath. 'I'm not afraid of you, Jules. I just don't want to waste my time on you.'

Jules seemed to deflate as the fight went out of her, as though her attitude had all been so much hot air. 'Please,' she said, begging now. 'It's important, or I wouldn't ask. If our friendship ever meant anything to you, please hear what I have to say.'

It was the tone in her appeal that got to Sarah. The sheer desperation. What could be so important? Forgiveness? No. She'd already tried that. She'd know it was pointless to ask again. And as for a favour to ask, what kind of favour could she possibly expect Sarah to agree to give her? Sarah didn't care, and why should she? Except that Floss—reliable, dependable, as good as married to Andy from the moment she'd met him Floss—had admitted she'd almost strayed. And Floss had tried to breach the chasm between Sarah and Jules.

Sarah licked her dry lips, curiosity driving her next words.

'All right,' she said. 'After closing this afternoon. But I'll come to your place.' She didn't want Dot listening in. 'Just because I'm agreeing to talk doesn't mean I'm going to say yes to whatever it is you're asking.'

Sarah didn't get a smile from Jules. She got the slightest of nods in acknowledgement and then a whispered, 'Thank you.' Jules turned and opened the door, and disappeared down the steps.

Sarah was left standing there, her blood churning. Because she wasn't just remembering their friendship, she was trying to make sense of other stuff too, like the day they'd all done a trek up to the top of Mount Gower. It had been the perfect day to climb, no cloud hanging over the island to obliterate the view from the top and spoil the experience or their photos.

There'd been Floss and Andy, Sarah and Richard, and Jules, who'd just broken up with her latest boyfriend, a Swedish chef called Björn who was working at Halfway.

Things between Richard and Jules seemed to be going better that visit. Jules had promised to Sarah that she'd try to get on with Richard and, while she was terse with him, she wasn't out and out rude. Not until they reached the top and were making their way through the fern-shrouded jungle. It had been the perfect day to climb, with no cloud hanging over the island to obliterate the view from the top and spoil the experience and their photos.

Sarah had been holding hands with Richard. 'Look at that view,' she'd said. The length of the island was laid out before them, an emerald green arc surrounded by water the colour of heaven. 'It's beautiful.'

'You're beautiful,' he'd said, and dropped to his knees and pulled a ring box from his pocket, snapping it open. 'Will you marry me?'

And she'd said yes and he'd pulled her into his kiss. The most magical kiss she'd ever had after the most magical proposal, right here at the very top of this most magical of islands. Everyone had clapped and cheered, even Jules, though her smile hadn't equalled the others'. Life had seemed perfect in that moment, and it wasn't until everyone had finished with their photos of the view and it was time to make their way down the mountain again, that Jules had manoeuvred alongside Sarah, and said,

'Are you sure about this?'

'What?'

'Marrying Richard.'

Sarah had scoffed. 'Of course, I am,' Sarah had scoffed. 'Just because you don't like him?'

'He's not good enough for you. He's a jerk.'

'What's wrong with you? Why would you say that?'

'I just think you could do better.'

'You don't know him.'

'I know enough.'

Sarah had looked sideways at her then. 'What's that supposed to mean?'

But Andy and Richard had caught up with them, and Jules had dropped back, and it was only later, when they were back in Richard's cabin, that Sarah had related what had happened on top of the mountain and asked him why Jules would say what she had.

Richard had pulled her onto his lap and smoothed the hair from her brow and kissed her, before saying, 'She's just jealous because she can't keep a boyfriend.'

'I don't know.'

'Of course she's jealous. Floss is married to Andy and now you're marrying me, and she's going to be the odd one out.'

'She always said she never wanted the whole marriage and kids deal,' Sarah had said, remembering.

'There you go. But now she feels bad. She just doesn't want anyone having something she doesn't want.'

'Do you think that's all it is?'

He pulled her closer. 'Hey, we got engaged today. Do you expect me to talk about some other chick all night, or …'

'Or what?'

'We could celebrate getting engaged.'

'Yeah,' she said, looping her arms around his neck, because that was a far better idea. 'Let's do that.'

She'd thought her life perfect in that moment, and, to be fair, it had been pretty much perfect for a long time. They both had good jobs, great pay, a beautiful home and a fantastic North Sydney lifestyle. Tennis for her on the weekend, golf for him. Absolutely picture perfect lives. Until the moment they'd decided it was time to share their lives with a small person, and disappointment, frustration and the infertility journey they found themselves on had turned their lives mental.

Infertility journey.

What a joke. Where were the happy-clappy blogs from people for whom IVF never worked? How could it be called a journey when you never arrived at the destination?

Sarah sighed and looked at the cloth in her hand, trying to remember what she was supposed to be doing before the thunderbolt called Jules had come walking into the store.

What was it that she'd missed, that had caused her life to go so wrong?

Della was waiting for her in the car, closely studying Jules's empty hands as she climbed in, as if expecting a treat. 'What did you get?'

'Sorry, sweetheart, I wasn't shopping.' But she'd had a win of sorts —Sarah had agreed to come and talk. Although that wasn't entirely a comforting thought and Jules's pulse was already racing at the prospect. She glanced in the rear-vision mirror, ostensibly to reassure her daughter, and was struck by a tsunami of doubt so enormous that it was a wonder she wasn't washed from the car to go tell Sarah that she'd changed her mind.

Della was just a child. Was it fair to her to involve her in all this?

'Don't worry,' she said shakily, half to herself. 'I'll get you a treat at the museum.' Jules was stopping by to pick up a key so she could open the next day. As well as catch up with any news she'd missed while she'd been away.

A short distance down the road, Jules stopped again, and Della, once free of her seat belt, bolted inside. 'Watch out for visitors!' Jules called uselessly after her. Jules had a pretty fair idea where she was headed: no doubt to show Horny her new jumper. The girl had barely taken it off since Jules had arrived home.

She followed Della inside, only to be humbled by the welcome and the hugs she received from the staff. They swarmed around her as if she'd been gone a year rather than a few weeks. By the time they were finished, she was dewy eyed and sniffing, reaching for a tissue as she assured them that she was fine. It was over and she couldn't wait to get back to work.

'Excuse me,' said an American voice, interrupting the little get-together. 'Where can I find that darling sweater? The one that little girl's wearing. Do you have that in boys' sizing?'

As one, the group looked around to see Della emerging from the museum room wearing her horned turtle jumper.

'I'd like two if you have them out the back somewhere. My grand-sons are crazy about dinosaurs. They'd love those.'

The staff looked blank. Jules smiled weakly. 'Oh, no. I made that,' she said.

'You did? Well, maybe I could order them from you direct. I'm happy to pay for postage.'

And just like that, Jules had sold her first two horned turtle jumpers, with an order from the museum for a dozen more in different sizes.

46

Spring was edging into summer, the weather becoming less change-able, bringing more sunshine and an increasing stream of visitors to the island. Sarah passed a mob of them taking photos as she rode her bike to Jules's place. They'd been in the shop earlier, buying snacks and having coffee on the veranda and they waved as she passed.

That was something she'd miss when she got home to Sydney, where avoiding eye contact was almost an art form. But she would get herself a bike. She'd forgotten how much she'd enjoyed cycling, and how good it was for fitness. Maybe she might even think about riding to work if she got that job closer to home.

Then again, cycling in Sydney? Maybe not.

She stopped pedalling just short of Jules's driveway and took a deep breath. At least in Sydney she wouldn't have to worry about surprise visits and mystery requests from people she'd prefer to avoid.

She dismounted and pushed her bike the rest of the way. She wasn't in that much of a hurry to get there.

Jules was waiting for her on the veranda. She nodded and Sarah nodded back. Excellent, that was the pleasantries taken care of.

She kicked down the stand on her bike and took off her helmet, dropping it in the basket.

'I'm here,' she said, 'but I warn you, if you're going to start blaming me for what happened again, I'm going.'

Jules blinked, a slow blink. Sarah saw her chest rise and fall with it. Jules looked like she'd lost weight. Because of her treatment? So what?

'Come inside,' Jules said, 'I'll put the kettle on.'

'Have you got anything stronger to put in it?'

Jules looked over her shoulder and shrugged. 'Sure.'

Sarah bypassed the milk and poured a slug of scotch into her coffee, nursing the mug in her hands, letting its warmth seep into her. 'So what is it you want?'

Jules bowed her head as if looking for absolution, and Sarah thought she was on a hiding to nowhere there, but when the other woman looked up, and she realised that she must have been summoning strength, because it wasn't meekness she saw in her eyes, but a sheen of steel.

'I don't want to waste your time, so I'm going to cut right to the chase,' she said. 'I need to make some plans, in case something happens to me. I have to make arrangements for Della.'

Sarah was fixated on the first bit. 'What's going to happen to you? I heard the radiotherapy was just for mopping up, and that you'd be fine.'

'But it's not just the cancer, is it? Because even if it doesn't come back and it isn't breast cancer that takes me out—and touch wood it won't be that now—it could be any of a dozen other things I don't even see coming. I can't rule anything out.'

'Aren't you being a bit melodramatic?'

'Am I? We're all dying, Sarah. It's only a matter of time.'

Sarah was still struggling to make sense of why she was here. She sipped her coffee, relishing the peaty burn of the liquor. 'Still, what's this got to do with me?'

'All this time, I never had a will, which is daft, but in making one, I have to think about Della. If something happens to me, I need to have guardianship arrangements in place.'

The first infusions of unease started seeping through Sarah's blood. *Surely she couldn't mean ...* There was no way. 'So where's the problem? Surely Pru would look after Della, if anything happened to you?'

'Pru can't.'

'Why? She's, what? Sixty? She's young.'

'Pru is out of the question.'

'But she's Della's grandmother—'

'Pru can't do it, okay?'

Sarah reeled from the force of Jules's attack. 'But there has to be someone else. What about Floss?'

Jules looked at her as if she'd just arrived from Mars. 'Floss has five kids, a mother with MS, and a business to run, and you want to wish another child onto her? Do you really think she'd welcome another child into the family?'

'I'm not wishing anything. I just don't understand why you want to involve me in this plan of yours.'

'Because you were wronged, Sarah, and I thought—I hoped—that this might be a way to offer you—'

'What?' Sarah was horrified. 'You mean like *compensation*? Is that what you're saying?'

'It's not like that at all.'

'Then what *is* it like?'

'I was thinking—hoping—that it might be a kind of atonement. I can't make up for what happened, but I can—'

Sarah shot to her feet. 'No!'

'Sarah!'

'No! You can't do this to me. You can't have the baby I couldn't and then give it to me in the event of your death like some kind of consolation prize. "Oh well, you were in the race, but it didn't happen for you, never mind, here you go, every player wins a prize!"'

'It's not like that! Sarah, listen—'

'It's ridiculous, that's what it is. I live in Sydney for a start.'

Floss swallowed. 'I was hoping that, if something happened, you would bring her up on the island.'

'What, you mean live here? For god's sake, get Pru to do it. She's her grandmother, after all. She's the obvious choice.'

'She's an alcoholic, Sarah.'

'What?'

'A functional alcoholic. She can't let herself do it, because she's sixty and she'd afraid she won't last another twenty years without a drink while Della grows up.

'And I *need* someone who can be her guardian if something happens to me. It might not be cancer that kills me, I might not die before Della grows up, but I just thought, that if I did, it was only fair that her guardian should be you. I'm sorry. I was wrong.'

Sarah looked at Jules, with her sunken eyes and too-prominent collarbones and bizarre bequest. 'I'll say.'

47

'I'm sorry you had to come pick it up,' Jules said, heading into the kitchen, when Floss dropped by to pick up her casserole dish.

'It's no trouble,' said Floss. 'I was passing anyway. How are you feeling?'

'Getting there,' she said. 'Feeling better every day.'

'I imagine it knocks the stuffing out of you.'

'You know, I think it's the being so far from home that makes it so tiring. Anyway, I'm just so grateful I didn't have to go the whole chemo route. Avoiding that is kind of like winning the cancer lottery.' She found the dish in the kitchen and handed it over. 'Best pasta bake ever. Della loved it too. Thank you for thinking of us.'

'Least I could do.'

Floss turned to leave, but Jules caught her arm.

'Floss, I just wanted to say I'm sorry about that serve I gave you the other day, questioning your motives for coming over. It wasn't fair. You didn't deserve it.'

Floss smiled. 'Oh, I think I did.'

Jules frowned.

'Long, sad story,' said Floss, with a shake of her head. 'Maybe one day I'll tell you the gory details.'

Jules's eyebrows shot up, then she smiled. 'I think I want to hear it. Sometime.'

The sight of Jules's smile warmed Floss through to her bones. She'd missed it. 'In that case, you probably will. But it will require wine, and lots of it.'

'In that case, I *definitely* want to hear it.'

The women laughed, and it was like something had broken, a layer of ice on a frozen brook, the water free to gurgle and sparkle underneath the sun.

Floss stopped laughing. 'It's nice to see you again, Jules. I'm hoping—'

'That we can be friends again?' Jules said. She pulled Floss into a hug. 'I'm thinking we already are.'

4 8

There was a voice crooning in Italian on the music system, a warm breeze drifting through the window and a naked man in her bed. Life was pretty much perfect. Sarah lay there panting, buzzing her way down from the heights, her body still humming.

'I missed you,' Noah said, breathing hard against her neck where he'd slumped after making love to her, his fingers turning lazy circles around her nipples.

She kissed the tip of his nose. 'I missed you too.'

'Why do you have to live so far away?'

'Hey, you're the one who moved. Anyway, it won't be long and I'll be back. At least, back on the mainland, close enough for more regular conjugal visits.'

'I can't wait for that.' He pulled her into his kiss.

Yep, life didn't get much more perfect than this. Little had she known when she'd been railroaded into going back to the island that she'd actually find something—*someone*—to make her trip worthwhile. She had Lord Howe to thank for Noah. And then another thought struck her and she chuckled in the midst of his kiss.

'What's so funny?'

'I was just thinking, if my mother hadn't broken her hip, I wouldn't have had to go to Lord Howe and I wouldn't have met you.'

'Why's that funny?'

'Only that I might actually have to thank her.'

He chuckled too. 'I might have to as well.'

On Saturday they hiked a stretch of the coastal walk that in places reminded Sarah of Lord Howe Island, and then Noah took her to the cute Tacking Point Lighthouse. On the drive back to his place, he surprised her by pulling into a supermarket.

'Big night planned?' she said with a wink. 'Stocking up on supplies?'

He grinned. 'Nah. Come on, I've got someone I want you to meet.'

Noah's mother was pint sized next to her rugby player–sized son, but Sarah could see where he got his readiness to smile. Sylvia was warm and welcoming and delighted to meet Noah's friend.

'Do you always take your girlfriends to visit your mother?' Sarah asked when, hand in hand, they walked back to the car.

'No,' he said, leaning down to kiss her. 'Only the important ones.'

Warmth bloomed in her chest.

That night he took her to a posh restaurant overlooking the serpentine Hastings River where they dined on premium Riverine beef. 'My mother sent me a text,' he said, when she returned from the bathroom. 'She likes you.'

'I like her too.'

'She thinks I should snap you up, before some other lucky guy does.'

'She said that?' It was way too early to be suggesting anything of the sort, even if she was secretly thrilled that Noah's mother approved of her. 'So what did you say?'

'"Why buy a book when you can join a library?"'

She punched him on the arm. 'You did not!'

He rubbed his arm like she'd actually done some damage, and

smiled before his eyes turned serious. 'No. But you are important to me, Sarah. I can't wait for there not to be an ocean separating us.'

She sighed. 'Me too. Not long now and I'll be back.'

On Sunday, Noah pulled out the pièce de résistance: lunch at a French restaurant tucked inside a winery that was lined with mature jacaranda, poinciana and magnolia trees. They dined on Basque-style chicken and slow-cooked lamb shanks.

It was there that Sarah admitted her first regrets about leaving Lord Howe: that it was almost sad to be going when she was finally enjoying the new beginnings of a friendship with Floss.

That's when Noah asked about Jules.

Sarah sat back in her seat. 'Jules is in a different category.'

'I guess.'

And because he sounded like he didn't quite believe it, Sarah said, 'I didn't tell you what happened this week. Jules asked to see me again. She actually asked me if I'd be guardian to Della, her daughter, if anything happened to her.'

'Wow,' he said.

'I know,' she said, 'how mental is that? As if she can sweep the past under the carpet and pretend it never happened.'

'Then again, she's trusting you to bring up her child if she's not there to do it herself.' He shrugged. 'That's a pretty heady responsibility. That's kind of special.'

'She's trying to buy me off.'

He pulled the wine from the cooler and poured a little of the ruby-coloured cabernet sauvignon into each of their glasses.

'She *is* trying to buy me off—you do see that?'

He shrugged again.

'Hey,' she said, adding a bright smile to her upturned hands, 'whose side are you on?'

'Why do there have to be sides?'

She snorted, picked up her glass and downed a swig.

'Can I tell you something?' Noah said.

'Only if you're not going to tell me what I should do.'

'No, not at all. It's about my father. I went looking for him when I turned eighteen. I got wind of him living in some kind of commune near Byron Bay.'

'Really? I didn't realised you'd ever met him. What was it like, meeting up with him for the first time?'

'It went better than I expected. He seemed genuinely happy to meet me. We hung out at the beach. Went surfing together. It was cool.' He took a sip of his wine. 'For a while.'

'What happened?'

'I woke up one morning to find him gone. Along with my Subaru and my wallet and my faith in human nature.'

'Wow, that's awful. That must have really twisted you up in knots.'

He shrugged. 'It did for a while. But then I realised he didn't care, and the only one hurting was me.'

'What did you do?'

'I let it go, Sarah.' He looked levelly at her. 'I forgave him.'

'Just like that? After all he'd done to you?'

'I was sick of shouldering it all and feeling bad. And I decided that it might have happened, but I wouldn't let it rule my life.'

'I'm sorry that happened to you,' she said, getting to her feet. 'Excuse me, I have to go to the bathroom. I'll be right back.'

She stared at herself in the mirror as she washed her hands, feeling disconcerted. She didn't know what Noah's story had to do with hers but there was one thing she knew: nobody understood. Not Floss. Not her father and certainly not her mother. Not even Noah seemed to understand. What happened between his father and him—it wasn't the same thing at all.

Forgive and forget. What a joke that was. She couldn't forget. Every time she thought about Jules or Richard, every time she saw Jules or Della, the past slapped her in the face.

If she couldn't forget, how the hell was she ever supposed to forgive?

Five stages of grief, her father had said, probably equated to five stages of forgiveness. She took a deep breath, and jiggled her shoulders up and down to release some tension. Even if her father was right, you had to want to get there first.

It was hard saying goodbye again to Noah, but it would only be a few weeks and she'd be back permanently. She flew into Sydney on Sunday evening and trained it across the city to the North Shore, so it was late when she let herself into her house.

'Welcome home,' she said to herself, as she crossed the threshold of the Kissing Point Road house she'd bought with Richard. 'The worst house in the best street,' he'd said. 'It'll be a great investment. We'll do it up and make a killing.' So they'd polished floorboards and built a big veranda before adding two more bedrooms and doing up the kitchen and it was worth something like four times what they'd paid for it.

Her house now. Richard had signed it over to her when he'd walked out. She thought about having Noah here. Hmm. Maybe it was time to think about cashing in and getting something smaller. It wasn't like she needed a family home.

Her university student house sitter wasn't home. She'd warned Kylie that she'd be staying a couple of nights, and the girl had taken that as a hint and gone to stay with her boyfriend. Sarah looked around. If the place was always this clean and tidy or whether she'd had to panic clean, Sarah didn't care. There was a bunch of fresh flowers in a vase on the table, so Sarah gave the girl extra points for that.

She headed for her bedroom, which she'd simply shut the door on when she left. Tomorrow she had to look corporate professional. It was time to go digging through her wardrobe for something to wear.

Monday at noon the sushi bar was bustling, filled with serious men in dark suits and women who looked like they'd just stepped out of the boardroom of one of the big four banks—and probably had. Frankie had been clever enough to snaffle a booth. She waved and Sarah wove her way past the crowded bar to get to her. She air kissed Frankie and then flopped down with a sigh of relief. She wasn't used to wearing heels, even workaday mid-heels that used to be her comfortable go-to standards. Even one of her favourite suits felt foreign. She'd grown slack while on the island. She was going to have to get used to power dressing again.

'You look great,' said Frankie. 'Island life must suit you.'

Or the hot sex, thought Sarah. A weekend of hot sex with a gorgeous bloke would put a sparkle in anyone's eyes. 'How are you?'

'Good. Apart from work. You have been sorely missed.'

Sarah smiled. She doubted it, but it was nice to hear it anyway. 'What's going on?'

Frankie rolled her eyes. 'Where to start? The tax department is a mess.'

'Oh?' It had been running fine when she left. 'Why?' And then she held up one hand. 'Actually, don't tell me. I don't want to know *anything* about the office.' She wasn't interested. She was handing in her resignation today and then heading to Chatswood for her interview. Meanwhile there was a sushi lunch to be enjoyed. They ordered green tea and chose a selection of dishes and got stuck in.

Sarah swallowed down her prawn dumpling and let her head fall back with a sigh. 'You have no idea know how much I've missed our lunches.'

Frankie smiled and poured more tea. 'Me too.' She took a sip. 'So how's it going over there? You surviving? You weren't that keen on going at first.'

Sarah thought back to all the reasons she hadn't wanted to go back to the island and all the things that had happened that had proven her concerns right. 'It hasn't exactly been a cake walk,' she said, 'but Mum's getting stronger. She won't need me in a few weeks.'

'So tell me about this job you're going for.'

Sarah filled her in, unable to keep the excitement from her voice. The job sounded perfect for her and she was going to do her damnedest to get it.

Twenty minutes later, Sarah sat back, hand on her belly. 'Oh my god, I am so full. I'm going to have to undo the button on my skirt.'

Frankie laughed. 'But what a way to go, eh?'

'True.' They gathered their things while the waitress totted up the bill. 'I'll come back to the office with you. I've got a date with Philip.'

'Good luck with that.'

'Thank you. They're probably half expecting it. But no doubt he'll make me feel guilty for thinking about leaving, or something like that.'

Frankie laughed. 'That, or tell you how ungrateful you are after all they've done for you.'

~

Philip answered her knock with a 'Come.'

He whipped off his reading glasses and jumped up from behind his desk to greet her. He held her hand between his and smiled widely. 'Sarah, so good of you to come.' He gestured towards his conversation table and chairs. 'So how goes it on Lord Howe Island?'

'Good. Mum's doing well. I'll be back in Sydney by late December.'

'Excellent. That is good news.' He looked at his watch. 'Simon should be joining us in a moment.'

'Oh, there's no need for that.' Sarah just wanted to hand over her letter, discuss her termination details and catch a taxi to her interview.

But then Simon was there and heartily pumping her hand too. Okay, so they'd both hear the news at the same time.

'The reason I asked to see you,' Sarah started, reaching for the envelope in her bag after they'd all sat down again.

'Before we get to that,' Philip said, exchanging a glance with Simon, 'I don't know if you've heard, but there's been a bit of shemozzle in the office.'

'Oh?'

'And we find ourselves with a vacancy,' Simon said.

She said nothing. Little did they realise they were about to have two.

'Yes, young Dillon didn't work out quite as well as we expected.'

Go figure, she wanted to say, and in spite of his amazing golf average and Twitter skills too. 'Oh?' she said instead, knowing she was at risk of sounding like a broken record.

'Well,' Philip said, his pen twirling so frantically in his fingers Sarah figured it must be punch drunk, 'the thing is—'

'We made a mistake,' Simon said.

'Yes,' Philip said, frowning as if the words were unfamiliar, 'we made a mistake. But that's in the past.'

It was like watching a tennis match, Philip serving one over the net and Simon lobbing it back.

'And so,' Simon added with a smile, 'you coming in today was inspired.'

She smiled weakly. 'Well, that's good then.'

'Because,' Philip said, 'we'd like to offer you a partnership. Congratulations, Sarah.'

'What?'

'It should have been yours all along. What do you say?'

Sarah blinked, totally blindsided. 'I don't know what to say.'

'You could say yes,' Simon suggested.

'I'm sure we'd even accept a thank you,' added Philip.

'Thank you,' she said with a smile, because she could say that. She thought about the letter of resignation burning a hole in her bag. 'I'll think about it.'

'Why didn't you tell me Dillon was gone?' Sarah said to Frankie when she stopped by her desk to tell her the news on the way out.

The other woman grinned. 'You were the one who said you didn't want to hear about work.'

Sarah sent her a death stare. 'What happened to him?'

'One of the big clients arrived home to find Dillon giving his wife a little extra help in the—' she made quote marks in the air with her fingers, '—insolvency department.'

Sarah's eyebrows shot up. 'Doing a bit of overtime, was he?'

'He was asked to hand in his resignation. Kevin from tax was asked to take over his duties, but that's left tax short. Looks like they've found just the person to clean it all up. Are you going to take it?'

'I told them I'd think about it.'

'They're lucky you didn't tell them to shove it where the sun don't shine. Good luck with the interview. Let me know how you get on.'

49

'Coffee or tea?' Floss asked.

'Coffee.'

'White with one, right?'

'Spot on,' said Jules, flashing a smile as her knitting needles click-clacked. 'Don't forget to ask for my discount.'

Floss had picked up Della from Pru's house and they'd met Jules at the museum café when she had finished her shift. Della and Mikey were busy at a kiddie table, colouring in together and getting on well.

'They'll both be at school before long,' said Jules when Floss returned. 'It's nice they'll know each other a bit better.'

'That it is. Sorry I didn't bring Mikey to play group. It was a bit—'

'It's okay, Floss. I know. And you were busy with all the stuff you have to do. I don't know how you do it all.'

'You get used to it, I guess,' Floss said with a shrug. 'You squeeze the hours for all they're worth. Which makes it all the nicer when you stop for ten minutes.' She smiled. 'Like now.'

'Thank you,' Jules said. 'Again.'

'Hey, forget it.' It was so lovely to be on speaking terms again. You couldn't have too many friends, Floss figured, that you could afford to lose any of them.

Their coffees were ready so Floss went to collect them, sorting out an argument over the red pencil between Della and Mikey on the way.

'You're so good with kids,' Jules said on her return.

'Hah. You have five and see how good you get.'

Jules grimaced. 'I didn't think I'd have one.'

'Yeah.' Floss looked over at the table where the kids were hunched over their pictures. 'But look at how gorgeous Della is. You've done an amazing job, Jules, for someone who never wanted kids.'

Jules stopped knitting to gaze at Floss. 'Why do I feel the need to keep saying thank you to you?'

'Because I'm the good fairy, of course,' Floss said, holding out her hands. Then she chuckled. 'I wish you wouldn't, though, because that makes me feel like I was a total bitch to you all those years.'

'Oh no, don't think that.'

'I can't help it. Wasted years. I'm sorry, Jules.' She sighed. 'I just wish Sarah could be with us.'

Jules shook her head. 'She won't meet with me again. She won't forgive me. I've tried.'

'Maybe she just needs more time?'

'I can understand it though. Would you forgive me, if I'd slept with Andy and got pregnant when you were desperate to have a child and couldn't have one?'

Floss stared blindly at the table, struck dumb. She'd always planned on being a mum, but the very idea that she couldn't have kids and that Andy and Jules might have—God, that brought things way too close to home.

'You see? So why would she forgive me? Why should she?' Jules sucked in a breath and found a smile to paint on her lips, no matter how thin the coat was. 'But it's okay. Nobody can say I haven't tried.'

For a moment the prospect of the three of them never being friends again weighed heavily on Floss's heart. It didn't seem right that they had come this far and there was still this final bridge, this final stage to broach. But maybe Jules was right. Maybe the triangle of their friendship was irrevocably broken.

That didn't mean she couldn't be friends with Jules. 'Oh hey, did I tell you I'm going to be a grandma?'

50

Sarah had such a good feeling about how the interview had gone she almost floated out of the office. The two principals—a man and a woman (imagine that!)—were both in their early forties and looked like the kind of people Sarah would mix with at tennis. They were only interviewing three candidates for the senior role that was designed to be a stepping stone to partnership, and they'd undertaken to get back to her within forty-eight hours, but they'd given her the impression that she was at the top of the list.

Even the shower of rain as she stepped outside couldn't put a dampener on her mood, not until cab after cab crawled by, ignoring her. Of course there'd be no cabs, she realised, it was raining. But god, the traffic. She'd forgotten about congestion and traffic fumes.

When the next cab crawled by without stopping, she thought, *Damn it, I have my umbrella, I'll walk, and test out just how long it would take to walk to work.*

Halfway home, her shoes were rubbing and her feet were killing her. She'd have to wear sneakers if she got the job.

She let herself in and kicked off her shoes to examine her ankles. Blisters. Big ones. No wonder her feet had hurt so much. She headed for the kitchen. She'd spied a bottle of wine in the fridge and she was sure Kylie wouldn't mind if she helped herself to a glass.

Then she flopped into an armchair to call Noah and rub her poor feet.

'I miss you,' Noah said, picking up on the first ring, his deep voice making Sarah forget all about her aching feet.

'I've only been gone one night.'

'Feels like longer.'

'Greedy,' she said.

'You bet. How did you go today?'

Sarah told him about her amazing day with one unexpected partnership offer and potentially a second job offer.

'What are you thinking?'

'I don't know. Once upon a time a partnership with FRL was my dream. But now they've finally offered it to me, I don't know that I want it. I'll see what happens with this other job.'

'Maybe you should turn them both down and check out what's on offer up here at the Port. I liked having you here.'

The idea was not without appeal. It wasn't as if she was tied to Sydney and there was direct access to Lord Howe, so she'd still be close if her parents needed her. 'Maybe I should.'

'You definitely should,' he said. 'We're good together.'

He made her promise to call the next day to let him know she'd got safely back to the island, and said goodbye.

We're good together. She sat there a while considering what she'd thought had been a throwaway line about looking for a job in Port Macquarie. Now she didn't think it had been throwaway at all.

Theirs had started as a casual hook-up. She hadn't thought it would last until he'd have to return home. But it had, and beyond then, too: a weekend with him at Port; plans being made for when she returned to the mainland. Now he was suggesting she think about getting a job in the same city as him and she hadn't summarily dismissed the notion. Because when it all came down to it, she didn't actually mind the idea. It would be nice to spend time with Noah on a more permanent basis. It wasn't like she was bound to Sydney, and it would be nice to get away. She'd forgotten what a pain the traffic congestion and the fumes and so many bloody people everywhere were.

She sipped her wine. Port Macquarie wouldn't be such a bad spot to live. Anywhere that Noah lived would be just fine with her. Because he'd suddenly become very important to her too.

She sat up quickly as her heart tripped a couple of beats. Oh, boy. Talk about unexpected. Here she was, a grown woman, and she was feeling like a teenager falling head over heels for her crush.

She held the glass to suddenly heated cheeks and smiled. How about that? She'd gone and fallen in love with Noah.

Half an hour later, she was deep in her wardrobe, sifting through her clothes. She pulled out a couple of linen shirts that would do in the store and a light zip-up jacket that would be perfect when riding her bike. But so much of her stuff looked wrong for the island. It looked too … North Shore, designed to be shown off with chunky beads and clanking bangles in some swanky café overlooking the harbour. Sarah couldn't remember when she'd last bothered with jewellery.

She stood back to better scan the contents of her wardrobe.

That's when the box on the shelf above caught her eye.

Oh, hell.

That box.

Surely that wasn't still there? Hadn't she ditched that before now?

She looked away. Tried to concentrate on the job at hand, sorting her wardrobe, choosing things that would better suit the warming climate for the remaining weeks she'd be on the island.

But the damned box kept bringing her back.

Until, her heart thumping, she could look nowhere else. The bloody thing wasn't going to go away. She had a good mind to toss it in the bin. In fact, she would.

She growled, and went off to find the stepladder.

Then she was back, climbing the steps and pulling the box from its resting spot on the shelf. A shower of fine dust fell from the top as it tilted. Okay, so it had been a while, but that only made her even more annoyed she'd left it that long. Annoyed and grumpy, she spat out dust. This box was going straight to the bin.

She stepped off the ladder and turned, dislodging the lid in the process. She reached down to pick it up, and that's when she saw them, the tiny pink and blue onesies she'd bought when she'd discovered she was pregnant; one in each colour, hedging her bets. The tiny onesies that had never been worn.

Her hand moved of its own volition, pulling one out. So soft.

Size 0000.

So tiny.

She sat on the bed, put the box next to her and held the suit up with both hands. Across the front was embroidered *Worth the Wait*.

She squeezed her eyes shut, bowing her head and hugging the suit to her chest. It would have been. It would have all been worthwhile.

Eventually, she took a deep breath and opened her eyes. She hadn't cried. How about that?

She laid the suits on the bed, pink and blue, side by side. Found the baby bonnet with the frilly edge and matching cardigan and bootees her mother had crocheted the minute she'd heard she was going to be a grandmother at last.

She rifled through the box. There were other memories she'd kept for whatever reason. Maybe just because she couldn't bear to part with them. A dummy she'd found in a baby store that said *Daddy's Little Princess*.

She rifled through the assortment. A bib saying *Nom nom* that had made her smile. Even a syringe, a reminder of the thousands they'd used to coax her ovaries into coughing up a few precious eggs. God, what the hell had she been thinking, keeping that?

And there, in her hand, an envelope. It was addressed *To Baby*.

Don't go there, said a tiny voice in the back of her head. *What's the point, when you're going to chuck all this stuff anyway?*

But no, her fingers were already working at the flap, removing the folded page. Just the one.

To my unborn child,

Your daddy and I waited a long time for this miracle and the happiest day in our lives was the day we learned you were coming. I want you to know that no matter how you were conceived, you were brought into this world through love, probably a lot more than many others.

And we both want you to know that you are, to us, our most wanted and cherished baby.

Thank you for coming in to this world and making our lives complete. We can't wait to meet and cuddle you in person.

We love you.

Mummy and Daddy.

Sarah blinked as she blew out a long breath. God, the rubbish she'd kept!

She gathered up the things on the bed to put back in the box, putting aside the bootees and the hat, Dot might want to give them to Deirdre for Tammy's baby. But it really was time to ditch the rest.

Then she pulled out the bib and the dummy for good measure.

Except there was something else in the box. Two envelopes, bound by a rubber band.

Her heart squeezed tight.

No.

But she couldn't stop herself. She picked the bundle up and turned it over. Jules's handwriting stared back at her.

Her heart thumping, her mouth dry, Sarah turned the envelope over, breaking the seal. She opened the pages and another folded page fell out onto her lap. She ignored it, already captured by Jules's *Dear Sarah.*

She read the letter, written all those years before. The letter she had never been able to bring herself to open before now.

I'm so sorry this letter is needed. I'm so sorry for the agony and hurt and the betrayal that I know you are feeling.

'Huh,' Sarah snorted. Sorry. Everyone was sorry. It didn't help any. It didn't change anything.

It was grief sex, Jules wrote.

It was wrong and a mistake and it should never have happened, but it did. It was one time only and nobody would ever have known. Until I discovered I was pregnant.

It was never an affair. He came to the island to be with Della.

I don't expect you to believe me, but it's the truth, and you deserve to know.

I'm sorry, Sarah. For everything. Truly sorry that I have lost you and, I fear, lost you forever.

Your friend,

Jules.

The hand holding Jules's letter dropped to her lap. *Grief sex.* One time only? Who was Jules trying to kid? Richard moved there. He'd left Sarah. He'd lived with Jules.

None of it made sense. It was Jules who'd told her not to marry him. It was Jules who'd told her that Richard wasn't good enough for her. Ironic that it was Jules who'd slept with him in that case, and proved her theory true.

Sarah sniffed. She'd never been able to work out why Jules had said that.

She picked up the other paper, expecting it to be spouting similar garbage from Richard. Making excuses. Saying sorry.

A thousand times sorry.

Bingo!

Because sure enough, there it was, right at the top of the page.

I'm sorry I have to write this down. I tried, you know I've tried, but I just can't talk to you any more.

Hang on.

I couldn't live with you any longer. I didn't recognise you. I didn't know who you were any more. And I know you didn't see me.

What?

You know I was over the moon when we got news you were pregnant. I thought we'd done it. I thought things might go back to normal, like they'd once been before all the hopeless and ultimately futile heartbreak of IVF. But they didn't go back to normal.

For a long time, I'd felt like I was a walk-on extra in your life. The way you changed after you became pregnant confirmed it. You were a stranger in our bed, and I knew then that I'd lost you.

I know it's been rough on you. I know you were shattered. But don't blame Jules. She doesn't deserve it. She wouldn't have kept the baby but for my insistence. She knew what it would cost her. She knew that in keeping Della, she would be sacrificing your friendship.

I'm the one you should hate. I'm the coward. I saw a way out of an endless cycle of misery, and I took it.

I'm sorry, Sarah. I love you—at least I did before IVF railroaded our marriage. I don't know what I feel right now except an overwhelming sense of sadness about what happened to our marriage. I know it's selfish of me, and I'm not proud of myself, but I just can't be with you any more.

Shell-shocked, Sarah slid from the bed, landing with a thump on the polished timber floor.

He couldn't talk to her? But he'd been so happy when she'd become pregnant. She'd thought things had gone back to normal. He was so thoughtful and romantic. He'd taken her to the Opera House, to a concert and dinner, and everything had been wonderful. Just like old times.

And then, when they'd got home, he'd kissed her so tenderly, his hands on her body, her changing breasts and over the sweep of her belly beneath which lay their baby. He'd wanted to make love to her.

And she'd said no.

'The baby,' she'd said, laughing as she'd pushed him away. 'We mustn't do anything that might harm the baby.'

She could still see the hurt in his eyes, hear his argument that it was safe, but she was insistent and she knew he would understand eventually. That it was worth it, just to be sure.

You were a stranger in our bed.

Okay, so maybe she'd been a bit careful, but that still didn't excuse him jumping straight into bed with someone else.

Grief sex. How did that work? What was that if not just a pathetic excuse? Sarah clutched the letter to her chest. So many questions without answers. Maybe it was time she found some.

51

Jules was casting off a pair of sleeves on the verandah alongside Pru, while Della zipped around the furniture in her kiddie car. Jules sighed as she knotted off the final stitches and snipped off the wool. Now all she had to do was stitch the pieces together and she'd have another jumper finished- and then she could start on the next one. 'I must have been crazy to take this on. I'm never going to get all these jumpers finished.'

Pru looked over from her magazine. 'You need to find someone who can help.'

'Yeah.' Jules had been thinking the same thing. 'But who?'

'What about me?'

'You?'

'Why not? Like you said, your grandma used to knit, so it can't be that hard. I might be a bit slow to begin with, but I'm sure I'll pick it up. Besides, it'll give me something to do. I've been feeling a bit bored lately. There's only so many banana cream pies one can make.'

'If you're sure,' Jules said, 'That'd be great.

'Of course, I'm sure,' Pru said, putting her magazine aside. 'Now, show me what you want me to do. If you haven't got any spare needles, maybe I could start stitching those pieces together so you can get a head start on the next one.'

Half an hour later, Jules was ribbing the next back, Pru busy with a darning needle when Della said from her kiddie car, 'Mummy, it's that lady again.'

Jules looked up, her smile ready, thinking it must be Floss.

Except it wasn't.

Sarah walked up the driveway and stood just short of the steps, her eyes like dark holes, her mouth twisted as though she'd been chewing on the inside of her cheek. And the only word Jules could think of to describe her was 'tormented'.

'We need to talk.'

Jules slowly stood. 'Okay.'

'Della,' Pru said, 'how about you and me go inside and make some scones?'

'Scones!' squealed Della. 'Yippee!' She clambered out of her car, all knees and elbows, and bolted inside.

Jules threw her mum a look that said *Thanks*. Pru squeezed her arm and disappeared.

'Come and sit down,' Jules said, worried Sarah would fall down, she looked such a wreck.

Sarah slowly ascended the steps, but she refused to sit. She stood by the railing clutching something in her hands. A letter.

That letter.

Jules looked from the envelope to her visitor's face. 'You told me you'd burned that.'

'I know what I told you. I found it and I opened it. I read it. Every word.'

Jules waited. If that were true, she had nothing else to say. Sarah looked like she was struggling to breathe, the muscles of her jaw painfully tight.

'You told me not to marry him. Right up there on top of Mount Gower, on the very day he proposed to me, you told me he wasn't good enough for me. Why did you do that? What did you know that I didn't?'

Jules shook her head, confused. This was history. Ancient history. She'd expected Sarah to launch straight into the letter.

'What happened?' Sarah pressed.

'All right. It was at your twenty-first. Richard followed me into the kitchen when I went to get more vodka. Björn had just left the island without saying goodbye and Richard said that I must be shit at sex if I couldn't keep a boyfriend. He pushed me into the corner and said he could do me a favour and show me what men like.'

She heard Sarah's shocked intake of air. 'He was drunk!'

'He wasn't *that* drunk.'

'We were all pissed that night, every last one of us. But he didn't mean it. He was just trying to wind you up. Like he always was.'

'Yeah,' Jules said on a sigh. 'I know that now.'

'So why did you say what you did?'

'Because I knew that once you married Richard, you'd be gone from us. You'd live in Sydney and you wouldn't come back, and I hated him for doing that to us. So I blew up what he'd said and made it my solemn duty to warn you. Not that you listened.'

Sarah rested her hands on the railing. 'Jesus, Jules. Maybe I should have.'

There was silence then, but for the swish and slap of palm leaves in the breeze. A kind of peace until Sarah's head swung around.

'So how did it happen?' she said. 'Tell me.'

'God, Sarah, why torture yourself? Didn't the letter explain?'

'Damn you, I *need* to know.'

Jules recoiled, but, 'All right,' she said. She cast her mind back to that night, aware that Sarah would want the unsanitised version, warts and all. 'Richard had finished work for the day and I'd made dinner. It was only soup.'

She sniffed, thinking, trying to get the order right. 'He was quiet. I knew he wasn't himself because he hadn't once taken a potshot at me or made some snarky comment. I'd never seen him like that. He seemed sad. Lost.'

She dragged air into her lungs and walked to the railing near

Sarah, but not close enough to touch, and looked out at the rainforest garden.

'We were talking over dinner. About the baby. About his despair. And about you. He broke down, Sarah. I've never seen a man cry, not like that. Great heaving sobs that sounded more like they were coming from a wounded animal than a man, almost like they were torn from him. I didn't know what to do. All I could think of was to try to console him. I put my arm around him and the next minute he was clinging to me, tears streaming down his face. He said he felt helpless. At the end of his tether. He said he couldn't see a way out. And he said, he said—' She was close to tears herself now, feeling the despair of that night somehow clinging to the air.

'What did he say?' Sarah's voice was barely a whisper.

She turned to her former friend. 'He said he was tempted to end it all.'

Sarah reached for the arm of the chair next to her, collapsing into it.

Jules saw the shock on her face, and felt her pain. 'Sarah, I didn't know what to do. I held him while he cried, I rocked him. But as a friend. And I don't know how it changed or why, but suddenly he was kissing me and we were on the floor.'

She paused, trying to collect herself. 'It was all over in five minutes. He didn't make love to me. It was grief sex, life-affirming sex—call it what you like. And afterwards, we were both mortified. We couldn't look at each other. We knew what had happened was wrong and we thought if we just shut up about it and pretended it never happened, it would go away. Richard went away. He went home. To you.'

'Except, then Della happened.'

Sarah covered her face with her hands.

'I told him, because I thought I owed him that much and because I wanted an abortion. I asked him to help me get to Sydney to see someone. But he begged me not to, and I couldn't go through with it. Not after what he'd been through, even though … even though I knew it would kill our friendship.'

Sarah nodded. You said it was Richard who insisted.'

'He did. He wanted the baby desperately.' Jules bit her lip. She so wanted to leave it there, to let Sarah think that was all, that it was all down to Richard and what he wanted. It would be so easy to leave it there. But that would be wrong.

'There's more,' she said. 'You know it was never my intention to have a child. I didn't want Della, not then, not at first. But I was selfish enough to realise that if I had to have the child, at least it would give my parents the grandchild they would never otherwise have. It was selfish of me, I know, but at the time I had to find something positive in the decision, something to make up for the pain of losing you.'

Sarah turned to her, her agony-filled eyes studying Jules' face as if testing the veracity of her words, before she sat back, raising her tear-streaked face to the heavens. 'Yep,' she said at last. 'I guess that makes sense.'

She made a move to get to her feet and Jules knew she couldn't let the woman go without one more detail.'Richard slept in the spare room, Sarah. He never came near me again, except when it involved Della. She gave him a reason to live. So you see, he never left you for me. It was never me. He loved Della. He delighted in her. But you were the only woman he ever loved and he thought he'd lost you. He just didn't know what to do.'

Sarah looked up and nodded. She sucked in a deep breath and this time rose to her feet before reaching across the space between them to squeezed Jules's hand. 'Thank you,' she said, her vision turning misty. 'I think I've heard enough.'

Jules stood there a while after Sarah had been swallowed up by the rainforest.

Pru peeked out of the door. 'Has she gone?'

Jules nodded. 'Yeah.'

'How is she?'

Jules sighed. 'I honestly don't know.'

5 2

Sarah walked. Down past the store where Dot was happily serving behind the counter again—at least twenty-five per cent of the time. Past the museum and along Lagoon Road and the loop it made around the airport, and still she walked, until she reached the gate where the guided tours of Mount Gower began and where unaccompanied access was denied. She leaned on the gate as the sun warmed her face and the breeze tugged at her hair. The rhythm of her steps had been a gentle balm to her troubled and tangled soul.

She'd driven Richard away. She driven herself mad in her single-minded pursuit and she'd driven away her husband in the process.

She'd never failed at anything she put her mind to, but she'd fucked up majorly at holding her marriage together. Then again, she hadn't even tried to save it. She'd been oblivious to the danger. Oblivious to the cracks. She who'd always prided herself on her eye for detail, which was so useful in the world of numbers and balance sheets. She'd been so obsessed with having a baby that she'd missed the signs her marriage was at breaking point. She'd let it splinter and shatter and fall to tiny shards around her, and then she'd made out like she was the victim.

'I'm sorry, Richard,' she said, looking out to the sea that had swal-

297

lowed him up, and it wasn't lost on her that, for once, she was the one saying the words she so abhorred. 'I'm sorry I made you feel so bad—so stuck and so unwanted. I'm sorry I did that to you. I was lost in my own orbit. If I could do anything to make up for it, I would. In a heartbeat.'

But there was nothing she could do. Nothing that could bring him back or make things better.

She took a deep breath of the clean, salt air and said, 'I loved you, even if I lost sight of that. I'm glad you had six months with your beautiful daughter. She's grown into a beautiful young girl. You'd be so proud of her.'

And then she turned around.

It came to her on the way back, filtering down through the flotsam and jetsam of her shattered life like the island breeze filtered through the loose strands of her hair—a sense of relief. Almost as if the oppressive weight of half a decade of bitterness and acrimony, resentment and injustice was budging. Lifting from her shoulders and sweeping clean the poison from her heart.

Acceptance? she asked herself as she walked, questioning this unfamiliar lightness of being. But no, she'd reached acceptance before, and that terrain had been flat and dull and monochrome.

This terrain was rich with colour and fragrant with scent, just like the island she was on, the green of the palms and the turquoise of the sea, the salt in the air and scent of the earth, rich and fertile. She breathed deep the fresh sweet air, and for the first time fully understood what Noah had been trying to tell her at the restaurant at Port Macquarie. That there was a time to let go, a time to move on.

This was no mere acceptance, she knew.

This was forgiveness.

For Richard.

For Jules.

For herself.

And there was one thing she could do to show it.

～

Jules was surprised to see her again when she came to the door. 'Sarah, what is it?'

'I'm sorry. I have something I need to tell you.'

'What?'

'Well, I haven't worked out all the details,' said Sarah, moisture blurring her vision, 'but if the offer is still open, I'd be honoured … if you still wanted …' She had to fight to get the words past the lump in her throat. 'I mean, if you still wanted me to be Della's guardian.'

'You mean it?' Jules's voice sounded like she thought there had to be a catch, like there was something she was missing.

And there was. Kind of.

'But only on one condition,' Sarah said. 'That it's never needed. Because *nothing* is going to happen to you, okay? You promise me that? Because I am never going to lose you again.'

Jules was blinking as much as she was, and the smile through her fingers was tremulous, before she suddenly pulled Sarah into her arms and hugged her tight. 'I'll do my best, okay?'

Sarah felt the arms of her friend around her and drank in the scent of Jules she knew so well, the scent she'd thought consigned to the past, and forgiveness had never smelt so good.

5 3

'Hey, Flossie girl,' said Neill when she stepped into the office. 'Have you seen this?'

She looked over her father's shoulder where he sat at his desk. 'What is it?'

'It's the summer edition of *Far Flung*, that holiday magazine.'

Floss stopped, a sickening chill sliding down her spine. 'Oh?'

'That bloke who came, remember him?'

Oh, yeah. Floss shut her eyes. Oh, yeah, she remembered him all right. She'd been trying to forget. She'd hoped he'd forgotten about the review.

'He's done a write-up. Four pages, Flossie, and loads of pictures. How about that?'

'Let me see that,' she said, trying to wrangle the magazine away.

Neill Beckinsale was having none of it. 'Wait your turn,' he said, swatting her hand. 'Sit down, I'll read it to you.'

Oh, god, please no. 'Dad—'

'Shh. Listen. "Lord Howe is a fine name for an island, but the islanders know a better one. They call it Halfway, because it's halfway to heaven, and after my visit to this amazing destination, I believe they're right. Here are my top ten reasons why—"'

She cracked open one eye. That didn't sound too bad.

Her dad reeled off each point: Kim's Lookout; Ned's Beach; the twin peaks of Mounts Gower and Lidgbird; and on and on. Floss started to relax. Until her father got to number ten and stopped.

'Oh wait—you rate a mention here, Flossie.'

'Dad, how about—'

'"Floss Miller,"' her dad read, '"is a pocket-sized rocket who almost singlehandedly"—huh!— "runs the finest little guesthouse you could hope to stay in. Clean, comfortable and home-away-from-homely, Beached is a gem of a spot to stay. Tell Floss I sent you, I owe her one."'

Her father looked up, frowning. 'What on earth does he mean by that? Why would he owe you one?'

Floss blinked, able to breathe again, and gave her father a shrug. 'Because we gave him free accommodation,' she said. 'What else could it be?'

'Oh, righty-oh.' Neill looked back down and smacked the pages with the back of his hand. 'Five out of five stars, Flossie, what do you say about that?'

Apart from it being a humongous relief? 'It's great, Dad,' she said, looping an arm around her father's shoulders as she checked out the photos. There was a selfie Matt had taken at the top of Kim's Lookout, looking back over the island to the twin mountains at the other end. He was cute, in that lumbersexual kind of way.

But he wasn't a patch on Andy.

'Have you decided which job you want?' Noah asked when he called from Port Macquarie on Friday night like he'd promised.

Sarah had heard yesterday that she'd been offered the position in North Sydney, but she wasn't as excited about it as she'd expected to be. 'No. I keep thinking about what you said about looking for something in Port Macquarie.'

'Well, I don't want to throw a spanner in the works, but something else has come up.'

'What?'

'The cop on Lord Howe who was taking long-service leave. Turns out he's got some ongoing health issues that haven't resolved. He's decided to retire.'

'On Lord Howe?'

'Yeah, sorry. I'd go back in a heartbeat, but know it's the last place you want to be.'

Well, that wasn't strictly true any more. She'd had a few days to process it, so she told him about the box she'd found, and the letters and how she'd gone to see Jules.

'Wow,' he said, when she'd downloaded it all. 'Well done you.'

'Thanks. It feels good. You were so right, there's a time to move on.

I wish somebody had told me that earlier.'

'Don't beat yourself up. You probably weren't in the right mind to listen earlier, at least not until you came back to the Island and were forced to confront the past.'

Wasn't that the truth? 'Wow, when did you get to be so wise?'

He laughed a little, low and sexy down the line. 'Normally I'd crack a joke there, about how I've always been wise, but maybe my year six teacher was right. Maybe sometimes you have to be serious.'

'What on earth are you talking about?'

'Just that I'm just tossing up whether or not to throw my hat into the ring.'

'For the job on Lord Howe? Is there any point? I thought they preferred to have a family man as the permanent appointment, rather than a single man.'

'Yeah,' he said, 'that's a problem, all right. So I got to thinking how I might possibly become a family man. So that I might qualify, I mean.'

'What?'

'I know it's wrong to do this over the phone ...'

Her extremities tingled. Her mouth went dry. 'Noah Lomu, you are not making any sense here.'

'Marry me.'

She collapsed into the nearest chair.

'Sarah?' Noah said, when she didn't respond. 'Did you hear me?'

Oh, she'd heard him all right. She just didn't believe it. She swallowed. 'You can't be serious.'

'Never been more serious about anything in my life. I'm asking you to marry me.'

'You want to marry me so you can apply for a job?'

'Well, there is that,' he conceded. 'But what it all boils down to is I want to marry you because it turns out I love you.'

Bam. She closed her eyes. What he was asking was too crazy to contemplate.

'But I don't have to apply for the job,' he added. 'I don't want to give you a reason to say no.'

'But Noah, even if I did say yes, you'd still hardly be a family man. You know I can't have kids.'

'I know. Doesn't matter. We'll still be a family, just a family of two, you and me. What do you say, Sarah? Will you do me the honour of becoming my wife?'

A bubble of laughter escaped her mouth. 'You really are serious.'

'You're killing me here. What's it to be? Yes or no?'

'Yes,' she said. 'One hundred times yes. I—' She stumbled. These were words she hadn't used for such a long time, words she'd thought tarnished and scrubbed from her lexicon. 'I love you too.'

'I'm getting married,' she said to herself, testing it out loud to see how it sounded, to see if she believed it.

She walked into the dining room where her mother and father were sitting at the table, intently poring over a brochure, mentally preparing herself to tell them the news, willing her mother not to snipe, just this once.

'What are you looking at?'

'Our itinerary.'

'What itinerary?'

Sam looked up, a grin from ear to ear. 'We've booked a cruise on the *High Seas Magic Carpet Ride*. Around the world, one hundred and six days.'

'What?'

'Don't say what, dear.'

'But—'

'You see,' her father said, 'Dot's well and truly on the mend now, and we've looked around at all our friends—the ones who are still here that is—and decided that if we don't do it now, we never will.'

'But one hundred and six days, that's what? More than three months. What about the store?'

'Don't fret,' said Dot. 'We've got that planned, haven't we, Samuel?'

'That's right,' he said. 'We're going to ask Danny.'

'What about me?'

'Pooh. You've already done more than enough,' Dot said. 'You've be the first to agree with that.'

'That's right, lovey. You've put your career on hold for us once before. It's not fair to expect you to do it again.'

'But what about Silvio? You know you hate Silvio being here with Danny.'

Her mother pursed her lips. 'But we won't be here, will we? We'll be off on the *High Seas Magic Carpet Ride*.'

It was impossible. Danny would never agree, and even if he did … 'Forget Danny,' she said. 'I'll do it. All you had to do was ask.'

Her thunderstruck parents looked at each other. 'Well, if you're sure?'

'I'm sure,' she said, and left them to go and call Noah.

5 5

On Christmas Day, they all went to Ned's Beach after lunch with their respective families: Floss and Andy with their tribe of kids, Annie showing a neat little baby belly and being doted on by Trent; Jules with Pru and Della; and Sarah and Noah.

While Pru watched over the kids splashing in the shallows and feeding the fish like Sarah and Jules and Floss had done when they'd been their age, the men gathered around the barbecue, nursing cold beers and cooking sausages nobody could possibly squeeze in, but that would probably disappear regardless.

The centrepiece of their picnic table was the Knitivity, the secret project Jules had begun knitting while she'd been undergoing radiotherapy. She'd knitted Mary and Joseph and an even tinier baby Jesus, the Three Wise Men and the shepherds who watched their flocks by night. There were sheep too, and a donkey and a camel and, just for Della, there was an ancient horned turtle guarding the cradle, a feat that had given Jules no end of grief because she'd had to make up the pattern herself.

Floss picked up the turtle and put it on her palm. 'I never knew they had a turtle as part of the nativity scene.'

Jules sniffed. 'If they could have a lobster in the nativity play in *Love, Actually*, I figure anything goes.'

Floss laughed as she put it down. 'You're going to be famous soon. Those jumpers of yours are being spotted all over the world. I don't know how you keep up.'

'I couldn't do it without, Pru,' Jules said. And it was true. Knitting had saved Jules while she'd been stuck in Sydney so far from home, and now knitting was saving Pru, one jumper, one evening at a time.

'Oh,' said Sarah as Annie and Trent ran up from the beach for a drink of water. 'I've got something for you.' She dug through her bag until she found the small package. 'Here you go, Annie. Happy Christmas.'

'For me?' Annie said.

'More or less.'

'Wow, thanks!' She sat cross legged on the grass and eased off the sticky tape before peeling back the wrapping paper.

'Oh my god, they're gorgeous. Look, Mum!' Annie held up the white crocheted bonnet with the frilly edge, the bootees laced with ribbon and the sweet cardigan. 'They're so tiny. They're beautiful, thank you.'

'Dot made them,' Sarah said, maybe just a fraction too brightly but she hoped nobody would notice. 'I was hoping they'd come in useful one day.'

Annie jumped up to give Sarah a hug and kissed her on the cheek. So different to that first wary reunion at the store, Sarah thought, before both Annie and Trent ran back to join the others in the water, leaving the three women on the grass.

Floss looked at Sarah. 'Dot made those for you, didn't she?'

'Yeah.' Sarah's breath hitched, and she gave a tight smile. 'I figure I don't need to hold onto them any more.'

'You okay?' asked Jules.

'I'm all right. It comes and goes like a wave.' She shrugged. 'I guess it's something that will always be lurking in the background, I just have to learn to ride it. Accept it.' That fifth stage of grief was a long one.

But if her dad was right that, like grief, there were five stages of forgiveness, and that you had to get to acceptance before you could deal with it, before you could move on—well, if her dad was right, somehow forgiveness was turning out easier than she'd ever thought possible.

She took a deep breath of the sweet scent of freshly mown sweet grass beneath her overlaid with the tang of salt and sea.

'You're really something,' said Jules, smiling warmly. 'You know that?'

'Yeah,' said Floss. 'Amazing.'

'Hardly,' Sarah said, shaking her head while she took in the scene around her—a scene that would have been unthinkable only six months ago—with Jules and Floss and the men around the barbecue and Pru and the kids mucking around in the water, Della squealing in delight as the fish nibbled at her ankles. 'But I do feel whole again, being back here on the island, having you as my friends.'

'Hey,' Jules said, hooking her little finger around Sarah's and linking the other with Floss, who quickly hooked onto Sarah's spare, forming a wonky circle. 'Best friends in the world, right?'

'Best friends in the universe!' said Floss.

There was moisture in her eyes as they shook their linked hands three times, the way they'd done since they were in year one, the way they would always.

Sarah smiled as the words left her lips. 'Best friends forever.'

LIKE WHAT YOU READ?

Then be sure to check out *The Trouble with Choices*. Read on for an excerpt.

TRISH MOREY

the trouble with choices

THE TROUBLE WITH CHOICES - EXCERPT FROM CHAPTER ONE

SOPHIE

Nan started playing 'Here Comes the Bride' on the organ up front, while the words going around and around in Sophie Faraday's head marched to a different tune.

I'm just not that into you.

Sophie swallowed against the lump in her throat. A fine time for Jason to realise that little fact, the night before her brother got hitched. Tears pricked at the corners of her eyes, but she wouldn't cry, not now, not when she was about to walk down the aisle at Dan and Lucy's wedding. Even if she had blown five hundred dollars on a spa suite at Mount Lofty House, where she'd now be spending the night alone.

Five hundred dollars!

She lifted her face to the blue sky and breathed deeply. Oh God, don't cry! If she started now, she'd never stop.

She blinked hard as Siena started down the red carpet, barely registering the oohs and aahs over how grown up her ten-year-old niece looked today in her lilac-coloured junior bridesmaid gown. A gentle puff of spring breeze, the air sweetly scented, sent white cherry blossom drifting over the congregation, their petals landing on shoulders and in hair.

And even from the depths of her own personal hell, Sophie had to hand it to Dan and Lucy. It was genius to get married in the orchard in springtime. It was the perfect venue for a wedding. So beautiful. So utterly romantic.

So unlike Jason. *Sniff.*

What had he told her when she'd asked him why? That she was too demanding. Too needy.

Of course, she'd been needy!

She'd needed him to get on that plane and arrive back in Adelaide from his fly-in-fly-out job like they'd arranged. She'd needed him to be her sexy, loving partner today, to pull her against him and tell her how much he'd missed her these last three weeks they'd been apart. She'd needed him to smile down at her and laugh at her jokes like she was the only woman alive.

Most of all, she'd needed not to be dumped the night before her own brother's wedding.

And that somehow meant she had a problem?

Siena reached the front and peeled off to the left, and Beth was the next to follow her daughter down the aisle. The organ kept right on pumping out the notes and Sophie watched her sister as if on autopilot.

Three months they'd been together. Three months and four days to be exact since Jason had seen her profile on the dating site, HEA.com, and messaged her, wanting to meet up on his next break. The start of a beautiful relationship, he'd told her as he'd gazed into her eyes the very first time they'd met, he was sure of it. And she'd believed it was, meeting every break since, bar one, until that beautiful relationship had crunched to a sudden halt less than twenty-four hours ago.

So much for happy-ever-after-dot-com. More like happy *never* after, the way her luck was going.

She gripped the posy in her hands that much tighter, imagining her fingers wrapped around Jason's throat right now. He might have waited until after the wedding. Could have left his 'I'm just not that into you' speech for another time. Surely, he could have pretended to be into her for just one more day, not to mention one more very expensive night?

Five hundred dollars!

'Sophie!' her older sister Hannah hissed behind her. 'Get going!'

She snapped to with a start, saw Beth already at the front and everyone looking expectantly her way. Even Nan missed a couple of notes because she was looking over her shoulder. Crap!

She took off too fast and wobbled on her heels. *Whoa*, she thought, clutching onto her posy like a lifeline and using all of the pause before the next step to steady herself. Maybe she shouldn't have downed that last glass of champagne. Or the one before it, for that matter. But then, it was a day for celebrating.

Not to mention a day for drowning her sorrows.

Still, it wouldn't be a good look if she fell flat on her face during the bridal procession. She almost snorted at that, though snorting would hardly be a good look, either. But at least now she didn't have to force a smile. The mental image of herself face-planting into the red carpet during the wedding march saw to that.

Wagner's famous processional sounded through the valley, and the soft air rippled the silk of her gown and sent another sprinkle of cherry blossom4 raining down onto the proceedings, as Sophie methodically—meticulously—put one foot in front of the other, and slowly made her way forward. By the time she got near the front without disgracing herself, her confidence was building and she was grinning in triumph. Dan was frowning a little, but that was no surprise—he was her older brother after all, and he'd have found something to be annoyed about—probably Nan missing those notes. She sent him a wink, and only then noticed the best man standing beside him, almost missing her next step. Because Nick Pasquale, she couldn't help but notice, had scrubbed up well for the occasion, so well she almost hadn't recognised him. She added a few more watts to her smile and aimed it in his direction in appreciation.

There was definitely something sexy about a man all gussied up for a wedding.

Hello...

The lightbulb smacked her right between the eyes, her realisation sparking a new resolution.

Stuff Jason!

Because this was a wedding and there had to be lots of eligible men here, and all of them dressed up for the occasion. Not Nick, of course—he'd always treated her like a little sister, and she had a spa suite going begging and wasn't planning on being treated like anyone's little sister tonight—but it was a wedding and she'd dropped four kilos in the last month, and she was a pretty hot-looking bridesmaid if she did say so herself. And if she couldn't get a shag at a wedding when she was a bridesmaid and looked this good, she really was hopeless.

Fired up with her new resolve, she winked at Beth as she took her place alongside, but her sister was staring into space, lost in her thoughts, Siena in front of her busy plucking at her unfamiliar skirts.

So when Hannah arrived, Sophie grinned at her instead. Now there was only Kate, Lucy's friend and matron of honour, to walk down the aisle before the bride made her entrance. Before long, the formalities would be over with and Sophie could get stuck into the serious business of finding herself a suitable candidate for the night.

She caught Hannah peering strangely at her before glancing back over her shoulder down the aisle. Leaning closer, she whispered, 'Are you okay?'

'Yup,' Sophie said, 'never better,' and Hannah was already straightening, seemingly convinced, except Sophie hiccuped and Hannah must have caught a whiff of alcohol because her eyes opened wide in disbelief.

'Oh God. Please tell me you're not drunk!'

This time she did snort, just a little, because the idea was so ridiculous. Of course she wasn't drunk. A little tipsy maybe ...

'How could you be so stupid?' her sister hissed.

'What's wrong?' whispered Beth, who'd suddenly decided to pay attention.

'Sophie's drunk.'

It was Beth's turn to look appalled. 'What?'

In front of them, Siena turned, her big brown eyes blinking up at the three sisters. 'What are you all whispering about? Who's drunk?'

'Shhhh,' Sophie said, putting a finger to her lips, loving how it would be damn near impossible for anyone to tell if she was slurring that, while her twin sisters either side glowered at her. Then, Kate took her place at the front, and Sophie welcomed the new arrival with another grin and shrugged at the question in the other woman's eyes, as if she didn't know what was going on. Meanwhile, the collective gasp behind them told her that the bride was on her way.

Saved by the bride, Sophie thought, thoroughly amused by her own wit. What was Hannah's problem? Clearly, she couldn't be *that* drunk. She turned to watch the woman who would soon be their sister-in-law, and swayed a little as she did, earning herself another glare from Hannah in the process. She raised her eyebrows and grinned back, before the approaching bride snagged her attention.

Because wow, what a bride. Lucy looked amazing as she walked down the aisle on the arm of her mother. Dressed in a cream-coloured lace sheath over a miniskirt, and with cherry blossoms artfully woven into a circle on her head, Lucy had never looked happier or more gorgeous. The bridesmaids had all helped Lucy get dressed and played fetch for the hairdresser and makeup artists, who had arrived early in the morning, but none of them could take one shred of credit for how radiant she looked right now. It was all down to Lucy herself, and the love that shone from her eyes and radiated from her smile.

The love she felt for Dan.

Sophie sighed wistfully. And to think her crazy brother had let Lucy walk away when last cherry season was finished and risked losing the love of his life forever.

Sophie glanced over at her big brother, saw his eyes similarly full of admiration and love, and wanted to hug him right then and there for putting this right. Getting Lucy back had been like a magician pulling a rabbit from a hat, and now marrying her—well, that was no cheap trick. That was pure magic.

The pair reached the front, and if the look Lucy and Dan exchanged wasn't enough to melt the most cynical of hearts, it sure was enough to peel back the fog of alcohol and let back in the pain of Jason's betrayal. Sophie choked on a sob, once again fighting back the tears. Was it so unreasonable to want the same kind of love for herself? Was it so unreasonable not to want to wait until she was a crusty old thirty-seven years old like her brother to find that special someone to share her life with?

No, it damned well wasn't.

The organ music faded away and Nan took her seat next to Pop in the row behind. It was birdsong that played the accompaniment while the celebrant welcomed everyone. A simple service, Lucy and Dan had planned. Short and to the point, with just the important bits included to share with family and friends.

It wouldn't take long and then Sophie could get stuck into the serious business of man hunting. She needed to mingle and check out who else was on the guest list she'd paid only lip service to before today.

And then she felt a familiar pressure and found another reason for hoping the ceremony wouldn't take too long. She crossed her legs under her gown and pressed her thighs together as inconspicuously as possible. Because all that champagne was doing more than just kicking in.

Right now, she really needed to pee.

ACKNOWLEDGMENTS

A funny thing happened on the way to getting this book to publication. Well, maybe not in a tickle your funny bone kind of way, more a peculiar case of life imitating art.

It was July of 2018 and I'd just handed in the first draft of this story, and, giddy with relief and the pressing need to catch up on life, the universe and everything I'd been neglecting for way too many months, I set about tackling the round of duties and appointments I'd been putting off. The usual but necessary stuff. Like taxes. The dentist. Along with dealing with the pink Breastscreen reminder that had been sitting on my desk glaring at me. Given Jules' brush with breast cancer in the book, there was a reason I wasn't going there while writing it. I didn't want to jinx myself. Ha!

When the "possible abnormality" recall notice arrived a week or so after my screen, I was more than a little miffed. It was my eighth mammagram after the seven before had come back clear, and I had no lumps or bumps to suggest anything was wrong. I was determined to be in and out of that appointment in no time. I wasn't. A double biopsy followed and a week later came a diagnosis of DCIS – Ductal

Carcinoma in Situ – and I was duly handed a "My Journey Kit". Welcome to the club.

What followed was referral to a surgeon, an MRI, a lumpectomy, and the follow up radiotherapy course to blast any of those remaining little suckers into kingdom come. With complications, the whole experience took around 7 months and was a steep learning curve, and certainly more a pain in the arse than any kind of "journey", but I was lucky that it was caught early which meant I dodged the chemo bullet, and for that I will always be grateful to Breastscreen for all those free regular screening mammograms. (And if you haven't had yours lately, or you've been putting it off – take it from me, call and make that appointment. Far better to deal with it before it becomes something a whole lot more sinister.)

Readers often ask how much hands on research is needed to write a book, and whether it's okay to use the internet rather than going somewhere or experiencing something for yourself. I've always said the internet is great, but that nothing beats being there. I'd been to Lord Howe Island twice – in 1988 on our honeymoon and again in 2016 on a research trip with fellow author Fiona McArthur, and I couldn't have attempted to capture the Island's magic without those visits. But never once had I expected to experience breast cancer for myself. Hands on research. You can't beat it. Though if I'm going to tempt fate, next time I might just write me a book about a woman winning the lottery...

While all the aforementioned was going on, I was lucky enough to have the amazing support of so many people. To the crew at Harlequin Mira/Harper Collins, to my editors Rachael Donovan and Julia Knapman at Harlequin Harper Collins, who made so many fabulous suggestions and edits, thank you for your support and for hanging in there while the sodding "journey" took its course. To Kylie Mason, structural and copy editor extraordinaire, to Christine Armstrong for my sublime cover, to proof readers (including my sister, Toni, who did an awesome job!) and all the other amazing people in the team, thank you!

To my fabulous agent, Helen Breitwieser, who was there every step of the way and so supportive, thank you. I am really looking forward to working with you on our upcoming books.

To Pat at Somerset Apartments who was a wealth of information, thank you! To Doctor Frank Reed at the Gower Wilson Memorial Hospital on Lord Howe who gave me amazing info about what a woman presenting with a lump would encounter and how her case would be managed, to Ros who happily showed both fellow author Fiona McArthur and me around your amazing facility when we popped in unexpectedly, and to Kara who kindly read an early version of this story, thank you – the story is enriched by your contributions. Anything I got wrong on hospital or medical procedure is my mistake!

To the people of Lord Howe Island, thank for your warm hospitality, your generosity and kindness, and thank you so much also for being the guardians and caretakers of this most gorgeous island, a jewel in Australia's crown and a credit to you all. Please be assured, I never once met anyone like Dot on my visits there – she was purely a figment of my own (admittedly warped) imagination.

While I'm here, I'd like to thank Robert Parkyn, surgeon par excellence. Thanks to you and your team for your expertise, your humour and your advice, because what's the good of being a patient if you can't ask what ifs about your fictional patients as well?

To my amazing writing family, the Maytoners, who made me laugh and cry as they card-bombed my letter box with well wishes and nick knacks and even a rainbow coloured Flamingo (that I'm still trying to work out what to do with), I love you all, you crazy, mad, amazingly talented bunch of women. So blessed to count you among my friends.

To my long-suffering husband and four amazing daughters, who are my everything, thanks for still loving me after the complete insanity that is this writer on deadline. I love you all so much.

And last, but certainly not least, to the readers. Authors would be nothing without readers picking up books and turning the pages. Thank you so much for picking up this one.

Trish
   x

ABOUT THE AUTHOR

Trish always fancied herself a writer, so she dutifully picked gherkins and washed dishes in a Chinese restaurant on her way to earning herself an economics degree and a qualification as a Chartered Accountant instead. Work took her to Canberra, where she promptly fell in love with a tall, dark and handsome hero who cut computer code, and marriage and four daughters followed, which gave Trish time to step back from her career and think about what she'd really like to do.

Writing fiction was at the top of the list. Since then, Trish has sold more than 38 books, to Harlequin Mira/Harper Collins and Tule Publishing, with sales in excess of seven million globally, her books printed in more than thirty languages in forty countries worldwide.

Four times nominated and two times winner of Romance Writers of Australia's Ruby Award (the Romantic Book of the Year) Trish is also a 2012 RITA finalist in the US.

You can find out more about Trish and upcoming books at her website at www. trishmorey.com, and you can email her at trish@trishmorey.com.

Trish loves to hear from her readers.

The Ruthless Greek's Virgin Princess

The Italian Billionaire's Bride

Forced Wife, Royal Love Child

Back in the Spaniard's Bed - in The Latin Lover

The Italian Boss's Mistress of Revenge

The Sheikh's Convenient Virgin

The Boss's Christmas Baby

The Spaniard's Blackmailed Bride

The Greek's Virgin

A Virgin for the Taking

For Revenge…Or Pleasure?

The Mancini Marriage Bargain - The Arranged Brides
Bk 2

Stolen by the Sheikh - The Arranged Brides Bk 1

The Italian Boss's Secret Child

The Italian's Virgin Bride

The Greek Boss's Demand